ONE LITTLE SECRET

a novel by

Allison Bottke

BETHANY HOUSE PUBLISHERS
Minneapolis Minnesota

Published by Bethany House Publishers
11400 Hampshire Avenue South
Bloomington, Minnesota 55438

Bethany House Publishers is a division of
Baker Publishing Group, Grand Rapids, Michigan

Printed in the United States of America

ISBN-13: 978-0-7642-0058-8
ISBN-10: 0-7642-0058-5

Library of Congress Cataloging-in-Publication Data

Bottke, Allison.
  One little secret / Allison Bottke.
        p.   cm.
  ISBN-13: 978-0-7642-0058-8 (pbk.)
  ISBN-10: 0-7642-0058-5 (pbk.)
  1. Housewives—Fiction. 2. Singers—Fiction. I. Title.

PS3602.O875O64   2007
813'.6—dc22

                                                        2007014090

---

dedication

To every woman who has ever had a dream.
With God, all things are possible.

1

Nik peered out from behind the heavy velvet curtains, straining to see the audience. What a rush! Every time he looked from the sidelines into a packed auditorium he remembered his first time—when he was seven years old and looking out from behind the legs of his famous father. It brought back memories that ran the gamut of emotions from fearful to euphoric.

"So what do you think, kid?" his father had asked.

What did he think? Did his father really want to know? How should he respond? Nik never knew what to say to his father—what would set him off. He had looked out at the crowd of screaming girls and found it both fascinating and frightening. Without question, being admired seemed thrilling; but then he recalled the fight his parents had had the night before and knew it wasn't always good.

Nik brushed off the memories like he would unwanted lint from his Armani jacket. Tonight, the crowd was here to watch him perform his Grammy-nominated song—not his father. Tonight, millions of viewers around the world were watching an annual telecast known as "Music's Biggest Night," broadcast live from the Staples Center in the heart of Los Angeles.

Activity backstage was frenzied, something the TV viewing audience never saw and the thousands of attendees sitting in the auditorium couldn't care less about as they did their best to gawk without appearing to gawk at the celebrities sitting among them.

From the moment he'd stepped out of the limo and onto the famous red carpet, Nik had but one thought on his mind: how to begin his acceptance speech. He wasn't concerned about his live performance; he'd do great. It was the speech that weighed heavily on his mind. Every time he'd rehearsed it the past several weeks he'd altered the first sentence—never feeling quite comfortable with his choice.

"Oh, darling, you'll be wonderful. Whatever you say will be wonderful." Everything was wonderful to Candy, and it was driving him nuts. He could hardly wait to break up with her. It had been coming for weeks, but he couldn't risk the bad publicity of dumping her before the Grammys.

"I don't care what you have to do," his manager told him sternly, "but don't even think about giving her walking papers until after the ceremony. Do you hear me?"

Nik had heeded the advice from Arnie. He'd grown up with the media lurking over his shoulder—waiting for some screwup they could blow out of proportion. As a kid it had really ticked him off that he always had to be on his best behavior because of his old man's career.

Now, following in the footsteps of the famous Cristoff Prevelakis, Nik fully understood the power of the press—and how his every step was vulnerable to public scrutiny. So he'd walked on egg-shells the past few weeks—behaving himself, staying out of trouble. For him that meant staying home. At least Candy had made the self-imposed exile somewhat tolerable, but he was sick of playing house.

At this very moment Candy was sitting in the audience with Arnie, waiting to hear Nik's name announced in the category of Best Solo Rock Vocal Performance.

"This is your year, Nikky," his mother had slurred sweetly at dinner last night, fishing the lone olive out of her Waterford crystal martini glass.

Nik started to agree with her. His fellow nominees were dinosaurs in the business; he couldn't believe they were still performing—let alone touring, as some of them were. No doubt about it, it was time the Grammy in this category went to a hot young talent.

"I don't know," replied the Great Cristoff, a multiple Grammy Award winner himself. "Could be Bruce's year again. It's anyone's guess with this lineup. The Vegas odds are all over the board."

Leave it to his father to throw ice water on the smoldering fire of desire that burned in Nik's heart.

As if being nominated alongside Bruce Springsteen wasn't enough, Eric Clapton and Neil Young were also on the nominee roster. Still, Nik thought his old man could feign some encouragement on his behalf.

Turning her attention toward her husband of thirty-plus years, Isabella Prevelakis had turned on the charm that, even after several Van Gogh vodka martinis, was as precise as a finely tuned Stradivarius violin. "Cristoff, you know as well as I do that this is Nikky's year. He's earned it, and he deserves it. Now be a good puppy and get me another drink, please?"

Only Nik's mother could get away with calling Cristoff Prevelakis a puppy. Large pit bull was more like it. At almost seventy, he was still a formidable presence—exuding sophisticated sensuality like Ricardo Montalban. Cristoff had been a Hollywood heartthrob for more than five decades, but now he was nurturing a slight paunch. He didn't sing in public anymore. The media frequently suggested that his voice had been trashed by years of hard living and was no longer as strong as it had been when he came on the scene with Frank Sinatra, Tony Bennett, and Dean Martin. Nik guessed the reason had nothing to do with his voice and everything to do with his poor memory—he didn't want to embarrass himself by forgetting the words, but how would it look for the Great Cristoff to use sheet music?

Following in his father's footsteps was a journey prescribed to Nikolai Cristoff Prevelakis—known as Nik Prevel to his fans—long before he took his first step or sang his first note. He'd often wondered how his relationship with his father would have been different if Nik had not been gifted with an exceptional voice. But Nik didn't dwell too much on that because the fact of the matter was all the critics agreed that his talent far exceeded Cristoff's. That had made for some tense years as Nik's star was rising and his father's was sinking quietly into the twilight of his career. Only the fact that Nik sang rock and roll while Cristoff specialized in love ballads had eased the simmering animosity between them.

Tonight, when he held the long-awaited Grammy in his hands, Nik would thank his fans for making him number one on the charts. He'd thank his mother for her unconditional love and support. He'd thank his manager, Arnie Shapiro, and his band. He would even thank Kitty Thomas, his hairdresser. Through it all, the nation would wait with anticipation to hear what he had to say about his famous father. He would surprise them all by saying nothing. It wasn't because of his father that Nik had achieved success—it was in spite of him.

He wouldn't thank Candy. No way was he going to give her any credit in front of millions of viewers. She was pretty, yes—pretty useless. After the ceremony, and the after-parties, he could send her packing.

As expected, his song went off without a hitch. The applause afterward affirmed what he already knew.

"Good luck, bro," said Bono, last year's winner for Best Male Vocalist, as he walked past Nik backstage on his way to open the envelope and announce his successor.

"Thanks, man," Nik replied, trying to remember the name of the woman at Bono's side who was presenting with him. Norah somebody? He'd made a pass at her a few years back, when she first came on the scene. She was a pretty package with a modest voice, so he'd been surprised the year she won Best Female Vocalist.

As Bono and the woman made their way to the podium, Nik once again cleared his throat and, waiting in the wings, mentally practiced his acceptance speech.

"And the winner is . . ."

2

"Pizza's here!"

"Don't shout, Valerie. I heard the doorbell," Ursula said with a laugh, handing her daughter money. "Here. Make sure to give him a tip."

"Get a decent job—that's the tip I've got for him," Victor opined, grabbing paper plates and napkins from the cupboard. "Where's the Parmesan cheese?"

"In the refrigerator, where it always is. And might I refresh your memory, dear son, to the years you delivered pizza?"

"My point exactly. It's a crummy job."

"It's honest work, and there's nothing crummy about that—you've turned out okay in spite of the hardship," Ursula protested as she grabbed his face between her hands and kissed his cheeks in the way only a mother could.

Her children had turned out better than okay. With a desire to teach, Victor had decided to get his Master of Music Theory and was about to head off to U.C. Berkeley, no longer her little boy. Out of high school less than one year, Valerie had been accepted as an intern for the Youth With a Mission organization and would be leaving for a short-term missions trip in Australia later in the month. They were partnering with a Doctors Without Borders group, and Ursula suspected that was Valerie's calling—medicine. Time would tell.

"He was cute, the pizza guy," Valerie sang. "A definite McDreamy." She entered the kitchen balancing the large pepperoni with extra cheese and mushrooms high above her head on one hand like an Italian chef in a TV commercial.

"Everyone's cute to you, oh-ye-of-little-discernment," Victor mocked, taking the pizza from her hand and distributing it onto paper plates.

"That's not true. Mom, do you think I think everyone is cute?"

Ursula shook her head. "You and your brother keep me out of your arguments. Now, come on. It's almost showtime. Hey, bud, don't be stingy with the pizza. Give me another slice."

Grabbing a soda pop, Ursula made her way into the living room. Grammy night at the Rhoades house was an annual party—along with Oscar night, the Super Bowl, the Miss America Pageant, and the Olympics.

"This is so cool," Valerie oohed, checking out her ballot form. "Thanks for printing these out, Mom."

"You're welcome, honey." Earlier that day, Ursula had downloaded the PDF ballot form from the official Web site for the Grammy Awards. Everyone had a copy on a clipboard along with an ink pen.

"Is Dad gonna be here?" Victor asked to no one in particular, paging through his ballot.

"You know your father doesn't share our sick obsession with award ceremonies," Ursula replied, settling with a swoosh into the ultrasoft Bernhardt leather sofa and pulling up a lap blanket. "Maybe we'll convert him one day, but not tonight."

"I've got my choices picked out." Valerie checked off boxes one by one.

"Yeah, I'm sure you do. Nik Prevel, Nik Prevel, Nik Prevel. Do you seriously think he's gonna win over Bruce Springsteen? I highly doubt it. What do you think, Mom?"

"I don't know what to think about music these days. I'm out of touch."

"Yeah, right, like you could ever be out of touch with music," Victor replied, throwing a piece of popcorn that landed in Ursula's copper-colored hair.

Ursula tossed the popcorn back at him. He was right. After her family, music was Ursula's life. Every Tuesday and Thursday she taught voice and piano lessons from her home, tutoring students referred to her by local public and private schools, as well as an occasional student sent her way by Philomena Petrovia, a client of Don's firm and a well-known opera singer who frequently came across young talent not quite ready for her tutelage.

There had been a time when being a member of the Metropolitan Opera was all Ursula had dreamed about. She'd been working on her Master of Fine Arts when she met Don and dropped out of school—and she'd never really looked back. If it came down to holding a degree or the heart of her beloved, there was no contest.

She gave private lessons because she loved it, not because she needed the money. Don's salary as an attorney, combined with their real-estate investments, allowed them to live more than comfortably in Bel-Air.

"Earth to Mother." Victor interrupted her reverie with another airborne kernel of popcorn.

"Enough of the food fight, children. Can we get serious?" Valerie scolded.

Serious was the last thing Ursula wanted to be. She wanted to bask in these final days of enjoying her children while they still lived at home. It always amazed her when she overheard her friends talking about communication problems with their kids. Ursula couldn't relate—the bond she shared with her family was a gift from God, and she'd never once regretted the decision to give up her youthful dream of singing professionally. *Thank you, Lord, for giving me these precious years with my children.* She could hardly believe that soon the kids would be gone, pursuing their own dreams.

That was what made the Grammys so exciting—seeing people's dreams come true.

3

"It's a travesty. That's all there is to it," Arnie sympathized when he caught up with Nik backstage after the ceremony ended.

Nik's fury was barely contained behind his thin smile.

"So what's the plan?" Arnie asked. "Do you want me to take Candy home? I could—if you want to make yourself scarce."

Nik felt his face grow hot. "I'm not ashamed. I don't have to hide."

"That's not what I meant. I just figured you might . . ."

"Might what?"

"Never mind, Nik. I'm just sorry, that's all. I'm really sorry. You deserved it."

"Yeah, well, apparently Bruce deserved it more. His thousand other awards were getting lonely."

And so they went from one party to another into the wee hours of the morning, ending up at the Sony BMG bash at the Hollywood Roosevelt Hotel. Candy, to Nik's great relief, disappeared early in the night; but Arnie was in for the long haul—probably protecting his client from drinking too much and behaving foolishly in front of the cameras. Photographers lurked everywhere—waiting for the perfect candid shot of someone doing something they wouldn't want captured on film.

Some losers had chickened out, opting not to attend the bevy of parties taking place all over Los Angeles; others, like him, made the rounds congratulating their peers with well-practiced good wishes. Some performers actually looked as if they believed what they were saying as they gushed over the other people's gramophone statuettes.

By the time his chauffeur dropped him at his palatial mansion in Malibu, the sun was rising, and Nik wanted nothing more than to crawl under the covers and forget about the past twenty-four hours.

Another year without a win. How was that possible?

4

It was a beautiful Southern California day. The kind of weather that made vacationing Midwesterners envious—balmy and warm, with just a slight breeze to stir the air. In March, no less.

Ursula adroitly maneuvered around her well-appointed kitchen like a ship's captain on the bridge, preparing an Ash Wednesday feast for her family.

Andrea Bocelli's latest CD played on the stereo, but she was listening to Victor and his band rehearsing in the garage.

Victor had been her first student—the reason she'd decided to teach voice in her home so many years ago. Her son was truly gifted. She'd watched him blossom not only as an amazing singer with perfect pitch but also with an ability to play virtually any instrument he picked up. He wrote music that made her cry. If he wanted to, he could put to shame any of the singers they'd watched a few weeks ago on the Grammys.

It was no secret that Don wanted his son to get an advanced education. Ursula understood that—but she still made it clear to Victor that she would support him in whatever decision he made. He'd decided to go back to school and that had surprised her. Had she secretly hoped he would choose the more uncertain path of a singer/songwriter? What kind of mother was she?

I just want him to be happy.

This dinner will make Don happy, she thought to herself, as the rich smell of barbecue brisket filled the kitchen. He loved her good old-fashioned Texas barbecue and her homemade corn-bread muffins. The aroma in the kitchen warmed her heart. She set the table using her good Lenox china and Michael C. Fina sterling-silver flatware. Ursula had long believed that saving the good stuff for special occasions sent the wrong message to her family. "This family is a special occasion!" she had exclaimed many times. "We deserve a lovely table as much as, if not more than, holiday company, don't you think?"

She admired the table as she picked up the phone to call her husband on his private line. He answered after two rings.

"Hello there, partner," she whispered a tad seductively into the phone. "Guess what we're having for dinner tonight?"

"Honey? Has there been an oversight?" Don responded in clipped legalese that came from years spent in the courtroom. "I'm having dinner with Carl and Sam tonight—remember?" His perfect enunciation and brusque demeanor were as much a part of him as the crooked smile she loved, and it belied the genuine warmth she knew he possessed.

Drat! She'd totally forgotten about his meeting with two of the three senior partners of the firm. They'd talked about it last week.

"That means you won't be able to go to church with us either, right? It's Ash Wednesday."

"I'm sorry. I thought we'd discussed this. . . ."

"No, don't apologize. You're right. We did talk about it. I just mixed up my days. It's my fault. I'm the one who should be sorry. Don't worry, really. I'll fix you a plate you can nuke when you get home—if you're still hungry. I made brisket."

"Don't tell me that! No fair. I'll cancel. Hold on."

"Yeah, right. You get right on that and let me know how it goes."

They both laughed at the absurdity of the thought.

Don's allegiance to the firm of Carpenter, Haggerty & Pillsbury was legendary. Years ago he had been the youngest attorney ever to be invited to join the prestigious firm specializing in entertainment law. It seemed that all his dedication was about to pay off—Don was certain this was the year he would be offered a senior partnership.

Ursula was blowing kisses into the phone when Victor came in from the garage. "Gotta go, lover boy. The other fella in my life just walked in. You're old news." She hung up the phone and watched her son walk to the refrigerator and peer into it with intense contemplation.

How many times over the years had she watched him do the same exact thing? He took stock of everything—methodically assessing his options before selecting something to snack on. She would miss him when he moved out. Anxious to get a head start, he'd already rented an off-campus apartment in Berkeley with three other roommates and planned to find full-time employment. He'd have time to earn some good money before classes started.

"What smells so good? The guys sent me in to find out."

Ursula laughed. "The aroma you smell is coming from the oven, not the refrigerator. It's brisket. It'll be done at five, in time for us to make the seven-o'clock service tonight. The fellows are welcome to join us for dinner if they'd like. Your dad has a meeting."

"Uh, Mom, remember I have a gig tonight? That's why we're rehearsing. See here, it's even written down," he said, pointing to the big Anne Geddes calendar on the wall.

Sure enough, in blue ink it read: *VR—Newport Beach Tennis Club.*

"Is your suit clean?"

"Yes, Mother."

"How about a shirt—do you have a clean shirt?"

"Mom, I've got it handled. I've been dressing myself for years. Chill. Is there anything we can munch on? Crackers, dip, anything?"

"I'll see what I can find and bring out a tray, okay?"

"Thanks, Mom." Victor kissed her on the cheek and slipped back into the garage as quietly as he'd entered the kitchen.

Well, it looked like it was going to be a mother-daughter dinner. That would be nice. It had been a while since she and Valerie had spent a quiet dinner alone.

Moments later, Ursula's cell phone rang.

"Mom, is it okay if I hang out at Kelly's house for dinner?" Valerie asked. "Her aunt and uncle are visiting from Africa, and I really want to talk with them."

"The aunt and uncle who are missionaries?"

"Yep. They've been home for a couple weeks already and are heading back out in a few days. This is the only chance I'll have to talk with them. Is it okay?"

It would be good for Valerie to have a chance to talk with folks who shared the same passion for mission work. "Of course, honey. You enjoy yourself. I'll wait up for you."

"Thanks, Mom. See you later."

"Bye, sweetie. Love you."

Alone. Better get used to it. She pulled a tray from the cupboard and began to prepare a snack for the guys in the garage.

5

🔊 Nik woke up and rolled over to find himself face-to-face with a strange woman. He stared, trying desperately to remember her name and where they'd met.

Oh yes, the Hyde Lounge on the Sunset Strip. The last thing he remembered was finishing off the golden bottle of Patrón Añejo, the 100 percent de Agave tequila she had introduced him to. Sleeping peacefully, she looked pretty—long blond hair splayed across the red satin pillowcase.

There's no such thing as an ugly person in Beverly Hills, he thought as he watched her sleep. *It's as though DNA in this town is special-ordered, like a custom-made XKR Victory Edition Jaguar.* He got out of bed quietly, not wanting to wake her up. Grabbing the bottoms of his pumpkin-colored Charvet pajamas, he tiptoed out of the room in search of his live-in butler, Winston.

"Good morning, sir. Will your guest be joining you for lunch?"

"Lunch? What time is it?" Nik asked, pouring himself a cup of coffee.

"Two o'clock."

"What time did we get in? Were you up?"

"About six o'clock this morning. I was getting the newspaper. We passed in the foyer."

"I saw you?"

"Yes, sir. We exchanged pleasantries."

He searched his memory and didn't recall talking to Winston any more than he recalled the name of the mysterious woman in his bed.

"Uh . . . Winston?"

"Yes, sir?"

"Do you have any idea who she is?"

"Not a clue, sir."

"Okay, then. I need your help. I've got a concert tonight at the Hollywood Bowl and I don't have time for this. Wake her up and put her in a taxi. Tell her I had an appointment. I'll go upstairs and shower."

Getting rid of groupies was never a pretty experience, but it was much easier when Winston did the honors. Easier, but not always safer—the last woman had thrown an expensive vase of silk flowers at him on her way out the door.

Nik laughed on his way to the bathroom as he recalled the event. Winston was used to handling delicate situations. He had worked for Isabella when Nik was a toddler. He'd been with the Prevelakis family for years, and Nik knew he'd still be working for his mother if it wasn't for his father.

Young Nik had overheard his father instructing Winston one day. "You're not to tell Isabella what goes on here when she's away. Do you understand?"

"Yes, sir, I understand," Winston had responded, but Nik could tell that he didn't.

That was when his mother had started to drink. Isabella and Cristoff pretended to be happily married, but it was pure and simple deception. When Nik was old enough to move out on his own, Isabella insisted that Winston go with him.

Transferring butlers from generation to generation wasn't unheard of. In fact, Nik knew that Winston's father had worked for the same family as his father and his grandfather before him. Nik was happy with the arrangement, and other than the occasional "unfortunate girl incident," he was sure Winston was equally content.

He knew from experience that the women Winston sent off would never tell their friends the butler put them in a taxi. They'd make up some sort of story that fit their personal fantasy. That was fine with Nik. Being with him was every woman's fantasy, and he enjoyed making dreams come true. Besides, cavorting with so many women was the only thing he did that made his father take notice.

"I don't know how he does it! A different girl every time we see him, that young Casanova."

"That makes you proud?" Nik had overheard his mother say to her husband when he was visiting their home last week.

"At least he likes women, Izzy! Look around you. It's getting acceptable for boys to like boys—have you noticed? Look at that cowboy movie—an abomination!"

"I know he likes women, Cristoff. I just wish he'd like fewer of them and settle down."

"What's so special about settling down? Highly overrated."

Nik wanted to knock his father flat on his backside for hurting his mother yet again. He knew his father's words had hurt her as surely as he knew she would pour herself another stiff drink to try and forget them.

He couldn't remember a time when his father had been faithful to his mother. He grew up hearing the kitchen staff talk about Cristoff's newest mistress, and he'd fished out more than one gossip column from the trash to read the headlines about paternity suits involving the Great Cristoff Prevelakis.

He would never get married and do that to his wife. Even though he was approaching his thirtieth birthday, he was happy being single. He heard the front door slam just as he stepped into the shower—no discernable sounds of shouting or breaking glass. *Thanks, Winston.*

Ursula woke up and rolled over to find Don gone. She wondered where he was, then smiled, knowing he would be on the golf course, working out his nervous energy with the new Scotty Cameron club she'd given him as a gift the night before. The salesman had told her it was the PGA's most played putter, and Don was like a kid with a new bike when she'd presented it to him.

"Tomorrow could be it," he'd said to her last night as they snuggled together before nodding off to sleep. They were hosting a dinner for his firm at their home; Ursula had been planning it for days.

"Well, it's about time. You deserve that partnership more than anyone else."

"Thanks, hon." Don kissed her forehead and held her a little tighter.

"Well, you do. You've been with the firm for years. It's the logical next step. You've always told me the law is nothing if not logical."

"I said that?"

"Yes, sir."

"I like it when you call me sir. Sounds so . . . royal."

"Oh yeah? How's this for royal," she'd said as she pulled away and tossed her pillow at him, starting a pillow fight that ended with them tangled up in a heap on the floor laughing. As corny as it sounded, she loved her husband more after twenty-one years of marriage than when they were first married.

"I thawed a turkey. We're going to have a full Thanksgiving meal," she'd told him as they returned to the bed to burrow under the covers. "With all the trimmings, no holds barred."

"But it's March."

"It's time for you to reap what you have sown," Ursula said confidently. "A Thanksgiving meal typically brings back good memories. It's predictable . . . it's evocative . . . it's sensory."

"It's a bird, dear."

"It's a symbol of celebration."

"I'll trust your instincts." Don leaned over to kiss his wife. "You're the boss." And with that, he'd fallen asleep in her arms as she gently ran her fingers through his hair.

Over the course of their marriage, Ursula had thrown countless parties—from intimate dinners for four to elaborate soirées for hundreds. Most were for Don's business associates and clients. Some were exclusive fundraising events that made the L.A. society columns.

Between teaching her students, entertaining for her husband, and the volunteering for projects for her friend Dee, she was busier than many of her friends who had full-time jobs. Plus, she had always made sure she was available for all of her kids' school or extracurricular activities.

Don was golfing to calm his nerves, but she had work to do. Ursula got out of bed and reviewed the schedule for the day as she dressed in a pair of beige Marc Jacobs wide-legged pants, a white Liz Claiborne blouse, and Colin Robertson jute platform wedge sandals. Feeling very Katharine Hepburnesque, she added red lipstick, tied her hair back in a narrow white headband scarf and lavishly sprayed herself with Love in White, a new fragrance she was trying. She wanted everything to be perfect. Don wanted this partnership, and he wanted it badly; his courtroom face couldn't hide what Ursula knew to be true. Tonight, she hoped, would be the culmination of a shared dream.

Lord, let this be Don's day. He's worked so hard. We've worked so hard.

6

🔊 "That redhead has great hair," Nik said, peering out from the wings. "See her? In the center, in the emerald-green leather top with the zippers?"

Arnie looked, knowing full well he was going to have to send the girl a backstage pass before the concert was over, unless Nik found another woman who caught his eye. He squinted across the audience. It seemed every one of the twenty-five thousand seats at the Hollywood Bowl was occupied. The redhead was flashy all right, which meant she was most definitely Nik's type. There was a perky little brunette sitting next to her who Arnie thought was much more attractive. He squelched the thought. He'd been married to Raysha for twenty years, and she'd kill him if he so much as looked at another woman.

"I didn't think you liked redheads." Arnie sipped his diet soda and moved away from the sidelines.

"Who said I didn't like redheads? I never said that. I just find blondes more attractive. Anything wrong with that?" Nik smiled seductively at an attractive stagehand who seemed to be making a point of ignoring him.

"Not a thing." Arnie gestured toward Nik's head. "Fix your hair. It's sticking up in the back."

"Kitty!" Nik yelled in a whisper. "Come here. Fix my hair, will you?"

Kitty inspected his thick black mop of wavy hair, then added another coat of liquid spray lacquer. "It's *supposed* to be sticking up in the back. That's the look."

Nik had discovered Kitty Thomas years ago at the Frédéric Fekkai salon in New York. A brash New Yorker with a penchant for wearing outrageous stiletto heels and changing her hair color almost as often as her shoes, Kitty was also his makeup artist, clothing stylist, personal shopper, and occasional secretary. Arnie wondered if she ever felt like Sandra Bullock in that movie where Hugh Grant played her demanding boss and took advantage of her—but Kitty seemed to take it all in stride. She wasn't afraid to get in Nik's face and give him what for—one of the few women who could, or did.

Kitty handed Nik warm tea with honey and lemon, which he downed in a few gulps. Arnie knew Nik's after-concert drink would be straight Jack Daniels, but he never drank before or during a concert.

"If my kitten says I look great," Nik purred, "then I trust her. She's never let me down yet."

Arnie took the cup as Nik rolled his head and stretched his neck muscles. "Okay, folks, five minutes to showtime."

―――――――――

Nik watched what he could see of the audience as he sang the final encore of the concert. They were mesmerized. Like the Pied Piper, Nik had brought them from a frenzied pace with his Latin-infused rock-and-roll hits to an almost hypnotic euphoria with this well-known ballad. It was a song everyone knew very well, but one he'd never before performed in concert.

"Amazing." Arnie handed Nik a towel to wipe his sweaty face as he exited the stage and joined him on the sidelines. "Look at them."

"Yeah, they seemed to like it."

"Seemed to like it? They loved it! I told you they would! Does Cristoff know? I mean, did you ask him?"

"Since when do I need my old man's permission to sing a song?" Nik felt his face grow hotter. "He doesn't own it."

"Well . . . not technically, but I'm not sure that would hold up in a court of law."

"What're you saying? The old man's gonna sue me for singing a song?"

"He may not sue you—but I guarantee you'll pay a price for this."

"Give me a break, Arnie. It's just a song, for crying out loud."

"It's not just a song and you know it. It's your father's trademark song."

Nik had to admit that was true. For more years than anyone could recall, "As Time Goes By" had been Cristoff Prevelakis's closing song at every concert. It was his song as much as "Somewhere Over the Rainbow" was Judy Garland's song.

"Great job, Mr. Prevel," said one of the stagehands as he led Nik to his dressing room. Nik nodded his head in silent thanks.

"I've always loved that song," called one of the tech guys as he wound up cords.

"You made me cry!" Kitty exclaimed when Nik walked into his dressing room. "I can't believe you sang 'As Time Goes By'! I grew up with that song. It was my mom's favorite. They played it at her wedding. She talked about it every year on their anniversary. Did you see the audience? They were on their feet when you hit that last note!"

"Did ya hear that, Arnie?" Nik gloated. "If I can impress Kitten, I can impress anyone."

Smiling, Arnie reached to close the dressing room door, and Nik heard a snippet of conversation outside that caught his attention.

"Wait!" Nik held up his hand and walked toward the door. "Shh, let's hear what they say."

"That's one for the record books," said a gruff voice, one of the stagehands.

"That was history in the making," another voice responded. "If he goes back to singing that trendy teen trash, he's as ignorant as the tabloids say he is. That's the kind of music God made his voice for—not that garbage he's been singing for years. It's about time he grew up."

Nik reached angrily for the doorknob—but Arnie grabbed his arm. "Take it easy, Nik. I'm starting to get an idea here."

Nik spat, "What do they know? That 'garbage' made me several million dollars last year."

"Well, I'm out of here, fellows," Kitty quickly announced. "Great concert, Nik. You were fabulous."

Nik didn't even look at Kitty as she slipped out the door, her four-inch heels clicking on the tile. He stared at Arnie. And Arnie didn't flinch.

"I don't see you complaining about your paycheck," Nik ranted. "If you don't like my garbage, you can just—"

"Whoa, buddy. I'm not—"

"Did you see the audience tonight? They loved it!"

"Yes, they did. Especially your closing song. Nik, everybody has been covering old ballads lately—Rod, Barry, Julio, Harry, even that new kid, Michael Bublé. What if you tried it?"

"No way."

Arnie held up his hands. "Think about it. You're at the top of your game. You've been a teen idol for years. But your fans are growing up. This is your chance not only to keep them, but to woo their parents, as well. Baby boomers have the fattest wallets these days."

Arnie waited, his eyes searching Nik's face. He handed Nik a robe and perched himself on the corner of a tall stool while Nik changed. "Nik, you had them eating out of your hands with that song. Your dad would have been proud."

"I doubt that."

"Still, you were great."

"I was, wasn't I." He grinned into the lighted makeup mirror, inspecting the new cap on his front tooth.

"Yes. You were. How did it feel?"

How did it feel? It was nice to slow things down—he knew that much. Especially after two hours of a frenetic pace. He had to admit that "As Time Goes By" brought up mixed emotions for him. It was the song his mother had sung to him at night when he was a kid—when she was sober enough to tuck him in. And it was the song everyone associated with the Great Cristoff.

"Well?" Arnie prodded.

"Well, what?"

"How did it feel? Singing a love song for a change?"

"I sing lots of love songs." He poured himself a shot of Jack Daniels, swallowed it in one gulp, and sat on a stool next to Arnie.

"Your love songs are a tad fast, the words a bit hard for old geezers like me to understand." When Nik didn't respond, Arnie continued, "The country's in a tailspin, Nik. Folks don't know if we're about to enter World War III or if terrorists are gonna blow something else up. It's a scary world. We want to feel safe. We want to be comforted. We want to know we can live happily ever after."

"You're saying folks want to live in fantasyland?"

"That's exactly what I'm saying! And what's wrong with that? You're an entertainer, Nik. One of the best there is. So entertain them! Send folks back to a time when love meant something. When romance really mattered. When folks stayed married for life."

"Man, you sound like a commercial." Nik turned to look him square in the eyes.

"Are you buying what I'm trying to sell?"

"Maybe."

"You gotta do it."

"Do what?"

"You've got to record an album of classic love songs."

"Classic love songs."

"Yes."

"Such as?"

"Such as 'The Way You Look Tonight,' 'Someone to Watch Over Me,' 'All the Way.' You know what I mean. Songs like that. It could be very profitable."

"How profitable?"

"I'd bet Ardage Records will give you a cool three million to record it. Plus points. But there's one more part to it."

"What?"

"How about making it a duet collection—get a hot young female to sing alongside you?"

Nik cocked an eyebrow. "Who do you have in mind?"

"No one in particular, really. I can bet you Mariah, Natalie, or even Madonna would jump at the chance."

"Madonna? She's still on her Confessions tour. Like she's got anything left to confess."

"Okay, maybe not her—but you can pretty much pick and choose."

"What about Carlotta?" Nik grinned and got up to pour himself another drink.

Arnie stared at Nik with his mouth agape.

"You really are walking on the wild side, aren't you? You think he'd allow it?"

"What does he have to say about it? She's not his property."

Carlotta was an amazing Latin singer with a sexy voice equaled only by her luscious body. The fact that she had once been Cristoff's mistress was public knowledge.

"She hasn't had a hit song in a lot of years." Arnie reached into the nearby candy dish and popped a handful of M&Ms in his mouth.

"Precisely. But she can still sing the studs off a stuffed shirt."

"When did you last hear her?"

"I caught her in Vegas last month at a private party for the Wynns. She's still got the pipes."

Arnie reached for more M&Ms. He appeared to be considering something. He looked at Nik and smiled slowly. "Let's keep all of our options open, okay? I even wonder if there might be someone else, someone who hasn't been discovered yet. We could really get some publicity with that."

7

(())) "You've outdone yourself this time, Ursula."

"Thank you, Sam."

"No, thank *you*. A toast to our lovely hostess."

Samuel Pillsbury was a senior partner at Carpenter, Haggerty & Pillsbury, and his graciousness never failed to impress Ursula. An attractive man, he could have passed for one of the debonair and flamboyant actors the firm represented. As crystal toasted crystal around the elegant candlelit table, Ursula caught Don's eye. He winked.

"This was just like Thanksgiving at my grandma's house," purred Celeste Foster. Her blond head tilted up sweetly. The newest associate at the firm, she was far perkier than Ursula had anticipated—and far more dangerous.

"She's mighty young," Ursula had whispered to Don earlier in the kitchen.

"She's mighty smart, which is far more important."

"That wouldn't have anything to do with the fact that she's Carl Haggerty's niece, would it?" Ursula handed him the bowl of dressing and motioned for him to place it on the serving tray.

"I'm sure that's part of it, but if she wasn't good, he wouldn't put up with her. Trust me, she's good. She's going places."

Watching Don as he joined the party, she couldn't help but notice how the newest associate's beautiful face lit up when he entered the room—or was it only her imagination?

Celeste was impeccably toned in her incredibly tight little black Roberto Cavalli dress, her heart-shaped face lethally lovely. Ursula wanted to drop-kick her into next week.

"Whatever made you decide on a Thanksgiving theme?" Celeste asked as she looked up coyly over the edge of her wine goblet. She didn't wait for an answer. "Isn't it quaint, Samuel? Don, you didn't tell me your wife was such an excellent cook."·

She looks like a bobblehead, Ursula thought.

"Ursula is far more than a cook, dear child. She's a gourmet chef. Note the difference."

"Thank you, Julliette." Ursula hadn't expected Sam's newest trophy wife to come to her rescue. The gorgeous woman had given up a lucrative career as a high-powered executive at a huge advertising agency when she'd married Sam, and she had been nothing but disdainful toward Ursula up to this point. The fact that she interrupted conversations as a rule and not an exception and laughed at her own bad jokes drove Ursula crazy. But she was grateful for this interruption—until she realized Julliette had not finished.

"She made a luscious chateaubriand the last time we were here, with a crème brûlée that defied superlatives. Too bad everything was so horribly fattening. I could eat only a tiny bite."

"I envy a good cook," said Celeste. "I've never had time to learn. They didn't have home economics at Harvard."

"And a good thing too," Sam interrupted Celeste. "You'll make a formidable opponent in court. That's clearly your gift."

"And Ursula's gift is being the perfect housewife! Here's to Ursula." Julliette held up her Lalique crystal goblet.

Ursula wasn't sure whether to laugh or cry. Did Julliette honestly think being called a *perfect housewife* in that disdainful tone of voice was a compliment? Looking to Don for help, Ursula was stunned to see him smiling and holding up his glass in admiration.

"I don't think I've ever known anyone who was just a house-wife," Celeste said after everyone had toasted. "All the women in my family as far back as I can remember have been lawyers. They never had time to cook or clean or take care of the house."

"You've outdone yourself this time, hon."

Don's genuine sincerity was like healing salve on an open wound. Ursula felt the tension slip from her shoulders. "Would anyone care for some coffee?" she asked, standing up.

"Yes, but can you wait a moment, Ursula? I'd like to make an announcement."

"Of course, Sam," she said, smiling graciously. She sat down as Sam stood up, looking knowingly across the table at her husband. *This is it—what we've waited for.*

"I'll cut right to the chase. We all know what we're here for. It's time to make some serious changes at Carpenter, Haggerty & Pillsbury."

The room grew silent.

"We got the Chesterfield case." Sam grinned, his eyes gleaming.

"Felicia Chesterfield?" Don inquired, eyebrows raised.

"Is there any other Chesterfield case?" Sam boomed.

Felicia Chesterfield had been filming in New York when she fell off a motorcycle and broke her leg. It wasn't a particularly bad break, and filming could have continued until she was able to return to the set, but it was common knowledge that she and the director didn't see eye to eye. Their volatile relationship had been plastered all over the tabloids for months. He took no time at all in having her replaced, a fact her legal team claimed to be a clear-cut contract violation. A few days later the director was found stabbed to death on his Ferretti 830 yacht in New York Harbor. All evidence pointed to Felicia Chesterfield.

"And, Don, we want you to handle the case." Sam grasped Don's right hand with both of his.

Instead of a senior partnership, her husband was being offered one of the highest profile cases in years. Ursula looked questioningly at Don but couldn't catch his eye. He was in the fray of heated communication with all the senior partners.

Julliette leaned over and whispered to Ursula, "The Chesterfield case will put the firm on the map."

Sam's voice cut through the buzz. "It's going to require temporary relocation to New York City, where the trial's being held. I expect you should be able to tie things up before fall."

Before fall? That's six months away! Ursula was used to Don's occasional travel, but a six-month case clear across the country? A host of questions ran across her mind, and she couldn't wait to get her husband alone. As always, they would discuss their options and make a decision.

"What do you say, Don?" Sam asked, still grinning.

"I'm honored, Sam, and you know I'll do my best."

Ursula's world began to move in slow motion as she watched her husband. Had Don really just made a decision of epic proportion before talking privately with her?

8

Ursula whirled on Don the moment she closed the door behind Celeste, their last guest to leave. "You should have waited to talk with me before you agreed to take the job. We always discuss things like this—you know that."

"I do know that, honey, and I'm sorry. I got caught up in the moment."

"I could tell."

"What's that supposed to mean?"

"That's not all you got caught up in."

His raised eyebrows showed no signs of comprehension.

"Don't tell me you didn't enjoy Madame Butterfly's batted lashes all night long."

"What are you talking about?"

"Miss Coyote Ugly. That's what I'm talking about."

"Huh?"

"You know darn well she was flirting with you all night long!"

"Who?"

"I know this is Hollywood, but since when is it appropriate for an attorney to paint on her dress?"

"Very funny."

"I'm not laughing."

"You're being ridiculous, Ursula. Utterly ridiculous."

"And what about all that 'just a housewife' nonsense? Why did you let them get away with that?"

"I really don't know what you're talking about."

"Were we at the same dinner table? Between Julliette and Celeste, they insulted me all night long."

"Insulted you? Being my wife is an insult?"

"Don't twist my words, Donald. You know what I mean. They said *housewife* the same way people refer to the Black Plague. Trust me, from their lips it wasn't a compliment. Not in the least."

"Ursula, I don't know what to say. This is the case of a lifetime, and I'm sure it will lead to a full senior partnership when I get back. It's what we've always dreamed of."

"It's what *you've* always dreamed of."

Ursula regretted the words the moment they'd left her mouth. But why couldn't he see her point of view? Why couldn't he at least try to understand how hurt she was? If they really were partners, if it truly was what they had always dreamed about, then they should have made the decision together.

When she woke up the next morning he was gone. A note was pinned to his pillow.

Dearest Ursula,

Good morning, beautiful one. Please forgive me for being a rogue and a cad. I've gone to slay the wicked women who caused you such angst, if not literally with a sword, then figuratively with a nine iron. I'll be back late—don't wait dinner for me. Sam and I are meeting at the office to discuss the plan of action for New York. And, honey? You aren't just a housewife, you're my housewife, and I love you more than words can say. I am sorry we did not talk first. Everything will be all right.

Your humble servant and love slave,
Galahad

Oh, Don. Her smile was mixed with tears as she got up and began to make the bed.

She'd managed to shake off the gloom by the time afternoon rolled around, convincing herself that she'd been a total fool and that green was most definitely not her best color.

Victor was practicing in the garage with his band when Valerie came home from Tiffany's house. Ursula heard her singing a vaguely familiar song as she came into the kitchen, tossed her bag on the floor, and kissed her mom on the cheek.

"So how was the concert?"

"Rad."

"Do people still say *rad*?"

"Yep."

"So tell me about it. Did you have good seats?"

"Good seats? Mom! We were practically sitting in his lap. It was so amazingly cool. Tiff was impressed. Her dad never gets tickets from his company."

"Her father's in the military, honey. Uncle Sam doesn't usually get comp tickets to rock concerts."

"Yeah, that's too bad, huh?"

"Are you hungry? Can I make you a sandwich?"

"Nah, we stopped for a burger on the way. Hey, Mom? Nik closed with a song I never heard him sing before. It goes like this. Do you know it?"

After a few bars Ursula knew the song and began to sing along. Valerie cheered, and Ursula sang louder, not noticing her son and his bandmates standing in the doorway listening to her. The applause was mighty as she improvised on an impossibly high note.

"Wow, Mom, that was awesome!" Victor practically glowed with pride.

"Nik sang it lower than that, but that's it. What's it called?"

"'As Time Goes By,'" Ursula and Victor responded in unison. "It's his father's trademark song," Victor said.

Her son knew as much about the classic ballads as she did. His band—The Twilights—was in demand at private events all over the West Coast. They performed just about every classic love song known to man. She loved sitting in on their practices—and attended as many gigs as she could. Victor called her a "dedicated groupie."

"Hey, Mrs. R., did you hear we're playing in Pacific Palisades tonight?" Phil, the drummer, asked.

"Some ritzy place on Amalfi Drive," Victor chimed in. "Hey, Phil, can you go grab the playlist? I want to run it by Mom."

"Sure, be right back."

He returned with a sheet of paper and held it out to her. "Here it is. What do you think?"

Ursula put down her cutting knife, wiped her hands on the towel hanging from her belt, and took the paper. She read the list with genuine interest. "This looks great to me, but what if you swapped 'The Way You Look Tonight' with 'Time After Time'? I think the emotional flow would be better. What do you think?"

"I think you're right. Don't know why we didn't think of that," Victor said, and the guys nodded in agreement, smiled, and praised her as though she'd written the last bars of a symphony instead of merely suggesting a change in the song lineup.

"Okay, fellas, what's up?" Ursula crossed her arms, leaned back on the counter, and looked at the group of young men, who quickly averted her eyes.

Victor's words ran together in one long sentence. "Emily's in the hospital with a broken leg and she can't sing tonight. She's gonna be fine, but we're in a major bind. We don't know what to do."

"Oh, honey, I'm sorry." Ursula put her hand on Victor's shoulder as he looked down and twisted his high-school class ring on his finger.

"Hey, Mom, why don't you do it?" Valerie said offhandedly as she chewed on a carrot.

"Yeah, right." Ursula laughed as she resumed chopping.

No one laughed with her. Instead, the guys stared at her.

"What? What's the matter?" She stopped cutting and pointed the knife at her son. His intense gaze turned into a devilish smile.

"No. No, no, no. No. Don't even go there. I'm not singing at someone's Bar Mitzvah."

"It's a wedding reception."

"Okay, then. I'm not singing at someone's wedding reception."

"Why not? You'd be great!" Victor said.

"Yeah, Mrs. R., you'd be great," Cliff, the saxophonist, echoed.

Valerie rolled her eyes. "I was only kidding."

"I'm not," Victor insisted. "Mom, we need you. There's no one else. You know all the songs. It'll be fun. Kind of like a swan song for The Twilights, our last gig before I leave for school. Maybe Dad could come too."

Ursula shook her head. "He won't be home tonight. He's meeting with Sam about a new client." They hadn't yet told the kids about the New York case.

"Well, then, that's perfect. You'd be here all by your poor old lonesome self."

"Drop the old part, okay?"

"By your poor lonesome self. Waddaya say?"

She looked at the expectant faces of the four young band members and the silly smirk on her daughter's lips and made her decision.

9

"Oh, Nikky, did you think your father wouldn't find out?" His mother bypassed the Waterford martini glass and reached instead for a double old-fashioned in the same Lismore pattern, poured chilled vodka over crushed ice, added a single olive, and swirled the liquid in the elegant tumbler, not drinking.

"I wasn't trying to hide anything from him. How'd he find out so soon?"

It was early in the day for even his mom to be drinking. Nik took the glass from her hand and swallowed the icy concoction in a few gulps. "Thanks."

"Hmmm." She held the empty glass and stared at him. "Many of the stagehands at the Hollywood Bowl worked there when your father performed—did you forget? One of them was on the phone while you were still singing."

"Figures."

"Yes, it figures. Your father has some very loyal fans, Nikky."

"And I don't?"

"I will not argue with you, son. No one doubts that you have fans."

"Dad does. To hear him talk you'd think I was singing at some dive on Sunset Boulevard. The Bowl was sold out last night, Mom. You should have seen it."

"I did see it. I was there. I heard you."

Nik's jaw dropped. "Why didn't you come backstage?"

"For the same reason I just mentioned—your father has fans. They'd have told him. I didn't want to argue. I'm sorry."

"Yeah, me too." His own mother couldn't talk to her only son after his performance because her philandering husband would have been ticked off. *What's wrong with this picture?*

"So how mad is he?"

"Mad? I'm not sure he's mad, exactly."

"Then what is he? Where is he? I came here to get it over with."

"That's the funny thing about it. When I came home he was behaving like a trapped hornet. But by the end of the night he was fine."

"Fine? What did you say to him?"

"Assuming I said anything at all?" Isabella poured another drink.

His mother had learned long ago how to tame the wild beast that was his father. Did she think he didn't know how much influence she had? He didn't respond to the "innocent" act; a simple stare and crossed arms said volumes.

"Okay, maybe I did say a few things."

"Yes?"

"I reminded him of the time we saw Liza Minnelli sing 'Somewhere Over the Rainbow.' She hardly ever sings her mother's song, but it was a very special tribute and your father loved it. He wasn't the least upset that Liza was trying to steal her mother's thunder."

"Yeah, but her mom is dead."

"Exactly. I told him it was a shame that her mother would never have the chance to hear her famous daughter sing the song she had made famous. No matter how wonderful Liza can sing—and she can sing—we both knew there wasn't a single person in the audience that night who didn't flash back to the pig-tailed Dorothy standing in the farm field in her blue cotton dress. Judy made it famous—not Liza—and that would *never* change."

"He bought that story?"

"What's to *buy*? It's the truth. Nikky. You will never be your father, any more than Liza could ever be her mother."

"I'm not trying to be him."

"Then you have nothing to worry about. Neither does Cristoff. I told him it was a supreme honor that you bestowed on him last night when you closed your show with his song, and I yelled at him that he wasn't in the audience to applaud you."

"You yelled at him?"

"Okay, well not exactly *yelled*, but I was rather forceful."

Forceful and beautiful—a wicked combination. A stunning woman, Isabella looked like Catherine Zeta-Jones might in twenty years, and with her long black hair braided into a chignon at the base of her neck and wearing an elegant Oscar de la Renta lounging suit, she could have passed for Spanish royalty.

Nik kissed his mother on the forehead.

"Thanks, Mom. So how should I handle things?"

"Just be yourself, son."

"Like that's ever worked."

Isabella wrapped her arms around him and hugged him fiercely just as Cristoff stormed into the room.

"What the heck is that thing in the driveway? Looks like a Batmobile."

"That's Nikky's new car, and I think it's classy." Isabella winked at her son as she gently picked up Milan, her little Shih Tzu puppy, and settled into the corner of the plush sofa, placing her feet on the ottoman.

"What is it?" Cristoff walked to the window and peered out at the car, and Nik joined him.

"It's a Lamborghini Murciélago LP-six-forty."

"V-twelve?" his father asked.

"Yep. Six-forty horses, hits sixty-two in three-point-four seconds."

"Nice color." His father said, turning from the window and going to the bar, where he grabbed a handful of peanuts.

Was that a compliment? "Thanks. It's the same color as my first car, remember?"

"Yeah, what was that, anyway?"

"A Mustang convertible."

"That's right. The one you wrecked a few weeks later."

"Oh shush, Cristoff. He was only sixteen. Every young man needs to learn to drive, and it's the only accident he's ever had. It was a kind of rite of passage."

A rite of passage. Nik wondered if she called the beating his father had given him afterward a rite of passage too. No wonder he'd never had another accident—he'd learned the hard way how to pay attention on the road.

Cristoff poured two shots of ouzo and handed one to Nik. "Here's to you, kid."

"For what?"

"For another . . . rite of passage, did you call it, Izzy?"

"Yes."

Nik waited for his father to continue.

"I heard what you did last night."

"Uh, Dad, that's why I came over today . . . to talk to you about that."

"No need to apologize. Your mother tells me I should be honored."

I wasn't going to apologize. "I decided at the last minute. I just kind of felt the spirit move me, you know? I meant no disrespect."

"It was a beautiful evening last night?" his father queried.

"Yes," Nik responded.

"Under the stars of the famous Hollywood Bowl?"

"Yes . . ."

"And you were . . ."

"Inspired?" Isabella smiled as she interrupted, her chocolate brown eyes sparkling.

"I guess so. I remembered what it was like when I was a kid and I'd listen to you close your show with that tune. It just felt . . . right. You know?"

"Yes. I know. Drink up. Here's to 'As Time Goes By.' "

They swigged back their shots of licorice liqueur, and then Cristoff smacked his glass down on the table. "Just don't ever do it again, unless you ask me first. Got it?"

Nik should have figured there would be a restriction coming— a rule he would have to follow at the risk of crossing his old man.

"The love songs are mine—especially that one. You have your music, and I have mine. It's what the fans want—it's what they know. End of story."

"It's not the end of the story." Nik looked away. "I'm thinking of recording an album of old ballads."

"Over my dead body!" Cristoff's anger came from deep inside his belly, a sound that at once made both Nik and Isabella cringe. "Absolutely not. I will not allow it. End of discussion. Period."

Every now and then Nik found himself at a fork in the road—a place where his life stretched out in front of him—where he had to decide whether to walk on hot coals and get burned, or slide through the safe sand of the easier way out. This time Nik opted for the heat.

He didn't say it loudly, but he said it slow and clear. "It's not for you to allow or not. I'm not asking your permission."

"What did you say?" Cristoff furrowed his brow in a way that had make Nik shiver when he was younger, but this time the look made him realize how old his father had become. The deep

47

wrinkles in his forehead resembled a Shar Pei his mother had once owned.

"You heard what I said, Father. I'm thinking of recording love songs, and I'm even considering some duets. Do you know any female singers who might be interested? Maybe *Carlotta*?" He boldly stared his father down.

"Don't even think about it," Cristoff spat. "Get out of my house. Now."

"It's my house too, and you can go when you want to, Nikky." Isabella kicked off her sandals and tucked her legs up under her like a teenager. "Isn't that right, Milan?" She nuzzled her little puppy.

"Insolence! What is happening here—in my own home!?"

"Nothing is happening, dear. We're having a little disagreement, like a normal family, and everything will be fine. It's time we all stopped making mountains out of molehills. It's becoming quite tiring. Don't you agree, dear?"

Cristoff merely grunted.

"I have to go now, Mother. I'm going to Sasha's wedding."

"Wonderful. We decided to send a gift instead—your father and I didn't want to cause a scene and steal their thunder. It's their day, after all."

"Oh." Nik had honestly forgotten that his attendance at his cousin's wedding might cause a problem. After all these years, the attention was still a part of his fame that had not fully sunk in—that he couldn't even attend a party for a relative without everyone making a fuss. "Should I stay home?"

"I'm sure it will be okay. It's invitation only, and I'm certain they'll have security guards. You're taking your man with you, right?"

Nik's "man" was his bodyguard, Campbell, a trusted friend who accompanied him to most public places these days.

Nik's father walked with him to the door. Before Nik reached for the doorknob, his father grabbed his arm.

"Don't mess with me about this, Nikolai."

Nik knew he was treading on thin ice when his father used his Christian name. He didn't care. He was tired of the dance—the fork in the road had come and he was prepared for the worst.

"You will not record my music, and you will most certainly not contact Carlotta—and that is the end of it."

"I have no intention of messing with you, Father." Nik pulled away, brushed off his shirt, yanked open the door, and walked toward his sleek sports car. "No intention whatsoever." He slid behind the scissor door, climbed into the low cockpit, fired up the powerful engine, and sped off, leaving the Great Cristoff on his own doorstep, speechless and angry as a troll.

It was one of the few times that Nik had ever left his childhood home with a smile on his face.

10

"We're as ready as we're going to be," Ursula declared after a short rehearsal. The boys had been absolutely right: she knew the entire playlist and relaxed as her confidence grew. "You fellows are really very good. Are you sure you don't want to pursue music full-time?"

"Only your mom would be encouraging us not to go to school—to continue this nonsense." Phil smiled.

"It's not nonsense. I really think you guys would have a good shot at making it big."

"Give it up, Mom, okay? You better go upstairs and get dressed."

After finding out the boys were all wearing black tuxes and that the reception was for Sasha Angelis, the daughter of a well-known film producer, Ursula decided to pull out all the stops. She was inspecting the final results in the hall mirror when she heard her son.

"Come on, Mom," Victor yelled up the stairs. "The van's loaded, and we have to get a move on. You ready yet?"

"Ready or not, here I come."

All heads turned, and by the time Ursula reached the bottom of the steps, the young men had nearly regained their composure.

"Well?"

"Wow, Mom, you look . . . incredible."

"Thank you, Victor."

Ursula's hair was totally slicked back like Greta Garbo, with a pure white gardenia secured in it just below her left ear. Valerie had run down to a neighbor's house to ask if she could pick one from their flower bed.

Ursula wore a full-length cobalt blue satin gown that brought out the blue in her eyes. A short silver-sequined jacket secured in the front with a rhinestone clip caught every ounce of light and would sparkle from the stage. Her jewelry was a vintage set of Eisenberg with matching earrings, necklace, and bracelet. A very expensive pair of crystal Miu Miu open-toed shoes she bought at one of her friend Dee's silent auctions sparkled on her size-seven feet.

Her makeup was heavier than she usually wore but would work perfectly for tonight's event. A brilliant deep red lipstick from MAC made her lips look more full and vibrant. She looked every inch a diva.

"You look like you stepped out of a movie, Mrs. Rhoades," Cliff whispered. "One of those old Bette Davis ones my mom always watches."

"Thank you, dear." She ignored yet another "old" comment. "Hadn't we best get moving, gentlemen? And might I add that you young men look particularly dashing yourselves."

They stammered and blushed and teased all the way out to the van.

The Angelis mansion was one of the most exquisite and opulent Ursula had ever seen. The reception was being held in an adjacent tent that must have cost fifty thousand dollars to rent and set up. Straight out of *Father of the Bride* without the rainstorm, it was fantasyland personified. Gossamer panels floated over a sea of teal and silver tables set with crystal and fine china. Candles placed among long-stemmed red roses decorated the tabletops. The dance floor and stage were huge and the sound system would have made George Lucas proud. The overall ambiance was perfect. *Dee would love this.*

While the boys set up their equipment, Ursula sipped on a cup of hot tea with lemon and honey that one of the waitstaff had graciously brought her.

"You look like you stepped out of an old Joan Crawford film," the waiter said, pouring her tea.

"Thank you, I think. The boys in the band pegged me as a dame from an old Bette Davis movie; someone else said I looked like the cover of an old Billie Holiday album. Good thing I'm secure in who I really am, or I'd be suffering an identity crisis." The waiter smiled and excused himself as she shook her head and laughed aloud. *I wonder what Don would think about this.*

11

By the time Nik got to the reception, it was already dark. The applause coming from the dance floor caught his attention as he walked to the bar to order a drink. He peered toward the clamor, trying to gain a glimpse of the band, able to see only a couple young boys onstage.

"I thought the Clayton Brothers had been hired for this party," he said to the bartender, a lovely young woman barely old enough to drink herself.

She jumped a little when she recognized him but managed to stay in control. "They were," she answered, "but they canceled when Stowell got arrested."

"That's right. Forgot all about that. Can't very well sing from prison."

"Unless you're Johnny Cash."

"Touché—good one."

"Thank you, Mr. Prevel. I saw your concert last night at the Hollywood Bowl. You were fabulous. They should have hired you to play tonight."

Ignorant girl. Aristotle had the money to afford him, but Nik no longer played at wedding receptions. *What an insult.*

"They any good?" He nodded toward the band.

"They're very good. The singer is amazing."

He couldn't see a singer from where he stood.

"Do you know 'Stardust'?" someone yelled toward the stage as Nik walked to get a closer look. It was an old but well-covered song Nik remembered from when he was a kid, one of his dad's favorite tunes. *Not likely this band of young kids will know it.* He couldn't see the singer, but he heard her voice booming from the speakers.

"You'll have to try harder than that to stump us. Play it, gentlemen!"

And within seconds Nik was transported back in time as the band expertly struck the chords of "Stardust" and a deep, throaty voice that sounded like a cross between Brenda Lee and Rosemary Clooney began to sing. It was a voice that made a person stop and take notice.

The little bartender—Ashley, her name tag had read—was right. This dame had to be a pro, but he didn't recognize the voice, and he was usually good at identifying singers. It wasn't easy getting close to the stage, as it appeared almost everyone from the party was standing a good ten people deep on the dance floor, circling the bride and groom as they alone danced to the romantic tune.

He was moving to the side of the tent to get a better view when he saw her.

She was magnificent.

Like a ghost from an era long past, the woman onstage could have stepped out from an old RKO film. Were it not for the modern cordless microphone she held, he would have felt as though he were a little boy watching a torch singer. He could almost smell the fragrance of what he was certain was a white gardenia in her cinnamon-colored hair. And those lips—red, full, and fabulous—were matched only by the way she belted out the song.

Calling out one classic tune after another, the crowd was unable to stump the band or the singer as Nik watched mesmerized. One song after another sent him reeling back in time as she sang "Someone to Watch Over Me," "I Only Have Eyes for You," and "I've Got You Under My Skin." He'd found a relatively safe place to the west of a huge potted plant dotted with tiny white twinkle lights where he could stand almost undetected. Campbell hovered inconspicuously nearby, quietly maintaining distance yet close enough to reach Nik's side in a few broad steps if needed. The people who did notice him were respecting his privacy—he had expected that he'd be safe around a crowd of this caliber.

What he hadn't expected was to discover a voice that would take him prisoner.

Who are you? And where have you been hiding?

When the band took a break, Nik wasn't sure what he was going to say when he reached her—only that he had to find out more about this vivacious vamp.

"Excuse me, have we met?" Nik asked.

———————

Ursula vaguely recognized the handsome young man in front of her but found his pickup line a bit lame. He was surely half her age and should be ashamed of himself for coming on to her. Still, she was flattered.

"I don't think so. But thanks for the effort. Maybe you know my son; he's closer to your age." She pointed toward the stage where the boys were preening in front of the youngest bridal party attendants.

"Your son? Which one?"

"The one with the wavy hair."

"The piano player? He's good."

"Yes, he's a natural, all right."

"You're the one who's the natural. Mighty nice set of pipes you've got there."

The reference to her "pipes" was not lost on Ursula, and she bristled at the jerk's comment about her chest.

"If you'll excuse me, I need to make a call before our next set. Have a good evening."

———

Nik watched her walk away, breathing deeply the fragrance of gardenia, wondering what he'd said wrong while he speed-dialed on his cell phone.

"Arnie, where are you?" he whispered.

"Home. Sitting on the deck with Raysha, enjoying the stars. Where are you?"

"At a wedding reception."

"How quaint. Whose?"

"Sasha Angelis."

"That's tonight? Darn it, Raysha," he yelled, "the Angelis wedding reception is tonight. I thought I told you to put that on our calendar. I wanted to go. Where's it at?" Arnie questioned Nik.

"The Palisades. That's why I'm calling. You can be here in no time—come on down. It's late and most folks have lost the tux jackets and ties, so you're probably safe with an Armani."

"I'll be right there."

"I've got a surprise for you."

"You know I hate surprises."

"Not this one you won't."

———

By the time Arnie arrived at the reception, the band was well into their last set for the night. He greeted Nik and then watched the dynamic songstress captivate the crowd with her wit, wisdom, knowledge of music, and sheer vocal prowess. A powerful mezzo-soprano, her range was phenomenal. It had been a long time since Arnie had heard such a pure voice. She was truly charismatic onstage in a self-effacing kind of way—the crowd loved her.

"You're right. This is my kind of surprise," he told Nik. "She's stunning."

"Yeah, thought you'd like her. How old do you think she is?"

"Hard to say, could be in her late forties, maybe even fifties."

"No way, really? That old?"

"Like I said, it's hard to say these days. This is Hollywood, remember? All is not as it seems in the world of broken dreams."

"Now that's original."

"Thank you." He grinned.

"The kid at the piano is her son. He looks about twenty."

"That might mean she is in her early forties, provided she got married right out of high school."

"Who said she had to be married? You're so old-fashioned, Arnie."

"It's hard to miss the significant diamond on her left hand, see?"

Nik looked surprised. He had been watching her all night but apparently hadn't noticed the off-limits sign flashing before him. Marital status had never been a big concern to him. Arnie suspected he actually preferred married women, considering they gave him far less hassle in the long run.

"Any final requests from the crowd?" the young pianist queried.

" 'La Vie en Rose,' " Nik shouted, easily projecting his voice from the back of the tent.

All eyes turned to him as his name was whispered throughout the room. Arnie groaned inwardly. Did Nik have to pursue every fleeting desire he had?

Mother and son exchanged a few words as she raised her eyebrows briefly.

"Thank you, Mr. Prevel," the pianist said loudly.

With that, the beauty stepped forward and called the room to attention. She intentionally avoided eye contact with Nik Prevel. "Thank you, ladies and gentlemen, for a splendid evening. God bless the happy couple and may they long remember this special night spent with family and friends.

"First recorded in 1945 by the great Edith Piaf, a petite singer from France nicknamed The Little Sparrow, 'La Vie en Rose' became her signature song and was voted a Grammy Hall of Fame Award in 1998. We hope you enjoy this rendition, and we hope you've enjoyed your evening. Drive safely, and God bless and keep you."

Arnie was more than impressed, not only with her voice, but with the fact that she switched seamlessly from English to perfect French—captivating the crowd. Guests began to sway and couples cuddled close on the dance floor—a perfect ending to a breathtaking event. It was one of those rare vocal performances that gave him goose bumps and made the tiny hairs on the back of his neck stand up.

Nik appeared to be in a trance when Arnie tapped him on the shoulder. "Are you thinking what I'm thinking?" Arnie whispered.

"Probably."

"So who's going to ask her? You or me?"

"I don't think Raysha would be happy if you brought her home with you."

"You're going to try and pick her up? You're not serious."

"Of course I'm serious. I never joke about women."

"She doesn't look your type."

"No such thing as not my type. She fascinates me. I want her."

"But that's not what I'm talking about—that wasn't at all what I was thinking."

"I know, Arnie. I'm not a dimwit. Leave it to me."

Arnie watched from the sidelines as Nik and the singer talked when she came offstage—and was amazed when she hauled off and smacked him square across the face. It was like a scene from one of the old movies she appeared to have stepped directly from. He laughed—something Nik was not doing as the singer walked away from him.

Arnie immediately went in search of the host to find out more about the woman, feeling certain that if he had anything to say about it, this wasn't the last they would see—or hear—from her.

12

🔊 Ursula settled back into the chair, watching Don frying bacon—a task he tackled only on Saturdays when he cooked the family a full breakfast, including blueberry pancakes and eggs. She tried to imagine what he would say if she told him Arnold Shapiro, the manager of the great Nik Prevel, had been calling all week, wanting to meet to talk with her about "an important project."

The calls had begun the day after she'd met his client.

"How did you get my cell phone number?"

"The father of the bride, of course. You weren't that hard to find, Mrs. Rhoades. Your band was on the payroll for the night, remember?"

"It's not my band."

"I understand. Your number was on the contract your son signed for the engagement . . . as an emergency contact."

"I see."

"Mr. Prevel was impressed with your voice, as was I. He'd like to talk with you about the possibility of working with him on a project he's got in the works."

"Nik Prevel wants to talk with me?"

"Correct."

"About a project."

"Correct."

I'll bet he does. "Mr. Shapiro—"

"Arnie, please."

"Mr. Shapiro, I appreciate your interest, but you've got the wrong girl. I was just filling in for the night—a one-time deal. I have no interest in *working* with Mr. Prevel."

What do they take me for? A fool? She'd read about managers acting as pimps for their famous clients—but she wasn't at all impressed with the possibility of being a notch in any rock star's belt.

"All I'm asking is that you meet with me, for just one hour—lunch somewhere. Let me tell you more about the project before you make your final decision."

"I've already made my decision and it's final. I'm flattered, but my husband is about to begin an important case and he needs me."

"Your husband is a lawyer?"

"Yes."

"You're a lawyer too?"

"No . . ."

"I'm confused. Why does your husband need you?"

"Mr. Shapiro, as I said, I appreciate your position, but my personal life is none of your concern."

Various conversations of the same ilk had occurred every day for the past week. The pursuit would make her angry if not for the fact that the man was somewhat endearing in his devotion to either Nik or to the mysterious project he was firmly refusing to discuss over the phone. She couldn't be sure which.

"Breakfast is served, m'lady." Don interrupted her thoughts. He set the plate in front of her and kissed her on the forehead.

"Yum. This looks wonderful, sweetheart. What am I going to do without you for so long?"

"You'll be fine. You'll come to the city from time to time—when I can get away—but I probably won't be cooking much. Once I get a feel for how the trial's going, I'll have a better handle on what, if any, free time I'll be able to squeeze in."

"All work and no play, you know what they say." She let the crisp bacon melt in her mouth as she watched Don. He was clearly looking forward to his trip.

"This is a very big deal, Ursula. There are guys who would kill for a case like this."

"A bit dramatic, don't you think?" She nodded yes to more coffee.

"Not at all. I don't think you understand what this means. This case is going to be all over the news—already is. This is my future, Ursula, my chance to show them what I've got."

"It's *our* future, and they already know what you've got or they wouldn't have entrusted this case to you. You'll be fine; stop worrying." She had never seen her husband so agitated. "So what kind of team has Sam assembled for you?"

"The typical guys, plus some new folks on the East Coast. I'll meet them first thing on Monday. Should be interesting."

Ursula was taking Don to LAX later that day. Valerie would be flying out of the same airport tomorrow for Australia, and a few days after that Victor would be on his way driving to Berkeley. Her head swam at the immensity of the changes occurring all at once.

"I still think they should have leased you an apartment or condo. Extended hotel living can't be very comfortable—not to mention costly."

"Hon, I don't think the expense of our housing is at the top of the list for concerns right now. Besides, hotel living is very comfortable, especially where we'll be. They've got the team in adjoining suites at the Trump International Hotel and Tower, right in the heart of the city on Central Park West. You know Sam and

Donald are friends. We'll have access to a full conference room, business center, restaurants, bars, and the works."

"I'm surprised Sam's never considered a New York branch for the firm."

"He's discussed the idea from time to time, but something keeps holding him back. I'm not sure what it is."

"Well, maybe this will be a deciding factor." Neither she nor Don cared much for New York, so she hoped a branch in that city wouldn't transpire. But one never knew how things would shake out. "I'm so proud of you. We've worked really hard for this—I just know they're going to offer you that senior partnership when you get back."

"Hope so. Thanks for the vote of confidence. So what do you plan to do with your spring and summer? It's going to be mighty quiet around here. You should think about getting yourself a hobby or something."

"I have plenty of hobbies—including taking care of you and our children and our home. I also tutor students, remember?"

"I thought all your students were on hiatus this summer."

"Yes, they are." She didn't remind him of the reason. Knowing this would be their first summer as "empty nesters," they'd decided to use this time as a kind of second honeymoon, taking some of Don's well-earned vacation days to spend together. But he'd become obsessed with the Chesterfield case since Sam had placed it in his lap, and nothing else seemed to matter—not her, not the kids, nothing. This total focus made him the outstanding lawyer he was; but even after all of these years, she had a tough time not feeling insecure about how easy it was for him to shut out everything else.

She joined him outside as Don loaded his luggage into the car. Her throat felt tight, and she sensed herself tearing up. "Honey, I'm going to miss you."

Don wrapped her in his arms, the smell of Aramis, her favorite men's cologne, heavy on his clothing.

"I'll miss you too, honey. You can fly out when I have a better feel for the case, okay?"

"Sure. Maybe I'll tackle that major closet reorganization project we've been talking about for years."

"I think that's a great idea. That should keep you plenty busy."

Keeping busy was never a problem. She could always find something to do in a house the size of theirs. Plus, Dee had been after her to chair another fundraising event; maybe she'd look into that, as well.

"Don, did you know Marge is going back to school?"

"Who?"

"Marge Kendall. My friend from the Junior League."

"Oh yeah? What's she taking? The art of buying shoes?"

"Very funny. She's going back for her Master's in Biology."

"Biology? You're kidding, right? Are we talking about the same Marge? The one with all the jewelry?"

"Yep. Same one. Still waters run deep."

"There's nothing still about that character!"

"Don . . . what would you say about me going back to school?"

"What would you take?"

What would she take? "Music, of course. What else?"

"To what end?"

"What do you mean, to what end?" She sat on a stone garden bench just outside the garage, and Don joined her.

"I mean, what's the point? You can tutor as many students as you'd like. All you have to do is make a few calls and you'll be busy the rest of the summer. You're the best tutor in the four-county area, and everyone knows it. What more education do you need?"

"I was thinking about studying under Philomena Petrovia."

"The opera singer? Our client?"

"Yes."

"What for?"

"What do you mean, what for?"

"Does she train private tutors now? I thought she was a professional singer."

"She is."

Philomena Petrovia was known as the Soprano Superstar; her legendary voice made her one of the most sought-after performers in opera. She took on a limited number of private students during her summer hiatus. Earlier in the year, half serious and half joking, Ursula had asked Philomena to put her on the list if she ever had an opening for a *seasoned student*. With rather auspicious timing, Ursula had been informed a few days before that she was on the short list.

"So what could she teach you about tutoring?"

"I didn't say anything about tutoring! I'm talking about advanced vocal training, for me."

Don looked at her as though she had lost her mind. "Is this about that party you and Victor played at last week?"

"Well, maybe . . . a little . . . It was fun. You should have—"

"Don't be foolish, Ursula. You're almost fifty years old—hardly the age to get started as a singer—let alone opera. You're pulling my leg, right?" He stood and rummaged around in the trunk to ensure everything was accounted for. "You've been out of school for decades. Honey, I don't mean to sound harsh, but that kind of education is for youngsters. You've got enough to keep you busy. Didn't you say you had some remodeling to do?" He shut the trunk and placed his briefcase on the backseat of the car. "Besides, there will be a great deal for you to do when I get the senior partnership—you know what is expected. Come on; let's beat the traffic."

Ursula bit her tongue to keep back a sharp retort. She was fuming inside, but the fact that he might be right shut her up like a Ziploc bag. The drive to the airport was chilly, in spite of the warm weather outside the car.

Traffic to the airport was horrendous. By the time they arrived, it was clear there would be no time for Don to park so she could accompany him at least as far as security—to give him a more personalized send-off than simply taking over the wheel and leaving him at the curb. Yet that was what had to happen.

"It's okay. I'm fine getting out here. We always do it this way. What's the big deal?"

"The big deal is you're going away for months, not days!" *And Valerie leaves tomorrow, and Victor leaves next week, and I'm feeling disconnected—don't you understand anything?* "I just wanted to make this a special send-off for you."

"Honey, I appreciate that—really I do. But this is okay. I'm going to be late. I have to run."

As they pulled his luggage out of the trunk, she looked up to see Celeste Foster and two other associates from the firm get out of a taxi a few cars away.

"Is that Celeste?" Ursula nodded toward the woman pulling her Louis Vuitton case into the terminal. "Don, I'm talking to you. Did I just see Celeste Foster go into the terminal? Is it a coincidence, or is she part of your New York team?"

"She might be. Sam is really impressed with her work."

"Did you know about this? Why didn't you tell me?"

"Ursula, I really have to get inside. This is a non-issue. I work around female associates all day long—it's never concerned you before. Why are you picking fights today?"

"Why are you avoiding the question? That feline Delilah has her claws out—ready to sink them into your sweet flesh at the first opportunity."

"You're being ridiculous and you know it."

"I am not being ridiculous and *you* know it."

"I will not have this discussion with you, Ursula. Go home, take a hot bath, and chill out. You are overreacting."

"Do not patronize me!"

"Then stop behaving like a child."

"I am not behaving like a child. I am your wife, and I'm concerned that you can't see that you're the next meal for that . . . that tigress!"

"Enough, Ursula! I'm late and I'm leaving."

He kissed her perfunctorily, patted her arm, and threw an "I love you" over his shoulder as he hurried into the terminal. As she watched her husband rush away, Ursula felt for the first time in her marriage that maybe things were not as perfect as she'd thought.

13

"I said to forget about her!" Nik was tired of hearing about Arnie's failed attempts to pursue on his behalf the selfish witch he'd met at the wedding reception. Who did she think she was? "I don't beg anyone to work with me. We'll find someone else."

"I wasn't begging her."

"How many times have you called?"

"I don't know."

"You're a Jewish lawyer in L.A.; you make a record of every call you place and you know it. How many?"

"Seven."

"Has she ever given you the time of day?"

"No."

"Agreed to meet with you?"

"No."

"Enough said. End of discussion.. We'll find someone else. In the meantime, what do you think of these songs as a starter?"

Arnie reviewed the list Nik had developed after hours of listening to old show tunes, movie tunes, and Big Band Era torch songs, songs like they'd heard Ursula sing at the reception and other American standards such as "You Send Me" and "If I Loved You."

"Check on rights and see if anything is in public domain," Nik said.

"Yeah, right, like that's gonna happen." Arnie shook his head. "Public domain is hardly an option with these tunes. Hymns, maybe, but not these."

"That'll be my next project—Nik Prevel Does the Hymns We All Know and Love. Has a nice ring to it."

"Except you don't *know* any hymns, let alone *love* any."

They both laughed at the absurdity of the suggestion.

They talked briefly about other potential female singers—unimpressed by any of their suggestions.

They sat back listening to an old Bessie Smith recording. It reminded Nik of Ursula and her fabulous voice. He couldn't get her out of his mind. "I still find it weird she wasn't at all excited about recording old standard tunes," he blurted. "She seemed to have a real passion for the era, knew every song they tossed out. I'm really surprised she wasn't open to the experience."

"I wouldn't know if she was open to the experience or not. I never had a chance to find out," Arnie complained.

"What do you mean? She knows what we have in mind, right?"

"How could she? I've never gotten her to agree to a meeting to discuss it."

"Wait a minute. Are you telling me she has no idea that I want her to record an album of love ballads with me?"

"Well, not really."

"What did you talk about for seven calls?"

"I told her you appreciated her voice and that you wanted to discuss a possible project with her."

"For crying out loud, Arnie! *A possible project?* After what I said to her at the wedding, I can just imagine what she's thinking."

"What did you say?"

"Never mind! Just get on that phone right now and tell her *specifically* what we have in mind. Then set up a meeting to talk more about it. Better yet, I want you to go over to her house and tell her in person, enough of this cat-and-mouse game."

"Are you sure this is the way you want to go? I mean, you said so yourself, she's pretty old."

"She's hardly old, Arnie. What's your problem, anyway? First you complain they're too young, now too old. What's just right, Papa Bear?"

"All right, all right—have it your way! I'll go see her."

Nik smiled, content that Arnie would get him what he wanted—and he wanted Ursula.

14

She got the call the day after Don left and immediately invited Dee over to share the news.

Dee started speaking before she'd even closed the door behind her. "I want the whole story. Start at the beginning. Philomena said she'd take you on for private lessons?" Dee put her purse on the counter and walked to the coffeepot. "May I?"

"Of course. I set out your mug. Yes, she did."

"That alone should give you all the affirmation you need. How many private students does she take in a year?" She carried her mug of steaming coffee and sat next to her friend.

"Two."

"Ursula! You have to be a nut case not to do this. Is it the money? Can you afford her?"

"It's not the money. I can afford her—financially. Just not sure if I can emotionally afford her."

Dee studied her, and Ursula knew her best friend understood. Dee was a partner in LeGrande Enterprises, a special-event firm based in Los Angeles, but she lived down in Orange County, where her firm had a satellite office just off the historic circle in the quaint town of Orange. Ursula enjoyed the time spent chatting with Dee, catching up on each other's lives. Dee wasn't like the Junior League crowd Ursula usually associated with, or like the associates' wives at Don's firm. She was real people—down-to-earth. Ursula trusted her implicitly.

"What does Don say?" Dee asked, reaching for an oatmeal cookie. "May I?"

"Of course. Be careful, I used a lot of butter and sugar."

"Thanks, I think I've got a handle on this now."

It had been quite a while since Dee had undergone gastric-bypass surgery, but Ursula knew firsthand what too much butter and sugar did to her friend.

"So don't change the subject. What does Don say?" Dee nibbled at the cookie.

"Nothing positive—that's for sure."

"Have you been praying about it?"

"Almost continually."

"And what is God telling you?"

"He's being rather quiet these days."

"Ah, I know what you mean. That's how I felt when Lyle and I first split up—like God left me at the same time."

"And now?"

"Now it's like we're connected via two-way radio. I've never felt more strongly that I'm walking in God's will. It's a good feeling after so long. Don't worry, Urs, you'll know what to do when the time comes to make a decision."

"Maybe I should have taken that meeting with Arnie Shapiro—at least listened to what he had to say. He hasn't called in a while. I think he got the message."

"I wish I could have heard you that night. Several of the committee members for the new golf course were at the reception—said you blew the roof off the tent with your voice. What was Nik Prevel like? Is he as gorgeous in person?"

"Valerie flipped when she found out he was there and she could have met him. She's a big fan, you know. I've heard some of his stuff, but frankly, I prefer his dad's music."

"When do you have to make a decision about Philomena?" Dee reached into her Fendi handbag and pulled out a nail file.

"Soon. By the end of the week. She gave me until Victor was on his way to get back to her."

"So you're almost an empty nester. How do you feel?"

Don had been gone for only five days, but it seemed like five weeks. She was still angry with him for not telling her about Celeste. Their one phone conversation since he'd arrived in New York had been strained. She'd vowed not to call him again until he called her, wondering how long it would take—and if she could hold out.

She'd cried the day after he left as she put Valerie on the plane. And Victor would leave in a few hours.

"I feel . . . mixed. Not sure what I'm supposed to do, you know?"

"I know what you mean. Kelsey and Kent love their condo, and Lyle and I are wondering what to do with all the space in our house. Did I tell you he turned one of the guest bedrooms into a walk-in closet for me? It's totally grand! I feel like a queen."

"You deserve it, Dee. I'm glad things are working out for you two."

Dee and Lyle had been separated for almost one year, and if Dee would have had her way, they'd have been divorced. But Lyle hung on—a decision that saved their marriage.

They prayed before Dee left, and Ursula felt more convicted about her decision to take private lessons. She would break down and call Don tonight. Surely he would eventually be supportive, even if he didn't understand why she was taking the lessons. He just couldn't grasp the love she had for music and singing.

Waving good-bye to Dee as she pulled out of the driveway, Ursula was surprised when a silver-gray Jaguar pulled into the space Dee had just vacated. Without her glasses it was difficult to see who was driving. She walked down the front steps to greet her guest as an impeccably dressed little man got out of the car and walked briskly up the walk with outstretched hand.

"I'm sorry to drop in like this, Mrs. Rhoades . . ."

She recognized his voice immediately.

"I'm Arnie Shapiro. I really need to talk with you. Do you have a few minutes? Have I caught you at a good time?"

Ursula sighed and accepted his handshake. He wore a khaki pinstripe suit—Dolce & Gabbana, perhaps—with a red-and-white-checked shirt and white tie. He reminded Ursula of Richard Dreyfuss in *Mr. Holland's Opus*.

"You're a mighty tenacious fellow, aren't you, Mr. Shapiro?"

"I suppose you could say that. I come on behalf of my client. He wants me to tell you that he would like you to work with him to record a collection of classic love-song ballads. This is not a smokescreen. It's a business proposal he would like you to seriously consider. He would like to meet with you in person to discuss said possibility."

Ursula cocked her head and furrowed her brow. "He wants to record an album with me?"

"Correct."

"Mr. Rock is going Pop?"

"Actually, it's called Traditional Pop, but yes, that's correct. Would it be possible to go inside, Mrs. Rhoades? It's a lovely Southern California day, but I'd prefer to discuss business inside, if it's all the same to you. I'm perfectly safe, housebroken even."

"I'm quite certain you are, Mr. Shapiro," she said with a smile. "Come in. I'm fascinated to hear what you have to say."

Arnie pulled out all the stops in his presentation and got Ursula to admit the offer was flattering. Still, she told him in no uncertain terms that she was not interested, that her husband was involved in a high-profile court case that required her not only to maintain a low profile but to be able to fly to New York City on a moment's notice.

"In addition to all those reasons, and this really is the deciding factor, I've been given a once-in-a-lifetime opportunity to study under Philomena Petrovia this summer, and I've decided to accept it."

Arnie wasn't surprised to hear this talented woman was on her own track already, but he pressed on. "Opera? Why choose the unlikely success of opera over the sure success of recording with Nik Prevel?"

Ursula only laughed at his attempt. "Opera was my major before I married Don. It's a longtime passion of mine. Please let Mr. Prevel know I really am honored. You know as well as I do that he'll have no trouble finding someone to sing with him—someone far younger and more talented."

Arnie knew that Nik would not be happy with her decision, but he had to admire the strength of this woman. She was clearly a person of deep conviction. He would like to have had the opportunity to get to know her better.

————————

Ursula tried several times before she connected with her husband later that evening. She tried to shake off the notion he sounded less than happy to hear from her.

"Guess what?"

"Honey, I don't have time for guessing games. I'm on my way out to Cipriani's for dinner with the team."

"Philomena Petrovia has invited me to study with her for the summer."

The silence was deafening.

"I thought we already discussed this."

"Yes, we did, but I wasn't aware we had definitive closure."

"Invited you? What does that mean exactly? Like a guest?"

"Well, not quite. I'll be one of her private students. She only takes two a year."

"How much will that cost?"

"Don, when you took putting classes with Jack Nicklaus, did I ask you how much it was going to cost? When you decided to train under Terry Paulsen, did I ask you how much it was going to cost? It's not about cost! This is a once-in-a-lifetime opportunity, and I'm going to take it." There. She'd said it. She held her breath, wondering what he would say.

"Congratulations, then," Don said flatly.

She wanted to tell him about Arnie's offer—which really was exciting news—but somehow the timing just didn't seem right.

"Don, what's the matter?" This wasn't the man she knew and loved. "I'm sorry I raised my voice. I'm sorry we argued at the airport. It's just that . . ."

"Ursula, honey, I'm late. I really have to go. This is a stressful case—you have no idea what it's like up here. We took on this case late in the game. You know that. We've got twelve attorneys and a half dozen researchers and associates working around the clock to get ready before the trial starts next month. If you want to go sing an Irish jig from the top of Mount Everest, you have my blessing. Just don't ask me to get excited about it, okay? We're fighting for someone's life, for crying out loud! I'm sorry, but right now your whims are not in the same league."

My whims?

She was fighting for her life too. He just didn't know it—or he just plain didn't care.

15

Clearly Nik was going to have to take matters into his own hands. This entire situation was out of control.

"She said no?"

"Yes, she did."

No one says no to Nik Prevel. "So what does she expect us to do now?" Nik folded the *Billboard* magazine in half and handed it to Arnie.

"What do you mean?"

"Surely she doesn't really mean no. I'm assuming she's waiting for us to make our next move?"

"I don't think so. I don't think this lady is playing games. No reason for her to do that. She's quite serious. Her life is her husband and her family, and she appears happy with that." Arnie sat down and perused *Billboard* while Nik paced the room like an expectant father.

"Oh, please. You can't be serious," Nik said.

"It might surprise you, Nik, that not everyone is on your same wavelength. Some folks have other priorities."

"What are her priorities? Since you've apparently come to know her so well."

"Her family."

"But you said everyone was gone. Husband out of town, kids gone. She's alone, correct?"

"Yes, but she's studying under Philomena this summer."

"Petrovia?"

"One and the same."

"I told you she was good!"

"I never doubted she was good. I heard her too, remember?"

"If Philomena is taking her on as a client, she's more than good. I want her, Arnie."

"I know you do. But she obviously does not want you."

"Give me Philomena's number."

"What are you going to do?"

"Never mind. Just give me her number. Get her on your cell phone. I know you have her number."

Arnie dutifully dialed up the number and handed the phone to Nik, shaking his head. "I don't have a very good feeling about this."

Nik pasted on a smile even as he listened to the rings. He had to play this right. "Hello, Philly? Is it really you? Yes, it's Nikky. How have you been? It's been far too long, my sweet beauty. I have a favor to ask of you, my dear. Will you please indulge me, your most humble servant?"

16

Ursula was putting the final touches on the luncheon table when she got the call from Philomena Petrovia's assistant informing her that Madame had decided not to take on two students this year.

"But . . . I just spoke with her. . . ."

"I understand, Mrs. Rhoades, and Madame Petrovia has asked me to extend her most sincere apologies. In closer assessment she has decided to cut back this year and retain only one private student. She's already been working with Miss Mabee, so it is only logical she would retain her as a student. She wishes you all good things with your career and asks that you connect with her at the end of the summer."

My career? What career? She didn't have a career. She'd never had a career, not really. She had quit school and married Don.

When the doorbell rang she had to dry her eyes and put on a game face. Eleven women were joining her for lunch today—a special luncheon at which she had planned to announce her private internship with Madame Philomena Petrovia, the grand diva who had just dumped her.

Two hours later Dee stood at her shoulder on the front door-step as Ursula waved good-bye to the last of her guests, including Julliette, who had managed to survive a vicious beating from Ursula's inner child.

"She really is insufferable, isn't she?" Dee continued to wave and smile.

"She makes me want to sneak into her house and wash all of her Ann Taylor suits in hot water."

"So why didn't you tell them about Philomena Petrovia? I thought that was why we were here? You haven't changed your mind, have you?"

"I didn't, but she did." Ursula fought back tears as she hung her head and leaned into the open arms of her friend for a much-needed hug.

"Oh, Ursula, I'm sorry!"

"Dee, I don't know what's happening to my life. I feel like a ship bobbing along in the ocean without a course to follow, without a sail, without a map. . . . I don't even have a navigator!"

Dee put her hands on Ursula's shoulders, held her at arm's length, and looked her square in the eyes. "Don't say that. You'll always have a navigator. God has not forgotten about you."

Ursula sighed deeply, grateful for her friend's faith at a time when she needed it most. She wanted to talk with Dee about what troubled her most—the suspicion that her husband might be hav-ing an affair with an associate at the firm. If anyone could under-stand this, it would be Dee. But she couldn't say it out loud—not yet. It was her worst fear—and she prayed she was wrong.

"Sweetie, I'm sorry, but I have to head out. Just remember, when you think you've got it bad, think about me dealing with Julliette almost every day as she chairs the Diamond Ball com-mittee this year."

A few minutes later Ursula was staring at the table trying to decide what to do first when someone knocked on the front door. *Go away. I don't want to talk to anyone.* She began to put plates on a tray to carry to the kitchen. Whoever it was soon discovered the doorbell and began to ring it in earnest, hitting a feverish pitch that didn't bode well for whoever was on the other side. *This better be good. . . .*

17

"Good afternoon, Mrs. Rhoades. May we come in?" Arnie extended his hand.

"Hello, Mrs. Rhoades." Nik smiled as she stepped wordlessly aside, taken off guard by her visitors.

Ursula was glad Valerie was gone. She'd have been going crazy to see Nik Prevel standing in her foyer. Ursula, on the other hand, didn't know what to think as Nik walked past her into the living room as though he'd visited countless times.

"Lovely home. It looks like you. Is that a Kandinsky? I love his work." Nik admired the painting, chatting like an old friend.

"Excuse me." At a loss for words, she returned to her task like a Stepford wife, moving to the dining room and placing dishes on a serving tray. She was behaving poorly—and knew it—yet it was as though she was having an out-of-body experience.

Nik followed and peered down at the leftovers still covering the dining room table. "Is this crawfish étouffée? Looks like it—smells like it. Rather ambitious dish—did you order in or have someone prepare this in your home?"

"I made it myself."

"I'm impressed. Did your guests enjoy it?"

"Yes, I believe my guests enjoyed it. But they eat like birds; it's hard to tell. I was just clearing the table. . . ."

"Here, let us help you." Nik motioned to Arnie, and they both began to pick up stemware.

Ursula's mind finally kicked into gear. "Gentlemen, what are you doing here? Please don't do that." She pointed to the glasses in their hands, indicating they should return them to the table.

"Just wanted to help, ma'am." Nik showed Ursula a lot of teeth.

"Thank you. But I already told Mr. Shapiro I wasn't interested in your offer. It sounds like it could be fun, and I wish you great success, but the timing is off for me. Please don't take it personally. I just have too many irons in the fire."

She began to stack plates on a tray as the men stood back and watched her work.

"Sure we can't help you?" Arnie asked.

Ursula smiled and shook her head.

"Arnie was telling me you'll be studying with Philomena Petrovia this summer. Congratulations."

"Uh, well, er, thank you. I was surprised when she accepted me."

It was none of their business that she'd been dropped.

"How did you meet the reclusive Philomena?" Nik asked.

"My husband's firm represents her. We met at a fundraiser years ago. She found out I tutored young people and began to send me students—those not quite ready for her private tutelage."

"Interesting shift, your going from teacher to student, wouldn't you say? Smart move, though; you have an amazing range. Have you taken vocal lessons before?" Nik inquired.

Having filled the tray with dishes and flatware, Ursula wiped her hands on a linen napkin and turned toward Nik. "Mr. Prevelakis, why are you here?"

"Nik. Please call me Nik."

"What is it you want? Nik."

She looked at both men standing in front of her. Arnie appeared sheepish—a bit embarrassed, it seemed, to be back in her house discussing something she had in no uncertain terms declared was out of the question. Nik, on the other hand, was bold and steadfast. He stood before her with broad shoulders, square jaw, cleft chin, and almost blue-back hair that could have come from his Spanish lineage on his mother's side or the Greek heritage on his father's side. Most intriguing, however, was the color of his eyes—no photo she'd ever seen of him had accurately captured his icy blue eyes. Like those of an Alaskan Husky—eerie . . . cold . . . distanced—his eyes made you want to stare.

"My father is mostly Greek, but at some point in our family history there was an influence of Austrian blood. The eyes come from a blond-haired, blue-eyed vixen who forever altered our gene pool. May she rest in peace, whoever she is."

"I'm sorry. I didn't mean to stare. . . ." Ursula stammered.

"It's okay. Most folks do."

The real Nik was certainly something to write home about. His crisply tailored suit looked Italian to her—most likely Prada. The tan color set off his dark wavy hair and olive complexion perfectly. The open collar of the crisp blue shirt was tilted at just the right angle. She couldn't identify his cologne, but he smelled expensive. The only incongruity was the Ferragamo loafers worn without socks—but it was L.A. and he was, after all, Nik Prevelakis.

He raised his arm, running his fingers through his thick hair. His style was at once disheveled and sexy—a look she had no doubt he used to his utmost advantage.

"I want you to sing with me. What's it going to take for you to say yes?"

"Tenacious." Arnie smiled at Ursula and nodded toward Nik.

"I'd say so. How do you stand him?"

"Years of practice." Arnie folded his arms, exposing a beautiful Patek Philippe gold watch.

"Mrs. Rhoades, I'm serious," Nik interjected. "What's it going to take? Bottom line."

Ursula felt her resolve failing. She sank into a dining room chair—and her uninvited guests followed suit. Nik reached over and boldly plucked a croissant from a basket. "May I?" he asked.

"Be my guest."

Perhaps it would be fun to record with Nik. Fun, but impossible.

"Allow me to spell it out for you gentlemen," she said. "As flattered as I am and as exciting as it sounds, I am *unable* to join you. My husband is the lead counsel on the Felicia Chesterfield case. He is working with a team of lawyers in New York City as we speak, and will most likely be there until August or September. Surely you've seen this on television."

Nik nodded. "Yes, I've seen it. What does that have to do with you?"

"You might be used to having your face splashed all over the tabloids, but I can't afford to have that happen to me right now. It could be disastrous for my husband, and he's worked too hard for this case—it could make his career. Please try to understand."

"You're saying that your husband's career is more important than your own?"

"I'm saying I don't have a career. I told you I was standing in for my son's lead singer who'd had an accident. I don't sing for a living."

"But you could—you should. This is your chance."

"It's my husband's chance, and that is far more important."

Arnie smiled appreciatively. "It's called sacrifice, Nik. And I must say it looks very good on you, Mrs. Rhoades. Your husband is a lucky man."

Nik shook his head in amazement.

"Thank you, Mr. Shapiro. I don't know how much luck has to do with it. We've been very blessed. Don is so close to becoming a senior partner in his firm, and I won't jeopardize that."

"Do you really mean all this?" Nik looked truly flummoxed by the situation.

"I've got it!" Arnie shouted as Ursula and Nik glared at each other. "I have an idea." Arnie's eyes lit up as though he'd had a most brilliant insight. "Hear me out, folks, okay? If I understand you correctly, it's your husband's high-profile career you're concerned about—that perhaps being associated with Nik would somehow cast a pall on Mr. Rhoades."

"Hey, that's not fair. Being associated with me could make her a star."

"That's exactly it, Nik—she doesn't want to be a star."

"Bingo! Now you get it." Ursula was beginning to like Arnie.

"Who wouldn't want to be a star?" The possibility was clearly beyond Nik's comprehension.

"What if no one knew who you were, Mrs. Rhoades?" Arnie's eyes were bright with excitement.

Ursula and Nik looked blankly at him—not yet comprehending where he was going.

"What if you were a mystery woman? What if your identity was kept a secret?"

"How do you propose to do that?" Ursula asked.

"Easy! We control everything from the get-go—with a plan of action that keeps your identity a total secret. No one knows your real name—except us, of course. We give you an alias—we create a bio for you. We don't use your face on the cover. In fact, we can let folks think they know who you are—that maybe we've used a famous singer who wishes to be anonymous. Let the public write your story for us!"

"You're nuts." Nik shook his head.

"I'm brilliant. I can see the press now! We'll get more media attention this way than if folks knew she was just a housewife."

"Don't you call me that!" Ursula shouted and stood up.

"I'm sorry, Mrs. Rhoades, I only meant . . ."

"I know what you meant! And I'm sick of hearing it!" She once again began stacking dishes onto the serving tray, but she couldn't help watching her uninvited visitors.

Nik and Arnie didn't move. They simply stared at each other—Arnie's eyes lit in expectation and Nik's brow furrowed in concentration. "You really think it could work?" Nik asked his manager quietly, as if forgetting Ursula was present.

"I know it could work. What do you think, Mrs. Rhoades? If we can guarantee your privacy?" Arnie asked, grinning broadly.

Ursula stopped clearing the table and slowly smiled as she found herself actually considering their offer. Excitement swept over her. *This may be just where the Lord is leading me, why He allowed the change in plans for studying under Philomena.*

"Okay, I tell you what—I'm not promising anything yet, but tell me what you have in mind. I'm willing to hear you out. And please call me Ursula—all this Mrs. Rhoades stuff is making me feel very old."

Arnie and Nik jumped from their chairs and practically hugged each other. Ursula laughed and led them to the living room, where they proceeded to communicate their vision of the project. Ideas flew back and forth, making Ursula's head swim.

"It doesn't take long to lay down vocal tracks. You can be done with your part by the time your husband is back home. He'll never be the wiser," Nik promised.

"Are you proposing I keep it a secret from Don?"

"Uh, no, just saying you wouldn't have to tell him if you didn't want to."

"We don't keep secrets."

"Then tell him," Nik said. "That's fine—your choice. But what about Philomena? You won't be able to do both."

Arnie looked sharply at his client.

"Oh, I almost forgot . . ."

"I'm sure you did." Nik smirked.

"I'll have to think about that." Ursula looked at the men, who had grown quiet and were now staring intently at her. She began to wonder if perhaps she had made a mistake. "This is crazy, guys. I just don't know if—"

"Nik," Arnie interrupted, "you know we haven't even heard you two sing together. We're assuming your voices will mesh, but perhaps we're being premature." He turned to Ursula. "What do you say, before you make a decision one way or the other, that you and Nik have a little jam session?"

"Great idea, Arnie!" Nik interjected.

"Come over to the studio tomorrow and we'll see if you two can even put it together. Then decide. How would that be?"

"That's perfect!" Nik enthused again.

Ursula wasn't so sure. "Well, before we even take that step, what are you proposing to pay me for this job?"

Arnie raised his eyebrows.

What was she thinking? She had gotten carried away in the moment. She wasn't qualified for this. She'd just make her services far too expensive so they'd go away and leave her alone.

She knew more about music than they probably thought. She wanted to make that clear. She was married to an entertainment attorney—she understood contract negotiations. "Would you want me full- or part-time while we're laying the vocal tracks?"

"Full-time," Nik said.

"For how long?"

Arnie answered, "Normally we're talking a few weeks, but considering you're new to this . . ."

"So how long?"

"A couple months max." Arnie looked at Nik, who nodded.

"You're right, I am new to this, so I don't want to be rushed. And I do have other commitments. What if I agreed to give you a few days every week?"

At that comment, Nik looked ready to explode. Arnie moved to stand in front of him. "Mrs. Rhoades . . . uh, Ursula, if we move ahead on this project, it will require significant production expenses on the part of my client. We don't typically work on a project a few days every week. We start a project and work it full-time until it's completed."

She looked at both men and realized for the first time in her life what it meant to be in the driver's seat. They needed her. Yet they were used to negotiating deals where they controlled everything and held all the cards. Ursula suddenly knew what poker players must feel like when they hold a royal flush.

"Gentlemen, I'm sorry, but I have other commitments. I could give you three days every week for the entire summer. It's that—or nothing. I'm sorry."

"Starting when?" Arnie asked.

"Starting now. I will do what needs to be done, but I must be finished with the project by the time my daughter returns from Australia on the first of August." She doubted Don would be done with the trial before then.

"That's five months. More than enough time to complete an album. What do you think, Nik?" Arnie asked.

"I'd say so, yes." Nik all but bit his lip.

"In that case, I think a hundred thousand would be acceptable," Ursula said boldly.

Nik didn't blink. "That's fair. What do you think, Arnie?"

She was playing a game, but they acted as though she hadn't priced herself out of the ballpark. Surely they weren't serious?

"How do you wish to handle profits? What percentage did you have in mind?" Arnie began jotting notes on a small pad of paper he'd pulled from the inside breast pocket of his jacket.

Wait a minute. What just happened? They can't be serious. They aren't really agreeing to pay an unknown singer a hundred thousand dollars and a percentage of the profits? "Stop playing games, guys. Do you expect me to believe you'd pay me a hundred thousand?"

"I never play games where money is concerned," Arnie said.

ALLISON BOTTKE

"Okay, enough is enough. I'm flattered by the attention—really I am—but I'm just not interested in you, Nik. I know it's hard for you to comprehend, but I'm a married woman."

Nik's eyes sparked, but he looked as if he was trying to rein in his anger. "This might surprise you, Mrs. Rhoades, but I want your voice, not your body. We're buying your talent—not you. Trust me—I'm no Ashton Kutcher."

"Are you insinuating I'm too old for you?"

"Lady, it's not about me wanting you, okay? I'm sorry to burst your bubble. It's about your voice." Nik crossed his arms.

"Truce!" Arnie shouted, which didn't do much to relieve the tension in the room. "How about if you two sing a few songs first and see where it goes from there, okay?" Arnie wiped his glasses on a monogrammed handkerchief. "We might be putting the cart before the horse if your voices don't mesh. Can you at least try that much?"

Nik and Arnie stared expectantly at Ursula.

Are they really serious? "Okay. What time? Give me the address and I'll be there," she said.

They agreed on a time and Arnie gave Ursula directions. "I'm sure you won't have trouble finding it. We'll see you tomorrow." Arnie reached for her hand in a strong shake that cemented the end of the discussion.

Nik walked toward the door. He gave a casual wave as though he couldn't care less. "Oh, and Ursula?" Nik said over his shoulder. "Wear something a little sexier. The musical muse needs excitement, not sedation."

Arnie abruptly apologized and pushed Nik out the door, leaving Ursula standing in the foyer, wondering what had just happened.

18

Ursula put on the third CD in the Rod Stewart collection of love songs and began to sing "Embraceable You" as she loaded the dishwasher. *Lord, I love this kind of music. You know that. Please give me a sign that I should do this.*

She picked up the phone for the hundredth time in the last three hours but only got Don's message once again. *Where are you?* She'd already left three messages. *What if this was an emergency?*

"Hello, Counselor, it's me again. Are you okay? I'm sorry to bother you, but I've got some really exciting news to share with you. Please call me back. Love you."

That was the last time she would call him today. He must be really busy, as he usually checked in several times throughout the day—if only to say hello and tell her he loved her. It was his habit—their habit. Come to think of it, they hadn't spoken in a couple days.

"I'm knee-deep in reading discovery and depositions," he grumbled when he finally returned her call.

"Hello to you too—is that any way to greet your wife?" Ursula forced a smile into her voice.

"I'm sorry, honey. It's just that this is more of a mess than we'd initially thought. We may need to file an extension. I can't imagine we'll be ready for trial next month."

He sounds so tired. "I'm sure you'll do what needs to be done. I miss you, baby."

"I miss you too." He sighed. "Sam flew in for the day. That's why I couldn't get back to you sooner. We were in meetings since he arrived."

"That's funny. Julliette was here for lunch today—she never said a thing about Sam being in New York."

"Assuming she knows."

"Why wouldn't she know?"

"He owns one of the biggest entertainment law firms in the country; he doesn't need to check in with his wife every time he goes somewhere, does he?"

Ursula bristled but quickly reminded herself of the pressure her husband was under.

"What's the matter, Don?" she asked quietly.

"Nothing's the matter."

"Are you sleeping enough? Eating right? I'll bet you're living on hotel junk food, and—"

"Jean Georges is hardly junk food."

She'd forgotten the flagship Jean Georges restaurant was in the Trump Tower. She and Don loved visiting the one in London, and they'd most recently eaten at the one in Las Vegas.

"Ooh, lucky you. I slaved over a hot stove all morning for the ladies. It was a great time, by the way."

"That's good, honey. Is that your news? What you needed to talk with me about?"

"No, there's more." Ursula ignored the frustration in his voice and couldn't help smiling as she took a deep breath, ready to plunge in. Don was going to be blown away. "As I was cleaning up the dishes—"

"Hon," Don interrupted. "I'm sorry, but will this take long? Sam just walked in, and it looks like he needs me. I have to get back to work. We've added a few more associates to the mix, and I have to brief them in fifteen minutes."

What if I need you too? "So I have a whole fifteen minutes to talk with my beloved? To share my big news?" She tried to smile.

"Actually, I can give you about five minutes. Sam and I are going over a file with Celeste before the briefing."

Five whole minutes. She'd almost forgotten about the cat woman. "Is Celeste being helpful?"

"As a matter of fact, she is . . . very helpful."

"I'll bet."

"Ursula, please. Come on—just tell me. What's your exciting news?"

How could she tell him while under a time crunch? "Never mind. We can talk about it later. When you have more time."

"Okay, then. I'll call you tonight when I get back to my room—if it's not too late."

"Call either way. I don't mind if you wake me up. Take care of yourself, okay? We don't need you getting run-down and sick. Have you been taking your vitamins?" When he was home she set out his daily vitamins and supplements by his cell phone. When he walked out the door in the morning he swallowed a handful and kissed her good-bye. It was a time-honored ritual she loved.

"I'm not a child, Ursula. For crying out loud! I'm sorry. There's just a lot of pressure right now. Try to understand, okay?"

She was worried. This wasn't like him. "Do you want me to come out for a few days? Maybe we could spend some quiet time late at night—if you know what I mean?" Ursula loved the late-night evenings they spent together—cuddling and being close. "Maybe you need a little TLC. I'll be glad to oblige, Mr. Rhoades. I could be there tomorrow."

"Thanks, hon, but what I need is to get off this phone. We'll talk later, okay? Love you. Bye."

She heard the dial tone before she even had time to say good-bye.

Could a dial tone be a sign from God?

19

Nik and Arnie worked all night on a contract draft, drawing up acceptable terms for the proposed partnership. Normally, they wouldn't have moved so quickly, but they wanted Ursula to know they were serious. Plus, her husband was an attorney, so they figured the sooner he could get a draft the better—no telling how long he would hold things up.

"Do you think she'll show?" Arnie wiped his glasses on his jacket sleeve.

"I'd bet on it. Did you see her eyes light up when we started talking about the project? She wants to do this."

"Hmmm." Arnie looked at his watch.

"I've never met anyone like her. She's fascinating." Nik leaned back, clasping his hands behind his head.

"And so not in your league."

"What's that supposed to mean?"

"Don't even think about it, Nik. Don't look at me like I don't know what I'm talking about."

The intercom bell interrupted them. "She's right on time," Nik said looking at his new Baume & Mercier watch—a recent gift from his mother. "I told you she'd come." He pressed the button to open the automatic gate.

———————

Ursula had left her car in a park-and-ride lot and taken a taxi to Nik's Malibu home. After donning large black glasses and a funky Eugenia Kim straw fedora hat, she looked like any number of Hollywood actresses. Not even the taxi driver could have identified her.

"What's with the getup?" Nik quizzed as she entered the foyer.

She couldn't speak right then. She was looking from the foyer through the living room to a wall of glass overlooking the ocean, offering exquisite views of the Pacific—from Catalina to the Channel Islands.

"Brilliant!" Arnie held out his right hand in welcome. "I didn't recognize you."

"Ah," Nik said. "Getting into character, eh?"

Regaining her composure, she heartily shook Arnie's hand. "I've read all about these cab drivers and utility men and such who get paid big bucks to disclose private information about big rock stars like you. If we're going to do this successfully, we have to start now to guard my privacy."

"Of course there will always be staff around," Arnie said, "but we should start right away by using your stage name. Just act natural—no need to arouse suspicion by whispering and lurking in corners. So who do you want to be? Nik and I have been talking about your name."

"I've been thinking about that too. What do you think about Alexandra Arcano? We could use only the first name on the album cover . . . maybe call me Alex for short?"

"Like Celine, Barbra, Mariah, or Madonna." Arnie nodded. "I like it."

" 'Nik and Alexandra Sing the Classics,' " Nik said. "I like the sound of that."

"What about switching that around: 'Alex and Nik Present,' " Ursula chimed in.

"Don't press your luck, lady." Nik grinned.

The butler interrupted the group as he walked into the foyer. "Good day, Miss . . ." He gracefully bowed.

"Arcano," said Ursula. "Alexandra Arcano."

"Alex, this is Winston," Nik said. "You'll be seeing a lot of him. Winston, meet the talented woman who will be recording my next project with me."

"Who *may* be recording your next project with you." Ursula corrected Nik and extended her hand.

Arnie excused himself. "I'll be in the studio."

"I am pleased to make your acquaintance, Miss Arcano. May I take your hat?"

"Uh, no, that's okay. I think I'll hang on to it for now. Thank you, Winston. But please call me Alex."

"Very good. Where will you be meeting today, sir? I will prepare a tray of refreshments."

"In the studio. Come this way, Alex. I'll give you a tour."

Ursula had seen photos of Nik's home in an issue of *W* magazine, but nothing could have prepared her for this opulence. She lived in a rather fine home in Bel-Air, not a shabby suburb by any stretch of the imagination—and several of the ladies she volunteered with lived in what were unmistakably mansions—but this home was in another league altogether.

It featured an open floor plan, high ceilings, and glass walls everywhere. Natural materials and massive sliding doors opened almost every room to breathtaking views. Although she had never been a fan of contemporary furnishings and modern art, it worked in his house. Bold, stunning, edgy—and a bit in-your-face—it seemed to fit Nik's personality.

Primary colors abounded, including a red grand piano in the main living room.

"Do you play?" Nik asked, noticing her attention on the instrument. "It's a custom-made Schimmel. Paid sixty-five thousand for it a couple years ago. Spared no expense."

"I teach piano and voice, remember? May I?"

"By all means." Nik pulled out the bench, and she sat down and began to play.

"I don't recognize that. What is it?" Nik cocked his head. "It's got a powerful melody."

"A Darlene Zschech piece called 'Shout to the Lord.' Very popular."

"Not in my circle." Nik grinned. "You're good. Play something with lyrics."

"This has lyrics." She sang them with passion.

Nik had never heard anyone sing about God in such a way. The song actually made his knees weak, and he found himself fighting back the urge to weep. It was unfamiliar territory for him.

"Is that what they call contemporary Christian music?" Nik sat next to her, trying to conceal his discomfort and regain his composure. "I know they have a category for it at the Grammys, but I haven't paid much attention to it."

Ursula laughed. "They have their own awards show too. It's called the Gospel Music Awards, and it used to be called the Dove Awards. Surely you've heard of it?"

"Maybe . . . Play another."

"Okay, this is called 'Give Them Wings to Fly.' It's my favorite Bonnie Keen tune."

This time Ursula was crying when she finished the song.

"Um, sorry. That always happens. She wrote it for her own kids, I think. Always chokes me up. It's on her *Marked for Life* CD.

Want me to make you a copy of it?" She wiped her eyes on a tissue she'd pulled from her jacket pocket.

"No copies! That's bootlegging, and we don't do that. Got it? But I'd like to hear some of her stuff. Make a list and I'll have my assistant pick them up or download them to my iPod."

Bet that's the first time a contemporary Christian medley has been played on that puppy, Ursula thought as they continued their tour, excited to think she was introducing Nik to music that just might change his life. She began to make a mental list of all the artists she wanted to share with him: Michael W. Smith, Third Day, Sandi Patty, David Crowder, Kathy Troccoli . . .

She stopped in front of a particularly spectacular painting. It appeared to be an original. "Is this a Matisse?"

"Good eye." Nik peered over her shoulder. "I've begun to collect his great-granddaughter's work too. What do you think of this one?" He pointed to another wall. "It's called *Blue Nude.* Her name is Sophie—not the nude, the artist—Sophie Matisse. I just bought this from the Francis M. Naumann gallery in uptown New York. Spared no expense."

Although she cared little for modern art, the colors of the piece were brilliant and she could clearly see the influence of the elder Matisse in his great-granddaughter's work.

Along with the Matisse, Nik had an original Andy Warhol, two Picassos, and a host of other smaller pieces, all open to multiple interpretations.

"My decorator says these are important, but I can't decide if I love them or hate them," he said, looking at two large R. Douglass Rice oil paintings that Ursula thought resembled work Valerie had done as a preschooler.

Nik Prevel's entire home was a work of art. She knew Don would love the pair of Charles Eames black-leather-and-rosewood lounge chairs with matching ottomans that flanked the massive fireplace, and the sleek Rodolfo Dordoni sofa that took up the rest of the room. Nik's kitchen had enough accoutrements to make any Iron Chef salivate.

"It's a Flux kitchen, the latest Scavolini model, created by Giugiaro Design. It's totally multifunctional. What do you think?"

Having just read a profile in the latest issue of *Elle Décor*, Ursula knew just enough about the innovative, avant-garde kitchen designer from Italy to know the room they were standing in was filled with the latest in technology and ergonomics.

She wanted to take more time looking around the high-tech visual candy store, especially once she noticed the Impressa Z5 Jura-Capresso one-touch cappuccino system she had been coveting for months, but he rushed her through the room as though he had something to hide. Clearly, this was his least favorite room in the house.

The next area on the tour was Nik's in-house recording studio. It was clearly his pride and joy.

"I had this built a few years ago when I bought the house from Johnny Carson's estate. Spared no expense."

She was beginning to think he sounded an awful lot like the wealthy visionary from *Jurassic Park*—"sparing no expense" was growing old.

The studio comprised the entire lower level of the home. The walls were filled from floor to ceiling with gold and platinum records, photographs, awards, and star memorabilia. Ursula wanted so much to check it all out but forced herself to appear coolly detached, lest he label her a groupie.

"It's lovely." She smiled.

"So what do you think?" Arnie's voice startled her. She hadn't noticed him sitting at a table in the far corner of the room. Surrounded by his briefcase, a laptop computer, a stack of papers, and a steaming mug of coffee, he was clearly ready to conduct business.

"It's a bit overwhelming. You are most certainly blessed, Mr. Prevel. Do many singers have studios in their home like this?"

"A few, not all. I prefer the privacy. Can we get over the Mr. and Mrs. formality? Can we be Arnie, Nik, and Ursula? Once and for all?"

"No," Ursula responded. "But we can be Arnie, Nik, and *Alex*."

"Okay, Alex." Nik directed, "Let's get our groove on."

There was a host of costly electronic equipment set up, but he sat down at an acoustic Steinway—on which he'd spared no expense—and without sheet music gracefully moved his fingers over the keys to create a lovely rendition of "Someone to Watch Over Me." He sang the lyrics from memory, as well, clearly impressed with himself.

"Waiting for an invitation?" Nik inquired of Ursula.

"Now? You want me to join you?"

"Unless you're here to give me a back rub or to clean the house or walk the dog or something else?"

"Very funny, wise guy." She smiled and joined him, taking a seat on a stool next to the piano.

"Do you know 'Till There Was You'? Nik asked.

"The better question is, do *you* know how to play it?" Ursula teased.

Moments later, right on cue, their voices joined, and at the first note, goose bumps crawled up her arms and onto her neck.

For the next hour, taking turns on the piano, Ursula and Nik sang one song after another—like kids at karaoke. Arnie applauded and took notes on his BlackBerry. "What do you think?" he asked after they finished a phenomenal rendition of "What a Wonderful World."

"I think she'll do," Nik said to Arnie while staring at Ursula. He grinned.

Ursula felt as though she were sixteen and sitting behind her first set of wheels. "Let's have a look at the contract and get this show on the road!"

$$20$$

Arnie was surprised by how quickly things went south. At first everyone was amazingly accommodating, but it soon became apparent that Ursula had her own ideas about what would be expected of her. He could see that his client was getting edgy. Nik wasn't used to a woman who spoke her mind—other than Isabella and Kitty—even if she did it in a soft-spoken manner. He also wasn't used to taking things slow. Nik was accustomed to projects that operated at a fast clip, and Ursula was making it abundantly clear that she wanted to take her time. In fact, she wanted to work part-time, only on Tuesdays, Wednesdays, and Thursdays, giving her long four-day weekends to visit her husband in New York or handle other personal issues. Arnie had to give Nik credit for not blowing his stack when she informed him, albeit sweetly, of her preferred schedule. Singers who worked with Nik typically worked 24/7 from start to finish—and were glad to do so. Some even moved into his home during the project—a fact Arnie hoped Ursula wasn't aware of and that Nik wouldn't suggest.

When Ursula started asking about how they intended to handle the actual production phase and began to share how she imagined it might go, Nik cut her off at the pass.

"Here's how it will go," Nik said testily. "We'll hire an arranger or an orchestrator—I'm not sure yet which way I want to go. Make a note, Arnie, that I want to talk with you about Jay and Greg."

"Will do." Arnie added this directive to the notes he'd already taken.

"Then we'll decide on the songs we want and rough out the best keys while meeting with the orchestrator to discuss arrangements and tempos. I've got a great technical engineer and recording engineer. We'll bring them in a day or so before we record. We'll use my guys to record. They're pros, the best studio musicians in the business. All they need is a few hours with the charts the day of production. . . ."

"Hold on a minute," Ursula interrupted. "It's going to take some time to decide on the songs. We have a lot to choose from, right? And . . . are you saying we won't have rehearsals with the band before we start recording? I don't mean to cause trouble, but I've never done this before. I was kind of figuring we'd spend time carefully selecting the songs and then take time rehearsing with the band or orchestra or whatever it is we call them, long before we started recording."

Nik tilted his head and crunched his eyebrows. "How long before did you have in mind? And how much rehearsing will you need?"

They spent the next twenty minutes listening to Ursula's rationale for taking their time, for methodically planning their every step. Arnie could see it for what it was—she was terrified—but he doubted if Nik had the same sympathetic understanding as he watched him get more and more agitated. By the time she stopped talking, it appeared that what Nik and his crew could have accomplished in six weeks maximum was going to take the entire spring and summer if Ursula had her way.

"I don't see any reason to rush things. I have until August first when my daughter returns from Australia, and it doesn't appear my husband will be done with the trial before then. I say we use all the time we have and enjoy ourselves. What's the hurry? But August first is my final date—I won't work another day once Valerie comes home."

Thanks to Arnie's ability to moderate the discussion, he managed to keep his client from exploding while at the same time assuring Ursula they would indeed consider her suggestions, but the second she slipped away to the ladies' room, Nik grabbed Arnie's arm.

"What the heck is all this about? She's a no-name telling me how to run a project? Giving me deadline ultimatums? You know darn well this is crazy, dragging things out like this. What does she expect me to do on her days off? Twiddle my thumbs just waiting for her royal highness to come back to work? Part-time, my eye! No way! This is not how it works, this is not how it's going to be!"

"Calm down and breathe. Your face is the color of your blue jeans. You heard her, Nik. She's got a lot of volunteer commitments, and she has a life outside of all this. A life she wants to keep." He waved his hand. "Stick with it, Nik. You're the star. I know that, you know that, and—trust me—she knows that too. But she has the right to make sure this fits her needs as well as ours."

"This is going to be career suicide." Nik hung his head in his hands. "How did I let you talk me into this? I've kissed any chance of a Grammy good-bye, and this is not the kind of music my fans want to hear."

"I beg to differ. I think you're selling your fans short. Nik, look at me." He leaned over and, in a tone of voice that always made Nik pay attention, said, "Remember your closing number at the

Hollywood Bowl? Remember how your fans were on their feet? Just a couple hours ago I sat right here listening to a vocal match made in heaven. You've been at this a long time, Nik. You know magic when you hear it—and you two are magic together. You bring out the best in her voice. And we're going to milk this mystery woman thing for all it's worth. Trust me when I say it's going to bring you more attention than you can imagine."

"You really think so?"

"I know so. And so do you. So bite your tongue when she comes back. Humor her, okay? When all is said and done, you'll have the final say. Just hear her out. We don't want her to walk."

"You think she'd actually do that? Walk?"

"I don't really know, but I think we have to be careful. This isn't some starstruck pop princess. She doesn't *need* this, Nik."

"Oh, I beg to differ. I think she needs this very much. I think she's lived under the shadow of an oppressive husband long enough."

Arnie wondered if that was really the case. Was Don Rhoades a bad guy? Did Nik see his mother in Ursula? They were both talented women who made a choice early in life to support the men they loved. Raysha had done the same for him, but for some reason that arrangement didn't seem to bother Nik.

Ursula came back, and they spent over an hour reviewing a calendar and hashing out a time frame. If Ursula noticed Nik's change in attitude, she didn't mention anything.

They allowed themselves two weeks to select songs, taking them into the first week of April. The remainder of April and all of May would give them eight weeks to review possible arrangements and keys, and to rehearse and practice with the band—about six weeks more than they needed. But Nik didn't comment, and he made one concession after another, including bringing the band in early. *Totally unnecessary,* Nik mouthed to Arnie when Ursula reached into her purse for a tissue, but she seemed adamant about the practice time. The entire month of June would be used to record all the songs. They factored in July to fine-tune specific songs and to rerecord tracks if needed. By August first, Ursula would be done with her part. The mixing engineer would take over, and when he was done they could release the project.

"I have one more thing," Ursula said.

Nik sighed and leaned back in his chair. Arnie held his breath.

"I'd like you to add my husband's name on the contract and on any checks given to me, as a partner in the venture."

Arnie shot a surprised glance at Nik. "Are you sure about that?"

"We are life partners, and I intend to keep it that way."

"So that means you'll have him look over the contract before you sign it?" Nik asked.

"Of course I will, and whoever else he might suggest. When you get the final copy worked up, I'll make sure he reviews it before I sign it. When do you expect it will be ready?"

"Since we wish to keep this as private as possible, I'm making all of the revisions myself," Arnie said. "I'll have the next draft done the first of the week. Is that okay?"

"That should be fine," Ursula agreed.

"I'm certain your husband can be trusted," Arnie said, "but any advisors he selects to review the contract will need to sign a confidentiality statement. A lot depends on your identity remaining secret."

"Of course, but aren't lawyers bound by privacy statutes?" Ursula asked.

"Only those officially hired as legal representation. Confidentiality doesn't always hold up for people asked to review contracts or give advice. I just want to make sure we are all on the same page about the need to restrict disclosure."

This was a perfect segue into a discussion about how best to handle the media, as well as some creative brainstorming regarding marketing and promotions. Arnie was in his element as he encouraged dialogue and took copious notes. He wished his assistant was there, or at least Kitty.

They came up with a bio for Alexandra Arcano, and Ursula was unyielding in her insistence that it not contain any blatant lies. In reality, it was a sketchy overview of Ursula's actual background and talents, minus a few details—like her real name, her marital status, her children, and where she lived. Arnie's office would distribute a series of releases, each adding a bit more information to keep the media beast sated.

"How long do you really think we'll be able to maintain the ruse?" Ursula asked. "I mean, once the project releases, won't people want to see the real Alexandra Arcano?"

"They might," Arnie responded. "But by then the trial will be over, and protecting your husband will no longer be the principal issue. That is your main concern at this point. Am I correct?"

She smiled. "That is correct. Thank you, gentlemen, for this opportunity. I know you've been biting your tongues all day. Don't look surprised. I was born at night, but it wasn't last night." The men laughed as she continued. "Don't think I don't know this is a chance of a lifetime, but this trial is also Don's chance of a lifetime. I don't want to do anything that might jeopardize his career. I'm not saying this project is a bad thing—that we need to be ashamed of it, or that you, Nik, are a bad person or anything like that. It's just that . . . well . . . I read entertainment magazines and I know how things can get blown out of proportion. The more dramatic the media can spin things, the better. I know sex sells—real or imagined."

"You read the Hollywood gossip rags? A good Christian woman like you?"

Arnie could tell by Nik's tone that he was joking, but Ursula didn't laugh.

"Let's get something out on the table right now, okay?" she said. "I know you don't share my faith, and that's okay—I will respect your choice. But I will not allow you to make snide remarks about my being a Christian. Is that clear?"

"I wasn't being snide. I just didn't figure you for someone who read that slop, that's all. I'm sorry," Nik said.

"Mostly I look at the pictures." She grinned, realizing how silly that sounded. "You know, to see who's wearing what. Anyway, apology accepted."

"Well, then," Arnie said, "I think we have a deal."

Nik watched from the window as Arnie closed the taxi door and waved as the cab pulled away. They met in the foyer on Arnie's way back inside.

"She wasn't wearing a wedding ring," Nik said casually.

"Nik, I know what you're thinking. Stop it. She's happily married with two children. Raysha takes her ring off all the time—to clean, or garden, or any number of things—and then forgets to put it back on. It's not a signal that she's ready to throw herself at your feet."

Nik wasn't about to be distracted from Ursula. "Her children have already flown the coop, and I'm not so sure about the happily married part. Didn't you notice how she kind of bristled every time we mentioned her elusive husband?"

"He's hardly elusive, Nik; he's lead counsel on one of the most high profile cases in the country. I admire her for protecting him from the media machine that surrounds your every move. We have to be careful about this. There's a lot at stake here. Don't mess with things."

"She's different, Arnie. She's . . . special. I've never met anyone like her."

"I'm sure you haven't—she doesn't travel in your crowd."

"Then it's time to change my crowd."

"Nik, she's almost old enough to be your mother."

"She's sexy and you know it."

Arnie shook his head and issued another stern reprimand. Nik didn't listen. He wondered what it would be like to have a woman be as devoted to him as Ursula was to her husband. Did her husband know how lucky he was? Probably not. He would use that as leverage. He would show her how much he appreciated her talents. How much he appreciated her. He would make her feel like a queen when they were together—which, when all is said and done, was what any woman wanted.

He'd been treating the women in his life like pawns on a chessboard. What did it matter? He didn't care for them. But this one was different. He needed to play a different kind of game with this one—a game he had no intention of losing.

$$21$$

"Thanks for squeezing me in." Ursula pecked the cheek of the attractive man in his trademark straw cowboy hat and eagerly sat in his famous chair. "I'm all yours. I want a new look. Just leave my length in back so I can still put it up, okay?"

She'd left the meeting with Nik and Arnie and immediately used her cell phone to see if she could book an appointment. Then she'd driven directly from the park-and-ride lot to 224 Rodeo Drive in Beverly Hills. While the three-block stretch of shops, boutiques, and salons constituted the most famous shopping district in America, for Ursula the opulent salon nestled between Cartier and Christian Dior was her home away from home. José Eber was known as *the* hairdresser to the stars, but after she'd met him back in 1990 at a fundraising event held for the opening of *Pretty Woman*, he had become one of Ursula's closest friends. José had been after her for years to change her style—and he finally had his chance.

The next morning she jogged two miles on her treadmill before showering, doing her hair, and driving to the park and ride. It was fun styling her new hairdo. Formerly all one length, her hair now had layers on top and bangs. Previously halfway down her back, her thick tresses now skimmed her shoulders in a Lana Turner–like pageboy. She wondered what Nik would think.

"Well now, that's . . . interesting," he said of her new hairdo when she arrived at his home later that day as scheduled.

"Interesting is an entirely mundane word—a superfluous word, really, as it means absolutely nothing. Tell me what you really think."

"I'm not sure yet. I kind of liked the way you had it when we met—slicked back with the gardenia, like a chanteuse."

"Have no fear, I can still pull it back. That's a good word—chanteuse. What does it really mean?" Ursula's excitement made her talk quickly. "Do you have a dictionary in this place? Where's Arnie? And Jeeves?"

"His name is Winston. He'll flip if he hears you calling him Jeeves. They both went out but will be back soon. We're all alone. . . . Are you afraid?"

Ursula did feel something like fear as he stepped toward her, but she laughed it off and waved him aside. "Come on, Casanova, let's look at songs. I brought some of my music like you suggested. Perhaps we'll find something in here." She held up a large pink fabric bag stuffed with songbooks and sheet music.

Yesterday had been a good day—they had accomplished a lot. She wasn't sure how they'd take her requests, but she needn't have worried—things couldn't have gone any better. It felt good to be a part of a team where her contributions were respected. Nik had behaved strangely a few times, and she figured it must have something to do with how poorly he ate and the energy drinks he downed like water. When she got to know him better she would suggest better nutrition and maybe some vitamin supplements. He really needed to take better care of himself if they were going to have productive sessions.

Nik pointed. "That's a mighty big Victoria's Secret bag. What the heck did you buy?"

"You know where it's from?"

"Any man worth his salt in Hollywood knows where the closest Victoria's Secret is located. Plus, I used to date one of their models."

That's right. She'd read about the romance in *People.* It had been a huge scandal when the girl left Nik and went back to her old boyfriend, who then dumped her a few weeks later.

"Sorry, I forgot."

"Not a problem. No need for you to keep up with my love life—I can barely keep up with it myself. So were you able to run the contract by your husband? Does he have any suggestions?"

"I'm not about to bother him with any contract discussions until Arnie makes all of our changes and the next draft is ready to read."

"But you talked to him yesterday after our meeting, didn't you? What did he say?"

"I called him, yes. But with all due respect, Nik, I'd prefer to keep my private life separate from our business arrangement. Okay?"

She wasn't lying. She had called Don. But once again her call went directly into voice mail. She'd left a message, but so far he hadn't returned her call.

Nik shrugged his shoulders as though it didn't matter one way or another. "Alrighty, then. Let's see what you have in the bag. Arnie went shopping last night at Tower Records and bought a boatload of CDs for us to review. We don't want to duplicate too many songs that have already been covered, so let's look for ones that haven't been done for a while."

"Sounds good to me."

"That computer"—he pointed to a built-in desk area she hadn't noticed yesterday—"is online, so we can Google titles for past history. Arnie also left a list of Web sites where we can get info on artists, composers, and copyrights."

"He sure is on top of things. Bless his heart."

For the next couple hours they paged through old songbooks, hummed melodies, plucked out tunes on the piano, conducted Web searches, took notes, and sat back listening to songs on the killer sound system Nik had in his studio.

"That is amazing," Ursula exclaimed when he popped in a Dean Martin CD and the sensuous sounds of "Moonlight Serenade" filled the room. "It's like he's in concert right here with us. I've never heard speakers like that—it's like they're everywhere, but I can hardly see them. Wow."

"It's a custom system. I had one of the best studio designers in L.A. put it in—spared no expense," Nik boasted.

I'm sure you didn't. If there was one thing about Nik Prevel that was going to drive her crazy it was his almost constant bragging about how much things cost. If she didn't know better, she'd think he came from poverty.

By the time Arnie arrived, they had a list of about one hundred songs. They were aiming at twenty songs total, so it would be a process of elimination.

"What about Broadway show tunes?" Arnie asked.

"We wondered if we should include them," Ursula said.

"That could be another project if this one takes off." Arnie made a note as Nik nodded.

"No, you don't," Ursula interjected when she saw their minds churning. "I can only do this one, guys—you know that."

"Don't stress. It's only the first day. Take it easy." Nik laughed.

Arnie looked at the schedule they'd developed the day before. "We've given ourselves two weeks to make the final song selections."

All three were paging through old songbooks when Winston startled them. "May I get you anything?"

"Yes, you can get us a crystal ball so we can see which of these songs will make a hit record. Better yet, you can get us that psychic chick on Hollywood Boulevard. The one everyone claims is so good. She can help us."

"You're not serious?" Ursula furrowed her brows.

"Uh, well, no. But it couldn't hurt, could it?" Nik joked.

"It most certainly could hurt. Scripture is very clear about soothsayers."

All three men stared at her. Ursula felt a blush on her face. "What? What're you looking at?"

"Will you be needing anything else, sir?" Winston knew when it was time to go.

"Not now, thank you."

"You're saying it's against your religion if we consult a reputable psychic?" Nik turned to Ursula when Winston left the room.

"A reputable psychic? That's an oxymoron."

"Okay, no psychics," Arnie interjected. "By the way, Alexandra, I like your hair—very chic."

She liked the sound of her new name—it went with her new hair. "Thank you, Arnie. I figured it was time for a new look. Don will blow a gasket, but he'll have to get used to it."

"You didn't ask his permission first?" Nik asked, reaching for another songbook.

Where did that come from? Had she given the impression that she was entirely dependant on Don? "No, I didn't ask his permission. I do have my own mind, you know."

"Sorry. Just didn't know how far all of this Christian two-becoming-one thing went. I'm trying to figure it out, you know? No disrespect intended."

He was probably just trying to get a rise out of her. But maybe he really didn't understand the kind of relationship she and Don shared. "Arnie, how long have you been married?"

"Over twenty years. We met in college."

Ursula smiled. A good, long marriage like hers. She couldn't wait to talk to Don tonight. She needed to get his take on all this. He might not understand at first, but once she cast the vision for what was happening, she knew he would be excited for her.

Please, Lord, let him be excited.

By the time she got to the park and ride and then back home, it was late. She'd left her cell phone on her kitchen counter, and when she was finally able to figure out how to check her messages on the new BlackBerry 8700c that Don insisted she must have but that she really hated, she saw he had called several times.

It was after ten, West Coast time, when she reached him.

"Hi, sweetheart. Sorry I missed your calls. I left my phone at home and it took me forever to figure out how to retrieve—"

"Where have you been?" he interrupted, his tone of voice scaring her.

"What's wrong?" Visions of something happening to Valerie while she was in a remote area of Australia filled her mind.

"I'm in a bind, honey, and I need you to do me a favor right away."

"You're angry because you need me to do you a favor?"

"I'm not angry."

"I'm sorry, but you sounded upset. What do you need?"

"You need to ship my passport tomorrow. Send it overnight mail to the hotel."

"What do you need your passport for?"

"We're going to Venice to talk with the Chesterfield family."

"Who's going to Venice?"

"A few of the team."

"Who, Don? Who is going to Italy with you?"

"What does that matter, Ursula?"

"She's going, isn't she? You're going to Italy with Medusa."

"I don't have time for this, Ursula. Where were you, anyway? I've been leaving messages all day."

Ursula felt a pain in her chest for the first time in years—wondering if she mattered at all to this man who was becoming a stranger to her. He'd become so distant from her. Looking back, she realized it had started even before he took this assignment in New York, but now, since taking up temporary residency in New York, he seemed to have turned downright rude.

"I was out, listening to some music. A friend of mine is doing a concert kind of thing and wanted my help selecting songs." She instantly regretted the little white lie—but she smarted too much to correct herself.

"Well, can you get the passport in the mail first thing tomorrow? We're going to fly out this weekend."

"Of course."

"Thanks, honey. I'll let you go now. You sound tired. We'll talk tomorrow. I love you. Bye, babe."

Once again the dial tone greeted her before she could say goodbye. This was becoming a habit in their communication. There was a time when she would have been hurt—a time when Don would have cared that he'd hurt her. *Is that time over?*

I could use some discernment here, Lord. What's going on with my husband? Have I lost him to Delilah?

22

It had been two of the best weeks Nik could remember having in his entire life. Every day Ursula arrived right on time and raring to go. Her excitement was contagious. Equally contagious was her level of optimism. She was clearly a woman who saw the glass half full as opposed to half empty. Always quick to respond with something positive, she never let him get away with any sort of negativity. And she did it in a gentle way—not at all reprimanding. She was a little neurotic about some things—wound a bit too tight—but the longer they worked together the better she got.

He was also learning more about the Bible than he'd expected to learn. It was apparent that not only did Ursula believe in God, but she also had an understanding of the Bible that confounded Nik.

"'For where your treasure is, there your heart will be also,'" she said with a wink after admiring a new car he just added to his collection.

"What's that supposed to mean?"

"It's Scripture. Matthew chapter six, verse twenty-one. It means we shouldn't let the things of the world become more important than what really matters."

He didn't want to get into a theological discussion with someone who could quote a specific chapter and verse number from the Bible by memory, no matter how much she fascinated him. Yet he thought about what she said long after she was gone.

A few days into the first week, they'd begun to make a game of her disguises and the way she arrived and departed. If a taxi continued to be summoned to and from the same park-and-ride lot on a daily basis, consistently dropping her at the drive of his Malibu compound, it would only be a matter of time before someone would catch on—the paparazzi were a clever hive.

Therefore, some days she'd go to Arnie's place in Brentwood and drive in with him; other days she'd leave her car at a shopping center and he would pick her up. The taxi worked from time to time, but she'd learned to have them occasionally drop her down the hill in front of someone else's home and, after making sure they had driven away, she would walk up the hill to his house.

"I love the walk. I need the exercise, and I really don't mind," she said one day, changing from her well-worn Nikes to a pair of multicolored satin-and-leather Louis Vuitton sandals in the foyer. She'd told him she'd been religiously exercising on her treadmill for an hour every day.

Most of the women Nik knew had trouble walking from the car to the restaurant entrance, fearful their expensive Manolo Blahniks would somehow be damaged. Ursula Rhoades had no pretenses, and Nik found that very attractive.

Everything would change today, if Ursula had anything to say about it. The past two weeks had been like consistent false labor for Ursula. In fact, she was hard-pressed to recall two more difficult weeks in her entire life. No matter how hard she tried to be positive, no matter how much she praised and complimented Nik, he was an insufferable, egotistical cad. If she heard "spared no expense" from him one more time she would scream. She was sick and tired of hearing how much he paid for this or that, what brand name was the best, and how much better he and his stuff were than his peers or their stuff.

Besides, he was completely disorganized. Nik was accustomed to having things done for him, but since they were keeping this project a secret, additional administrative help had not been hired. Their workspace was a huge granite game table in Nik's studio, covered with dozens of songbooks and stacks of sheet music. Materials spilled over onto the floor as well. CDs were everywhere.

Her first stab at efficiency was to pick up a thirty-five-dollar portable CD player at Wal-Mart and place it on the table between them. Instead of trying to figure out where a particular CD was in the cartridge of four hundred CDs in Nik's seventy-five-thousand custom-built setup, a total waste of time and energy in her estimation, they simply popped in a CD and hit Play, never leaving their seats. Of course, it wasn't the same sound quality, but it suited their purpose just fine.

Ursula's second attempt was to take Arnie aside early the second week, explaining that someone had to track and organize the songs they were selecting. "I can't work this way, Arnie. Look at this mess! We spend more time paging through Post-it notes, trying to recall where we first located a song. He acts like it's a game. I can handle the administrative things if he'll let me."

It wasn't just because of her husband's position with Carpenter, Haggerty & Pillsbury that she was consistently asked to chair major fundraising events. She was very good at planning, organization, and follow-up and wasn't accustomed to having these gifts ignored or underutilized.

"I'll talk to him," Arnie promised.

The next day, Nik announced he had a brilliant idea, declaring that Ursula was perfect for the task of organizing this phase of the project, and would she kindly consider being their administrative guru? Arnie had winked at her, and their friendship took another step forward.

She quietly agreed to do it, praising Nik for his foresight—and from that point on they began to use their time together far more efficiently.

Since then, they'd managed to cull fifty songs from their list of one hundred. And now they would begin to individually dissect each of those fifty songs. Ursula had developed a list of ten things to look for in each song and had created a rating form for them to use in the next phase, to help when the time came to select the final twenty or so songs. She was excited to share her system with the guys.

But it took them an hour and a half to go full circle and come back around to the system she initially proposed, all because of Nik's ego and insecurity. It was like textbook psychology—as long as she couched her suggestions in such a way that he felt they were really his ideas, all was well. It was maddening. They still had months to work together and already this man was driving her crazy.

———

"I can't help it. I'm crazy about her. She's amazing. Have you ever met anyone like her?" Nik whispered to Arnie as Ursula left the room to get a diet soda from the kitchen.

"She's one of a kind, all right, but get the idea out of your mind right this minute. She is off limits. Period. End of story. Don't screw this up, Nik. This isn't an Elvis movie."

Once they agreed on how to use the forms she had developed, they spent the better part of the day fine-tuning the system. Nik had to admit that when they were done, it would be easy to select the top twenty tunes using the judging criteria she had devised.

"You have a dinner party tonight at the Chateau Marmont," Arnie announced. "Tori's birthday. I picked up a gift for you to give her, a little something from Tiffany. I must say, I have a new appreciation for Kitty these days."

Since they wanted to keep things as private as possible, Nik had given Kitty the summer off with pay when they decided to record this album. But they were missing her efficiency, if not her ever-changing bizarre hair styles and notorious shoes.

"You're changing the subject, Arnie. No matter what you say, I'm still crazy about her."

"Crazy about who?" Ursula asked as she returned with a tray of refreshments Winston had prepared for them.

"Kitty." Arnie smiled. "We're both crazy about her. Not sure we can keep up without her." He looked sternly at Nik.

"Is there anything I can help with?" Ursula handed Arnie a glass of tea.

"Sure, I have something." Nik smirked at Arnie.

"What might that be?" Ursula dipped a chip into fresh guacamole.

"Help me pick out something to wear to Tori's party tonight."

"Tori? As in Spelling?"

"Yep. Wish you could meet her—you'd like her."

"I'm sure I would. Thanks but no thanks on the wardrobe-mistress job."

"Aw, come on. Some girls would give their eyeteeth to wander through my closet. Help a fellow out, would ya?"

Ursula began to collect her things. "It's time to head out for the day, fellows. Tell Winston thanks for the snack. It was a really productive day. I think 'Time After Time' is gonna be a keeper." She bussed Arnie on the cheek and he smiled like a kid in a candy shop. "I'll see you guys on Tuesday. Have a great weekend."

As she passed him on the way out, Nik took Ursula's arm and attempted to pull her into an embrace. "Don't I get a kiss good-bye?"

He shouldn't have been surprised by her response, but he was. "Cut it out, Nik! I'm not one of your party girls. You try that again and this project is over." She rolled her eyes and slammed the door in his face.

"You got what you asked for, buddy," Arnie said.

No I didn't, but I will. I will!

23

By the time Ursula got home she wondered if she had over-reacted. After all, she had hugged Arnie good-bye almost from the day they first met. With Arnie it was a natural, brotherly kind of thing—no ulterior motives—but she had been fending off Nik's inappropriate comments and advances from the first day. It was clear he was used to getting his own way, and the more she ignored his sexual innuendo, the more determined he seemed to become.

It took a little over an hour to go through her mail, check voice messages, and answer e-mail. Being able to correspond with Valerie across the world via the Internet was a big plus, and although her daughter's posts were brief, it warmed her mother's heart that Val took the time to let her know all was well.

Victor had also sent an e-mail. Although still sweet, his was a tad less warm and fuzzy.

Dear Momza,

Got a second call-back for the job. Things look promising. Stop. I'll let you know when I hear something. Stop. Thanks for the genetic predisposition for cleanliness and organization—these guys I live with are total Neanderthal slobs. Stop. Please

122

send a care package of dried fruit, peas, and nuts from Trader Joes. Stop. I miss you. I miss Dad. Don't miss Val, but I already told her that. Stop. Later gator. Stop.

> Love,
> The Maestro

She checked the private e-mail account Don had set up for their personal communication while he was on the road. The in-box was empty. The last entry had been written at 3:15 A.M. three days ago. She read it again and sighed.

From: Trump International Hotel and Tower
Sent: Tuesday, April 04—3:15 AM
To: URmywife@tellnet.net
Subject: Checking In

Hi, Honey. It's been a long day. Back from Italy with not a whole heck of a lot more information than we had before we left. This is one bear of a trial. Wish I could tell you more—but you know the story. Did the pool guy ever come? Make sure Stan knows about the broken sprinkler head by the front door. Hope you're having fun relaxing. You deserve it. Bet you don't miss your students—I sure wouldn't. Give kids my love when you talk to them. Take care. Love, D.

That's how little you know. Of course I miss my students. For the past twenty years Ursula had been tutoring students in piano and voice two days every week. She went on hiatus only when she and Don took the kids for their annual summer vacation. Making the decision not to take students this summer had been a major thing for Ursula, but at the time she'd thought she would be spending the summer with Don.

When she had told Don she would not be studying with Philomena Petrovia after all, he'd sounded almost glad—as though the great diva had taken her on as some kind of charity case and had suddenly decided to let her down easy before she got her hopes up. Although Ursula greatly struggled against the feeling of pride, she wanted her husband to understand what a good singer she really was.

Nik Prevel did. He believed in her. Even if she couldn't let on publicly that she was the mysterious Alexandra, it made her feel good that she was being taken seriously as a singer by Arnie and Nik. She had a one-hundred-thousand-dollar cashier's check in her desk drawer to prove it, given to her after signing the contract she never did run by her husband for review.

Plus, she felt sexy, desirable, and appreciated when she was in the studio. It had been a long time since she'd felt that way—was that so wrong?

The phone rang just as she hit Send on a brief message to Don, wishing him well on the case and telling him she loved him. Their phone conversations had become tense, and e-mail communication was safer these days.

"Ursula, he didn't mean anything by that. He was only being friendly."

"Thanks, Arnie, but his kind of friendly and my kind of friendly are two entirely different kinds of friendly. You don't have to apologize for him."

Along with everything else he did in the course of the day, Arnie had become a kind of buffer between her and Nik. "He's not a bad guy, Ursula. He—"

"He's incorrigible. I can't believe his pickup lines actually work on women. Is it true what I just read in *E!*, that he's seeing Naomi Watts? When did that happen?"

"It didn't. Trust me. Since you two started this project he's been like a hermit, which is not a good thing from a PR standpoint. That's why I made him go to Tori's party tonight."

"He managed to dress himself? Hopefully he'll stay out of trouble."

"A little trouble is good for a man like him. People expect it—the media expect it."

They visited for a while about their families. She told him Don was doing fine, but that due to the nature of the trial, she couldn't share anything more with him. In reality, she really didn't know anything more.

Arnie shared about his wife's recent award for her work on breast cancer awareness. She'd had a bad scare a few years ago and become involved in the Susan G. Komen Race for the Cure.

"So is everything okay? You're not mad?" Arnie asked.

"Don't worry about it, Arnie. I'm not quitting. Just tell him to lay off the smarm, okay?"

"You think he's smarmy?"

"You don't?"

The silence between them smiled.

"I'll talk to him this weekend. What's the plan for Tuesday? Want to drive in with me?"

They made plans for a top-secret rendezvous, and she hung up looking forward to a long, quiet weekend. She loved having four days off between their sessions.

After removing her makeup and applying a new Chanel night cream, she settled under the covers with a cup of hot herbal tea to read a book she'd recently picked up from her church library called *The Potluck Club*. She was unfamiliar with the authors, but the title was cute and the cover quote was from Graham Kerr.

She fell asleep reading, and when the doorbell rang at 5:00 Saturday morning, her book fell to the floor as she stumbled out of bed, the hairs on her neck standing up. *It must be an emergency.* She instantly became hyperalert, grabbed a housecoat, and ran down the stairs, taking them two at a time. *Please, God, don't let it be my family.*

$$24$$

Seeing Nik standing on her doorstep in the first light of dawn made her blink twice.

This better be good. "Nik, what are you doing here?" she called through the door.

"Invite me in. It's cold out here."

"Go home. It's five in the morning!"

"Please, Ursula. We gotta talk."

What should I do, Lord? She certainly couldn't leave him bellowing on her doorstep.

"Just a minute, Nik. I'll be right back." She returned to her bedroom to quickly change into jeans and a sweater, and when she returned, Nik was sitting on her front steps with his head resting in his hands.

When she reluctantly opened the door, he stood and walked past her, smelling of booze and cigarette smoke.

"You're drunk. How did you get here? Where's your car?" She peered out the front window.

"Taxi."

"You need coffee. Go sit down." She pointed him toward the living room.

He followed her into the kitchen instead, placing himself on a stool while she made coffee.

"Nice kitchen. Is that a Bosch?" He pointed to the new dishwasher.

"Yes. What do you want?"

"Is that a Sub-Zero?" He stared at her refrigerator.

"Yes. Now, I doubt you've come over to identify my appliances. What's up, Nik?"

"Wow, a Capresso coffee maker; not like mine, but I'm impressed." He looked around her well-appointed kitchen in amazement, as though he were the only person in Southern California with good taste. "Really impressed."

"Is that so? Well, I'm not the least bit impressed with you." She tried to make her voice stern, but he only smiled. "We have a business agreement, Nik, and it doesn't include you coming to my home at dawn. So, unless there is an emergency or you have something earthshaking to impart—which in your current condition I highly doubt—I suggest you drink a cup of java and sober up. I'll call you a taxi."

"Ouch. You are a demon with your words."

"Don't call me that. I'm not a demon." She pointed her finger at him.

"Oops, sorry. Forgot about your whole religion thing—demons mean a whole different thing to you folks, don't they?"

"Nik. What. Do. You. Want?"

He looked at her with lids half opened. He wore a deep purple satin YSL shirt open to the navel, a chunky David Yurman chain around his neck, black Brioni slacks with a Brighton belt, and his signature Ferragamo loafers on bare feet. She wondered if Ferragamo paid him a handsome sum to be a walking billboard.

"I could have slept with Stephanie Hampshire last night. She was all over me at Tori's place. But I said no. We even went to the Cat afterward, and I left alone. What do you think about that?"

"I'll alert the media."

The Cat & Fiddle was a popular industry hangout on Sunset Boulevard for music types like Nik.

"You don't think too much of me, do you?" He leaned his chin on his palm.

She didn't know what she thought of him—he was often positively beastly, other times pathetically sweet, and sometimes incredibly attractive—so she said nothing. Instead she put a mug of steaming coffee in front of him and pulled up a stool across the bar from him.

"You didn't call a taxi," he said quietly, after a moment.

Ursula quickly stood up, but he reached out and caught her arm. "I don't want you to. Not yet." He stared at her a moment before letting go of her arm. "I want to call a truce. That's why I came over."

Ursula spoke loudly. "A truce implies some sort of altercation has occurred, doesn't it?" she said. "I'm not aware that we've had any such altercation."

"Ah, but that is where you are mistaken." He leaned in and used a husky voice. "A truce means a respite from a disagreeable state or action—and I think our state is disagreeable. I want a respite."

She smiled at his response but didn't sit back down.

Nik squirmed. "I'm serious, Ursula. Arnie told me you were ticked off. You really need to lighten up. I was just kidding. We have a long road ahead of us and I don't like the friction—it makes things difficult for everyone."

She took a deep breath before she spoke. "I think that's what you do like, Nik. Friction."

Nik blushed, and Ursula pressed on. "Do you have any female friends you haven't slept with?"

"Who's talking about sex?" He looked surprised.

"You are. Answer my question. Do you have any female friends you haven't seen naked?"

"I don't take every woman I meet to bed."

Ursula shook her head; she didn't believe him. She stepped toward him and looked directly in his eyes. "Nik, you're not going to take me to bed. Not today. Not ever. I am committed to my husband, and frankly, I'm not attracted to you."

"You're not?" He looked honestly amazed at this.

"And even if I was—which I'm not—I would not engage in sexual immorality. This may sound strange to you, but God's rules make my life better. He is good!" Even now, she felt joy and peace flowing through her. "I may sound like a Pollyanna to you, but once you start walking with God, you realize how wonderfully freeing it really is."

Nik frowned. "You don't beat around the bush, do you?"

"Not at five in the morning when someone who has obviously been drinking all night knocks on my door and wakes me from a sound sleep, ticked off because I'm not throwing myself all over him like some cheap trollop."

He began to laugh. "Do people really use words like that? Cheap trollop?"

"Well, you know what I mean." She joined him in laughter. "Stop laughing at me. I'm serious."

He didn't stop laughing, and neither did she. Instead of picking up the phone, she brewed a full pot of coffee and they talked about friendships, relationships, his parents, and her marriage.

"Don is my best friend," she said. "I'm so sad he's gone. Tomorrow is Palm Sunday, and he won't be here to share it with me."

"What's Palm Sunday? You got palm readers coming to church?"

Ursula didn't laugh at that one. She simply explained the meaning of Palm Sunday, launching them into another conversation. Nik even asked several questions.

Nik was sorry when it was time to leave Ursula's—and realized that he had forgotten all about his goal to get her into bed. As he walked out the door, he knew he was not the same drunken womanizer who had walked in her door. For the first time in his life, he had a female friend. He wasn't quite sure what to do with her, but there was time to figure it out.

The cab dropped him off at home, and he immediately felt oppressive emptiness. He looked around at the priceless artwork on his walls, the custom-designed furniture, and the view out the wall of glass and wondered what had changed.

He shook out a hearty dose of aspirin and swallowed them without water.

Ursula had said tomorrow was Palm Sunday. Was there a Catholic church in town having a service? Did Catholics even celebrate Palm Sunday? He searched his brain, trying to recall the details of a time in his youth when his mother and father had dragged him to a church service on Easter. All he could remember was the way women had hovered around his father like carrion birds, smothering him with compliments, talking about his newest recording, or telling him of some TV show they'd seen him on. He hated how his mother, his beautiful mother, would be pushed slowly to the side—observing from a distance the meteoric rise of her megalomaniac husband. As a child, Nik had clung to her hand, watching them both from his unique position.

He pressed his thumbs against his eyes, knowing he must get some sleep. But something hovered in the back of his mind—some alien thought he felt he should recall. Walking to the sink to get a drink of water, he noticed for the first time the sound of his heels on the Mexican tiles. Catching his reflection in the stainless-steel doors of his Sub-Zero refrigerator, he realized how much he was like his father—and was revolted. The realization that he might be turning into Cristoff was almost more than he could bear. He'd spent a lifetime insisting he was anything but.

He squeezed his eyes tightly—forcing the hot tears back—refusing to feel the pain that struggled to be set free like a caged wild animal.

He looked at the clock. It was almost eight, and for some reason, the visit with Ursula had made him want to call his mother. Isabella. His most vivid childhood memory of his mother was her beauty—that and the ever-present martini glass that was as much a part of her as the costly diamonds that adorned her long, delicate fingers and dripped from her alabaster neck and ears. His childhood friends loved his mother—but they were afraid, though in awe, of his father.

He listened to the phone ring as he settled back into the corner of his leather sofa, prepared to leave a message on his mother's personal voice mail.

"This is Isabella," she answered.

"Hello, Mother."

"Nikky! Is anything the matter, dear? Where are you?"

"Home. I'm fine. It is kind of early for me, isn't it? I didn't wake you, did I?"

"No, dear. I've been awake for a while. I'm making baklava for your father. What are you doing up at this hour?"

"Haven't been to sleep yet."

"Ah, I see."

I doubt that.

"And where is Patriarch Prevelakis this lovely morning?"

"Sleeping, of course."

"What's happening with the project Sony wants to do? Is it a go?" Nik was selfishly curious.

There had been some talk about another greatest-hits project featuring his father's past Grammy Award songs. They'd repackaged some of his best-loved songs a few years ago in a holiday gift-box collection, and it had sold over two million copies—and had won a Grammy Award.

It had been that way from the start. In 1958, at the age of twenty-two, Cristoff had won his first Grammy at the very first

Grammy Award event ever held. Over the past several decades he had gone on to become one of the most Grammy-awarded singers in history. Everything Cristoff Prevelakis touched turned to gold . . . except his son.

"I'm not certain," Isabella whispered. "Don't quote me, but I don't think it's going to happen."

"That's too bad." Nik smirked, glad his mother couldn't see him. Cristoff's time was over; it was his turn now.

"Yes, it is too bad. It would have been good for him."

"He'll find something else to do, I'm sure."

"I'm sure too. Nikky, are you okay?"

"I'm fine, Isabella. Stop being motherly."

"Ah, but I am your mother, Nikita." She seldom lapsed into his nickname these days.

"Say, Mom?"

"Yes?"

"Do you have a few minutes? I mean, can you talk?"

"Of course, dear. Let me put this filo dough away and wash my hands and I'll call you right back. No. Hang on. I will put the phone down and be right back. Don't go away."

He was bone-tired but they talked for almost an hour. He shared as much as he could about the project he was working on—all the time calling Ursula by her alias. He didn't disclose the musical genre and she didn't ask. If she thought he was recording another rock album, so be it. Although he trusted his mother, he knew better than to ask her to intentionally keep anything secret from Cristoff.

"So it sounds like you like this Alexandra?" she said. "How about you bring her over for dinner one night?"

"Oh no, I don't think so." His tone of voice said it all.

"Nikky, that was such a long time ago. You must not hold things against your father. He can't help himself—he said he was sorry."

Every time his mother made excuses for his father, she did him more harm than good. Couldn't she see that?

"Nikky, you know he won't be around forever."

We should be so lucky. He'll probably outlive all of us.

"And he does love you."

"Yeah, right. Easy for you to say."

"Do you really think so, Nikky? That it is easy for me? All of this?"

They never talked about his father's long history of mistresses. Not really. He remembered innocently asking when he was a little boy, but the pain from his father's hand falling hard on his cheek was no match for the pain on his mother's face that cut like a scalpel into his heart. He never asked again.

He just watched and learned. He made excuses for his father's behavior.

Until the day Cristoff tried to seduce the first girl Nik had ever loved.

Nik had brought Elizabeth to dinner at his parents' home, and within the hour his already drunken father was making blatant advances. His inappropriate behavior only worsened. Elizabeth had rushed out in tears. They broke up shortly thereafter.

Things had always been tense between him and his father, but to Nik's tender heart, the seismic activity of that night had fashioned a chasm far too wide to ever traverse.

That had been eight years ago, when Nik was barely twenty-one years old. As his own star rose high in the Hollywood sky, he'd vowed never to be like his father. He would remain single forever because then he would never be the cause of the kind of pain he'd so often seen on his mother's face.

Deciding it was too late to go back to bed after Nik left, Ursula began early and spent all day Saturday doing chores while listening to praise and worship music blaring from her not-as-expensive-as-Nik's sound system. Their early-morning conversation rolled back and forth in her brain, and she wondered how someone so fortunate could be so unhappy. She realized how easy it had been to misjudge him—taking at face value the persona he wanted her to see instead of what was really inside his heart. Not that she had a clear understanding of what was really inside his heart, for the walls he had built were sturdy and high, not only keeping others out, but holding himself prisoner. She'd never before met anyone so lost—so empty of soul.

Ursula wanted to call Nik and invite him to Palm Sunday service with her. The more she thought about it, the more she understood how difficult it must be to live his life. They couldn't be seen together for the obvious reasons. If he wore a disguise and accompanied her to church, there would still be a problem—people would want to know who Ursula's mystery man was. Not a good thing, considering her husband was out of town.

Perhaps the real question was whether he would be receptive to going to church if she asked. Had she really seen a glimmer of interest in their early-morning conversation? Could someone so entrenched in a skewed belief system make a U-turn? Ursula thought about the apostle Paul. If he could turn his life around and make a difference for God, surely there was hope for Nik Prevel. She decided against asking him to Palm Sunday service and prayed instead that he would be led to worship on this solemn day in his own way.

She looked forward to Tuesday with a renewed sense of excitement—believing that God was indeed working in mysterious ways. The more she concentrated on Nik and his salvation, the less time she had to think about what might be happening between Don and Celeste.

Nik slept the remainder of Saturday and dreamed about his talk with his mother. In his dream she said all the right things, he responded as a loving, dutiful son, and his father wept, begging for forgiveness. It was a dream worthy of Paramount Studios, and when Nik awoke late in the day, he laughed at the absurdity of it all.

He thought briefly about going out, but he had hours of Iron Chef, Emeril, Wolfgang Puck, and Rachael Ray recorded on TiVo and decided instead to make paella for dinner and watch TV. Winston had stocked the kitchen with ingredients before leaving for the weekend, and Nik could create one heck of a feast.

"Free for dinner tonight?" he asked Arnie, the phone cradled against his neck as he cut mushrooms into delicate pieces with his new Kyocera knife.

"Sorry, buddy. Raysha and I have an anniversary party to go to. Give me a rain check, okay?"

"Hey, Arnie? Do you celebrate Palm Sunday, or is that not a Jewish thing?" Nik tried to sound casual, but he felt ignorant and weak.

They visited a bit about Arnie's Jewish roots and Nik shook his head silently. He knew so little about the man who was so much a part of his life he would be hard-pressed to function without him. When they said good-bye, Nik vowed to stop taking his relationship with Arnie so lightly.

There. Are you satisfied, Ursula? I've changed something about my vile character after all.

By mid-Sunday, Nik was feeling more normal. Who did Ursula think she was, anyway? Trying to make him feel worthless and out of control. He was a successful man with a life most people envied. She was just a housewife with too much time on her hands. She could pretend all she wanted that she wasn't attracted to him, that her religion somehow made her better than he, but there was no denying the chemistry between them and he was tired of playing games. He knew what she needed, and he was just the man to give it to her.

25

The Monday morning board meeting for the Palmcrest Children's Center had been rescheduled for Tuesday and ran well past ten o'clock. During a break, Ursula had tried calling both Nik and Arnie, but neither had answered, so she left voice-mail messages. By the time she arrived at Arnie's house to carpool to Nik's, Arnie had already left. There was a note addressed to her taped to the door.

> Alex, tried calling but no answer. You really need to get a cell phone that (1) actually works, and/or (2) you know how to operate. ☺ Had to meet with Nik. Call a taxi from here and leave car in back. Door open. See you soon.
> Arnie

She pulled her phone from her purse and didn't know whether to laugh or cry. No wonder she hadn't heard back from Don, or the kids. She'd forgotten to recharge her phone, and it was dead. How she hated cell phones! It was almost noon when she got to Nik's place—so much for an early start. She hated being late but made the decision that it wasn't going to stop her from having a wonderful day. Sunday's service at Dee's church had been so uplifting. After the Palm Sunday service, she'd accepted Dee and Lyle's invitation to brunch at The Arches in Newport Beach. Later in the day, she'd spoken on the phone with both Don and Victor and had received a lovely e-mail from Valerie. It had been a good Sunday—a very good Sunday indeed. She wondered how Nik had spent the day.

The door to Nik's house opened before she could knock.

"Good morning, Winston. Did you have a nice weekend? You went away, didn't you?"

"Yes, ma'am. Very nice. And you?"

"Fabulous."

"Very good, ma'am. You're wanted in the study."

The study?

The air in the study was heavy. Nik and Arnie were sitting tensely in armchairs. Arnie stood as she entered the room, and her memory was immediately transported to the principal's office where a detention assignment was about to be meted out.

"Good morning. Sorry I'm late. The Board—"

"Ursula. We need to talk."

Arnie's use of her real name made her pause. He'd always been so careful about using her alias. He walked over to the door and closed it behind her. Nik got up and poured himself a glass of water, avoiding eye contact.

"We've been talking this morning, and we feel it's going to be necessary to amend our contract regarding the days you work." Arnie cleared his throat.

"What do you mean? Am I being put on probation for being late?" She giggled.

"My client has been waiting since nine this morning."

"Your client?" She raised her eyebrows, no longer laughing. "Nik, what's this about? I'm standing right here—you can talk to me yourself. You don't need Jim Henson. Sorry, Arnie, no offense."

"Do you realize any number of pros would give their eyeteeth to do this project?" Nik hissed. "If you're not going to take this seriously you might as well tell us right now."

Ursula jumped at the electric anger that sparked from his tongue.

What happened? She chose her words carefully. "You know I'm serious. Now tell me what's happened—why are you so angry?" When Nik did not respond she turned to Arnie. "Arnie, what's the matter? We've been working together for almost three weeks. Something has clearly happened, and don't tell me it's because I'm a few hours late—I left messages for you both."

"My client feels that—"

"Enough with the 'my client' malarkey. We can behave like adults. Spit it out."

"We've hardly worked together *for three weeks*." Nik sneered. "It's been three weeks since our first meeting, but you've worked a sum total of nine days. I don't think you understand what's on the line here!" Nik shouted. "This isn't a karaoke booth in the mall where you put in a five-dollar bill, sing a song, and out pops a CD or cassette tape. Do you know who I am?"

"I know exactly who you are, Nik."

"Then act like it."

"What's that supposed to mean?"

"Arnie, go get a cup of coffee and let me talk with Ursula alone for a minute."

When Arnie showed no sign of moving, Nik crossed his arms, his chin upraised in defiance. "It's okay," he said.

"It's not okay." Arnie crossed to where they were both standing, firmly putting his hands on his hips.

"I'm not going to go get coffee so you two can beat each other up and say something stupid you'll both regret. Everyone knows you are the boss, Nik. Everyone knows you hold all the trump cards—that you pay the bills and call the shots. We all know you are *the star.* Ursula knows how it works, but she also knows how to push your buttons and enjoys doing it."

"Hey—"

"It's true, Ursula," he said, shaking his finger at her. "You know exactly what I'm talking about. And you"—he pointed to Nik—"must stop feeling threatened by this woman. She is not a threat. She's a talented singer that you discovered, and you are going to make millions on this CD if you both get your egos out of the way and stop acting like children!"

Nik and Ursula stared as he continued.

"What he's really ticked off about, Ursula, is this three days on and four days off thing. And frankly I don't blame him. We tried to give you everything you wanted, but this schedule isn't working. So the two of you talk it out and figure out how to make it work. Now maybe I will go get myself a cup of coffee. In fact, I'm going out for lunch. I'll be back in an hour. Start without me if I'm late."

It wasn't until the door closed that either of them spoke.

"Now look at what you've done!" growled Nik.

"Look at what *I've* done?" she spat back at him. "You're just like a child. When you don't get your way, you either pout or throw a tantrum or—" She stopped short. *Oh, Lord,* she prayed silently. *This is wrong. Help me say the right words.*

"Or what? Go on, say it, Little Miss Perfect." Nik stepped closer to her, anger burning in his eyes. "What else am I doing wrong besides being a spoiled brat? You're mighty quick to condemn, oh ye of Christian love and nonjudgment. If that's what it means to walk in faith, I don't want any part of it!"

His cruel words bit her as she fought back tears. But he was right. She had judged him—before she'd even known him, she'd judged him. What right did she have pointing out any of Nik's faults, when in reality she was keeping this entire project a secret from her husband?

"I don't blame you," she said softly. "I haven't been setting a very good example, have I? I'm sorry, Nik."

He stared at her and then turned sharply away.

"Nik, what happened?" Ursula pleaded to his back. "When you left my house on Saturday I thought we'd reached another level of understanding. Did I say something wrong? I'm sorry if I came on strong about my beliefs. I didn't mean to appear judgmental—"

"This has nothing whatsoever to do with Saturday."

It had everything to do with Saturday—how could he say that? *Unless something happened on Sunday?*

"Did something happen on Sunday? I thought about inviting you to church with me, but I didn't want to appear, you know, pushy."

"I drove by your home on Sunday."

"You did? When? Why didn't you stop in?"

"You know why I didn't stop in. You had a visitor. I saw him, Ursula. And it didn't look like any photo of Don I've ever seen, although you looked chummy enough to be married. Did it ever occur to you that making out on your front steps with a man who isn't your husband might be frowned upon by your neighbors?"

"What in heaven's name are you talking about, Nik?"

"Don't play games with me!" He grabbed her by the arm. "I saw you."

She didn't know whether to laugh or cry when she realized what he had seen.

"Did you also happen to see my alleged lover's wife sitting in the car?" She pulled away from him and stepped back. "I went to church and then to brunch with Dee and her husband, Lyle. When they left my house afterward, she forgot her purse. Lyle came back to get it. We hugged good-bye on the front steps. Is that what you call making out, Nik?"

"Then what about Monday?" he asked. "What's your excuse for that?"

"What do you mean?"

"You said you had a board meeting every Monday—that's one of the reasons you insisted on having Monday off. I called Palmcrest to talk with you and they told me there wasn't a board meeting."

"There wasn't. They moved it to today, and it went long— which you would have known if you listened to your voice mails. That's why I was late. As it turns out I spent the better part of Monday morning at the dentist having a broken filling repaired and the remainder of the afternoon sleeping off the Novocain in the steam room at La Petite Retreat! Although I must say I did have a mighty fine massage by Bruno before I came home—do you by any chance have a grainy black-and-white spy photo or two of that illicit behavior? I'm sure his life partner would be interested in seeing our tryst." She began to collect her songbooks, throwing them into her bag.

"What are you doing?" Nik whispered.

"You're right—this isn't working. I'm leaving."

"I thought you were playing me."

"And why exactly would I do that?" It was all she could do not to throw a songbook at him. "Have I ever led you to believe we were anything more than singing partners, Nik? I'm a married woman. I love my husband. And you're acting like a jealous boyfriend."

Nik sat down and put his head in his hands.

Ursula could hardly get herself to say it, but she knew she had to. "Nik, I don't think I can work with you under these conditions. You can't drive by my house like a stalker and accuse me of infidelity. It's not right . . . it's not healthy . . . for either of us. I haven't cashed the check, and we can tear up the contract and call it quits. I can walk away now and consider myself fortunate that I had the chance to meet you and sing with you these past weeks. I can't give you what you want if what you want is me."

Nik turned toward her, his face tormented. "I don't know what I want," he said quietly. "I only know that when you're around me I feel good and when you're gone I feel empty. You make me happy, Ursula."

As soon as he said it she knew what this was really about. Nik didn't know what true happiness was or what it would take to achieve it. What he wanted was something to fill that empty place in his heart that only a relationship with God could fill. He was spiritually empty and thought she was the one filling that emptiness, when in reality it was so much bigger than that. God was working on Nik and using her as a tool. *Can I really walk away now?*

Nik might be almost thirty years old, but in many ways he was still a boy. She had seen glimpses of the man he could become, but the two of them were traversing uncharted territory. Did God really intend to use her as an instrument when she was clearly in conflict in her own marriage? Could she really help Nik mature, or was she operating out of her own self-interest?

She never expected to find her answer so quickly.

26

She was still thinking how to respond when Nik sighed heavily. "Give me ten minutes, will you?" he said softly as he turned away. "But please don't leave—not yet. Okay?"

"I won't leave," she said softly. "You know, Nik, sometimes it hurts to grow." She slipped from the room.

Nik was sitting in the armchair with a legal pad on his lap when she returned exactly ten minutes later. She could see he had jotted down some notes. He stood up when she entered the room, something only Arnie usually did.

"I want to continue working with you," he said awkwardly without preamble. "If you'll give me another chance. I won't pretend I have all the answers right at this moment, or that I fully understand exactly why I've been a total meathead the past forty-eight hours. . . ."

Ursula gave him an encouraging smile.

"While you were gone I was thinking about something my mother once told me about life." He motioned for her to sit down and sat across from her. He leaned forward with his elbows resting on his knees and focused on the ink pen he rolled between his fingers as though he were speaking to it instead of her.

"I was just a kid, and I had a cocoon in a jar in my room—not an unusual thing for a kid to have." She nodded in agreement. "The day it hatched we were home alone, and Mom and I sat for hours watching that butterfly make its way out of what surely had to be painful confinement. Our eyes were practically glued to that jar, and all the while Mom gave me examples of the birth process of other things—you know birds, animals, and insects. I wasn't much interested in humans at that point. Did you know it can take hours for a baby eagle to peck its way out of an egg? Sometimes they're so exhausted they don't make it. Imagine that. All that work to get out of confinement only to breathe a short time and then die. It wasn't like Mom was trying to scare me or anything. I was curious about life and kept asking question after question. It was a beautiful monarch butterfly that emerged from that cocoon, and I couldn't believe my eyes that something so perfect—so exquisite—could have been coiled up and crumpled in that ugly brown shell for so long. But that day has stuck with me. I heard my mother's voice plain as day just now when you walked out of the room. 'Nikky, sometimes it hurts to grow. But if something isn't growing, it's dying.' "

There were tears in his eyes when he looked up.

"I think I'm growing, Ursula, but it hurts, and I'm not sure what to do about that."

If he was anyone other than Nik Prevel—if circumstances had been different—she would have reached over and held his hands, or wrapped her arms around him in a big motherly hug. He could sure use it. But she remained still, even after he jumped up and grabbed a can of soda from the small refrigerator behind the bar, took a big swig, and resumed his business-as-usual stance.

"Well, anyway, I'd like to make this work. If you're still game?"

"I'm still game."

"Good . . . that's cool. Glad to hear it. Uh . . . is there anything you need from me? I mean, anything I could do to make this . . . partnership . . . better?"

Ursula was impressed that he would even ask. And she knew exactly what to ask for. "I only have one small request. I'm not trying to convert you or anything like that, so please don't take this the wrong way, but it sure would help me if we could start with a short prayer every day before we begin working. Kind of like saying grace before you eat, you know? Nothing big or major, just a little request for our day to be successful and productive. Would that be okay?"

Nik looked at her as though she'd sprouted wings. "Pray?"

"This whole experience is totally new for me. You're a pro; you've grown up in this world. . . . You're a rock star, for crying out loud. But I'm in over my head. Do you think I don't know that?"

"And prayer helps?" He sounded skeptical.

"Well, God helps when we pray to Him. I'll continue praying on my own if you prefer, but this sure would help me."

Ursula tried hard to understand how Nik might perceive this suggestion—she could tell praying out loud was totally foreign for him, as it was for a lot of people. She didn't want to scare him or put him on the defensive.

"This is kind of what I have in mind." She clasped her hands, bowed her head, and didn't give him time to protest. "Dear Lord, thank you for giving us voices to sing. Thank you for the creative gifts you give to artists to bring joy into hearts and lives. Thank you for giving Nik insight and wisdom to move ahead on this project—he wants this album to bring the essence of love into homes around the world. Please, Lord, help me to grow in my ability to be the voice this project needs and the person Nik needs me to be in order to feel comfortable that he's made the right choice. Bless Arnie as he works with us and bless Winston as he takes care of us. Be with us right now as we make some important decisions that may set the stage for our time together. And, Lord, please forgive me for causing anguish to our team—help me to be the kind of professional this project needs. We owe our voices and this opportunity to you, and we praise your name for the abundant blessings you bestow upon us each and every day. In your name we pray, Amen."

She looked up to see that Nik was still standing behind the bar, his head bowed and eyes closed. She quickly stood and turned to get a glass of water. "Could we try it every day?" she asked as nonchalantly as she could manage. "You don't have to say anything. I'll do all the talking. If you're uncomfortable, we'll stop."

"We'll try it and I'll let you know." He came out from behind the bar and offered her a can of soda.

"Thanks."

"Not sure what Arnie will think; he's Jewish, you know."

"I know."

They talked at length about Ursula's schedule and the burden this placed on everyone.

"Just when we get started, you're gone for four days. We have three days of amazing progress—then four days of nothing. I can't sit around and do nothing for four days, so, unless you want me to work without you and make all of the decisions, we really need to rethink your schedule."

After some more talk, Ursula agreed to work Monday through Friday, with every other Friday off.

"And if you do go to New York for a long weekend, we can always work around you on that Monday—just let us know ahead of time. Is that fair?" he asked.

"That's fair." She extended her hand, and they shook on it.

27

Nik was feeling smugly self-assured and confident about the progress they'd made once he called Ursula's bluff and put his foot down. They'd tested sixteen songs in the last three days.

Ursula had finally started behaving like a professional since he'd almost fired her. Sometimes a guy just had to play hard-ball—especially with women used to having their own way. Ursula now arrived every day ready to work and vocally warmed up. They had the system of her travel pretty much worked out so as to confound the media. No one seemed to have caught on to their project, except Winston, who had subtly suggested to Nik one evening after rehearsal that he would gladly assist with the charade in any way he could.

Nik was even getting used to Ursula's daily prayers and had to admit it seemed to help her stay focused. Truthfully, he'd never heard her kind of prayers before; they were like a conversation with God, as if they were friends.

"Let's humor her with this prayer thing for a while, okay?" he'd said to Arnie—who agreed it might not hurt. In fact, Arnie seemed to be getting into it and always added a hearty amen.

Winston even hung around occasionally, reverently bowing his head.

"I can work a little tomorrow if I can take off early today—if that will work?" Ursula asked when she arrived on Friday. "It's Good Friday. I'd like to leave a bit early so I can attend church tonight, if that's okay?"

Nik planned to be home on Saturday because he was having his parents over for dinner.

"I suppose we could work a few hours in the morning, but I have plans for the evening."

"A hot date?" Ursula smiled.

He couldn't help but wonder if she was smiling extra hard to mask feelings of jealousy. "But, of course," he toyed, "it's Saturday night. Go ahead and leave early today. What exactly is Good Friday, anyway? Isn't every day supposed to be good for you Christians?" He immediately regretted asking the question in such a way. "Oops, sorry. I wasn't making light of your religion."

She smiled. "That's okay. I'm getting used to you."

———

Arnie wasn't able to join them on Saturday morning, and Ursula noticed how much more open Nik was to make inquiries about her faith when they were alone. He asked a lot of questions during the three hours they worked, and Ursula told him about the upcoming Easter Sunday service she was so excited about.

Once in a while, Nik slipped up to his kitchen. Ursula could smell a luscious aroma wafting into the room every time he opened the door, but when she asked what he was making, it was clear he did not want to talk about it. She began to think perhaps she had misjudged him and his picture-book kitchen. Could it be they shared a passion for cooking? Could it be he was actually comfortable in his kitchen and that she'd gotten the wrong impression during the tour on her first day? She tried to get him to talk about it, but every time she mentioned a favorite recipe book or cooking show, he clammed up.

By the time she left on Saturday, it was clear Nik had his mind on other things. She wondered who he was entertaining that night. He must be wooing some starlet. She felt a pang of jealousy and realized she was missing her husband and the life she used to have. She no longer had anyone to cook for—and she missed the breakfasts Don used to make for her on Saturday. Nothing was consistent anymore. She felt like a contestant on *American Idol*, not sure from week to week if she'd be asked back or fired on the spot.

———

Nik stared at his mother across the table and for the first time realized she was still a young woman—not much older than Ursula. She would turn fifty on her next birthday, the same day his father would turn seventy. August first was a special day in the Prevelakis family. Not only did his parents share the same birthday, but they had married on that same day when Isabella had turned eighteen. Growing up, Nik thought this was a cool thing because it was easy for him to remember the most important events in his young life, other than his own birthday.

He came to realize it was also easy for his father—a man with many women to remember, but only one who could make his life miserable if he forgot a special date.

Nik had been born two years later on August twenty-first and was glad he didn't have to share his birthday with a man as ego-centric as Cristoff Apollo Prevelakis.

"This is a wonderful meal, Nikky." His mother smiled.

"Thank you, Mother."

"Isn't everything wonderful, dear?" She leaned over to Cristoff and kissed his cheek. "Our Nikky made this all himself—from scratch, in his very own kitchen. What do you think?"

Nik held his breath and prepared himself. Why did she have to ask his father's opinion? Nothing he ever said was positive. Plus, his father was old school—how many times growing up had he heard that men who cooked were sissies? He'd done his best over the years to downplay this particular hobby—this gift. Nik braced himself.

"Very good, Nikolai. You must get your talent from my side of the family—the Prevelakises come from a long line of culinary masters."

Nik almost choked on the bite of spanakopita he'd just taken. *Did the Great Cristoff just give me a compliment?*

Tonight's menu was a traditional Easter soup called mayeritsa, Greek salad with feta cheese and black olives, spanakopita, dolmathes, moussaka, and baklava his mother had baked.

If his mother's baklava was Cristoff's favorite dessert, then moussaka was his father's favorite main dish. It had taken Nik months to learn how to make it. He'd worn out the videotape of Emeril teaching the class.

"Have you told your son the good news?" Isabella daintily wiped the corner of her mouth with the linen napkin.

"What good news?" Cristoff smirked.

"Oh, don't be coy!" She poked him on the shoulder. "Tell him."

Nik put down his fork and looked at his father.

"Sony has decided to release a collection of my greatest hits." Cristoff was nonchalant.

Didn't Mother tell me she thought that wasn't going to happen? How many special limited-edition packages could they milk out of his father's career? Apparently as many as they wanted.

"You don't sound pleased," Nik commented.

"Of course he is pleased," said Isabella.

"I miss Fogarty. It was easier to work with him. Not so many games." Cristoff reached for the bottle of wine.

James Fogarty had been the record label's executive assigned to work specifically with Nik's father for the twenty-plus years he was riding high at the top of the charts. He'd worked with Cristoff and his agent to put together dozens of projects—many of which had won multiple Grammy Awards. Fogarty had died a few years ago, and since then Cristoff had gone through more executive liaisons with his recording label than Donald Trump went through apprentices.

"What kind of games? I don't have any trouble with my label. They've been great on my newest project." Nik reached for more bread.

"Ah, but you are the new generation; they no longer appreciate the wisdom of a master."

Nik had never heard his father sound quite so resigned. It wasn't like him at all. Isabella must have sensed they were entering territory best left alone.

"And how is your project going, Nikky?" Isabella beamed. "You have been very secretive about this one."

Since their altercation after the Hollywood Bowl concert, he hadn't mentioned the theme of his next project, and judging by his father's lack of vehemence, he deduced that Cristoff had assumed that Nik had heeded his warning and returned to recording rock-and-roll music like a good little boy.

"Yes, how are things in the bat cave?" Cristoff added. He took another helping of the spinach pie he liked so much. That was compliment enough for Nik.

"Uh, things are going okay. We're going through song selections right now—deciding what to record."

"We?" Cristoff eyed Nik with suspicion. Their last talk had concerned Carlotta.

"No one you know. A total unknown, as a matter of fact— never recorded a thing in her life."

"Another one of those skinny little half-naked girls who scream into the microphone? I can't understand a thing they say."

As much as he wanted to tell his father he was recording famous love songs, he didn't want to risk an argument. The evening was going well—unusually so—and Nik didn't want to ruin anything.

Isabella held up her wine glass. "I would like to make a toast to my two favorite men." Nik and Cristoff held up their glasses. "May God bless each of you as you work on your new records. May they be more successful than you could ever dream. I love both of you. Here's to our family."

"To family," Cristoff boomed.

"To family." Nik swallowed back the lump in his throat.

"I am very proud of you two." Isabella set down her glass. "You have given me great joy in this evening, and I think it must be a gift from God."

The men looked at her with raised eyebrows.

"It is appropriate during this season, don't you think? To mention God? Tomorrow is Easter. The resurrection of the Lord—and tonight we have resurrected our 'old' family. I am happy."

Nik finally understood. All these years of watching his mother live out her faith, and it took a suburban housewife to open his eyes to it. Isabella was a Jesus freak too. She had the same strange peace Ursula had.

Ursula.

I love her. The words flashed through his head. It wasn't that he just desired her or even that he wanted to conquer her. He had fallen in love with Ursula Rhoades.

"Do you know what that kid at Sony told me?"

Leave it to Cristoff to return to the subject he loved best when things got emotional—himself.

"No, dear, what did he say?" Isabella took a tiny nibble of baklava.

"He says we may have a shot at the Grammys again this year, with this new release. They're rushing it through in time for the October nominating deadline. Seems they got wind of another copycat doing what everyone knows I do best, recording classic love songs. Most likely Rod Stewart again."

Isabella turned to Nik. "Will your album release in time to be nominated, Nikky? It would be so wonderful if both of you were nominated again, wouldn't it? They'd be in different categories, but even so . . . father and son, legendary crooner and contemporary rock star! I love it when that happens. Remember that fabulous article *People* did a few years ago when you were both nominated? What was it called again? *Two Styles—One Bloodline.*"

"Yeah, that's what they called it." Nik reached for a drink.

But not this year. This year there would be one style—one bloodline. Nik had given up his dream of a Grammy to record something different. Cristoff would most likely win yet another award, and so be it. He wondered which of his father's songs Sony planned to include on this Greatest Hits project. He'd have to see if Arnie could get his hands on a list before they made the final selection for their project. It was going to be bad enough once Cristoff found out what Nik was doing—no need to add fuel to the fire by recording the same songs.

28

Ursula turned from the bathroom doorway and walked out into the bedroom, where she sat down on the edge of the bed trying to wake up. The early-morning sun streamed through the stained-glass window, warming her face. Varying shades of lilac danced on her skin as the rays progressed westward. She'd had their bedroom suite decorated in a purple iris theme, including custom-made stained-glass accent windows that adorned either side of the fireplace. Having a fireplace in her bedroom had been a longtime dream—one Don had turned to reality with his hard work. Everywhere she looked in their home was evidence of her husband's desire to provide for her.

It would be a strange Easter Sunday for her—alone for the first time in . . . she couldn't count how many years.

The day after Easter would be the start of the trial, and although she understood on a conscious level why Don couldn't fly back to spend Easter with her, it was more difficult to convince her heart. The fact that both Valerie and Victor were gone increased the pain. Ursula and Don had raised their children as if they were baby eagles—preparing them from birth to eventually leave the nest and soar on their own—but now that it had come to pass, Ursula felt the sharp pangs of loneliness.

Ursula shook her head. Everything would be fine when this trial was over and her little project was over—Don and she would be together again. She stood up to get ready for church, wanting to simply worship the Lord and celebrate this day of resurrected new life.

She looked into the mirror and felt ashamed. Today above all days was about the truth of her faith. The truth of what Jesus had told His disciples—that on the third day He would rise from the dead. The Word of God was all about truth, and the knot in her stomach when she thought about the lie she was living made her physically ill. She must tell Don about her secret project with Nik Prevel. The longer she waited, the more difficult it became to tell him.

She was about to step into the shower when her cell phone rang. She immediately recognized the number on the caller ID as Nik's cell.

"I may not know what Palm Sunday is, but I do know Easter," he said without preamble. "Will you take this poor, unrefined sinner to church with you today?"

She laughed, but her heart lurched. Today, churches around the globe would welcome with open arms those folks who went to church only at Christmas and Easter. Ursula had read in the newspaper just the day before an estimate that some seventy-six million adults who rarely attended church would visit on Easter. While for many it would be little more than a quick sugar rush, for others it would be a time of spiritual renewal. Perhaps, for millions of seekers, like Nik, it would be a chance to find the missing piece of life's puzzle, the piece that could bring them peace.

Besides, she welcomed his company. Easter was traditionally a time to spend with loved ones, and right now, Nik was the person who best understood what was going on in her life.

Two hours later a taxi cab dropped him off, and although she knew it was Nik who stood in her foyer, her eyes beheld a stranger. "So how do I look?" he asked. "Will this work?"

She was so excited about bringing him to church, she had neglected to think about an issue that was as common to Nik as breathing: He was recognized wherever he went.

"Did you dye your hair?"

"Of course not; it's a wig. You like?"

She was speechless as she walked around him like a patron viewing art.

"This is amazing. Look at your eyes!"

"Contacts."

He'd changed his icy blue eyes to the color of chocolate kisses. His usual wavy brownish black hair was cropped short in a shade of dark caramel.

"Wow." She really didn't know what else to say. The overall effect was stunning—yet eerie.

"Kitty came over early and helped me. She's great, huh?"

"Did you tell her where you were going?"

"Are you kidding? And ruin my reputation? I didn't tell and she didn't ask. Anyway"—he awkwardly thrust out an orchid corsage in a clear plastic box—"this is for you." He shrugged. "I figured it must be some kind of Easter ritual or something because everyone was buying them when I was in the store."

"My kids used to always buy me an orchid corsage for Easter—and for Mother's Day. Thank you, Nik." She hugged him awkwardly, acutely aware that he was not her son.

She pulled away and began to remove the corsage from its cellophane nest. He reached over and took it from her.

"May I?" He didn't wait for an answer and in a few deft movements gently secured the fragrant blossom to the lapel of her Donna Karan jacket.

"I can't imagine what it must be like."

"What?"

"Having to go through this"—she stepped away from him and waved her arm—"every time you want to go out."

"I don't have to do this every time I go out—just when I don't want to be recognized, which isn't often." The right corner of his mouth raised in his trademark dimpled grin.

"Well, you'd better not do that while we're out," she said, grabbing her purse.

"Do what?" He followed her out to the garage.

"Smile. It's a dead giveaway." She tossed him her car keys. "You drive."

29

Ursula had two tickets to the annual Easter pageant at the Crystal Cathedral, a nondenominational megachurch in Garden Grove about an hour's drive south of L.A. She'd bought the second ticket hoping against hope that Don might fly back to join her for Easter.

"It's a definite God thing," she declared as Nik drove. "I thought I would have to go alone."

"Is this the place they show on TV?" Nik asked as they pulled into the vast parking lot, directed by a series of volunteer attendants in neon orange vests.

"You've seen the *Hour of Power*?" Ursula raised her eyebrows.

"Not really, but we had a housekeeper once who watched it religiously. She pointed out some fountains to me one day when I was a kid, and I remember seeing huge glass doors magically open and water shooting up to the sky. Pretty impressive. Do they still do that?"

Ursula assured him they still did. As they walked across the lovely grounds among a throng of people, Nik was all ears as Ursula talked a mile a minute like a child describing Disneyland.

158

"This is an amazing production—you aren't going to believe it. The *Glory of Easter* pageant is one of the largest and most spectacular Passion plays you'll ever see."

"A passionate play, eh?" Nik grinned.

"Nik, the term *Passion play* is used to describe a vivid reenactment of Christ's last days on earth—it's an interpretation of the week that changed the course of history forever."

He whispered in her ear as they entered the church, "Uh, okay, you'll tell me if there's something I'm supposed to do, right? Like kneel or something? So I don't look like a jerk?"

She smiled and assured him all would be well.

Nik wasn't sure what he had expected, but this wasn't it.

"The sanctuary seats almost three thousand, and that's among the five largest pipe organs in the world," Ursula whispered as they were directed to their assigned seats. "I remember those two facts from the tour I took a few years back."

Nik could only shake his head—he'd never seen a church or a pipe organ so big in all his life. Then he began to notice the people, and the diversity of the crowd impressed him. Yet, for all the differences in race, age, and even in clothing, there was a startling similarity. Everywhere he looked he saw joyful faces. He couldn't quite put his finger on it, but he found himself smiling. He wanted to burst out singing "Love Is in the Air"! Because that's how it felt—like love was all around him. People didn't behave like this in the church he recalled from his youth. The church he knew was a very quiet, very reverent, and very uncomfortable place to be. No one in this church appeared uncomfortable at all.

Suddenly music filled the church like nothing he'd ever experienced, and as the ninety-minute dramatic production opened, so too did Nik's heart.

The play even had flying angels soaring overhead and live animals parading down the aisles. Nik heard about Jesus, Pilate, Mary Magdalene, Herod, and Mary as the performers recreated the Palm Sunday procession, the Last Supper, the trial, crucifixion, and ascension.

Utilizing incredible special effects, the lifelike re-creation of earthquakes, thunderstorms, and lightning inside the all-glass building was astounding. With each enactment of the events leading up to Christ's crucifixion and resurrection, Nik could see Ursula becoming more overwhelmed. Tears gently rolled down her cheeks, and Nik had to fight back his own swelling emotions. When the stone rolled away from the tomb and Jesus in all His splendid glory stood before the audience, Ursula reached for a hanky from her purse to wipe her eyes.

It took every ounce of strength he had to halt the hot tears that threatened to burst forth from his own eyes. Ursula didn't seem to notice—or she was giving him space to sort it out as the production came to an end.

When the production ended and the lights came on, people all around him were crying, hugging, shaking hands, and greeting one another. Nik smiled and laughed right along with them, enjoying the chance to be greeted like a normal person and not a rock star. He felt as if he was part of something bigger, as if he shared a spiritual bond with these people. Something inside him had changed, and it felt good.

Ursula noticed first. A group of high school girls were huddled together, giggling and gawking at Nik.

"Uh, Nik." She pulled him by the arm and looked him in the eye. "Don't look now, but I think you've been recognized."

Immediately going into defensive mode, he tucked his chin down like a football player ready to run in the opposite direction and leaned into her.

"Okay, lead on. Get me out of here," he instructed.

She grabbed his arm and moved quickly through the crowd of people, exiting the sanctuary without trouble.

"Whew, that was close. I told you not to smile," she joked.

Nik was unusually quiet on the drive back to her home. He had a lot to think about.

"I'll call a taxi and head home," Nik announced when he pulled into her garage. "Thanks for taking me. I . . . uh . . . I . . ."

"Nik, would you like to stay and talk for a while? I think I have enough food. Would you care to join me for an omelet?"

"Only if you'll let me cook," he said, carefully pulling off the wig and running his hands through his hair. "Sorry, it was hot."

"Sure, no problem, but it's the brown eyes that creep me out. The hair I could live with."

Nik rummaged through her refrigerator, pantry, and cupboards—assembling a mishmash of ingredients on her Cambria quartz countertop.

"I hope you know what you're doing." She recalled how reticent he had been only yesterday to discuss his cooking talent. He was a mass of conflicted actions and reactions.

"I'll muddle through. You just sit down and take a load off your feet."

Ursula sat at the counter watching Nik move adeptly around her kitchen. He'd periodically ask where something was and she'd respond. As he cooked, they talked about his parents and what it was like growing up around the Great Cristoff.

"I had them over for dinner last night," Nik said. "Wasn't as bad as usual."

That's why he was so nervous.

Like old friends playing catch-up after years of separation, they shared childhood stories and talked about personal things, all the while laughing and carrying on.

"I seem to spill my guts in your house. Have you noticed that?" Nik didn't make eye contact.

"Spill away. God knows these walls have seen their share of emotions over the years." Sensing his discomfort, she got up and began to set the kitchen table. "So where did you learn to cook like this?" She watched him crush garlic expertly, slice mushrooms like Emeril, and mix spices like a chemist. "How come you never let on about your culinary acumen?"

"Some secrets are best kept as such—secret."

Ursula said grace before they dove in to their meals like starving island castaways on *Survivor.*

"This is amazing!" she gushed.

"But of course." Nik grinned, but his cockiness was visibly forced.

While they ate, she could sense he had something on his mind. As a mother she had developed a sixth sense when her children had heavy hearts and needed to talk. The key was to build the trust, encourage the freedom to ask whatever was on their mind, and to listen without judging. She'd had many a conversation across this very table and silently prayed to have the right words when Nik asked whatever was on his mind.

"So how long have you been a . . . Christian?" Nik asked without looking up.

"I went forward on an altar call when I was seven years old. I can remember it like it was yesterday."

"Tell me." He put down his fork and rested his chin in his hand.

For the next hour they talked about her faith and her family. They talked about Nik's early recollections of attending Catholic services and what he'd picked up being the son of a father with Greek Orthodox roots and a mother with a Spanish heritage that stretched back for generations.

"So if you had to explain it in a nutshell, how would you do it?" Nik slathered blackberry jam on a piece of toast.

"Explain what?"

"The bottom line of Easter—what the God thing is all about."

The million-dollar question. She smiled. "It's so simple really. God so loved us He allowed His son, Jesus, to become human and live among us. Then He loved us enough to withhold His awesome power and allow Jesus to die to pay for all the sins of the world. Then three days later, He used His power to raise Jesus from the dead—to prove He'd overcome sin and death. On Easter morning everything became new, just as each of us do when we believe and accept what God has done for us." She paused a moment to let this sink in. "Nik, it's not what denomination we are or what rules and regulations we follow. It's all about having a personal relationship with Jesus Christ."

She wanted to say more—to share how much peace her relationship with the Lord brought her. She wanted to tell him that when she was alone or afraid, nothing helped more than her belief that God was in control—that she knew He would never leave her.

But instead she remained silent, the Lord impressing on her heart the need to be still.

Even through the eerie brown lenses, she could see in Nik's eyes the effect her words—God's words—were having on his heart. He stared off into space, deep in thought. "I think that's the reason my mother has been able to stand my father all these years," he said absently. "I think maybe she has that relationship."

Ursula nodded.

"He's a tough guy to live with," Nik continued. "But there's no denying his music has had an impact. He's got a gift for sure."

Like the stranger who had stood in her doorway earlier in the day—the Nik talking now was like another person. She merely nodded from time to time as he shared his heart.

"I remember his first Grammy; he was so smug. It only got worse the more he won."

"Maybe that's why God has kept you from winning for so many years—He's preparing your heart to accept it with gracious thanksgiving."

Nik's silence was hard to decipher. She waited, taking a moment to pour more coffee. Perhaps she had said too much, overstepped her boundaries?

"When I was a little girl"—Ursula leaned in with her elbows on the table and chin in her hands—"all I ever wanted to do was sing. I used to dream about winning a Grammy."

Her secret was out.

"Then why did you give it up?" Nik questioned.

"I've never really given it up. I still sing . . . with my students."

"And with your son, now and then," Nik said smiling, reminding her of how they'd met.

"And I still kind of dream about winning a Grammy—only I do it vicariously through others."

"How so?" Nik cocked his head.

"Every year my kids and I watch the Grammys together. Val was sure you'd win last time. She was crushed."

"That makes both of us."

"You were crushed?"

"My father has won his share of Grammys. That's a hard act to follow."

"I can only imagine. But you're not doing so shabby yourself. He must be proud of you, even if he doesn't say so."

"Yeah, right. But seriously, you gave up a career to be just a housewife—who does that?"

For the first time in a while she didn't bristle at the housewife reference and instead found herself smiling broadly. "I found something better."

"Such as?"

"Such as love. I have a lovely home, lovely kids, and a basically lovely husband when he isn't wrapped up in a case, and I have a lovely Lord. All in all, I have a totally lovely life."

"You sound like a Hallmark commercial. Should we wrap a big red bow around you?"

"Sometimes I feel like a Hallmark commercial." She laughed.

Nik grinned and shook his head.

"And I get to have the great Nik Prevelakis as a friend. What more could a girl want?"

Nik laughed as he stood and began to clear the table. "Friend? Don't let that cat out of the bag; you'll ruin my reputation."

"Please don't do that!" Ursula implored, taking the plate from his hands. "In my house whoever cooks does not clean up. It's the rule."

"Okay, then. It's time for me to head back, anyway. I'll call a taxi."

Ursula put down the plate and placed her hands on the table. "Do you really think having a woman for a friend would taint your reputation?"

"I was just kidding."

"No, Nik, I don't think you were. Be honest."

"Frankly, I don't know what it would do—we're treading on unknown ground for me."

"I know we are, but I'm willing to see it through, to make it work. I've learned it's often friendships that help define who we are. In many ways friendship is as much about trust and commitment as marriage."

"Ah, but without the perks." Nik winked seductively.

"Stop that!" Ursula threw a nearby potholder at him as he took his cell phone from his pocket. And she started to clean the kitchen as they waited for his taxi.

"So what is it about this place that feels different from my place?" Nik gestured around her kitchen as he looked in the big mirror on the wall to put on his wig.

"Besides the lower square footage—and the lack of ocean view and decadent opulence?"

"You know what I mean."

"Yes, I know what you mean." She poured herself another cup of coffee and sat down. "You know that feeling we were talking about earlier, what you felt in church today? That feeling is alive in this house—it fills this house. It always has. Don't get me wrong, we've had our share of trouble over the years, and raising kids is never easy, no matter how good they might be. But, Nik . . . ?"

"Yeah?"

"It always comes back to God being in control. See that plaque?" She pointed above the kitchen sink to an elaborate *God Bless This Home* wood carving. "He has, and I thank Him every day for it."

Nik stared thoughtfully at the plaque as he leaned on the edge of a barstool.

"Nik? Would it be okay if I asked a friend of mine to call you? His name is Harvey Doyle—Pastor Harvey Doyle. I think you'd like him. He used to be a Catholic priest."

"What happened?"

"He left the Catholic Church years ago—you'd have to ask him for specifics."

"Another Martin Luther, eh?"

Ursula's raised eyebrows bespoke volumes, and Nik laughed. "I'm not a total imbecile; I do read from time to time."

"I'm sorry. I didn't mean to insinuate anything—it's just that you surprised me."

"Yeah, well, I surprise myself from time to time."

Ursula silently thanked God for placing the idea in her head to connect Nik with Pastor Doyle—she didn't know why she hadn't thought about it before. They were well suited for a spiritually empowering friendship. Nik would surely keep Harvey on his toes, and it was no secret that Pastor Doyle had a special affinity for sharing the gospel with Catholics, particularly lapsed Catholics like Nik.

The sound of the taxi pulling into the drive interrupted the moment, but Ursula felt that too was God's timing.

"Sure, tell him to call. Does he know about our little secret? Our project?"

"Not yet, but I've been thinking about telling him. Would that be okay? We can trust him." *I could sure use some spiritual guidance these days.*

"Whatever you think is best." Nik stood awkwardly. "Thanks for totally screwing up my life. Have a good day." He grinned as she playfully smacked him on the arm.

"Get out of here already. I'll see you tomorrow."

As she opened the door, he turned and gave her a quick hug void of sexual tension or feelings or innuendo and whispered in her ear, "Don't give up that dream, Alexandra. With a voice like yours, you just might win a Grammy one day. Stranger things have happened."

He strode down the steps and into the taxi and waved good-bye, leaving her standing on her doorstep with her mouth hanging open.

30

Something had happened between Nik and Ursula over Easter weekend; Arnie was sure of it. If he didn't know any better, he would have guessed they'd slept together. The level of intimacy shared between a man and woman when they cross that bridge was obvious to anyone with a discerning eye. And it was his job to have a discerning eye about everything that concerned Nik. But he kept his mouth shut. He had enough work to do.

Arnie was conducting advance copyright work on all the tunes they'd selected so they'd be ready to move when the time was right. He had called in a favor and acquired a list of the songs being included on Cristoff's Greatest Hits project—a project he was surprised to discover was well on its way to being completed. Fortunately, only three of the songs were on their list, and they found it easy to replace them with other tunes. He was also co-ordinating advance publicity and, with the help of hired profes-sionals, was developing a promotional campaign for the project—a sensitive task due to the nature of the "mystery woman" aspect.

Although overwhelmed with things to coordinate, Arnie was exhilarated with this part of the project. The pairing of Nik and

Ursula's voices was truly magical. They harmonized with exquisite blend and perfect pitch, and the emotions their music elicited transported him to his days courting Raysha. *Nik has no idea how lucky he is to have found Ursula. Then again, maybe he does.*

By the time Wednesday rolled around, Arnie decided his inner voice could no longer be ignored—it was screaming at him. Something was definitely going on between Ursula and Nik, and it was time to get to the bottom of it. Any manager worth his salt could not let things get out of hand. He cornered Nik.

"What's going on with you two?" He stared Nik right in the eyes. "Tell me you didn't sleep with her. And don't give me that wide-eyed innocent look. I don't buy it for a second."

"Oh, ye of little faith." Nik smirked.

"This isn't a joke. Any idiot can tell something's different."

"We're just enjoying ourselves—getting into our stride. You've been telling us for weeks to lighten up and have fun. So what's the problem?"

"I'm serious, Nik—you'll screw up more than this project. She's a married woman."

"Stop being a Jewish mother. You worry too much."

"Nik, if you've crossed the line—"

"Hey, Alex," Nik shouted across the studio, "Arnie thinks we've crossed the line."

"Shut up, Nik!" Arnie pulled him aside and frowned.

"Crossed what line?" Ursula queried.

"You know . . ." Nik teased.

Awareness dawned on Ursula's face. "Arnie! You're kidding?" She stepped over to him in double time. "You're not serious, are you? Do you think we've . . . been . . . well . . . you know . . ."

"Then what? Look at you two. You're like cats locked in an aviary with a gazillion canaries."

"That's an original analogy," Ursula said sarcastically. "You are so wrong it isn't even funny. Did you really come out and ask him if we slept together? Arnie, I'm ashamed of you!"

Arnie crossed his arms and stood firm, looking back and forth into each of their faces. "Listen, you two. I'm not kidding. I know your personal lives aren't ethically any of my business; but give me a break, and don't treat me like a fool, okay? I'm on the frontlines of what's going to be a major media blitz once this hits, and I need to know the truth."

"My personal life is going to be blitzed?" Ursula frowned.

"Not your *real* life—the life we're manufacturing." Arnie tapped his toe.

"Hold on. You're not going to lie about me, about us, are you?" Ursula questioned.

"Not lie; we just aren't telling the entire truth. We talked about this already. You are a mystery woman. Period. Your name is Alexandra Arcano and you are an unknown singer. Period. But all the orchestrating of press releases, fielding phone calls, co-ordinating the actual recording session, releasing bits and pieces of information to build the buzz—it all requires a lot of focus, a lot of work. My job is not as easy as you may think. And I need to know if it's going to get harder because of a change in . . . a change in . . ."

"Relationship?" Ursula asked, beginning to lighten up and smile.

"Exactly. Has there been a change?" Arnie asked.

"I'd have to say, yes." Nik put his arm around Ursula's shoulders. "What do you say, Alex?"

"I'd have to agree, but keep your hands off, buster." She pulled away and playfully smacked him.

"Oh, great." Arnie began to pace, running his hand through his thinning hair. He tried to focus on how this would affect business, but his heart was reeling with the news. He had thought better of Ursula. "Okay," he murmured, "let me think about how to handle this."

"Arnie, there's nothing to handle. It's not what you think."

"What do I think?" Arnie asked.

"You think Nik and I have committed adultery."

"Ouch. You could have used a better word." Nik grimaced.

"Why? That's the correct word, isn't it?" Ursula raised her eyebrows.

Arnie threw up his hands in utter confusion. "So what are we talking about, then?"

"Should you tell him, or do I?" Nik smiled.

"Oh, by all means you tell him. I'd love to hear your explanation of the change in our relationship." Ursula sat down and put her feet up on the table while Nik cleared his throat as though preparing for a speech.

"Well, we've decided to . . . be . . . friends." He grinned broadly, crossed his arms, and stared at Arnie.

Arnie looked back and forth at them. What was Nik saying? "I thought you already were friends? What have you been all these weeks? Strangers?"

"I'm not sure what we were. I was too busy fantasizing about what I wanted us to be." Nik winked at Ursula.

"Ah ha! The truth comes out at last!" She threw a wadded-up tissue at him.

Arnie watched them banter like kids and didn't know what to believe.

"So really, that's it? You've decided to be friends? Do you know how to do that?" Arnie raised an eyebrow at Nik.

"He certainly does!" Ursula stood. "Although I'll admit it took a bit of work to convince him of that."

Arnie sat down and put his head in his hands as Ursula sat next to him at the table.

"Arnie, it's true. There's nothing going on between us. At least not what you were thinking. Really. Look at me. Would I lie to you?" She put her hand atop one of his. "Nik, tell him not to worry."

"Oh no. Don't have him tell me not to worry—any time he tells me not to worry is when I know I need to worry. I'd prefer to hear it from you."

With impeccable timing, Winston knocked at the door and announced lunch.

"Sounds great. Bring something in and we'll work around it. Thanks, Winston." Nik dismissed him and looked to Arnie. "You've been after me for years to grow up, and now that I'm trying, you're unhappy."

"I'm not unhappy, Nik. I just need to have a clear vision of who and what it is I'm working with."

"What you're working with"—Ursula put both hands on the table and leaned in—"is two talented and committed people who want to make the best record possible."

Arnie smiled wryly at the pair as an idea began to form in his mind.

31

"You know as well as I do we have more than enough time to get this project completed and released by October first. We could do two projects in the time she's insisted we take. So what do you say? I say we go for it."

The "it" Arnie wanted to go for was to get the project completed and released in time to be considered for a Grammy nomination.

"You're not serious," Nik said. *I gave up my chance for a Grammy to record this CD.*

"Of course I am. Why not? Nik, you two are fabulous together! The press corps is going to eat up this 'mystery woman' concept— believe me. What do we have to lose?"

"My head when the old man finds out."

"Yeah, well, let's cross that bridge when we get to it."

"Fine." Nik felt certain this was not going to be the type of music to earn him his Grammy, but he didn't have the heart to dissuade Arnie.

"No need to say anything to Ursula, okay? She'll only get more nervous," Nik said. Truth be told, he didn't want to get her hopes up after what she'd said about her longtime dream. He'd meant it when he told her that she had the talent to win a Grammy one day, but she'd have to pay her dues before that happened.

They decided to bring in the band right away to begin cutting tracks, telling Ursula it was an early start on the rehearsal stage.

Ursula called Pastor Doyle and told him everything about her little secret project. While he was more than willing to contact Nik—and assured her he would do so within the next few days— he was more concerned about her marriage and strongly advised her to tell Don right away. "There's nothing to be afraid of," he told her.

Am I afraid?

Before she could contact Don, Nik and Arnie told her they had called in the band ahead of schedule. More and more people were learning about the project—except her husband. *I must tell Don soon.*

The band members looked decidedly confused when at last they met the secret singer.

"This is Alexandra Arcano. She'll be recording with us." Nik went around the room and introduced her as she took each member by the hand and spoke directly with him. She asked each one a little about his life, instrument, and history with Nik. It was clear she was not at all what they had expected.

"She's as old as my mom," Pete, the drummer, whispered a bit too loudly.

She laughed. "And don't you forget it."

"Sorry, m-ma'am," he stammered.

"No need to apologize. I am probably old enough to be the mother of most of you. But you fellows are the pros, and don't think I don't know that. I respect what you do, and I'm grateful

Nik is giving me this opportunity to sing with him—and to work with you guys. I'm looking forward to having a great time."

Nik chimed in. "You guys know my dad's old theme song. Run it through in my key one time, and then we'll give it a go and you can hear for yourself—then tell me if the Nikster has lost his mind."

The band played "As Time Goes By" while Ursula listened. It wasn't quite what she'd heard in her head when envisioning the accompaniment for their record, but it was a good start.

"Now let's hear some vocals!" Arnie said from the microphone in the control room. "Show us what you've got."

She and Nik stepped up to the boom-stand microphones and began to sing.

———

No one knew Arnie was recording.

With every note, the expressions on the faces of the band grew more astonished. The silence was deafening at the end of the song before Jonathon, the keyboard player, stood up and began to clap. Max, the guitarist, joined in along with Keith, the trumpet player. Pete struck his drumsticks together and Arnie's applause was visible if not audible from the control room. Nik and Ursula jumped up and down in their excitement. Arnie even thought he saw Ursula wipe a tear from her eye.

"That was bliss, pure bliss," Ursula was saying when he came out of the control room. Arnie made note of her sentiment on a piece of scratch paper, liking the sound of it. *Pure Bliss*. He interrupted the excitement: "Listen up, gang. I'm going to play it back." The group looked surprised but eager to hear the recording. Arnie hit Play and made a mental note to hang on to the recording. *This is history in the making.*

Of course. Everything Nik Prevel touched turned to gold.

32

It was a crazy week, but Ursula was thrilled by the progress. They juggled between reviewing and choosing songs to making demo recordings of the tunes they liked. Winston kept them supplied with food and beverages. The days were long, so several of the band members had spent a few nights in Nik's guest quarters. Arnie managed to go home each night—and gave Ursula a ride to her car—although it technically qualified as early morning on some days.

Keeping her identity a secret was a tad more difficult than they had expected once the band came on board because they couldn't reveal where she lived or why she arrived some days via taxi and other days with Arnie. She occasionally used the excuse that her car was in the shop, but she hated lying and told Nik and Arnie they would have to come up with a better excuse. A few days later Arnie handed her a set of car keys to a brand-new Lincoln Zephyr registered in his name.

"From Nik. It's a loaner until the end of the project. It can be traced back to me, which is okay; just be careful not to let anyone see you transferring to or from your own vehicle—your license plate will lead them to your real name."

Getting from her car to the Lincoln without paparazzi or media attention was relatively easy for the time being—but Arnie frequently warned her that would not always be the case—especially as more and more people joined the project and word began to leak out about the pairing of Nik and Alex. "Who is Alexandra Arcano?" would become the million-dollar question.

"I'm banking on it," Arnie told her.

By the end of the month they had a stack of Ursula's review forms completed and hours of pre-production demo tapes. They decided to get started recording their favorite songs right away.

"I'm not sure which is my favorite, but I'm glad we're doing 'What Are You Doing the Rest of Your Life?' "

"Yeah, me too," Nik said. "I'm also glad we're doing 'The Way You Look Tonight' and 'I Only Have Eyes for You.' "

"Well, since everyone is naming favorites, I'm rather partial to 'Till There Was You,' " Arnie chimed in.

Before they knew it, everyone, including Winston, was shouting his favorite.

She was sorry, in a way, that they had dropped her all-time favorite, "La Vie en Rose," when they discovered a duet with Carlotta was being included on Cristoff's collection. Yet she knew it was most likely the one song in which her family would surely have recognized her voice. The other songs were going to be more difficult to discern.

Winston broke open a selection of champagne, beer, and soda, and the entire group toasted the next stage of the project. Contrary to what Ursula had once envisioned, the group did not party all night with drinks and drugs. This was a rather wholesome lot—a far cry from what the media portrayed as everyday life in Nik's world.

Ursula was beginning to understand the vast difference between fact and fiction and would be hard-pressed in the future to ever believe another entertainment magazine. Nik's life was nothing like she'd read about—at least not while he was working 24/7.

She still hadn't told Don about the project. Ursula had scarcely talked with her husband since the trial had started. They sent brief e-mails late at night, and she saw more of him on the television than she cared to see.

"The dame should fry." Max had declared one night as they flipped through channels, stopping on live coverage outside the New York courtroom of Judge Cromwell. No one but Nik and Arnie knew Ursula was the wife of the lead counsel on the case, and this gave her a unique, though at times uncomfortable, position.

"We don't know the facts of the case," she'd said. "How can you say that?"

"She's guilty and everyone knows it," Jonathon put in.

"Is that so?" she questioned. "Then why the trial? Why not just tar and feather her?"

The conversation had led to a heated discussion on due process and the death penalty, which led to the beginning of a rather profound discussion on faith.

"How is it you manage to maneuver virtually every conversation to the subject of faith?" Nik remarked one afternoon when he'd joined a discussion she was having with the band about the Old Testament.

"I don't!" she insisted. "It just seems to happen that way."

"Oh yeah? Well, what started this one?"

"We were talking about *The Da Vinci Code* and Pete asked my opinion, so I gave it."

"I'll bet you did." Nik laughed. "Now, let's get back to work. The guys want to try something new on 'My Heart Stood Still.' "

In spite of the excitement of the past week, in spite of the long days and the amazing progress they were making, Ursula was very concerned about one thing. One major thing. Okay, including the fact she had yet to tell Don about the project, she was concerned about two major things.

She hated the sound of the band.

Not their capabilities—they were all excellent musicians. But they were *rock* musicians—used to playing backup for a rock star. She feared no matter what new thing they tried, it would still sound the same.

"Arnie," she asked quietly one afternoon. "Do you really think the keyboard sounds like violins?"

The keyboard in question was an amazing instrument, she had to admit that. It was a fully programmable electric Steinway with more technological gadgets than she had ever seen in her life, and Jonathon could make it sound like virtually any instrument on the planet. But to her ears it still wasn't quite right.

"It sounds like violins to me. And they'll lay down more musical tracks when they overdub. It's called the sweetening stage. It won't sound anything like this. You'll think there was a full orchestra behind you," Arnie assured her. "Don't worry."

But Ursula was skeptical.

They'd recorded over a dozen songs the past week as they narrowed their final song selections. She listened closely to the playbacks and knew she wasn't singing at her best. Something wasn't right. She couldn't *feel* the romance—it was as simple and as complex as that. She couldn't *feel* it.

But how could she tell Nik? What if she was wrong? After all, she was the amateur. They had all of May to rehearse with the band before the actual recording. She would give it a go before saying anything.

Nik's intercom bell rang.

"There's my taxi," she yelled. "See you guys."

"See you on Monday." Both Arnie and Nik pecked her on the cheek in a way that had become natural. Friendly hello and good-bye hugs and kisses were a part of every day, and Ursula's short morning prayer had continued with no resistance from the band. She even brought the guys homemade cookies fresh from the oven some mornings. She mothered all of them, but it wouldn't have meant a thing if she couldn't sing. Ursula knew that and was glad she had diligently exercised her voice over the years.

Nik walked her out the door as the car pulled up the driveway.

"I don't think that's your taxi"—he grimaced—"unless Yellow Cab has switched to using Rolls Royce Phantoms?"

She joined him on the doorstep and watched the luxurious silver car pull up. A liveried driver got out and actually tipped his hat at Nik. "Good day, Master Nik."

"Hello, Boris," Nik said.

"Boris?" Ursula whispered, trying hard not to laugh. "Did he really just call you *Master*? Who's in the car?" She couldn't see through the heavily tinted glass.

"Oh, you'll recognize him." Nik frowned.

A distinguished, silver-haired gentleman got out of the backseat with the help of Boris, who lent his arm as a sort of crutch. Ursula caught her breath when a ten-million-watt smile beamed from a suntanned face as the gentleman proceeded up the steps.

"Alexandra Arcano," Nik said, "meet my father, Cristoff Prevelakis."

The Great Cristoff grabbed her hand and pulled her brusquely toward him, planting a big, wet kiss on her cheek, throwing her off-balance. She stumbled back into Nik, who caught her around the waist to keep her from falling.

"So this is what you've been keeping a secret from your old man!" Cristoff boomed, laughing heartily. "I should have figured as much!" He reached once again for Ursula, who was still in shock.

"It's about time he smartened up and got himself a gal with some meat on her bones and who's old enough to stay out after ten!"

That's just great, Ursula thought. *I meet the king of music and he thinks I'm old and fat.*

Just then her taxi showed up. "How good to meet you, sir," she said. "Have a wonderful evening."

"Hold on, young lady," Cristoff began. "You're not getting away that easily. I've heard from reliable sources that you've been spending quite a bit of time with the kid. I want to know exactly what your intentions are." He guffawed and puffed up like a peacock as though he'd said something totally original and witty. Ursula was speechless.

Reliable sources? Who is talking?

33

Cristoff Prevelakis clearly was not used to having women run away from him. *Like father, like son,* Ursula concluded as she closed the taxi door and waved to the still-protesting man. She would hear soon enough what went down when she left.

On Saturday she ran two miles on her treadmill while she washed clothes. Her scale indicated a six-pound drop from the last time she'd weighed herself—which she celebrated with half of a Krispy Kreme doughnut. She paid bills, went grocery shopping, got her nails done, and also managed to squeeze in a massage and facial. She fell into bed exhausted but happy.

After church on Sunday, Ursula sat down in her favorite easy chair with a hot cup of Good Earth tea and called Don. It was time to tell him about her little secret. She felt certain he would be happy for her—she just had to make him understand why she'd waited so long to tell him.

What would he say about the hundred-thousand-dollar cashier's check that still sat in her drawer? She'd thought long and hard about what this would mean for their family. Sure, Don made good money and provided well for the family. But things were expensive in L.A., and their finances were carefully allotted—it was how they were able to live as comfortably as they did. The two biggest issues that kept them financially vigilant were the education costs for their children and planning for Don's eventual retirement. The money from Ursula's little recording project would certainly help, and if the CD did well, she stood to make more money from profits.

She listened to the phone ring and said a silent prayer. She was surprised when a woman answered.

"Hello, please hold."

She heard laughter in the background and the sound of several voices talking at once. *Did I dial the wrong number?* She was about to hang up when her husband's lawyer voice boomed into her ear.

"This is Donald Rhoades."

"This is Mrs. Donald Rhoades. How's it going, big guy? Who was that—housekeeping?"

"Hello, Ursula!" Don's rather exuberant greeting made her smile. She was glad she had caught him in a good mood. He'd been awfully tense the past few weeks.

"Nice to hear you laughing." She grinned as she pictured his big smile.

She waited for more, but when only the growing background noise of what she assumed was a party of some sort greeted her ear, she swallowed hard and jumped right in. "Hi, sweetheart. Have I caught you at a good time? I really need to talk to you about something. It's rather good news and—"

"I have some good news myself! That's why we're celebrating."

"Hello, Ursula!" She heard Sam's distinctive voice shout in the background.

"Tell Sam hi," she said, trying to make out the voices, wondering if *that woman* was there. *Could it have been Celeste who answered Don's phone?*

"We've been going over discovery and depositions for weeks and one of the team just found a letter that had been buried in a file—overwhelmingly strong evidence that's going to help our client in a major way."

"That is good news," Ursula said. "May I share mine?"

She heard more laughter in the background and could make out Sam's back-slapping antics even long distance. No wonder Don was distracted.

"It's more than good news, Ursula. This is monumental!" Don yelled into the receiver.

She heard cheers and clapping and could almost picture her husband taking a bow. His boisterous proclamation had clearly been said for more than just her ears.

"Ursula? Is that you?" Sam had taken the phone from Don and was shouting. She had to hold the receiver away from her ear.

"Yes, Sam, it's me. Congratulations. I hear things are going well."

"You could say that," he bellowed. "Your husband—"

"And my team!" she heard Don shout.

"And his team . . . have done it again! You should be proud of him."

"I am. Does this mean you've won the case? Will it be over sooner than you thought?" Even though there was no party at her house, she found herself shouting too.

"She wants to know if we've won!" Sam shouted to the crowd. *How big is Don's hotel room, anyway?* More laughter ensued as Don returned to the phone.

"We've hardly won the case. There's still a long way to go—and I don't think we'll be back any sooner. But things have just taken a very good turn for us—and for Felicia Chesterfield."

"Things have taken a very good turn for me too. Can I tell you about it?"

"That's good, honey. Say, can I call you back later tonight? It's hard to hear you."

I'll bet it's hard to hear.

"So who else is at your little party?"

"Everyone! We're all here, but it's getting a bit crowded. What do you say we head down to Jean Georges and break open some more champagne?" Don yelled to the people in his room.

"Are you even listening to me, Don? I have something exciting to tell—"

"That's nice, honey. Let's talk about it later tonight. Love you, bye."

"Wait, Don, don't hang up—" But he already had.

By the time he got around to calling her seven hours later, she had reached the boiling point and decided she simply wasn't going to tell him at all. It was more than obvious he couldn't care less about what she was doing on the other side of the country while he traipsed around the Big Apple with Celeste the she-cat and his team of groupies. By the time he returned home she would be done with her part of the project, and when the album released—if it ever really did release—her real name would never be associated with it, anyway, so no one would ever need to know.

As for the hundred thousand dollars, she'd open a savings account and put it in the bank. When the time came that they needed it—if they ever needed it—she'd tell him then.

34

Ursula arrived early on Monday anticipating details about Cristoff's visit. She didn't want to think about her weekend conversation with Don—or about her decision not to tell him what she was up to.

"You should have heard him. He grilled me like a prosecuting attorney," Nik explained.

"Don't mention lawyers." She frowned.

Nik raised his eyebrows. "Trouble in paradise?"

Ursula ignored him. "So your father was curious?"

"Curious!" Arnie shouted. "He was relentless—wanted to know all about you."

"Especially after he heard you." Nik grinned at her.

Ursula gulped. "You played our demos?"

"Everything except "As Time Goes By." You blew him away." Arnie stood up and slapped her on the back like a good old boy. "We're home free! Cristoff is the best litmus test there is. He was clearly impressed."

Nik appeared happy but was unusually quiet the rest of the morning.

"What's the matter, Nik?" she asked when Arnie left the room to get coffee.

"It wasn't near as pretty a picture as Arnie painted. He flipped out."

"What do you mean?"

"He assumed we were recording a rock album."

"You mean you *let* him assume we were recording a rock album. You never *told* him? Oh, Nik—"

"Don't 'oh, Nik' me—like your husband has been *in the know*?"

Wait. She hadn't told Nik that Don didn't exactly know about the project. "How did you know that?"

"Give me some credit, okay? You really think I'm an idiot, don't you?"

"No, I don't think you're an—"

"You never talk about him, what he thinks about what we're doing or anything. It's kind of like he doesn't exist."

"That's not true. . . ."

"It is true." Nik stood up and began to pace. "But that's your business; you told me not to pry."

"Thank you," she whispered—not wanting to talk about it. Besides, Nik clearly had more to say about his father.

"As if he's the only one who can record love songs! Like he has the market cornered on the genre! That jerk! Who does he think he is?"

Ursula did her best to stay calm as Nik worked himself up into a lather about his father.

"I don't need his approval to record this album!"

"No, you don't, but his blessing would be nice, wouldn't it?"

Nik stared at her for a long moment. "Blessing? Yeah, right—like that would ever happen. He's never blessed a thing I've done."

"When our son was a little boy"—Ursula waved her hand for Nik to sit down next to her, which he reluctantly did as she continued—"he exhibited an uncanny musical ability. Of course I was thrilled, but Don had another vision for his future. I tried to allow Victor, and later on Valerie, the ability to become their own persons, to not be influenced by what I wanted them to be when they grew up."

"Lucky kids." Nik put his elbows on his knees and his head in his hands.

"Luck had nothing to do with it. It was prayer and God's grace. One of the most important things parents can do is to identify the natural gifts God has given their children and encourage those gifts—but at some point they have to let their children make their own choices. Val was a missionary doctor almost from birth—she was evangelizing and healing her Cabbage Patch dolls as soon as she could talk. For Victor it was music—he knew he wanted to learn it and to teach it. I was hoping he'd be another Andrea Bocelli."

"That's a switch."

"Yeah, it's funny, I know. And up until he left for Berkeley, Don was still bribing Victor, saying he'd send him to law school all expenses paid if he would change his mind. It's hard not to have an agenda as a parent."

Ursula put her left elbow on the table and rested her chin in her hand. "God has given my son an incredible voice, but he's also given him a heart to teach, in spite of my dreams for him, and in spite of the career Don would have liked him to pursue."

"But your dreams weren't wrong, Ursula. You're a singer. It's only natural you'd want him to be one too."

"And Don is a lawyer, so it's only natural for him to want his only son to follow in his footsteps. That's the point." She sighed and leaned back in her chair. "Victor had to be stronger than both of us; he had to follow his own heart."

"You didn't *have* to let him—you *chose* to let him. You could have chosen to make his life miserable."

"Has your father really made your life miserable, Nik? Don't you want to sing?"

His answer was very quiet. "That's all I've ever wanted to do."

"And you're doing it, aren't you?"

"Yeah . . ."

"But?"

"But it would be nice if he didn't always give me such a hard time about everything." Nik stood up and began to raise his voice. "I don't sing the right kind of music, my band isn't good enough, the photos on my CD covers are never shot correctly, my clothes don't look good, and even my house isn't right! I live in a multimillion-dollar house on the beach in Malibu and it's still not enough!"

"And this won't be enough either if we don't get to work," Arnie cut in as he walked through the door. "Turn that passion into music. Let's go."

"It's just not working, Arnie," she whispered. "And I know you know it. I can see it in your eyes."

It had been two weeks since Nik had allowed her to view, if only briefly, the pain he felt concerning his relationship with his father. Since then, he'd thrown himself into the music. They all had—working night and day to get it right.

The band had quickly learned the songs they'd selected, and Ursula and Nik had developed some uncommon stylizations around the classic standards—making the songs uniquely their own.

But it still didn't sound right.

"I'm afraid to say anything to him," she continued, nodding toward Nik. "You know as well as I do how sensitive to criticism his father has made him. I don't dare tell him something's off. What do you think? Honestly?"

Arnie looked puzzled but then shook his head. "I'm afraid you're right. But I can't put my finger on it."

"Is it me?" Ursula bit her lip, dreading his answer.

"I don't think it's either of you. Your vocals are off-the-chart fantastic. Let's give it a bit more time."

She thanked Arnie and immediately started to pray. She continued to pray in her quiet time at the start of every day. *Is this how you want me to use my talent, Lord? If so, lead us to discover what's wrong. Is it just my own insecurity?*

She also prayed for her friendships and volunteer commitments, which were beginning to suffer in the wake of her commitment to this project. She was feeling stressed as her friends began to press her about what she was doing—being secretive was not her style.

Rubbing at her too were the frequent negative references Nik made about his father. Did he really mean all the horrid things he said about Cristoff, or was it a smoke screen to mask the pain? She prayed for discernment to know how to respond the next time he disparaged his father. No revelations came to her until one day when everyone was talking about Cristoff's theme song and whether or not it was a wise decision to include it on the album.

"Why not ask him?" she piped in.

Everyone stared at her as if she were a unicorn at the Kentucky Derby.

"I'm serious. It's his song—"

"He doesn't own it!" Nik spat out.

"Not technically, but 'My Way' isn't Sinatra's song and 'New York, New York' isn't Liza Minnelli's personal property, and we can't hear those tunes without thinking of them, can we?"

"And your point is?"

"My point is that he is your father and 'As Time Goes By' is his theme song. I think it would be respectful and honoring to ask for his blessing to record it."

"Respectful? Oh, now that's rich," Nik sneered. "Arnie, she thinks we ought to ask for his blessing! What do you think about that?"

When Arnie didn't respond, Nik walked over to his desk and picked up his cell phone. "Tell you what, Alex, why don't you do that?"

"Do what?"

"Ask for his blessing." He pushed a speed-dial button on his phone and handed it to her.

"He won't answer, but feel free to leave a message. I'd love to see his face when he hears it."

Ursula found herself holding the phone, and before she could say a word, Cristoff's voice boomed in her ear. "What is it, Nikolai? Come to your senses about that ridiculous plan?"

Caller ID made it impossible anymore to simply hang up when a person changed her mind. Ursula said a quick prayer and began to speak.

Nik couldn't believe she had called his bluff. He wanted to rip the phone out of her hand, but instead he just leaned back against the wall and closed his eyes. *Please, don't make it worse.*

"Yes, Mr. Prevelakis, this is Alexandra Arcano, the old fat gal recording with Nik. . . . Um, I'm sorry to bother you, sir, but we're all sitting here at Nik's house, and we were wondering something. . . . Yes, I'm calling from his phone. That's why you thought I was him. . . . Mr. Prevelakis, I won't waste your time. May I cut right to the chase?" She continued without taking a breath. "We'd very much like to record 'As Time Goes By.' But we won't do it without your approval."

Feeling as if he had been drugged, Nik opened his eyes and tried to cut Ursula off, but no words came. Everyone in the room was staring at her—as a collective breath was held.

"Hello? Sir? Are you there? Oh, hello, Mrs. Prevelakis. My name is Alexandra Arcano. . . . Yes, I'm the one Nik told you about. . . . Thank you. . . . Yes. . . . I appreciate that. . . . Thank you."

Ursula turned away from the others and walked toward the sofa to sit down.

Finally able to move, Nik strode toward her as she began to chat with his mother as if they were old friends. "What are you doing?" he hissed.

"Talking to your mother," Ursula mouthed, smiling and nodding her head. "Yes, ma'am. We'd like to record your husband's theme song, as a kind of tribute to him, but we won't do it without his blessing."

"Tribute!" Nik screamed a whisper as Arnie held him back. "What the heck—"

"Shhh!" Ursula wagged her finger sternly at him. "Yes, Mrs. Prevelakis. . . . Okay, Isabella. Yes, Nik asked me to call. . . . He's standing right here. Would you like to talk with him?"

"No!" Nik ferociously shook his head.

"Okay. That sounds lovely. I'll look forward to meeting you too. . . . Thank you. Good-bye." She flipped the lid on the phone and tossed it to Nik. "Catch!"

Nik grabbed the phone and almost threw it back—at her head—as she calmly poured herself a glass of water while everyone stared, waiting to hear what only she had been privy to.

"They're on their way over—should be here in a few minutes." She took a swig of water.

"Oh my!" Arnie whistled.

"Tell me you're kidding." Nik grabbed her arm. "Tell me you're not serious."

"Well, I'm outta here," Pete said, putting down his drumsticks.

"I'm with you, bud," Max said as he removed his guitar strap from around his neck.

"No one is going anywhere," Arnie interrupted. "We have a full day of rehearsing ahead of us. Take a break and get yourself some lunch. Winston has a boatload of food set out in the kitchen."

The guys exited faster than frightened cheetahs, and Nik felt like doing the same, but he had to stay and fight.

"Do they know something I don't?" Ursula tipped her head innocently.

"Do you have any idea what you've done?"

"You're the one who gave me the phone. What did you want me to do?"

"Okay, Arnie, how do we handle this?" Nik ran his hand through his hair and began to pace.

"I think we have to see what happens. Did he sound mad?" Arnie asked Ursula.

"He didn't sound anything. Once I told him, he either handed the phone to Isabella or she took it from him. I'm not sure which."

"So he was silent?" Arnie furrowed his brows. "Doesn't sound at all like him."

"What the heck was the tribute garbage all about? I won't give that old man any kind of tribute!"

"That's enough, Nikolai Prevelakis!" Ursula snapped.

She stood almost nose to nose with Nik, her hands firmly on her hips. He wanted to give her what for, to throw her out of his house for speaking to him like that. *Doesn't she realize who I am?* But all he could do was stare at her, with his face burning, while she lectured him as if he were a little boy.

"I will not tolerate any more disrespect for your father! Do you hear me? If we sing your father's theme song, a tribute is exactly what it's going to be—that or a slap in the face. And you can count me out if the latter is your intention!"

Arnie joined in. "If we pretend it's a tribute, it might be a way to get him to agree—"

She turned to Arnie and continued her tirade. "Stop playing games! We're not pretending! A tribute is an honorable thing—not bait to use to get someone to do what you want them to do. Listen to yourselves. I may not know the Great Cristoff as well as you guys, but I know a little about human nature and about being a parent. . . ."

She swung her focus to Nik, but he was ready now. "Why can't you give him the benefit of the doubt and ask for his permission as a loving son would ask a loving father?"

"Because love doesn't enter the equation," Nik spat back.

Ursula looked him square in the eyes. "Well, don't you think it's time it did?"

———

The first few minutes were tense, but after awkward introductions and insignificant small talk, once they all sat down and began visiting, things seemed to lighten up. They talked about the weather, Arnie's wife, and Isabella and Cristoff's recent trip to Spain.

Even Nik appeared to be relaxed as everyone sat in his well-appointed dining room around the huge hand-painted volcanic-stone table. The guys in the band were still on break, most likely with their ears pressed to the kitchen door listening closely.

It was Isabella who approached the subject of the elephant in the room with diplomatic aplomb. "So, Nikky, please tell us some more about this tribute you wish to pay to your father." Isabella looked expectantly at her son while petting Milan, who had snuggled into her lap and promptly fallen asleep.

Everyone including Cristoff looked at Nik. Nik, in turn, looked at Ursula. She could see his Adam's apple bobbing up and down his long neck and prayed silently for him to swallow his pride and say the right thing.

"Well . . . we figured . . . we . . ."

"Cat got your tongue, Nik?" his father chided.

It hadn't taken long for Ursula to make the assessment that Cristoff enjoyed baiting his son. While she didn't understand the reasons behind the behavior, she felt certain it kept father and son distanced in an emotionally damaging way. Why had Isabella allowed this verbal intimidation to continue over so many years? Ursula could see the color rise up Nik's neck.

"Go ahead, Nik," she encouraged. "Tell your father what we were discussing in rehearsals this morning—when we got to his song."

"We figured we should add it to the collection," he said apprehensively.

"Is that so?" Cristoff said. "And why is that?"

"You're kidding, right?" Ursula laughed and stood up. "Look at the facts. We have two of the most powerful men in musical history"—she waved her hand at both men while walking toward Nik—"each with his own unique style and audience." She stood behind Nik and placed her hands on his shoulders. "After making his name in the world of rock and roll, the famous son decides to walk proudly in his famous father's footsteps and record an album of romantic love songs." She slowly circled the table and walked toward Cristoff.

"I know as well as everyone here that I'm just background music to the project. The real draw is the Prevelakis name and the multigenerational talents of two amazing singers." She stopped at Cristoff's side, placed her palm on the table, and leaned in to him. "Sure, we could record the album without 'As Time Goes By,' and it would probably still be well received. But I've seen both of you perform, and I know how much you love your audiences. Your son inherited your genes—your phenomenal talent. Don't you think the fans that both of you have made over the years deserve to hear Nik sing 'As Time Goes By'?" She walked to her chair and sat down. "As a fan myself, I would feel cheated if he didn't include your song. What do you think, Isabella?"

"I would feel cheated too." Isabella wiped her eyes. "Nikky, this is very special."

Cristoff had been looking intently at Ursula all the time she spoke—his eyes had followed her every movement.

"You are very good, my dear," he said, shaking his head. "Where did you find her again, kid?"

"You wouldn't believe it if I told you," Nik answered tentatively, obviously still aware of what was at stake.

"A wonderful speech, Alexandra; but is that really how it is, Nikolai?" Cristoff turned to Nik. "Do you really want to record my song? Or is it some promotional marketing idea?" He looked at Arnie.

"Hey, leave me out of this—it's not my idea. I know better." Arnie crossed his arms and shook his head.

"Yes, I'd like to record it," Nik said.

"And if I say no?" Cristoff challenged.

"Cristoff—" Isabella reached for his arm, but he put one finger to his lips to silence her as though she were a recalcitrant child.

Cristoff glared at his son. "If I say no . . . then what, boy?"

Dear God, please put the right words into his mouth, Ursula silently prayed.

"Then we won't do it," Nik responded quietly.

Thank you.

The two men looked at each other over the table.

"Well, then!" Cristoff shouted and stood up. "That's it, then."

What's it, then? Ursula was unable to read his face.

"You can have my song," he said simply, without emotion, as if it were not a big deal. "But I have one condition: I want to sit in on a rehearsal today—you are still working today, correct? I want to hear this little lady sing in person." He grabbed Ursula by the arm and pulled her up from the chair. "Let's go, boy," he said to Nik, who still looked stunned. "Time is money. You have a band waiting to rehearse, no?" Cristoff pulled Ursula out of the room and toward the studio as everyone else followed.

35

They had great fun that afternoon, going through their list of selected songs and listening to Cristoff tell stories about times past when he or someone he knew had recorded the same song. He appeared genuinely impressed at how they had used Ursula's rating forms to decide which songs to record, and both he and Nik had several conversations about the rationale behind the selection and/or deletion of a particular song.

Isabella appeared more than content to sit on a leather side chair with Milan in her lap and listen to her men behave like adults.

They played the demos and rehearsed live. Cristoff offered comments and advice about each song. The band members listened to all of the feedback with genuine interest. Nik appeared cool as a cucumber, but Ursula was a nervous wreck, especially when she saw Cristoff and Isabella put their heads together and whisper.

Nik never gave his father the opportunity to offer his critique of his theme song. They never sang "As Time Goes By." "We're not ready yet," Nik had stated firmly. And Cristoff didn't insist.

"I wish I had a video camera," Isabella whispered to Ursula late in the afternoon, as they watched the father and son banter playfully. "Thank you."

"For what?" Ursula raised her eyebrows.

"For making this possible." She pointed at her family. "It is no secret they have been traveling on rocky roads for far too many years."

"It must be difficult for you to have two strong men with equally strong opinions."

"That is a kind way to say they are both pigheaded and pompous."

"Oh no! I didn't mean that at all."

Isabella laughed. "Not to worry, dear. They *are* pigheaded and pompous, and not only do I know it, but they know it, as well. I have long prayed they would put aside their differences and become friends. Especially now that Cristoff is getting older—that we are all getting older."

I wonder if Isabella knows the vital part she could play in the reconciliation. "Isabella?" Ursula whispered.

"Yes?"

"I have something to ask, and I know we are basically strangers, but I'm having some trouble with something, and I'm wondering—"

"I make it a point never to get involved in my son's personal life; I am sorry. I cannot tell you anything other than if Nik has chosen you to be in his life, you must be a very special woman."

"I'm afraid you have the wrong idea. We aren't involved in that way."

Isabella raised her eyebrows and smiled.

"I'm serious. I'm old enough to be his mother."

"A good thing, I think. His previous . . . girlfriends . . . have been babies. You seem to be good for him."

"Isabella, believe me; I enjoy your son very much—getting to know him and working on this project with him—but there is nothing personal going on between us." She wanted to disclose more about her life. That she was a married woman, that her husband was being impossibly selfish, that this secret was killing her. But she knew that was impossible.

"I believe you," Isabella said, clearly not believing her.

"As you were listening to us sing, was there anything you felt was . . . off . . . not quite right? I mean, Nik would never ask his father—at least not right now—but I saw you two whispering. Is there something I could do differently?"

"It is still early in your cutting phase, is it not?"

"Yes. We've been working with the band only a short time. Arnie tells me that a lot will be done in the mixing stages after everything is finished."

"When do you plan to record?"

"In June."

"Oh my, that gives you a great deal of time. You have the entire month to lay down the vocals—you will do fine. Your voice is truly a treasure—one of the strongest mezzo-sopranos we have heard in many years. You have perfect pitch and a most impressive range."

Cristoff scared both of them when he came up and shouted "Boo!" like a fun-loving child.

"Is this girl talk?" He smiled. "Or can a dirty old man join the fun?"

They laughed and chatted, and it suddenly struck Ursula how amazing it was that she was actually going to record an album with one of the most well-known rock stars of the decade and that she was standing an arm's length away from the Great Cristoff. *If only Don could see me now!*

"You and Nik have great chemistry," Cristoff said when Isabella left to visit the powder room. "Your voices are perfect together. He has a good ear—and a good eye for selecting his women."

"I am his singing partner—that's all."

He smiled knowingly at her, and she kept her mouth shut. She had bigger concerns on her mind. They stood in silence a few minutes as they listened to Nik singing with the band.

"He's good, isn't he?" Ursula murmured.

"Yes." Cristoff crossed his arms and stood listening.

"Very good," she added.

"He is a Prevelakis. I wouldn't expect anything less."

"Am I good enough to sing with him?" There—she'd said it.

Cristoff looked at her. "Why is it that women need a man to tell them they are good? To tell them they are beautiful? To validate them?"

"With all due respect, sir, I am not looking for validation." She was thankful he couldn't have guessed that a pang of desire for her husband's approval shot through her gut. "I am looking for a true critique from a master of the trade."

"Ah. Well, if that is the case, let me tell you exactly what I think."

36

Several days later she still found it hard to concentrate. Her mind kept thinking back to all Cristoff had to say about her vocal styling, volume, range, and breath control. He'd spoken to her as if she were a beginner. She'd managed to contain her indignation; after all, she had asked his opinion and knew there were a few things she could work on that would make her voice better. The past few days she had been working on those things . . . but something was still not right.

"I'm telling you, Arnie. This just isn't working," Ursula whispered as they settled in to watch *American Idol* after a long day of practicing. "I sound awful."

"No, you don't. Believe me, I would fire you in a second if I didn't think you were good enough."

Ursula smiled grimly before continuing. "What is it, then?"

"I don't know. But let's talk about it later. The show's starting."

She managed to forget her troubles when her favorite *Idol* singer was voted off the show. In a strange way she could relate to her— you never knew when the bottom would fall out.

Cristoff showed up the next day, with some different sheet music to one of their songs he wanted to share.

"I don't know what's gotten into him," Nik whispered to her. "This is totally unlike him. What did you say to him, Alex?" His eyes didn't leave his father.

"I didn't say anything to him. What do you mean?"

Nik smiled. "He's almost human."

"He *is* human. You two just needed some lessons in common courtesy. Your mother should have smacked you both over the head years ago."

"I'll smack the two of you if you don't get singing," Arnie barked. He was acting irritable, and the tension increased as the day went on. They clearly had a lot of work to do.

After they'd spent an intense morning working on "I'll Be Seeing You," Cristoff simply turned and walked out. During another run-through, Ursula broke down. "I'm sorry, guys. This is terrible! I don't know what's the matter with me." She sat down and cried. The band members shuffled uncomfortably, looking to Nik for direction. Nik left the band and sat down beside her.

"If it's any consolation, I feel something's off too," he said dismally. "Just not sure what it is."

They spent a while talking about the music, trying to put their finger on what it could be. No one had an answer.

They welcomed the interruption when Winston entered the room and stood stoically by the door with a phone in his outstretched hand.

"Your father, sir," he said to Nik.

Winston had never sounded quite so formal in his delivery, and the announcement made Ursula laugh.

"Please tell him I'll have to call him back," Nik responded.

"I do believe you will want to take this call, sir."

Ursula prayed there wasn't a problem and was relieved to see Nik smiling as he listened to his father, unable to get a word in edgewise. He hung up, shaking his head.

"Well, since we're not getting anything accomplished here, we might as well take my parents up on their offer. They've invited us to lunch." He made a sweep of his arm, pointing to everyone. "All of us."

"Very good, sir," Winston responded. "Should I bring the car around?"

The intercom bell rang. "No, that's a van. My father sent Boris to pick us up."

Pete stood from his drums and tapped his sticks together. "Cool. Road trip."

They all piled into the van and rode up Malibu Canyon to Cross Creek Drive and the Prevelakis estate.

––––––––––––

"Welcome to our home," Cristoff said as everyone gathered in the foyer. Ursula wasn't paying much attention to what he was saying; his home screamed louder.

It was straight out of *Lifestyles of the Rich and Famous*, and she half expected Robin Leach to conduct a tour. The enormous crystal chandelier hanging above the multistory foyer was magnificent. But it paled in comparison to the room-sized fountain that took center stage, flanked by elegant double staircases that stretched upward.

"This is fabulous," Ursula whispered to Arnie, who had come alongside her.

"It's a scale model of the Trevi Fountain in Rome," Arnie whispered back.

"I knew I recognized it! The one from the movie *Three Coins in the Fountain*, right?"

"Bingo."

In all its Baroque splendor, complete with giant Corinthian pilasters framing Neptune in the central niche, the striking fountain included carved Tritons, seahorses, chariots, and a host of other figures and features. Clear water tumbled from numerous outlets, cascading over rocks and marble, convening in a blue-bottomed pool complete with a collection of coins, no doubt tossed in by visitors. Lights were strategically placed both in and out of the water, and Ursula imagined it looked breathtaking at night. It was resplendent artwork that left her speechless.

"I'm afraid we've misled you," Cristoff announced, taking hold of his wife's hand.

Ursula watched Nik clench his jaw and squint his eyes.

"Lunch will eventually be served in the dining room," Isabella said.

"However," Cristoff picked up, "we first have a surprise for you."

"A gift for you," Isabella added, "a gift given to you in love."

Cristoff and Isabella walked down the expansive staircase, leaving Nik, Arnie, and Ursula standing in the cavernous foyer. Ursula looked around and noticed that Winston, Pete, Max, Jonathon, and Keith had all disappeared.

"Come this way," Isabella said.

"We're going to his studio," Arnie whispered to Ursula.

They reached an alcove, and Cristoff threw open a set of ornately carved double doors. The most beautiful music Ursula had ever heard burst forth.

"Wow, and I thought Nik's sound system was good. . . ." she whispered to Arnie.

Arnie just smiled.

They entered a huge room, almost a hall. At the far end of the room, a full big-band orchestra played. There must have been forty-five musicians playing violins, cellos, woodwinds, percussion—and in front of it all stood Nik's four band members, instruments in hand, joining in on "If I Loved You" from the musical *Carousel*.

"I believe they are waiting for you to begin," Cristoff said to his son.

"And for you as well." Isabella motioned to Ursula, quietly clapping.

Nik and Ursula looked at each other and silently walked to the microphones positioned in front of the musicians. They began to sing, and instantly Ursula knew this was what had been missing. She felt the music. She physically felt it as the talents of the orchestra and their vocals came together as one organism. She felt the passion that Rodgers and Hammerstein must have felt as they wrote the song so many years ago.

With each note—each bar—the emotion grew. She swayed to the music, singing effortlessly, powerfully, as the music culminated in a crescendo of passion that was the essence of love—the essence this music was intended to portray.

When the song ended, the room was silent. Ursula felt certain the beat of her heart could be heard by all. Then the musicians began to applaud, and everyone hooted and hollered as though a World Series favorite had made the winning run.

Isabella cried, Cristoff looked proud as a peacock, Winston and Arnie nodded like bobbleheads, and Nik looked at Ursula and whispered, "Do you feel it now?"

37

"Nikky," Isabella pleaded after they'd sung a few more songs, "please do not be angry with your father—or with me. We just wanted you to hear the . . . difference."

"This is what you need," Cristoff said.

Nik stared at the orchestra, which included his four band members, who appeared to be enjoying themselves to no end, and listened as they launched into a dazzling rendition of "I've Got You Under My Skin." Ursula felt awkward. She was intruding on a family moment.

"I understand things are done differently now than when I was your age, and your boys are very good," Cristoff said. "But some things cannot be improved upon—and this is one of them."

"It's like magic," Ursula whispered to Nik.

Nik remained silent.

"That was phenomenal," Arnie said as he embraced first Nik and then Ursula, grinning from ear to ear. "I wish we could hear that again—now that would be a demo recording that wouldn't leave you wondering," he added.

"We can." Cristoff walked over to an intercom on the wall and pushed a button as he talked. "Larry, please play that back."

Ursula noticed for the first time a glass-enclosed control room in the far corner—a room filled with six people.

"Come, sit down," Isabella said, leading Nik and Ursula to a huge circular conference table. Winston excused himself as they sat down.

"Ladies and gentlemen," a voice boomed from hidden speakers, "your attention please . . ."

The opening to the Broadway song began. When the vocals started, Ursula's jaw dropped. "Oh my . . . is that . . . us?" she said.

"None other." Cristoff cocked his head and listened, sitting beside Nik at the table. "Did that last note sound a hair flat to you, Nikolai?"

Ursula didn't think so, but at the moment she wasn't sure she was the best judge.

"Good ear," Nik said.

They listened to all three songs they had sung. When she looked up, Ursula could see Isabella was as overwhelmed with emotion as she was.

"I couldn't put my finger on it," Ursula said, "all this time! But that's it . . . that's it. We needed an orchestra!"

She watched Nik closely, still not certain what was going on in his mind. Was he angry at his father for going behind his back to coordinate this elaborate surprise? Would they be able to record the album using this orchestra? Would they all fit in Nik's studio? A dozen questions ran through her mind as she noticed Isabella prompting her husband to speak.

"Hey, kid," Cristoff cleared his throat. "I want to say something. Your mother has told me I have been a . . . what did you call me, dear?"

"A jerk." She smiled sweetly.

"Ah yes. She has a way with words."

Nik smiled.

"That was not my intention," Cristoff said quietly.

Nik looked at his father but remained silent.

"I was angry, that is correct, when I heard you were recording my music. . . ."

Ursula could see Nik bristle at the reference to the music being Cristoff's alone. She knew how he felt about that topic, and in her mind's eye she could see Nik ranting and raving about his father.

"Isabella—and Alexandra—have helped me to see that I have been wrong to think of you as . . ." He seemed to search for the word.

"Competition," Isabella inserted quietly.

"Yes, as competition. Please understand—when I started, I had to claw my way up. Things were different then. I always had to fight against copycats . . . against people who wanted to be me."

"I've never tried to be you," Nik said.

"Oh, Nikky," his mother said as she grabbed his hand. "It is okay for a son to want to be like his father. That is natural— a good thing. What is wrong is for a father not to want his son to follow in his footsteps." She looked lovingly at her husband. "Your father has been wrong, and I was wrong to let it go on for so long. Will you forgive us?"

Ursula started to stand; they needed time alone, as a family, to begin the healing process that had been years in coming.

"Wait!" Cristoff bellowed as she tried to escape.

"Uh, I really think you folks should . . . be alone . . ." she stammered.

The moment was lost, but Ursula could see the look of relief in both Nik's and Cristoff's eyes, if not in Isabella's.

"We can talk about these things later, no?" Cristoff asked Nik.

"Sure, later." Nik nodded.

"Now a decision must be made. Nik?" Cristoff puffed up. "I would like to offer you and Alex my musicians, my studio, and my experience as you record your album."

Father and son once again locked eyes. Ursula prayed hard. *Please, God, guide Nik's answer.*

"I'll need to discuss it first with my partner," she heard Nik say.

Where is Arnie, anyway? She looked around and saw he was talking with the guys in the control booth. "He's up there." She pointed.

"I meant you," Nik said.

"Me? Uh . . ." She pulled him aside.

"Well?" Nik asked when they were alone. "Should we do it?"

"You heard how we sounded; it was amazing. Would it sound that way after musical tracks are laid down—if we go back to your studio and use just your band?"

"Probably not. Close, maybe."

Ursula looked at the orchestra and nodded.

"You've been telling me for weeks that something wasn't right; I should have listened to you. You sang like an angel, Ursula. But when we sang with the orchestra, something was different . . . better."

"I know! It was pretty fabulous, wasn't it? I mean, it's been fun with the guys; but this was so exciting, so professional. Victor would love this—he would be right in his element."

"You were right in your element. I think we need to do it."

"Me too."

"But my father . . . I'm not buying his good-guy routine—not by a long shot."

"You don't think he's sincere?"

"I don't trust him. I've seen him in action. He's not an easy man to work with. If we agree to do this, we'll need to have Arnie nail down the specifics about how much control he wants to have."

"Can't you ask him yourself? He's your father; do you need your manager to handle that?"

"My father comes from the old school. Trust me—he'll be much happier ironing out the details with Arnie. I just don't want to find ourselves suddenly with a new producer who has a new vision. He has an agenda; we just need to be one step ahead of him. We need the control."

"We?"

"Yes, we."

Then it dawned on her. Nik considered her an equal in regard to this project. She wished Don was around to experience this moment—and Victor too. And Valerie? She would be starry-eyed and mushy. Ursula wanted her as far from Nik Prevel as possible. It was a good thing she was on the other side of the world.

38

They worked night and day the rest of May. And every session raised a new set of issues. Often a difference of opinion about how a song should be sung or an instrument played sparked the conflict, and of course, it was usually the two male stars in the room that caused the ruckus. The more Cristoff boasted, the more Nik had to show him up. They were as bad as kids on a playground. References to past relationships that both men had experienced, as well as frequent discussions by band members regarding who was intimately involved with whom, became as normal as discussing the weather. One day Cristoff and Nik would act like long-lost friends reuniting after years away, the next they'd be at each other's throats about something. Ursula had expected as much. Father and son had been walking on thin ice for years, and only a fool would think the volatile duo could put away their differences so quickly.

Ursula felt certain it was daily prayer alone that kept things from escalating past the point of no return. When she'd asked Nik if she could continue to begin each session with a short prayer once they moved operations to Cristoff's studio, he had agreed. If any of the orchestra members or recording engineers were uncomfortable, they were informed they could step out of the room and rejoin them when the prayer was over. No one ever left the room—not even Cristoff, who would ceremoniously cross himself at the end of every prayer, loudly proclaiming, "Amen!"

What Ursula hadn't expected was the overt sexual tension that filled the air like acrid fumes from a refinery. Cristoff was totally oblivious to acceptable boundaries.

"I've about had it with him," she told Arnie. "I'm not sure I can hold my tongue much longer. Do you have any suggestions?"

"I'd say ignore him."

"Easy for you to say. He's not draping himself all over your body every chance he gets."

Arnie patted her shoulder. "Perhaps you just need to lighten up a bit and go with the flow—we're almost done."

"We're not almost done, and this is not about me lightening up! It's about Cristoff keeping his hands off me."

"He's not that bad, Ursula."

"Yes, he is. I don't know how Isabella can stand it."

"He's Greek." Arnie shrugged his shoulders. "They're a touchy breed."

"Maybe so, but I'm German and we're not." She looked down and rubbed her toe on an invisible spot on the ground. "It's not just the touching, Arnie," she whispered. "He says inappropriate things."

"Such as?"

"You were standing right there yesterday when he said Nik should go out and 'get horizontal' so he could be in better shape to sing today."

"He was kidding."

"He was not kidding. I can't stand it anymore."

"But, Ursula, it's Hollywood. That's the way men talk."

"That is not the way men talk, Arnie! I've been around men all my life. I raised one, remember? *You* don't talk that way. The flagrant references to casual sex are wrong—especially in mixed company. How is it you people think this lifestyle"—she waved her arm—"allows you to live by a different set of rules?"

"You sound like Raysha."

"Good, at least I sound like someone sane. I was beginning to think I was a lone wolf in a pack of rabid dogs."

"It's not that bad, Ursula."

Arnie had begun to shuffle through papers in his briefcase. She placed her hand on top of the papers and leaned in to him.

"Arnie, it is that bad. Cristoff and Nik talk about sex like a . . . like a good golf game! They compare experiences, discussing women as though they were property. Sure, some of it is bravado—I imagine a lot of it is bravado—but that doesn't mean it's right. I can handle myself, for now. But I want you to know what's going on. I'm getting tired of deflecting the bullets every time he's around. And he's been around a lot."

Arnie groaned as Ursula walked away. The issue would have been easier to ignore if he and Raysha had not argued about the same thing more than once. He was thankful Nik wasn't nearly as bad as his father. It was bad enough running media interference around Nik's revolving door of relationships. He couldn't imagine what it had been like for Cristoff's management team during his heyday.

Sure enough, when Arnie began to take notice of Cristoff's physical proximity to Ursula whenever they spoke, he had to admit if he were a woman with Ursula's ethics and integrity, he'd be uncomfortable too.

Toward the end of the session Isabella walked up to him as he was watching Cristoff and Ursula talking with one of the sound technicians. She stood holding Milan, gently scratching under the dog's chin. Ursula and Cristoff were performing a delicate dance as Cristoff would place his arm around her waist and she'd remove it, moving away. He'd manage to inch close once again and grab her hand as they talked—a hand she'd gently pull away. Arnie crossed his arms, wondering how to handle the situation before Ursula did something drastic.

"I'd bet a twenty that Alexandra is going to slap him across the face before the week is up," Isabella whispered in Arnie's ear. "What do you think?"

"I'd say before the day's up from the look on her face."

"Doesn't she know the more she pulls away from him, the more determined he becomes?"

"Doesn't it bother you, Izzy?"

"He's harmless these days."

These days. "Yeah, but still . . ."

"Oh, sweet man"—she patted his cheek—"if I let it bother me every time Cristoff touched someone, I'd never have a sane moment. I wouldn't worry about Alexandra—she can hold her own."

"She's reaching the end of her rope."

"Then she needs to let him know it."

"Oh, I'm sure she will." Arnie bit his lip.

"Don't worry about it, Arnie. Cristoff really is a different man these days—and I am a different woman." She put Milan down on the floor and watched her saunter off to her velvet bed in the corner of the studio. She looped her arm around Arnie's as he watched the activity going on around them. "It is good to see him working again—even if he's not singing."

The scuttlebutt in Arnie's circles was that Cristoff's voice was gone. Years of smoking Turkish cigars, drinking, and partying had taken their toll—so it was being said. Arnie would never directly ask Isabella, and Nik was sensitive to anything that concerned his father, so it was never brought up. He didn't know if the rumor was true—but it explained a lot if it was.

"It's good to see them together this way, is it not?" she asked. "It has been such a long time."

Arnie silently nodded his head. In all of his years with Nik, he had never seen father and son work together—a sad thing considering how successful they both were.

"She is very good for Nik," Isabella said. "Times are changing."

Arnie knew she was referring to Ursula's age. It was no secret that in Hollywood the table had shifted for older women pairing with younger men. Demi Moore had made it more than fashionable.

"I am afraid my son is hopelessly in love."

Arnie raised his eyebrows and looked immediately toward Nik.

He and Ursula were going through music onstage, working on a chorus that had been giving them a bit of trouble. Nik and Ursula were both laughing. Cristoff had moved to the control room.

"I don't see that; how do you see that?" Arnie quizzed.

"Oh, a mother knows these things. We see with the heart as well as with the eyes. Trust me."

Arnie hoped with every fiber of his being this wasn't true— but something deep in the pit of his stomach told him to be on hyperalert. He needed to give Nik something else to occupy his mind. Something new that would put Nik in the public eye . . .

He moved to the table and began to shuffle through papers again, looking for something.

"I'm off to get my nails done." Isabella kissed his cheek. "Don't worry so much, and tell me if I win the bet."

He waved good-bye and smiled when he put his hands on the e-mail he'd been looking for.

Earlier that week, Sara Larquette's manager had mentioned a possible event Nik and Sara could attend together. Sara's newest CD was moving up the charts. She was single and gorgeous, a perfect fit for Nik. The fact that Nik couldn't stand her was irrelevant—he'd do it for the press.

Ursula might not appreciate the lifestyle that people like Nik and Cristoff lived, but Arnie had been in the business long enough to know that sex sold—and it was Arnie's job to sell his client to the public. It might be a bitter pill for some folks to swallow, but that's how it was. Nik occasionally had real relationships with women, but many were arranged pairings, strictly for photo ops. Arnie didn't doubt Nik slept with many of them—no matter the origin of the connection. But that wasn't his concern. Keeping Nik popular was his concern.

Time to get out and play, Nik. Arnie picked up his cell phone and called Sara Larquette's manager.

39

Ursula paged through the latest copy of *Us* magazine as José trimmed her hair. She stopped abruptly at the photo of Nik and Sara Larquette. The caption read: *Hollywood Playboy Serious About Sara?*

"They make a striking couple," José said, looking over her shoulder. "The dress doesn't leave much to the imagination though, does it?"

The woman on Nik's arm was stunning. She wore a form-fitting Vera Wang dress with a plunging neckline that clung to her curves. Her Balenciaga Meteorite sandals looked perfect on her; not everyone could get away with wearing a heavy metal-heel platform. The multicolored stones on the shoes matched the fabric of the dress. The look was very chic—and very expensive.

Ursula had no idea who Sara Larquette was. *When did Nik find time to go out on a date?*

"Have you heard *Can't Stop Crying*?" José wagged his comb at her.

"No, what is it?"

"Sara's newest album."

"Is it any good? What kind of music does she sing?"

"It's great. She sings a blend of jazz, pop, and opera."

"Opera?"

"I think she studied at Juilliard. Kind of reminds me of a young Carly Simon, although I absolutely hate it that I can recall what a young Carly Simon sounded like."

"Haven't heard her."

"My dear, where have you been, on Mars? You can't turn on the radio without hearing her."

"Hmm, been busy, I guess."

"They say he's recording some top-secret project with her," José added.

Is that so? Ursula couldn't wait to tell Arnie the buzz was already beginning, and in her own hair salon no less.

She went from the salon to the grocery store, where she was speeding around the corner of the spice aisle headed for the dairy section when she literally ran into Julliette Pillsbury.

"I stopped by your place on Wednesday," Julliette said after apologies and greetings as they stood together in front of the dairy case deciding on coffee creamers.

Julliette never stopped by unannounced.

"I'm sorry I missed you." Ursula put a bottle of hazelnut creamer in her cart.

"I stopped by last Monday too." Julliette decided against the flavored creamers and selected a pint of half-and-half. "And a few other times when I was in the neighborhood."

"Is there something you need?" Ursula pushed her cart toward the pasta aisle as Julliette followed alongside.

"Did you hear that one of the associates discovered an important document that may change the outcome of the entire case?" She picked up a bag of angel-hair pasta.

How long had it been since her phone call to Don that interrupted the celebration of that discovery? Ursula searched for lasagna noodles. She was going to make the band her homemade lasagna.

Rehearsals were officially over and they were about to enter the full-blown recording stage.

"I did hear that. In fact, I spoke with Don and your husband on the phone when they were celebrating," Ursula said. *Was that almost a month ago?*

"I know. I was there."

"You were in New York last month? In Don's hotel room?" Ursula stopped pushing her cart.

"Along with a dozen others—it was a major thing."

"I didn't know you were there."

"I called to see if you wanted to fly up with me on a red-eye and surprise the guys; you never called me back."

"I'm sorry. I didn't get your call. I have a new phone and still can't figure the stupid thing out." She pushed her cart down a new aisle, and Julliette quickly followed.

"I couldn't have planned my surprise any better—I arrived shortly after the party started, just as you called Don," she coyly said.

So then why had she just asked if Ursula knew about the document? What game was she playing?

Ursula hadn't spoken much with Don since that conversation. They'd exchanged a few e-mails, but she was busy and he was busy and . . . well . . . there would be time when he came home and after she finished recording to talk. But still, he'd never mentioned that Julliette had been in town. What other secrets was he keeping from her?

"You do understand, Ursula," Julliette whispered as she abruptly stopped in front of the spices again, "what this case means for your husband, don't you?"

"Of course. I'm happy it's going so well."

"We're just concerned. . . ." Julliette tapped her nail on her front teeth as she perused the Asian spice section.

"Who's concerned? About what?" Ursula questioned.

"I told Sam I've been unable to reach you—that you've been extra busy since Don left—and he expressed concern about it. That's all."

That's all, my eye. Ursula knew better than to play Julliette's game. She would not take the bait.

"No need for concern; all is well." She began to push her cart down the aisle, but Julliette once again followed.

"I'm planning a Fourth of July dinner celebration for the firm," Julliette announced. "Can I count on your help?"

"Will they be back? Don thought it would be early August before things were tied up enough to come home."

"No, they won't be back. The event will be held in New York. We're flying out all of the spouses of the partners and having a party. Donald has loaned us one of his country properties for the July Fourth weekend."

She said "Donald" as though they were old friends, but Ursula knew full well that Julliette had never met Donald Trump. He was a business associate of Sam's.

"How nice of him." Ursula grinned. "So what do you need me to do?"

They talked briefly as they stood together in the checkout line. Julliette had clearly given this soirée a lot of thought. She was planning to schedule events for the partners and their wives—including golf, tennis, massages, buffet breakfasts, catered lunches, and at least one formal dinner. The outdoor picnic with live musical entertainment, followed by the local community fireworks display on the Fourth of July, sounded like fun.

"I think we'll need to make a quick visit to the estate in June to see the accommodations," Julliette said, "but I might be able to do that on my own—if you're too busy." She batted her eyelashes and checked the time on her Rolex.

Ursula would be knee-deep in recording the entire month of June. No way could she fly out to New York, even for a day or two.

Then again, Nik managed to get away with Sara, didn't he? If he could still have a life, why couldn't she?

"I'll help all I can, but can I get back to you about the location trip in June?"

"Certainly, but whatever could be taking up your time? With Don and your children being away and all, I figured you would have a great deal of time on your hands this summer."

Ursula wanted to reach into her cart, pull out the banana cream pie, and shove it smack dab into Julliette's reconstructed face. She thought briefly about confessing, letting her in on the secret—she would be green with envy—but that was out of the question. Julliette was about as discreet as Sara Larquette's dress had been.

I'll just let her wonder.

40

Blissful Love. That was what Nik and Alex's CD would be called. Arnie had presented the title to the group for consideration, and it had been a unanimous decision. "You gave me the idea," he'd whispered to Ursula later that day, handing her a piece of scratch paper with the words *pure bliss* scribbled in pencil. "Remember saying it?"

She did. She figured when it was all over she would remember just about everything from this magical time in her life—with the help of her prayer journal, which had detailed, albeit sporadic, entries.

The atmosphere of their sessions had changed since they began the recording stage. Isabella hired a caterer to supply food to the group, meaning Winston no longer popped in with snacks and Ursula no longer stayed up late baking for the band members. The guys in the band had added suit coats to their usual ensemble of jeans and T-shirts, and the members of the orchestra dressed comfortably in black and white, as though they were performing at the Met. Ursula worked harder on her makeup and hair, and dressed up a bit more than she had during the rehearsal phase. To show off her newly toned figure, she began to wear mostly classic tailored suits from Jones New York, Ann Taylor, and Yves Saint Laurent paired with fun blouses by Elie Tahari, Diane von Furstenberg, and Tracy Reese. Ursula's two-tone classic spectator shoes with stacked heels from Lanvin greatly impressed Kitty, Nik's personal stylist, who, at Arnie's request, had returned to work.

While never an obvious presence, Kitty acted kind of as a stage manager to make sure everything was perfect, and resumed her job of taking care of Nik. She quickly let Cristoff know that she was *not* taking care of him, and he steered clear of her. Mostly, she helped Arnie, who visibly relaxed when she returned. Kitty did not know Ursula's real identity.

It was amazing how well the secret was being kept. No one questioned anything about Alexandra Arcano.

Every day virtually flew by as they sang song after song, recording hours of arrangements using dozens of variations. There were times when tempers ran short and when technical glitches held them up or unforeseen issues arose, but to Ursula, it was like living a fantasy—a dream come true.

On her birthday, Don sent long-stemmed red roses to celebrate every year of her life. They talked briefly on the phone on his way to dinner at the famed Russian Samovar restaurant on West 52nd Street in the heart of the city, a cursory conversation where all the right words were said without the right emotion. She wondered if he noticed it. She didn't inquire who comprised "the team" accompanying him out to eat.

She hadn't told anyone at the studio that it was her birthday, and it would have gone unnoticed by Nik and the gang had it not been for the fact that Arnie came by her house to drop off some last-minute changes to the recording schedule and saw the card on the flowers.

"Why didn't you tell us it was your birthday?"

"It's no big deal—that's why." She paged through the sheets Arnie had given to her.

The next day they'd celebrated with a surprise party at lunch-time, complete with a cake, balloons, and presents.

Nik bought Ursula a lovely Marc Jacobs clutch in a creamy shade of peach studded with crystals. "I have the perfect dress for this. Thank you, Nik." She hugged him, quickly pulled away, and winked at Kitty, who she expected was really responsible for picking it out.

Arnie and Raysha had bought her a gift certificate for a weekend for two at the Mil Amo Spa in Sedona, Arizona. They knew she and Don often drove to Sedona for weekend getaways.

Cristoff and Isabella had just returned from London, where they had attended an auction at Christie's. Two hundred pieces of jewelry from the late Princess Margaret's private collection had gone on the auction block. They presented Ursula with a lovely 1920s Art Deco diamond-and-sapphire brooch. "Don't tell us you can't accept this," Isabella sternly scolded before she could get the words out of her mouth. "We have a dreadful amount of money and few people to spend it on—allow us this simple pleasure. Now look what my Cristoff bought for me." And she proceeded to share her jewels with Ursula as if they were schoolgirls sharing a secret.

But the best gift was completely unexpected and came toward the end of the month when recording was just about completed.

They'd long ago decided to record "As Time Goes By" last. The major reason for the scheduling calisthenics was because Cristoff would be out of town the last two weeks in June. Even though he had given the go-ahead to record this *tribute,* it was still an obviously touchy issue. Everyone knew that recording it while he was gone would be the easiest and least stressful thing to do.

After several rehearsals trying various arrangements, they had decided it was best to simply alternate verses and combine vocals on the chorus. For some reason, deciding which verses to alternate was becoming a monumental issue.

Ursula sighed. "I'm sorry, fellows, it just doesn't feel right."

"I have to agree." Nik ran his fingers through his hair.

"Sounded pretty good to me." Kitty dangled a Michael Kors open-toe sling-back pump with a dangerously skinny heel from her tiny foot.

"Tell you what," Arnie said over the talk-back from the control room. "Why don't you each do it a couple times solo and then a couple times together, and we'll figure out what to do in the mix? No sense spending all this time trying to figure out what sounds best. We can do that later."

"So it's true, then?" Ursula asked Nik as she put on ChapStick.

"What?"

"That the songs we listen to most likely aren't recorded in one sitting. I mean, the singers don't get it down all in one take like they show in the movies."

"Sometimes they do. Remember how great 'Time After Time' went? And how about 'What a Wonderful World'? I'd be surprised if we don't use those two as is—from start to finish."

Ursula had to agree, there had been days when the recording sessions went without a hitch.

Then there was today.

"Okay, let's give it a shot like Arnie suggests. I'll start." Nik moved his headphones up from around his neck to his ears and positioned himself in front of the microphone as Ursula took a seat at the table next to Kitty. At Arnie's cue the orchestra began and Nik launched into the song that had made his father famous.

"He sure is one heck of a cutie, isn't he?" Kitty leaned over and whispered to Ursula.

Ursula raised her eyebrows and whispered, not taking her eyes from Nik. "Yes, I suppose he is; are you interested?"

"Not on your life! He's way too high-maintenance for me. I prefer men who know how to get their hands dirty, if you know what I mean. But still, what a voice . . . listen to that."

Everyone was so immersed in listening to Nik sing "As Time Goes By," no one noticed when Cristoff entered the room until he applauded at the end of the song, startling the group. The silence was as thick as Tammy Faye's mascara as he walked from the back of the room.

"Thought you could pull one over on me, did you?" He crossed his arms and stood directly in front of his son.

"No one was trying to pull anything, Cristoff," Arnie's voice boomed over the talk-back, the sweat on his brow discernable even from outside the control room.

"I can handle this, Arnie." Nik moved his headphones to his neck. "When did you get back?"

"We just landed. You're using my studio, my favorite musicians, and my home. You didn't think it would be common courtesy to let me know when you planned to record my song?"

———————

Nik bristled under his father's tone, but he wasn't about to get into another fight with him. Not today. They were recording the last song, they were ahead of schedule, and he was feeling good about his project—no matter what his father thought.

"Cristoff, so glad you could join us," Ursula said, jumping up. "Wasn't that great? I've never heard Nik sound so good. What did you think?"

Will she never learn? There was no point asking his father's opinion. He never had a positive thing to say—hadn't in all the years Nik had known him.

"I thought it was going to be a duet," Cristoff said.

"It is," Nik replied, "we've just decided to record multiple tracks and edit the final cut in the mix."

"So you can't figure out what to do, in other words—is that right?" Cristoff smirked.

"Yes, Father. That's right. You're right, as usual. Are you happy? We can't quite decide how to make this work"—he waved the sheet music in front of his father's face—"but we will, and when we do, it will be the best rendition anyone has ever heard—mark my words."

Cristoff reached over and plucked the music from Nik's hand, quickly scanning the page. "So that means you don't want me to tell you what I think you should do?"

Nik was livid. He was sick of hearing what his father thought he should do—in virtually every area of his life. He was always quick to offer advice he seldom followed himself. Nik had held his tongue for weeks, mostly out of consideration for Ursula, but he'd had enough.

"No, I don't want to *hear* you tell me what you think I should do—why don't you *show* me for once? If you think you can do it better, why don't you come up here yourself?"

The minute he said it, Nik was sorry. No matter how mad his father made him, it wasn't right to humiliate him this way. He hadn't heard his father sing in years—not many people had—and he wasn't sure he still could.

"Forget I said that, okay? It's been a long day . . ." Nik took off his headphones and placed them on the music stand.

"Do you have a pen?" Cristoff said, laying the music down on the table. One of the musicians jumped up and handed him a pen from his music stand. With concise strokes, Cristoff made a series of checks, scribbles, and drew lines through sections of music as Nik leaned down to look over his shoulder.

"How will that sound?" Nik asked.

"Let's see." Cristoff took the headphones from the music stand and put them on, all the while giving instructions to the orchestra, which they hurriedly scribbled on their own music.

"Okay, let's go. Cue them, Arnie." Cristoff pointed.

It all happened so fast. Suddenly, the room was filled with the mellifluous voice of the elder Prevelakis as he took command of the song like a battlefield general. Nik listened with a critical ear, but, if anything, his father sounded better than he had remembered.

When the song ended, the room burst into applause as people jumped to their feet. The Great Cristoff took a deep and stately bow.

"Come here, kid, I want you to try this. Look here." Cristoff indicated with his pen a section on the music. "Take it from the second stanza," he instructed the orchestra, and they began to play. He motioned for Nik to sing.

"That's it," Cristoff said when Nik finished. "Now try this . . ." Soon both father and son were singing together, each intent on looking at the sheet music. Nik followed his father's lead at various places when he veered from the course dictated by the notes. Cristoff would sing a verse and Nik would follow, then they'd try it together another way. Nik thought they sounded better each time. By the time they sang the song together from start to finish, Nik felt confident that his father's changes would make their rendition of "As Time Goes By" timeless.

When Nik looked out at their small audience, he saw Ursula wiping tears from her eyes. She didn't seem to hear when his father called her name.

"Earth to Alexandra. Come here, please." Cristoff waved her over like an impatient teacher in study hall. "Do you think you can try this?"

"What?"

"What could we possibly be talking about, Nikolai?" Cristoff joked. "Have I been remiss to think she was bright and beautiful?"

"I think he wants you to sing, Alex." Nik smiled at her.

"Me?"

"Yes. You," said Cristoff.

"You'll be fine, Alex." Nik reached over and put his arm around her shoulder. "Just follow his lead and see what it sounds like. It's just a practice."

In no time a second engineer had outfitted all three of them with headphones, and a third microphone and stand appeared as if from outer space. The energy in the room was palpable. The orchestra held themselves more erect than usual, seeming to understand their significant part in the unique moment.

Nik noticed his mother slip into the room with Milan. She sat off by herself in a Chippendale wing-back chair, watching from afar and nodding as the trio sang. He was glad she too would be a part of this moment.

For the next hour, Nik, his father, and Alex sang more renditions of "As Time Goes By" than Nik would have believed possible. When Cristoff abruptly excused himself, feigning a prior engagement, it took Nik and Ursula only a few more takes before Arnie assured them they had what they needed.

"I can't think of a better way to end this experience." Ursula reached for a tissue. "Looks like my job here is done. . . . Time for you and the guys to do your magic."

Nik turned to Ursula, his heart filled with emotion. "That was a . . . surprise" was all he could think of to say.

Ursula nodded without speaking, while Arnie grinned like a Cheshire cat from the control room.

41

🔊 Ursula never flew to New York for the Fourth of July celebration. She got a call on her way to the airport from Don, informing her that the entire team had to remain in the city. Apparently, knowing the principal partners would be out of town, opposing counsel had pulled a fast one and tried to slip something by them. Time was running out for them to file a rebuttal or something like that. Ursula didn't pay much attention to the specifics, but was grateful he had been able to reach her before she got on the plane. Sam had extended invitations to all of the spouses to take advantage of the Trump estate, and Julliette and several of the other wives still planned to attend, but Ursula thought she would rather have a bikini wax than spend four days with Julliette.

Ursula had never felt so distanced from her husband, and although she understood he could not be faulted for this sudden change in plans, she had grown weary of the constant need to accommodate his schedule—with little regard for her own.

She thought briefly about going to Nik's, but considering her frame of mind, she felt perhaps that would not be wise. And so she spent the entire holiday weekend watching old movies on the

AMC channel. A couple days she never even got dressed—lounging the entire day in the ratty old pajamas she reserved for times like this. She didn't even attend opening day at the Festival of the Arts in Laguna Beach, a longtime family tradition.

She missed her husband, her children, her students, and her life. And God forgive her, she missed Nik and the life she had in the studio. The ache of resignation that her world would never again be the same overwhelmed her. *I want to tell Don. I want him to know what I've experienced. Why is it so hard, Lord?*

42

"We don't need her," Arnie insisted.

"We do. It's not quite right. We need to cut that last verse again." Nik reached for the phone, but Arnie grabbed his wrist.

"Nik. It's fine. You know it's fine. She has a life away from all of this. You have to let her go."

He didn't want to let her go. Nik missed everything about Ursula when she wasn't around. The album could have entered the final mixing stage a week ago, but he wasn't ready for it to end.

"It's done, Nik." Arnie patted his back. "It's going to be phenomenal. You should be proud."

"It's not done until I say it's done!" Nik stormed from the room, cell phone in hand.

———

Nik's call on Friday morning complicated a day Ursula didn't need to have complicated. Valerie had been home from Australia barely one week and had just left to spend the night with Tiffany. Ursula planned to clean house all day and run errands. She had a facial scheduled on Saturday, as well as a manicure, pedicure, and hair color touch-up. It was an important day. Felicia Chesterfield was a free woman; her husband had won his case.

Ursula had an elaborate romantic evening scheduled for Don's return, including a candlelight dinner and a professional massage by a massage therapist who made house calls. Don would be tired after the flight, and this would be a good way to get him to relax. It had been so long since they had been together, and she wanted everything to be perfect.

"I can't do it today, Nik. Don is coming home tomorrow night."

"Yeah, so what's that have to do with today? We need you. Just this one last time. We can't finish this tune without another take—we sang the wrong melody."

It was August, and her contractual requirements were "officially" over. She looked at her watch.

"Okay, but I can't stay long. I have a lot to do here. Which song is it?"

They talked a bit longer about the song in question, and she agreed to go by the studio later that afternoon.

———

"Okay, what do we need to do?" she inquired of Arnie when she arrived. "I'm sorry to sound abrupt, but tomorrow's an important day, and I'm afraid I'm a bit preoccupied. Besides, I'm ready for my life to return to normal."

"Is that really what you want?"

"Yes, Arnie, it's really what I want. I've had a chance to be home the past few weeks and it feels good. My daughter is back, and I'd almost forgotten how much I missed her. I love my home, and believe it or not, I love the peace and quiet of my life. I don't know how anyone sustains a lifestyle like this." She swept her hand through the air. "This is as far from normal as it gets."

"Doesn't all that quiet get lonely?"

"Arnie, you're a wise man. You should know a person can be lonely in a crowded room. Look at him."

They looked at Nik, who was hunched over the console wearing headphones. A heated discussion was going on with the remix engineer, and Nik kept running his hands through his thick, wavy hair.

"He's the loneliest man I've ever met, in spite of what the tabloids say. Is he sleeping at all? He looks like death warmed over." Ursula bit her bottom lip.

"He's okay; he thrives on this process," Arnie said without looking up.

"Arnie. Look at him. Stop being his manager and be his friend. Look at his face."

"Yeah? What's wrong with his face?" Arnie tilted his head while staring at Nik.

"He looks tired. He has dark circles under his eyes. Was he out last night?"

"What are you? His mother?" Arnie laughed as she stuck out her tongue.

"I'm his friend, and I care. And so do you, in spite of the act."

"Ursula, he's fine. Cristoff stopped in earlier—he helped mix 'What a Wonderful World.' "

"How'd it go?"

"Stupendous! I think it's one of the best tunes on the album."

"That's terrific! So have they sung together since our session? I still have dreams about it."

"A little, but nothing like that day. Wish we had that on film."

"I figured once the ice had been broken they would, you know . . ."

"What? Turn into the Von Trapp Family Singers?" Arnie joked.

"Well, maybe not that sweet, but is it too much to expect that father and son could sing together from time to time? It's not unusual, you know."

"You're an idealist, dear girl. Do you know that?"

"Yeah, maybe so. But is that so bad? Why do you think Cristoff sang for us that day?"

"I think he was trying to impress you, and maybe Nik. He just turned seventy years old. I'm sure he's questioning a lot about his life these days, wouldn't you think? It was a serendipitous moment. Glad I was there."

"I'd rather think it was a God-cidence, if you know what I mean." They both smiled at her common reference to those divine appointment coincidences that she felt were things God planned.

They both watched Nik in silence as he worked, savoring what they knew would be the last days of a memorable time in all of their lives.

"Don't tell Nik I said so"—Arnie leaned in—"but Cristoff's help on this project has been priceless."

Ursula was glad to hear that, hoping that in some way the chasm between the men had been narrowed.

Nik noticed her and waved for her to come to the control booth.

It was hardly "one take." Well after midnight Ursula threw her hands in the air. "That's it—I'm done. I've wasted the entire night, and I'm going home. My part in this project is over." She began to retrieve her belongings.

"We still have a lot of work to do," Nik said, his brows furrowed.

"No, we don't. We're going over and over things we've already completed. You know that. This is ridiculous, Nik!"

Arnie had gone home at ten, after Nik assured him they would only be a few more minutes. Now, two hours later, he was still finding things to do to keep her at the studio.

"Nik, I have to go. My husband is coming home tomorrow. You don't need me anymore. It's time to move on. Please."

Nik looked at her with resignation as he stood up from the console.

"I don't want this to end," he whispered.

"I know you don't, Nik." She sat next to him and placed her hand on his arm. "There's a part of me that wishes it didn't have to end. But you have a life, and I have a life, and they are two different lives. This has been one of the best experiences I have ever had—but it's time for me to go." She twirled her wedding ring.

"Back to playing Barbie and Ken?" He stood up quickly, knocking the chair out from under him.

Ursula had been around him long enough to understand his temper tantrums. "If that's what you want to call it, then yes. I'm going back to playing Barbie and Ken. And you know what, Nik?" She stood almost nose to nose with him. "I'm looking forward to it."

She was on her way out of the studio when Nik yelled.

"It was me. I'm the reason Philomena changed her mind about you."

Ursula turned around slowly. "What do you mean?"

"I called in a favor. I asked her to dump you. It was my fault."

Ursula put down her Coach hobo bag and walked back over to where Nik was standing, head bowed.

"I'm sorry." He looked into her eyes with fear in his. "It was before . . . before . . . I knew you. I didn't want you to find out before I could tell you, but I didn't know how to tell you. I know studying under Philly was important to you. Please forgive me." He sat back down, placed his elbows on the console, and put his head in his hands.

"Nik, I knew about that weeks ago. I overheard you talking to Arnie about it."

He snapped his head up and stared at her. "And you didn't say anything? You weren't ticked off?"

"Of course I was, at first. But you did me a favor. I will never forget this amazing experience. You helped me rekindle a dream, and it felt good. No, more than good—it felt fabulous! But now it's time for me to wake up from that dream and get back to real life. And I'm not sad—and neither should you be. I really love my life, and I think you're starting to love yours too."

He looked shocked, like he'd expected her to get mad and begin throwing things. Probably because he was used to hanging out with volatile young starlets.

"Good-bye, Nik." She bent down and kissed him lightly on the top of his head. "I forgive you. Now forgive yourself and live the life God has planned for you."

43

Don was home! He told Ursula he'd barely recognized her when she met him at the airport. While her new haircut and weight loss made her feel sexy and young—it appeared to have the opposite effect on her husband, at least at first.

"I'm just not used to seeing you like this . . ." he'd stammered. But once the shock wore off, he admitted that she looked like the bride he'd married years ago. In fact, they behaved like newlyweds the first week he was home. It was a good feeling; she'd forgotten that blush of new love and what it felt like.

The evenings began to cool off as August turned quietly into September. Don continued to work like a madman, but they had resumed their long-standing tradition of a Friday date night, and Ursula found herself looking forward to it like a little kid. Victor sent daily e-mails from Berkeley, causing Ursula to wonder how he found time to study. Valerie spent a lot of time at the house, still trying to decide what she wanted to do with her life.

"Mom!" Valerie hollered one afternoon, running into the kitchen from the garage. "Listen!" She tossed her purse on the floor and quickly turned on the Bose Wave radio that sat on the counter, moving the dial to the channel she wanted.

Ursula smiled as the highly produced strains of "What a Wonderful World" poured forth. *I am on the radio!*

"Isn't it McDreamy?" Valerie spun around the kitchen like a ballerina as Ursula sat on a stool and leaned her chin in her hand, listening closely.

"It's from Nik Prevel's new CD, the one he did with that mystery woman—who does she sound like to you? I'm pretty sure it's Celine Dion. It kind of sounds like her, don't you think?"

Celine Dion?

"And she sounds a little like you too, Mom."

"You think?"

"Kind of . . . but not quite. You know?"

"Hmmm."

"Victor sings that song, doesn't he?" Valerie reached for a banana from the fruit bowl on the counter and sat next to Ursula.

"Yes, he does. Do you like it?"

"Are you kidding? It's almost as delectable as the singer. I want to have his children!"

"Valerie!" *Delectable? Children?*

"Just kidding, Mom. He's a hunk, though—you've got to admit that."

"I suppose that's one description of Nik Prevel."

They sat listening to the ending of the song as Nik and Alexandra merged their voices together in a crescendo of emotion that almost made her cry as she remembered recording it. She had to admit, hearing it now, that even she had a hard time recognizing her own voice. She'd had no idea how much technology enhanced a natural voice.

"I bought the CD yesterday. It's great. Wanna hear it?" She reached into her purse and handed the CD to her mother.

And there it was. In her hands. Her CD. Nik's face was on the cover, with the shadow of a mystery woman in the background. She wanted to cry big happy tears. Forcing the emotion back, she asked her daughter, "What do you think of the title?"

"Are you kidding? I love it—*Blissful Love*. Yum."

Nothing had prepared Ursula for this moment—how it would feel. It was hard for her to be objective, but she thought it sounded pretty good. She wanted to jump up and down and share her secret with her daughter, but instead she put down the CD and grabbed her Paula Deen cookbook and began to flip through it, looking for a new recipe to try out that night. She found a recipe she liked, but she'd need to go to the grocery store for a few of the ingredients.

Since returning from New York last month, Don had taken on more and more responsibility in anticipation of what they felt certain would be an offer of full senior partnership before the end of the year. But he kept his word and was always home in time for dinner on Friday night. It was nice having him home—it was nice to be home. But there was still one huge thing between them. She still hadn't told him her secret. And she was starting to think it would be best not to. There was also the lingering question of the time he spent with Celeste the she-cat in New York. Perhaps they both had secrets best left alone.

When school had begun earlier that month, Ursula had taken on ten new voice and piano students, an unusually high number of students for her, but she wanted to be kept busy. Her friend Dee had managed to get her to agree to co-chair another of her fundraisers, and that was keeping her busy too.

She'd seen Arnie briefly when he had dropped by to update her on the status of the CD, but she had refused to take Nik's calls, thinking it better that way. She did send him a nice card congratulating him on the release. She had recently read in *Hello!* magazine that he was dating Margo Conroy from *CSI: Las Vegas*. Whether it was true or not was anyone's guess.

44

The day *Blissful Love* hit number one on the Billboard Two Hundred chart, Nik was sitting at the breakfast bar in his kitchen eating a bowl of Honey Bunches of Oats cereal and watching Rachael Ray travel across Italy on forty dollars a day. He could never figure out how she did it. He spent forty dollars on an appetizer at The Ivy.

Arnie rushed into the kitchen waving the oversized glossy newspaper like a fireman fanning a flame.

"It's number one! You're number one!" he shouted just as the phone rang.

"Nikky? Did you see *Billboard*?" his mother practically screamed as Cristoff grabbed the phone from her and yelled to his son.

"I told you! Didn't I tell you this album would be number one?"

Nik couldn't remember his father saying anything of the kind; in fact he thought he had said just the opposite. There was a time when Nik would have pointed that out, but not anymore. Ursula had helped him see that his prior responses to his father's comments served no purpose other than to alienate them further. She had taught him that he was a smarter man when he could rise above it.

The last time he'd visited, Pastor Doyle had even prayed about that very thing—that Nik would find wisdom to respond with words that would heal and not harm when it came to his father. His friendship with Harvey Doyle had come as a surprise—a pleasant surprise. At first, Nik was certain Pastor Doyle and Ursula must be in cahoots, so alike were their views and beliefs. Until he came to see that the underlying messages of love, forgiveness, grace, and optimism were pretty much what Christianity was all about.

And so when his father said something that angered him, he had promised Pastor Doyle and himself that he would count to three and say something positive—no matter how hard it might be.

One, two, three. "Sure, Pop. It's pretty cool, huh?" Nik responded to his father as he and Arnie danced around the kitchen. The album had been out less than a month, and at this rate they'd go Platinum in no time.

"What does Alexandra think?" His mother had apparently stolen the phone back from his father.

"I'll let you know as soon as I call her."

"You're going to call her?" Arnie quizzed as Nik hung up the phone.

"Should I?"

"Well, you know what she said . . ."

Only too well. Her good-bye in the studio was still fresh in his mind, though it had been weeks ago. He had called her a few times, but she never answered her phone.

"I think it's best that we say good-bye at this point, Nik. We worked with her on this, and now we're done. There was a contract. She wants to return to her normal life."

Nik wondered if her husband knew how lucky he was to have Ursula in his life.

"Well, shouldn't she at least know we're number one?"

"I'll call her," Arnie agreed and dialed the phone.

45

Arnie arrived at the Music Box Theatre a full hour before the Grammy nominees would be announced. He knew from past experience that many artists, musicians, and agents would be in attendance. He sat in an aisle seat at the back of the theatre and crossed his legs, relaxing with the *Wall Street Journal*.

Nik and Ursula were up against a lot of tough competition, but Arnie was grateful for one thing—even though it wouldn't have been nominated in the same categories, the nominations didn't include Cristoff's Greatest Hits CD. The project had been delayed due to some legal issues. Surprisingly, Cristoff didn't seem overly upset about it, and Arnie wondered if there was something more behind it all. Was it possible that Cristoff had sacrificed his own project to allow his son time alone in the limelight?

"Pretty smart move on your part, old man—the mystery woman thing," Clive Davis called as he passed Arnie on the way to his front-row seat. "Catchy name, Alexandra Arcano. I wish the kid well." He extended his hand in a hearty shake.

"Thank you." Arnie nodded his head.

Everyone was a kid to Clive, a man who had been around the music industry almost as many years as the Grammy itself. Arnie knew if anyone in the business could appreciate the value and excitement of discovering new talent, it was Clive Davis. He'd discovered Janis Joplin back in '67 when he was president of Columbia Records, and the nineteen-year-old Whitney Houston in the seventies when he founded Arista. Arnie and Raysha had attended the gala celebration when he was inducted into the Rock and Roll Hall of Fame back in 2000. He had produced the hugely successful *Great American Songbook* CD series that had catapulted Rod Stewart back into stardom.

If Clive Davis stopped to talk, there was cause to listen. A feeling Arnie had had since the CD's completion grew stronger. *This is gonna be Nik's year.*

In almost no time the annual Grammy nomination program began to the pomp and circumstance befitting virtually everything that was done in Hollywood.

He managed to find a quiet place in the theatre to make a phone call after the announcements were made.

"We did it, Nik! Two of the biggies: Best Pop Performance by a Duo for 'What a Wonderful World,' and . . ."

"And what? And what?!"

"And . . . Best Male Pop Vocal Performance!"

Arnie could almost hear Nik holding his breath, waiting to hear him say the name of the song, yet knowing beyond a shadow of a doubt which song it was. There was only one solo on the CD.

" 'As Time Goes By'! Congratulations, Nik! You did it!"

After listening to hours of recorded mixes with Nik and Alexandra alternating verses and changing keys, the engineers kept returning to the recording Nik had done solo—the day his father had been in the studio coaching him. When Arnie had approached Ursula with the dilemma they were having over selecting a mix to use, she assured him there was absolutely nothing to worry about.

He kept forgetting her unselfish nature, that she really did want what was best for others.

"It's perfect," she'd responded. Ursula seemed genuinely pleased when they included Nik's solo on *Blissful Love*. Arnie knew she would be ecstatic over his nomination.

After doing their best impressions of sixteen-year-old boys who just got the keys to a vintage Mustang convertible, they calmed down and talked about what this would mean for Ursula.

"Come over for lunch. I'll call Ursula to see if she'll join us," Nik said. "Unless you think it will be better if you call her?"

"No, you go ahead and call—she should hear it from you. I'm on my way . . . as soon as I give our statement to the press." Arnie grinned broadly as he made his way through the crowd of people to the pressroom.

Thankfully, she was alone in her car when Nik called and was able to safely pull over to the shoulder after he blurted out the news of their nominations as soon as she said hello, giving her no time to hang up. "Come over for lunch; Arnie's on his way. We have to celebrate!"

She could hardly breathe as she clutched the steering wheel, tears coursing down her cheeks. "You wouldn't kid me about this, would you? You're serious, Nik?" She gulped.

"As a heart attack. Now get over here. No excuses."

She immediately forgot she'd been on her way to the Peninsula Hotel Spa in Beverly Hills as she turned her car around and headed to Malibu.

Ursula was practically dancing around Nik's kitchen as Arnie peeled off the black foil from the top of a champagne bottle and Nik closed his new Giada DeLaurentis recipe book, too excited to follow written directions and deciding instead to prepare something original from the ingredients he'd assembled. Some folks ate when they got nervous—Nik cooked.

"I figured champagne was in order." Arnie poured the light golden liquid into three satiny Lalique Diamant champagne flutes Winston had set out in anticipation of their celebration.

"So what exactly are we drinking, trusted manager o' mine?" Nik inspected the liquid.

"Veuve Clicquot La Grande Dame 1996." Arnie read the bottle. "I've always wanted to taste this—heard a lot about it." He peered at the bubbles through the exquisite French crystal.

They looked at one another and laughed as they toasted their nominations, all talking at once, too excited to think straight.

"Okay, will you two please sit down." Nik waved a rather large butcher knife in mock threat. "You're making me crazy—I'm trying to create!"

Ursula and Arnie complied, perching themselves on barstools at the granite countertop.

"You two will have to make a decision about how you want to handle your performance at the Grammys. I have no doubt they'll want you to be a part of the show. The main question now is, do we reveal Alexandra's identity before or after?"

"Wait. What performance?" Ursula suddenly sounded scared.

"Ursula. This is a Grammy Award . . . your dream . . . remember?" Nik laughed. "Live performances in the duo category aren't typically included on the telecast—but I think Arnie might be right. Our record has done so well, I have a feeling the Academy is going to jump at the opportunity to feature your first public appearance."

"I can already see the pre-show commercials hyping the unveiling of the mystery woman on primetime TV," Arnie added. "Mark my words—we'll be hearing from them soon. So let's decide our preferred strategy."

"Whoa, guys, I haven't agreed to any coming-out party."

Arnie pulled out his BlackBerry to take notes. "Don't be silly; of course you'll agree to appear live on the show. You're the biggest draw of the night—the mystery woman revealed!"

———————————

Ursula was speechless. She hadn't told her husband, and they were talking about telling the world?

Arnie pulled out three different press-release drafts from a file in his briefcase, reading them aloud for their feedback. She made him agree that Ursula would remain Alexandra Arcano up until the award ceremony. In the event a clever reporter uncovered her identity before the ceremony, they would have the appropriate press release ready. But the goal was to milk the publicity for all it was worth—to make her first public appearance at the Grammys, singing "What a Wonderful World," at which time they would announce her real identity.

I'll have plenty of time between now and then to tell my family.

"Okay, then"—Arnie jotted notes—"we'll distribute this press release after you sing." He drew a checkmark on one of the drafts, folded the other two, and returned all three to his briefcase.

"Whether or not we win anything," Ursula said.

"Correct." Arnie nodded. "There's bound to be at least one person watching the telecast who will recognize you. Once you perform on live TV your identity will be front-page news, winner or not."

"I hardly think I'll be front-page news." Ursula laughed.

"I wouldn't bank on that—the press corps will eat you up once they discover you are just a housewife." Nik batted his eyelashes.

"Very funny." Ursula feigned anger, but the excitement—and fear—in the pit of her belly was almost more than she could contain.

Even if they didn't win a single award, singing onstage at the Grammys would be a dream come true. *How do I tell Don?*

"Okay, I need to go," Arnie said. "Leave it to me to handle the media blitz until the award ceremony in February, but this means we have to be even more careful about protecting your identity. The hawks will be circling the ranch big time." He pointed at Ursula.

"I understand," she said, but she wasn't sure she did. *How bad is this going to get?*

After Arnie left, there was a brief moment of uncomfortable silence, but then Ursula hugged Nik and they began jumping, twirling, and chirping like magpies.

"I can't believe it! Two nominations! Can you believe it?" Ursula couldn't sit still, so she began cleaning the kitchen. She looked at Nik, but he wasn't smiling anymore.

"Ursula, your husband doesn't know yet, does he?"

Uh-oh. "Um, no. I haven't told him yet. I was waiting for the right time."

"The right time." He shook his head.

"I thought maybe I would never tell him." Her voice sounded small.

Nik shook his head again.

"I never thought we'd get nominated for a Grammy. I figured the album would eventually be forgotten and I could chalk it up as a pretty incredible experience, you know? The entire situation is such a mess." She slumped down next to him.

"Ursula, what's really stopping you?"

"I don't know."

"Pastor Doyle says every time I say, 'I don't know,' I'm really saying, 'I'm afraid to say it out loud.' "

"You're quoting Pastor Doyle to me?"

"We're talking about you."

She walked to the wall of glass and peered out at the ocean. Nik came up behind her and touched her shoulder, but she crossed to the other side of the room. "How can I choose, Nik?" Tears spilled from her eyes. "How can I choose between singing professionally and being—"

"Just a housewife?" Nik asked.

"I'm not just a housewife! I'm a valuable part of a partnership that has enabled Don to reach a level of success we've both dreamed of. I mean that, Nik. This has been a shared dream. I never minded the sacrifice—not really. I loved being home with the kids; I loved entertaining Don's business associates and clients; I loved making our home a safe haven for my husband after hours in the trenches. Don is at a place we've prayed for years to reach—this has been our life. I don't know how to do it all. What will happen now?"

"I don't know, Ursula! What will happen?" Nik yelled angrily. "Will the sky fall in? Will his precious career tank? Will you pass Go without collecting two hundred dollars, or are you going straight to jail?"

"You're talking crazy!"

"I'm talking crazy? Can you even hear what you sound like? I'm sick and tired of hearing you whine and cry about this! What is the big deal? You haven't committed a felony, Ursula! It's not like you've killed someone or committed some unpardonable sin!"

"But I have! Don't you see? I have committed a sin: I've lied to my husband and to my family for months. I've killed the trust we once shared! I should have told him months ago. I've dug a hole so deep I don't know how I'll ever get out."

"So let me get this straight: the forgiveness lessons you've been giving me for months don't apply to you and your family?" Nik stood in front of her and shouted into her face.

Ursula stared at him a long time before falling back into a chair with a sigh. "You're right. I just don't know where to start."

A phone call interrupted them—the first in a long line of congratulations. Word was spreading. They turned the conversation to lighter issues as Nik fielded phone calls and Winston accepted floral deliveries. One by one, the band members began to arrive—carrying champagne, flowers, and balloons.

By late afternoon a small crowd had amassed, including Isabella and Cristoff, who, by his slightly slurred speech and unsteady walk, appeared to be already well on his way into celebrating—or feeling sorry for himself. Ursula couldn't decipher which.

46

After being called Alex for several hours, Ursula acutely felt the pangs of dishonesty. Except for Arnie and Nik, the inner circle still had no idea her real name wasn't Alexandra Arcano—that she was really Ursula Rhoades, a housewife who lived in Bel-Air. There were so many levels of deception even she was getting confused.

Then there was the issue of Don.

Ursula went outside to sit on a chaise lounge on Nik's balcony. She was staring at the ocean when Kitty joined her.

"Wow, now, those are really something," Ursula said of Kitty's footwear.

"They are, aren't they?" She sat down and crossed her slender legs to better show off the signature scarlet sole of her spectacular new Christian Louboutin crepe de chine and leather pumps with criss-crossing gold straps on a black platform with spike heels that were at least four inches long. Ursula always marveled at how Kitty could stand in heels that high, let alone walk as gracefully as she did.

"I just saw those in *W.* How'd you get your hands on them so fast?"

"I've got a connection at *Vogue*, but keep that a secret." She smiled.

After Kitty extended her congratulations, they didn't say much, looking instead through the expansive glass wall into the living room, where the party continued.

"He's a different guy since you've been around, Alex. You know that, don't you?" Kitty said as they watched Nik banter with Cristoff. "You have no idea how the energy used to be when they were in the same room. It's like they're different guys—it's like magic."

"It's not magic, Kitty. It's God. He has a plan for that family."

"Does that plan include you? I think he wants it to, you know." She nodded toward Nik.

"Kitty, there is nothing between us. Not like that, anyway."

"It doesn't matter to me if there is, Alex," Kitty said with a coy smile.

"The truth is . . . I'm married." There. She waved her ring finger that sported her diamonds.

"Oh. That does complicate things."

"Kitty, I'm going to share something with you, and I need to trust that what I'm about to say will stay here—just between us, okay?"

Kitty promised.

"My name isn't Alexandra Arcano. It's Ursula Rhoades." She proceeded to spill out her secret. It felt good to say it out loud. By the time she finished, Ursula knew one thing: it was time to come totally clean—with her family and then with the public. She couldn't continue the charade until awards night. They would simply have to change their strategy.

She stood up and brushed imaginary debris from her Capris. "I need to leave now. I have to figure out how to tell my husband."

"Wait!" Kitty jumped up. "Can I help? I mean, is there anything I can do? This is a total trip! Not at all what I expected. I mean, we all figured you had some sort of checkered past; you wouldn't believe the scenarios some of the guys have dreamt up. But seriously, we figured the mystery-woman thing was a clever promotional ploy for the public. No wonder Arnie has been like a cat with a canary—this is so up his alley."

Tonight was the big night—when she planned to tell Don. Cooking was her way to relax and prepare herself for the confession.

The phone rang. It was Don, calling to say that he would be "just a little late." "Honey, I'm sorry. I know you have dinner planned, and I'll be there as soon as I can. I expect I'll only be a half hour or so late. Can I get anything on my way?"

"No, that's okay. I've got it handled." She wanted to be angry, but part of her felt some relief at being able to postpone her confession.

"I can smell it from here," he said with a laugh.

"We're in trouble if that's the case."

"Ursula?"

"Yes?"

"Sam wants to have dinner with us next month. He asked if you'd be open to hosting the partners and their wives at our place. What should I tell him?" She could almost hear his smile.

"Tell him it's about time! Do you think this is it, honey?"

"I certainly hope so."

Ursula knew the firm was finally getting back to normal after the Chesterfield case. As a result of the Chesterfield case, they had acquired several new high-profile clients and the business had expanded considerably. In fact, the senior partners were looking at moving their offices to a much larger facility. The timing couldn't be better to bring on a new senior partner.

"Baby, I hope this is it!"

"I know—me too. Sam's new secretary will be calling to schedule the date—I think her name is Linda. Okay, I must run. I'll see you soon. Is Valerie home?"

"No, dear, she isn't. She won't be home tonight, remember? We're all alone. I want to talk to you about something."

"Okay. See you soon, then. Bye, hon."

She tossed a few more herbs into the mushrooms, checked on the roast in the oven, and went upstairs to get ready.

———————

Four hours later, as Ursula began to put away the food that had now grown cold, things were far from okay.

"I'm sorry, honey. I have to get these papers filed tomorrow, and if I don't stay and write, it'll never get done. You understand, right?"

She understood. She always understood—that was the problem. For years she had been the understanding housewife, always amenable to missed dinners, changed plans, and waiting. She never made waves—it wasn't her nature. It had really seldom bothered her because she had grown accustomed to this way of life, and she'd always had the children needing her attention. But that wasn't the case anymore.

Don was a good man, a good father, and a good provider. But something had changed. This news she had to share with him had changed her life—it would change *their* life—and he wasn't the least concerned that perhaps she had something important to talk about.

Something she had been trying to tell him for months.

47

The entire Rhoades family spent New Year's Eve at their church. Victor played keyboard and sang on the worship team, Valerie performed in a skit with her youth group, and Ursula and Don sat holding hands—enjoying the night as though they hadn't a care in the world.

Their church put on this gala event every year, and they'd attended as a family for the past decade. With a buffet dinner, music, games for the younger kids in the youth room, and music for the adults and teens, it was a great alternative to New Year's Eve parties where alcohol would be served. The only proof around here was the proof that God was in control.

"Thank you." Don leaned in to kiss her cheek.

"For what?"

"For being the best wife a man could have, for being the best mother. If I make senior partner, it's because of you. You've always been here for me—for us."

He reached into his pocket and pulled out a small turquoise box.

"Tiffany's?" She smiled as he placed the box in her hand. "What's this for? We just had Christmas, Don, and you spent way too much money on me then."

"This is a special New Year's gift. I wanted you to have it. This is the year that will change our lives. The senior partnership means more money, a lot more money. I think we should begin to think about a bigger house, maybe, and trading in the cars, and—"

"Whoa! Isn't that a bit premature, hon? I mean, you haven't been offered the job yet. . . ."

"*We* haven't been offered the job yet, but we will. Just think about it, okay?"

"We really don't need a bigger house, do we? The kids will be gone; they're hardly ever around as it is."

"Ah yes, but now we'll be entertaining even more—and that's what this is for." He pointed to the gift. "Open it."

"Now?"

"Of course!" He grinned from ear to ear.

Don loved buying her presents; he was always very generous that way. Yet she wished there was some way she could make him understand that he didn't need to spend more money on her, that what she really wanted from him was time . . . and for him to listen to her. She'd begun to feel that he never really listened to her and felt partly to blame for that. She never spoke up, not really.

But she forgot all that when she saw the gift. The earrings were in the shape of stars, each about the size of a quarter. Brilliant blue stones set in what appeared to be platinum.

"Oh, Don, they're lovely, absolutely lovely."

"That's because you are my star!"

She jumped at hearing him call her a star. *Does he know?* Was this his subtle way of exposing her? She looked into his eyes but could see only love.

"They're sapphires," he whispered. "What do you think?"

"I don't know what to say." Her eyes filled with tears.

"They'll look great with that Ballentiny dress you have—the one we got in Paris."

"Balenciaga, and yes, they will go perfectly with that dress. Thank you, sweetheart. Thank you." She hugged him close, smelling his aftershave and feeling the pangs of guilt gnaw at her heart.

She straightened and wiped her eyes. "Don, could I tell you something?"

"Honey, look! It's the Nelsons. Sally! Mark! Over here." He stood and waved them over.

The remainder of the night was spent visiting with friends and enjoying the fellowship of their church family. Ursula couldn't help but think perhaps this was God's gentle way of telling her to just let it be. Perhaps she simply needed to forget about it once and for all.

Clearly God did not intend for her to tell Don the news; otherwise, why was it always an impossible task?

She could donate the money to charity, put the entire episode behind her as though it never happened, and pray no one ever found out. Arnie and Nik would be disappointed, but they'd have no choice but to understand. Nik could still win his Grammy—they might even win for best duet—but she had no intention of ever going public with who she was.

It took her a week to find the nerve to call.

"You can't be serious!" Nik shouted over the phone.

"I am serious. I need you to understand, Nik." She thought she heard a car pull into the driveway. "I might have to hang up; I think someone's home."

"Don't you dare hang up on me!"

"Stop yelling at me."

"I'm not yelling."

"You are, and I want you to stop it."

"I'm coming over there."

"No! Nik, you can't. Please . . . don't come over . . . please," she begged.

"You are a crazy woman! You're about to throw away the single most important thing in the world!" he hissed.

"In *your* world, Nik—the single most important thing in *your* world, but not in mine. The most important thing in my world is my faith, my marriage, and my family."

"You're nuts. You don't have a marriage."

"What's that supposed to mean?"

"You have a prison. No marriage worth its salt would take sacrifice to that extreme."

"And you would know about that, how?" she snapped.

"Hasn't this meant anything to you? Hasn't what we've accomplished together meant anything?" She could almost picture Nik pacing around his kitchen.

"Of course it has—you know that."

"Then why are you making this experience miserable for everyone?"

"I'm sorry I've made things *miserable* for you. That wasn't my intention. But I've finally realized that God has been sending me signs all along—I just wasn't paying attention! Every time I try to tell Don, it has been as if some supernatural force intervened. New Year's Eve was my final wake-up call."

"Oh yeah? Well, here's another wake-up call. You have a selfish, self-centered husband who doesn't give a rip about his wife!"

"That's not true! Don is a good man. Please try to understand. I had a wonderful time, but it's over. I have to go back to my own world—to the real world. I can't live in your world anymore; I just can't."

She looked up to see Valerie standing in the doorway with her arms crossed, staring at her, fighting back tears.

"I have to go now. I'll talk to you later." She hung up the phone and walked toward her daughter. "It's not what you think, honey—"

"Oh, it's exactly what I think. I heard you, Mother! With my own ears!"

"Trust me, it's not—"

"Trust you? Do you think we're all blind? I've been watching you since I came home—we all have. You're different! Look at you!" She pointed toward Ursula's new hairstyle and ran her eyes down her toned frame, clearly referring to her weight loss and new look.

"Because I change my hair and start taking better care of my body does not mean I am seeing someone. Is that what you think you heard?"

"So tell me, then, who was on the phone?"

Ursula sat on a stool. "It's a long story, Valerie—"

"I've got time."

"I can't tell you, honey. I have to tell your father first."

"No! Don't tell him! It will kill him. I won't say anything to him—I promise. You can't tell him, Mom—you can't." Her confrontational stance had transformed into a look of sheer terror, and it broke Ursula's heart. "Don't tell him, please." Tears spilled from her eyes.

"Oh, honey, I am so sorry." Ursula pulled her daughter to her chest and hugged her, aching to share the whole story. With great resolve, she pulled apart and looked directly in Valerie's face. "Listen to me, Valerie, and listen closely. I am not having an affair. I never have and I never will. You're right that something big is going on, but it's not that. I need you to trust me—to believe me. Have I ever lied to you?"

"Uh, no," Valerie whispered and sniffed as her mother handed her a packet of tissues from her pocket.

"I've been keeping a little secret from you kids and from your father, but it's not what you think—it's really a very good thing. I just need to tell your father first."

"When are you gonna tell him? Whatever it is." She was still crying.

"I wasn't going to, but now I see that was wrong. Soon, I promise." Ursula looked at her daughter and grinned. "Actually, when the truth comes out, you are going to freak out, but in an entirely different way."

48

🔊 "We have to contain this situation." Nik paced around Arnie's living room while Kitty sat nearby on a barstool, twisting her hair. "She can't refuse to perform at the Grammys. That would be career suicide for her and a nightmare for us. It can't happen. Period."

"I agree. But something's got her really upset," Arnie replied. "She said something about Valerie thinking she was having an affair and it had to stop. I could barely understand her."

"She's like Sybil! She's psychotic!" Nik ranted. "She changes her mind like she changes her shoes. One day she's telling him, the next day she's not. This has been going on since we started . . . back and forth and back and forth. Now she's dropping out of the event altogether? She needs someone to tell her what to do. I don't think she knows how to make her own decisions. She won't listen to me, but maybe she'll listen to all of us." Nik threw his hands in the air.

"Yeah, well, she's not expecting *all of us*. Maybe you two should go in the other room until I tell her you're here." Arnie pointed them vehemently toward the kitchen and turned to answer the door.

"Thanks for seeing me on such short notice, Arnie." Ursula kissed him on the cheek as he ushered her into the house.

"Not a problem, kid. Nik called too after you and I hung up. He was ticked off that you'd hung up on him, talking crazy. Can I get you something to drink?" He motioned for her to join him in the living room.

"No, I'm fine. And I didn't actually hang up on him. Valerie walked into the room; I couldn't talk."

"Did she hear anything?"

"Enough to get the wrong impression." She stared at the leather spines of a collection of first-edition books displayed on mahogany bookshelves.

"Oh, I see."

"No, Arnie, you don't see," she said as she turned, "and neither does Nik—and neither did I until a few minutes ago. I made a choice—a good choice—and now it's time to live with that choice."

"Okay, what's that mean, exactly?" Arnie popped a cashew into his mouth as he leaned on the bar. He had to agree with Nik: as together as this woman appeared most of the time, when it came to this issue, she was like a silver sphere in a pinball game, being slapped back and forth by flippers on opposing sides. If she had such a good marriage, why was it so hard to tell her husband the incredible news?

"On the way over here I got to thinking about my kids. I once told Nik that the hardest thing for a parent to do is step aside and let their children chase their own dreams, fulfill their own destinies, live their own lives. We can't force them, no matter how well intentioned, to take a path contrary to their nature just because it's where we want them to go. Well, we can try to force them—but that kind of coercion never works in the long run."

"Your kids are lucky to have you as a mom."

"I'm not so sure about that, but thanks. Valerie is trying to decide what she wants to do with her life. We've been talking a lot about the different gifts God gives to His children—how you just feel it in your gut when you know you're walking in His purpose for your life. Do you know what I mean, Arnie?"

"Yes, I believe I do."

"I've spent most of my life taking care of other people, and I don't regret one single choice I made to be with my family. But what's wrong with me doing something for me? What's wrong with me chasing my dream—fulfilling my destiny—using the gifts God gave me?" She pulled a lace hanky from her purse and dabbed the corners of her eyes. "On my way over I also got to thinking about how many times I've tried to tell Don about this project. On New Year's Eve I thought for certain I heard God clearly telling me to give it up—to stop trying. But what I was really hearing was my own fear at coming clean. I've been wrong to keep this a secret from Don, and I need to accept whatever the consequences are when I tell him."

Her bottom lip quivered as she took a deep breath.

"But the bottom line is I can't return to my old world—I'll never be able to return to my old world after this." She grabbed his hands. "Arnie, this project has changed me—and I imagine it will change my marriage. I'm scared to death—but I want to go for this. I know I'm like the boy who cried wolf, and I don't blame you for not believing me. But I've changed my mind. I want to go to the Grammys; I need to go to the Grammys."

"But I thought . . ."

"I was wrong!" Ursula shouted. "I've been wrong about a lot of things. But it's time I made things right."

Arnie practically jumped out of his skin when the kitchen door swung open and Nik rushed into the room.

"Well, it's about time you made a sensible decision!" Nik put his hands on his hips.

"I should have expected you'd be here." Ursula sighed as she sat on the barstool. "Come on out, Kitty. I know you're in there too."

Kitty sauntered in, the two kissed hello, and she wordlessly sat down next to Ursula.

"Forgive me, but can we recap the situation?" Arnie queried. "When you spoke with Nik you were dropping out. Now, if I understand you correctly, you're dropping back in? Ursula, I'm just trying to make sure we are all on the same page."

"Yes, we are on the same page. I'm sorry, Nik. I know you have no reason to believe me now. I know I've been a pill to work with. Please forgive me."

———————————

Nik wanted more than anything to wrap his arms around her and take in the scent of her perfume. But knowing all eyes were on him, waiting for him to spew an angry diatribe of reasons why he had been right and she had been wrong, he remained still.

"You're forgiven." He actually found himself looking ever so slightly toward heaven, as Ursula often did, and silently saying *thank you*.

"You have to believe me when I say I've tried to tell Don. It's beyond ludicrous how many times I've been cut off at the pass." Ursula gave them details of some of the times before the nominations when she had tried to tell Don her news.

"Since the nominations were announced, my elaborate plans to come clean have been foiled by a last-minute legal brief that needed to be filed and then running into friends we haven't seen in ages on New Year's Eve. It's always something—it's insane."

Kitty said, "With that many fiascos, I can understand how you might think it's God plan for you to forget about the whole thing."

"And now my daughter thinks I'm having an affair."

Silence fell on the group, and Nik wasn't sure what to say. "Ursula, do you want me to tell him? I'd be happy to pay him a visit."

"I'm sure you would." Ursula playfully stuck out her tongue.

"Don't look at me." Kitty raised her hands. "I'm not volunteering—no way."

"Thanks, guys, but I think I know how to finally tell my family."

"And that would be?" Nik raised his eyebrows.

Ursula smiled. "At the Grammys."

"No telling how your husband would take that, Ursula," Arnie said. "What if . . ."

"Arnie! I know it's the coward's way out—do you think I don't know that? When I'm here with you guys discussing it, I have all the resolve in the world. I make the decision that today is the day—today I'm going to march right up to him and lay it all out. But then something happens—there's not enough time, we get interrupted, the conversation gets tabled for later, but later never comes. Or when it does come I'm too scared or too ticked off to continue. It's crazy! This is the only way. I'll just have to suffer the consequences."

"Have you ever considered that the consequences might be good?" Kitty interjected. She crossed her arms and leaned back. "I don't know your husband or your family, but if I were them, I'd be tickled pink for you. You are genuinely a nice lady—a rare bird for this town. I can see that, and I've only known you a few months—they've known you for years. Don't you think perhaps they'll understand your crazy motives? It's not like you gambled away the family fortune or sold arms to the enemy. Sure, your husband might be angry at first—he might even be deeply hurt by your little secret. But for crying out loud, Ursula, give it to God, ask for your husband's forgiveness, and enjoy the moment! You're headed to the Grammy Awards, not the guillotine!"

Nik waved his hands to get everyone's attention. "I like Ursula's idea. The Grammys." He grinned. "I know just how to do it."

49

Blissful Love continued to top the charts as the Grammys approached. Speculation as to the identity of the mystery chanteuse was at a feverish pitch. A week didn't go by when Nik's face wasn't plastered on the cover of *People, Us, Entertainment Weekly, Star,* and a host of other entertainment and news weeklies. He appeared next to everyone from J. Lo to Dolly Parton.

"This exceeds anything we could have expected," Arnie had said to Ursula one day when he'd called to talk to her about the Grammy performance being planned. Sure enough, as Arnie had predicted, the Academy had asked them to sing. "Nik asked me to remind you to connect with Kitty about what to wear. He said you should look like you did when he met you."

Had it been only ten months ago that she'd sung with her son and his band at the Angelis reception? It seemed like another life.

"Tell him we're one step ahead of him—we went shopping a few days ago. I think she's planning to connect with Nik soon to coordinate his look. She picked up a couple Armani tuxes for him to try on. We're going classic black-and-white with red accessories."

They'd found a dazzling vintage Valentino couture gown in black satin at a consignment shop on Melrose that fit as though it had been made for her. Kitty loaned her a pair of red satin peep-toe Prada shoes that screamed Lana Turner—a perfect touch.

"He said something about a flower of some kind for your hair. . . . Ah . . . a . . ."

"Gardenia?"

"Yes! A gardenia, that's it."

They talked more about the awards ceremony, chattering like teenagers preparing for prom.

"No matter what happens," she said, "this will be a Grammy night the kids will never forget!" Just then, Victor came into the kitchen, and Ursula pretended to say good-bye to Dee. She wondered how much of her conversation he had overheard, hoping he wouldn't get the same wrong impression as his sister. She had finally managed to convince Valerie that everything was going to be fine. Their relationship was still a bit strained, but Ursula knew once she told her the truth, everything would make sense.

"Victor, what are you doing back so soon?"

"Okay, spit it out, Momza, why won't we forget *this* Grammy night?" He dropped his backpack on the floor and kissed her hello. "Other than I won't be home to grace you with my presence and voting expertise?"

"Well, you'll just have to make it home—it won't be the same without you." She got up and hugged him. "What are you doing here?" Victor had recently returned to school after winter break; she hadn't expected him back so soon.

"Hopped a last-minute ride with Blair. Figured I'd hang with you old folks for the weekend, if I'm not interrupting anything?"

"Don't be silly. Sit down—are you hungry?" She opened the refrigerator and began to remove sandwich fixings. "Must be nice to have a friend with a plane."

Victor had met Blair at school; they shared a few classes and hit it off. His parents owned a winery in Temecula, and he flew home almost every weekend in his four-seater Cessna.

"Don't change the subject—what about the Grammys?"

"Ah . . . I . . ." Ursula stammered.

Valerie came into the kitchen yawning and playfully punched her brother in the arm. "I thought I heard you. What are you doing home?"

"You're supposed to be sleeping," Ursula admonished. Still trying to figure out her future plans, Valerie was working at a local restaurant four evenings a week.

"I *was* sleeping; you guys woke me up."

"You're just in time. I was putting Mom on the spot." Victor smiled. "She was having some big secret phone conversation when I came in."

Valerie's head snapped up, eyes wide.

"Seems she has a surprise up her sleeve. So what is it?" Victor looked innocently at his mother, clueless about the salt he had just thrown on Valerie's still-raw wound. "Something about the Grammy Awards."

"The Grammy Awards?" Valerie raised her eyebrows. "Huh?"

Think fast.

"Uh, okay. I was going to wait to tell you . . . but . . . Dee just gave me four tickets to the Grammy Awards. I don't suppose either of you would like to go next week?"

Before she knew it, the kids were talking at once—jumping and squealing, making plans for what to wear, who they would tell, what it would be like.

"I'll need to get someone to cover my shift at work," Valerie said.

"I'll need to make sure I can get back here and make plans to get out of my Monday classes—no way I'll make it back to Berkeley in time."

"What does Dad think?" Valerie asked. "You know he hates award ceremonies."

"I only just found out about the tickets. I haven't told him yet."

One lie begot another and another, and by the time Don came home for dinner, her head ached from trying to keep all of her stories straight.

———

"Will I need to wear a tux?" Don reached for the salt as they talked about the Grammy Awards at dinner. "What's the dress code for peons?"

"We're hardly peons, Don," Ursula said.

"Well, I plan to dress up!" Valerie announced. "Can I borrow some jewelry, Mom?"

"Sure, honey."

"I can't afford a tux. Sorry," Victor said. "My good suit will have to do."

"I think it would be fun if you both wore tuxes," Ursula suggested, refilling Victor's glass with milk. "Anyone else care for a refill?" Valerie and Don shook their heads.

"The tux will be my treat," she said, looking at Victor. "You own yours, big guy." She playfully nudged her husband. "And won't you look handsome!"

"I can't believe Dee got us tickets," Valerie said. "She's, like, the coolest friend."

Uh-oh. I have to talk to Dee.

———

"I'm not happy about this, Ursula. You do realize that you're asking me to lie for you?" Dee's eyes were piercing as she sat across the table from Ursula.

"I'm not asking you to lie for me. I did all the lying already myself—God forgive me."

"God forgive you is right. How could you implicate me in this?" Dee crossed her arms and squinted her eyes.

Dee had been used more than she knew over the past months in covering up the little secret that had rolled into a great big monster-sized snowball of a lie. Ursula felt genuinely bad about it and ushered up silent prayers asking for forgiveness every time she used her friend as an excuse to cover up a meeting, a phone call, or a shopping trip. But she had to come clean with Dee.

"I didn't plan it; you have to believe me. I'm sorry I used your name. You're the only one who could feasibly get us tickets to the Grammys. It just tumbled out—I got carried away."

"Why can't you simply tell them the truth?"

"I will tell them the truth. Please, Dee! Just go along with this if you run into one of them before I have a chance to tell them, okay? Or if the kids should call to thank you. The awards are next week. I'll tell them soon, I promise. Please . . ."

Ursula fiercely hugged her friend when at last she reluctantly agreed.

50

The Grammys had finally arrived! Tonight the charade would end. At last her family would know, and just the thought lifted a weight from Ursula's shoulders. She was sorry it had taken so long to tell them.

The reality hadn't settled in until earlier in the day when she was getting ready and Nik had called her on her cell phone while Don was in the shower.

"I can't talk long, Nik. Don will be getting out of the shower, and—"

"Just wanted to tell you to break a leg! You'll be great."

The minute I step onto the stage my identity will be exposed to the world. "Oh, Nik, I've never been so scared."

"You'll knock 'em dead. Performing in front of that many people is such a rush. Enjoy yourself!"

"Easy for you to say—everyone in your family knows what's going on."

Nik had told his parents the truth about Ursula earlier in the week, and Isabella had called to lend her support, making Ursula feel even worse about her inability to tell her own family.

Nik's laugh brought her back to the moment. "Now listen to me, Ursula Rhoades. This is your dream! In a few hours you'll be singing onstage at the Grammys, not plopped on your sofa in a tattered housecoat eating chips and dip and playing armchair fashion police while you watch it on TV. Your family will be totally jazzed."

"How can you be so sure?"

"Trust me. Once the shock wears off they'll be blown away."

"I'm sure they will."

"All ready with your speech?"

"That's a bit premature, wouldn't you say? We haven't won anything yet."

"I meant your speech to your family."

"Oh, uh, yes—as ready as I'll ever be."

"Good. See you onstage!" Nik hung up just as she heard the water in the bathroom go off.

———

The entire evening had been carefully orchestrated, starting with Boris. Using Cristoff's driver and car had been Isabella's idea, one part of a series of elaborate plans for the evening.

As soon as they settled into the luxurious vehicle, Victor announced he had burned some of the Grammy-nominated songs onto a CD for traveling music, and before she knew what was happening they were all singing like campers around a roaring fire. Even Don, who hated award shows, seemed to be warming up to the excitement of the evening.

Nik had made arrangements to do the sound check at the Staples Center alone to keep her identity a secret. They wouldn't have an opportunity to sing together until they stood side by side onstage. Had things gone the way she'd rehearsed them in her mind countless times the past month, Victor and she would have been doing vocal warm-ups on the drive over. Alas, that wouldn't be happening. *But this singalong should be a perfect warm-up.* She found herself getting lost in the music as they alternately sang and listened to a collection of rock, jazz, country, pop, and one rap tune Victor quickly skipped when he saw his father's reaction. Suddenly, the car was filled with the melodic introduction to "What a Wonderful World."

"If I hear that song one more time I'm going to scream." Ursula gulped. "Please skip it, Victor."

"Sure thing." He pushed the button on the remote control, and the voice of a pop star whose name she could never recall came over the speakers. "Is that better?"

"Thank you." She smiled nervously.

"You're just as good as Alexandra Arcano, Mom. Seriously," Victor said over the music.

"He's right, honey," Don said, surprising her. "Sometimes it's eerie. Especially on 'Time After Time,' the way she sings the chorus reminds me of you."

Maybe they won't be so surprised after all! "Funny you should say that . . ." But her family ignored her as they chattered about the mystery surrounding Nik Prevel's singing partner.

Ursula smiled as she listened to her family talk about the mystery woman. She had plenty of time to break the news. What would they say when they found out the truth? She closed her eyes, prayed for strength, and went over the lyrics to the song one more time in her mind.

"Honey? We're almost there. Earth to Ursula; come in Ursula." Don's touch on her arm made her jump.

"Wound a bit tight, Momza?" Vic joked. "Relax. We need to prepare ourselves for the hike to our seats—we're in row XX; that's probably so far back in the nosebleed section we'll need oxygen masks, but it's still cool to be here." He handed the four tickets back to his father, who looked at the seat numbers and shook his head before returning them to his tux pocket.

Almost there?

"What kind of number is XX? Do they mean X as in the end of the alphabet, or is it the Roman Numeral X? Or what?" Don furrowed his brows. "We'd have been able to see better watching it on TV."

"Stop being a Scrooge, Daddy." Valerie playfully swatted her father. "I don't care where we sit, I'm just jazzed to be here." She grinned. "Tiffany is green with envy!"

What does he mean almost there? How can we be almost there? Had she dozed off? She looked out the window to see they were inching forward in a long line of limousines toward a literal fork in the road, where VIPs drove to the right, and everyone else drove left. Cars turning right would be met by security guards who would check vehicle license numbers against their list, inspect invitations for authenticity, and communicate the names of the vehicle occupants into headsets. Cars turning left, which included theirs, would drop occupants at the general-seating entrance, where red carpet formalities were nonexistent.

"Uh . . . I have something . . ." Ursula stammered as her family, glowing with excitement, looked at her. Her eyes felt wider than normal. "I have something to tell you. I—"

"Look!" Vic shouted, pointing out the window. "It's Mick Jagger!"

Sure enough, there he was—larger than life, sitting in the back of the limo they were slowly passing on the left, his window wide open.

Their limo coasted to a stop, and the tinted window separating the driver from the passengers quietly whirred open. "I believe we are here." Boris looked in the rearview mirror at Ursula, and their eyes locked. *Already? We can't be here already.* But even the depth of her fear couldn't knock the thrill out of her as she looked out to see the huge Grammy banners covering the front of the Staples Center.

In no time, Boris had opened the door, extending his hand to help her from the limo. Pretending to catch her high heel on the curb as she exited the car, she stumbled into Boris to keep from falling, allowing her to whisper in his ear.

"I didn't tell them yet. Get word to Arnie."

"Are you okay, hon?" Don jumped from the car.

"I'm fine, dear. Just took a little trip." She forced a giggle, feeling sick to her stomach.

She knew Winston would be on the lookout for them at the entrance door. He had the genuine tickets; the XX tickets were counterfeits.

When she saw him, she wanted to crawl into his lap and ask him to make it all better, but instead she managed to shoot him a look of utter terror she prayed conveyed to him the fact she had not yet disclosed the truth to her family.

"Good evening, sir, ma'am," he said, taking their tickets. "Please follow me."

"My, my, a private usher?" Don raised his eyebrows.

"Hon, please, I need to talk to you," she said quietly over her shoulder as she followed behind Winston, who had obtained clearance to escort them through a back entrance.

"Wait until we get seated or you'll fall and break your neck." Don laughed, pointing at her high heels.

After traversing several sections of the vast auditorium, they found themselves entering the lower level from an obscure side door. Winston handed Don four new tickets and gestured toward the center aisle.

"A gift from Mrs. Decker. Enjoy the show."

"Oh my gosh!" Valerie gushed. "Is he serious? Are we sitting down there?"

Raising his eyebrows at the seat numbers on the tickets, Don led them down the aisle, looking dashing in his tux. Ursula noticed people whispering with one another as they sat down, most certainly asking, "Who are these people and how did they get seats so close?"

"God bless Aunt Dee!" Victor exclaimed. "Check it out! We're in the fifth row, aisle seats to boot! Awesome!"

"Do you mind if I take the aisle?" Ursula gulped. "My stomach isn't feeling so great." She didn't need to lie about that.

After they were situated in their seats, Ursula put her hand on Don's arm. "Honey, I need to tell you . . ."

"Isn't that Tyra Banks?" Don whispered as he nodded to the seat directly in front of theirs.

Ursula would have laughed if she weren't on the verge of tears. This was utterly ridiculous.

"Yes, Don, I believe it is."

And a few seats down from Tyra, Janet Jackson and Jermaine Dupri were close enough to be occupying one seat, and directly in front of them sat the entire Green Day band. Their section was teeming with well-known performers from the musical realm as well as from the world of film and TV. Keith Urban and his lovely wife, Nicole Kidman, were in their same row, and if Ursula wasn't mistaken, the lead singer from Los Lonely Boys was sitting next to Victor. Everywhere she looked she saw stars.

"Ursula, these are prime seats. Who did you say gave them to Dee?"

"I didn't say . . . Don, listen to me. In a few minutes I'm . . ."

"What is it?" Don asked, his eyes darting around the room, clearly preoccupied.

"Hon, in a few minutes I'm . . ."

"Hey, Dad." Victor leaned over his sister and whispered, "Check it out at three o'clock. How does that stay on?"

They weren't the only necks in their section craned to the right as Pamela Anderson glided down the aisle. It was hard to understand the law of gravity that would permit the sheer leather and lace fabric strips to cover what little they were actually covering on the former *Baywatch* star's ample curves.

"Breathe, dear," Ursula instructed her husband, "and tell your son it's double-stick adhesive tape." She tried her best not to gawk and wondered what fashion policeman Robert Verdi would have to say in the tabloids tomorrow about Pam's nightmare partial-gown.

"This is amazing," Don whispered into her ear. "The kids will never forget this, but don't tell them I'm just as impressed. It's nice to see how the other half lives once in a while, eh? Now, what were you saying? I'm all ears."

Lord help me! No more lying! Time was quickly running out. She couldn't walk on that stage without first telling Don. She couldn't do that to him.

"You do look ill, hon," Don said, heaping burning coals on her in his kindness. "Are you going to be okay?"

"No! I'm not going to be okay unless you listen to me . . . now! I need you to focus, Don! I need to tell you something—" The lights dimmed suddenly as symphonic music began to emanate from the orchestra pit, making it impossible to be heard without shouting. The Grammy Awards had begun, and in just a few minutes the first commercial break would be her cue to excuse herself to the ladies' room. Except that wasn't where she would be headed.

51

Because it wasn't typically a part of the telecast, the only way the Academy could accommodate the addition of the musical performances of the five nominees for Best Pop Performance by a Duo was to have them as one of the first awards of the night. The nominees would perform live, one right after another in a musical medley. Other than artist introductions, there would be no breaks between the five songs. "What a Wonderful World" was the last song in the medley. She wouldn't have to wait long before her secret was exposed.

Ursula returned to reality and took a deep breath when she heard Queen Latifah, this year's mistress of ceremonies, end her opening monologue and announce the upcoming medley that would take place right after the break—Ursula's prompt to exit the auditorium. She leaned over to Don. "I have to run to the ladies' room."

"Now? You'd better hurry," Valerie leaned over to whisper. "Or you're gonna miss the unveiling of Alexandra!" Her daughter's incredulous look spoke volumes.

Ursula's guilt increased exponentially. "Not a chance of that happening."

"Do you need me to go with you?" Don asked.

"No, I'll be fine." Ursula hesitated. "Don?"

"Yes?"

"I love you. I really do. Don't forget that, okay?"

"Ah, sure, honey. I love you too." He patted her hand and turned to talk with Valerie.

"Listen to me, Don," Ursula said more urgently in his ear. "I most likely won't see you until the show is over, but I need you to know that I tried to tell you a dozen times. I really did. Please forgive me. I love you so much, and I love the kids so much. Please tell them." She kissed him hard on the lips and left him sitting there stunned—no time to tell him all that was on her heart.

Please, God, let him understand. Let them all understand.

She practically flew up the long aisle, and upon reaching the lobby was quickly met by an escort who none too gently grabbed her arm as she led Ursula through a door and down a corridor heading for backstage. Kitty met up with them halfway and thrust a short red sequin bolero jacket into Ursula's hands and pinned a beautiful fresh gardenia in her hair as they walked.

"Okay, this is it!" Kitty said, handing her a Chanel red lipstick and a hand mirror. "Nik's waiting in the wings. You're on in less than fifteen minutes."

Lord help me. "I can do this. I can do this," she chanted. "Can I do this, Kitty?" She stopped dead in her tracks and held on to Kitty's hand for dear life. "I am so scared."

"You'll be great, Ursula."

"Kitty! I didn't tell him. I couldn't! They don't know. This is awful."

"Listen to me." Kitty looked into her eyes. "Don't worry about them. They'll be all right. I'll go down to your seat right now—okay?"

"What will you say?" Ursula panicked.

"We have a plan. Don't worry. Concentrate on your performance. Don't stress your vocal cords. Ursula! You have got to calm down."

"Don is probably freaking out right now. I don't even know what I just said to him. What do you mean you have a plan?"

"We've got it handled—trust us, okay? I have to go." She kissed her cheek, spun around, and was gone in a flash.

Ursula looked up and discovered that she was backstage at the Grammys. The fact that she hadn't attended the sound check had sent the producers into a tizzy, but Nik had walked her through their performance over the phone twice.

"We're the last of the five songs," he had explained. "The producer wants us to cross to center stage from opposite sides of the wings—singing, no less. I'll begin by singing solo—walking under a follow spot. You'll join me after the first two stanzas. But here's the scoop: you start singing and walking in total darkness. It won't be pitch-black; my follow spot will guide you, and our final destinations will be identified with glow tape. So when you get to your mark, stay there. But your follow spot won't appear until you are almost center stage—the audience will *hear* you before they *see* you. Can you do that?"

"Sure!" Once she began to sing it would be fine. At least she hoped it would be fine.

"It's a dramatic entrance. Just don't jump when the light comes on. It's pretty blinding. And, the audience will probably cheer and applaud, so don't let that throw you. Just keep your eyes on me and pretend we're back in the studio, okay?"

"Aye, aye, sir." She laughed, assuring him she wouldn't let him down.

There was so much activity going on, she could barely see Nik across the stage as a techie fitted her with an earpiece monitor and handed her a microphone, whispering instructions at breakneck speed as the fourth nominees took a bow. She tried to ignore the people backstage who were staring at her, wondering who she was. She locked eyes with Nik across the stage, and he gave her a thumbs-up and blew her a kiss. She heard the music begin. *Oh, Lord, here we go!*

"Ladies and gentlemen, here to perform their nominated song, 'What a Wonderful World,' and appearing in public together for the first time, please welcome Nik Prevel and Alexandra Arcano!"

Nik's sultry voice filled the auditorium, as did uproarious applause. She said a silent prayer, took a deep breath, and began to sing on cue while walking in darkness—never taking her eyes off Nik's face.

———————

The applause was deafening when the spotlight came on as planned, timed perfectly at a vocal break in the song. She took the opportunity to look out at the audience while the orchestra played. No wonder stars were so comfortable doing this; she couldn't see past the first row. It was easy to forget that thousands of people were in the audience watching and millions were sitting at home as she and her children had done for years.

She wished she could see her family—then again, perhaps this was best.

She sang like she'd never sung before. She was no longer nervous as the song reached its crescendo. Their duet was magical. *Oh, thank you, God!*

It was the performance of her life—Nik's voice and hers blended together so full and rich. The orchestra was on target and the lights perfect. She felt like the heroine in a Fred Astaire and Ginger Rogers film, the way the lights worked and their soft-shoe choreography played out without a hitch.

She wondered what Nik was thinking as they took their bows, although his radiant smile spoke volumes. She wondered what people were thinking when they realized she was a total unknown. She wondered if any of her friends were watching from their homes. Mostly, she wondered what her family was thinking—what Kitty had told them, what they would do next.

She struggled to see them from the stage as she and Nik exited but could not.

She stood in the wings with Nik breathing heavily and grinning like a fool. Mariah Carey and Paul McCartney breezed past them, holding the envelope that could change their lives forever.

"Good luck!" Mariah said to Nik as she passed, giving him a seductive smile he likely would have appreciated at any other time but barely seemed to notice. He didn't take his eyes off Ursula.

"You look stunning," he whispered in her ear as she reached for a tissue from a box sitting on the prep table to dab the perspiration on her brow. "Here, let me get that." He took the tissue and, holding her chin in one hand, gently blotted her forehead with his other hand.

"We were great, weren't we? People liked it?" She began to catch her breath. "I wonder what Don and the kids thought. Oh, I wish I could see them." She craned her neck to look from the wings.

"Stay focused, Ursula," Nik said into her ear, pulling her close to him. "You were stupendous—you're made for this. I love you, Ursula."

She gave him a huge smile. "I can't thank you enough for this experience. It's—"

"No. Did you hear what I said, Ursula? I really love you. I've tried to do the friend thing and it's just not working."

"Oh . . . oh, Nik . . ." Ursula stammered. "I know you think that's what it is, but I can assure you—"

"No! It's not what I *think*; it's what I *know*. God did not bring you into my life to rub my nose into what I can't have. I won't believe that!"

"And I won't believe God brought us together to ruin my marriage! You don't know what you're saying. Let's just forget—"

"That's just it, I can't forget! God knows I've been trying."

"Shhh. Nik, people are listening."

All around them people had gotten quiet, straining to hear what they were saying. Then Ursula realized they were listening to the announcers. Her head snapped up when she heard their names announced, and suddenly the people in the wings were shouting and clapping and pushing them out onstage.

"What a Wonderful World" had won the Grammy for Best Pop Performance by a Duo!

"We did it!" Nik shouted as the applause out front along with the backstage ruckus drowned out any ability to even think straight. "Let's go!" He grabbed her by the arm, but she stood firm.

"Wait! What are you going to say? Nik, please don't say anything we'll both regret—please."

"Don't worry. Trust me." He smiled and led her back onstage. The applause was deafening.

Ursula had never allowed herself to think this might actually happen, and so she was more than happy to let Nik take the microphone on their behalf.

There she was—smiling like Vanna under the spotlight and praying she wouldn't trip or throw up or do something equally as drastic. She prayed Nik wouldn't use this platform to declare his love for her. She knew he wasn't serious—but he didn't know he wasn't serious.

What a mess this could be.

"A great man once told me," Nik began as he held up the gold gramophone statue in his hand, "that this award could make or break a career. Not the actual winning of it, but what the winner did with it once they won it. I learned a lot from that great man, and he deserves so much more than a thank you. You folks know him as the Grammy Hall of Fame winner who owns quite a few of these little guys. I know him as my father, the legendary Cristoff Prevelakis." Nik motioned to where he knew Cristoff and Isabella were sitting, waving his arm for Cristoff to stand up, which he did to the uproarious applause of everyone in the auditorium.

Ursula had no doubt that more than a few jaws dropped at Nik's declaration; it was so out of character for the old Nik, but she was proud of the man he had become. She knew this selfless act of publicly praising his father would be a milestone in their relationship.

As the applause ceased, he went on to thank his mother, Arnie, Kitty, the record label, his band, and a host of other people Ursula barely knew. She stood in a haze of disbelief as time stood still. Last but not least, revealing her real name to the public for the first time, he thanked "Ursula Rhoades, aka Alexandra Arcano," leaving out any reference to love, for which she silently thanked God.

When he stepped back and indicated for Ursula to say something, she was initially stunned but quickly seized the opportunity—understanding her time was being measured virtually in seconds. All around the world, viewers had been watching to see Alexandra Arcano revealed. While some were probably disappointed that she wasn't a recognizable celebrity, many were probably thrilled that she was unknown—for it brought hope to millions, hope that dreams can come true. She couldn't even think about what her family was doing at this moment—what they were thinking, saying. She prayed that Kitty had reached them and was at this very minute assuring them all would be well. *Please, God, let all be well.*

Tears cascaded unashamedly down her cheeks as she leaned into the microphone.

"Are you sure you don't want to thank your third-grade teacher, Nik?" The audience laughed, and Ursula's confidence buoyed. "This has been an amazing journey, and I thank the Academy for recognizing the work we've accomplished on *Blissful Love*. I want to thank my dear friend Nik Prevel for seeing in me something I was unable to see in myself—that when God gives us a gift, He intends for us to use it to bring Him glory. I'd also like to thank my family—I love you all so much. I hope you will always be able to see past this Grammy for who I am—your wife and mother. And to anyone out there who has a dream, I say this: it's never too late to make your dreams come true . . . never. God bless you."

She turned from the microphone, latched her arm through Nik's outstretched elbow, and to the roar of applause walked offstage and into another world. Like Dorothy going from a monochromatic world into the amazingly colorful land of Oz, she stepped out of her normal life and into fantasyland.

52

Don had no idea that when Ursula had rushed off to the ladies' room his life was about to change. Ursula's parting words had confused him. He thought for a moment perhaps she was leaving him, that she'd finally had enough of him and the long hours he worked at the firm. The past summer had taken its toll on their relationship, and he had to admit that she had been different when he returned from New York. He'd thought it was the Celeste thing and that eventually the entire misunderstanding would blow over. But it was crazy to think she'd choose to leave him at the Grammy Awards. No, something was wrong.

"Mom looked stressed; should I go find her?" Valerie had asked him as the commercial break ended and Ursula had yet to return. Had she really said she might not see him until the show was over? Surely he must have misunderstood her.

"No, honey, I'm sure it's all right. Besides, this is the part you've been waiting for, isn't it? The mystery woman is going to be revealed."

"Like you even know what we're talking about." She playfully punched his arm. "Have you even listened to the CD?"

He had to admit that he had heard the album and enjoyed it. One of the secretaries at the firm played it often in the lunchroom, and he'd noticed that more than one computer had the music playing in the background as paralegals and assistants worked. The songs took him back to a place in his youth that was pleasant—to a time when his mother had let him stand on her feet and she'd dance him around the living room. He especially loved "Someone to Watch Over Me." He thought he recognized the voice, but couldn't quite place it. Like he'd said in the limo, there were even times when she sounded a bit like his wife, although this woman's voice was more full-bodied, richer.

He looked back over his shoulder to see if Ursula was coming, hoping she wouldn't miss the performance that the kids—that almost the entire country—had been talking about for months.

They'd stopped whispering about who the mystery singer could be and were watching and listening to the performances of the nominees for Best Duo as one couple after another sang their nominated song. Then a lovely young woman sat down in Ursula's seat.

"Uh, I'm sorry but that seat is taken," he quickly whispered.

"By your wife, Ursula, right?"

Don looked at the woman but said nothing.

"My name is Kitty Thomas. I can't say anything else right now, but on the next break I will."

A few minutes later he watched—stunned—as Alexandra Arcano was suddenly bathed under a follow-spot that made her glow like an angel. He couldn't breathe. *Was that . . . ? Could it be . . . ?*

"Mom!" Valerie squeaked as she clutched her father's arm.

"Oh my gosh!" Don heard Victor say.

He leaned toward Kitty, never taking his eyes off his wife. "What do you know about this?" he demanded.

"Shhh, just listen. I'll tell you more when they're done."

Along with millions of viewers, Don listened spellbound as his wife sang "What a Wonderful World" with that young heartthrob Nik Prevel. With . . . Nik . . . Prevel! That's what was the matter! That's what she had tried to tell him. That's why she'd been behaving differently. She was seeing Nik Prevel—it was clear the way she couldn't take her eyes off him! Oh, she wasn't just *seeing* him; she'd apparently recorded an album with him! How in heaven's name could this have happened?

"I don't understand . . ." Valerie said.

"It's her! Mom's Alexandra Arcano! How cool!" Victor shifted excitedly in his seat. "Way to go, Momza!"

"No way!" Valerie exclaimed.

The three of them sat back shaking their heads, and when the song ended only Victor joined the audience in the applause. Valerie was dumbstruck, and Don gripped the armrests so tightly the veins in his hands looked ready to explode.

A few minutes later he watched in awe as his wife glided across the stage on the arm of Nik Prevel to accept the Grammy for Best Duo of the Year. He had never seen her look more poised or more beautiful. He listened to her tell the world that she loved him— loved her children—and watched as she shed tears of joy for all to see. He didn't realize that he too was crying until Kitty reached over and gently took his hand, placing a tissue in his palm.

"Come with me, all of you. I'll take you to her."

Nik and Ursula were shepherded immediately back to a media room where the lights, activity, and noise were beyond anything Ursula had ever seen.

Arnie met up with them as they walked, extending hearty congratulations before issuing instructions like an overcaffeinated drill sergeant.

"Kitty told me you never had a chance to tell Don," Arnie practically yelled over the din.

"What happened?" Nik asked.

"She didn't tell Don before she went onstage."

Nik just shook his head.

"What do we do?" Ursula held on to Arnie as the escort pulled them along.

"Not much you can do now except go with the flow. We distributed the press release here and over the wires. You can say good-bye to Alexandra Arcano. You're back to being Ursula Rhoades."

"No. I mean what do we do about Don and the kids? Where are they? I have to see them. Who are all of these people?"

"Think of them as bridges to your fans, my dear. They'll be all over you like shoppers the day after Thanksgiving. Let Nik do the talking."

"Stand here," the escort abruptly said, positioning them in front of the Grammy backdrop for photos as the camera flashes commenced—quickly making her dizzy as she tried to follow them.

"Don't try to guess which one's next; just smile and stay calm. You'll get used to it," Nik whispered. "I can't believe you didn't tell him." Nik posed, his arm around Ursula.

"I tried, believe me. I'm serious—who are all of these people?" she whispered back.

"I'm sure you did. These are the folks who keep your magazines fed. Keep smiling."

Reporters from dozens of magazines, television networks, newspapers, and tabloids all shouted questions to the pair. Nik responded to most of them.

Ursula was embarrassed at how personal some of the questions were, especially the ones regarding her relationship with Nik. No topic appeared to be off limits.

"She's a very beautiful woman, Nik," shouted a man who identified himself as Barry Koltnow from the *Orange County Register*, as though Ursula wasn't standing right in front of him. "Anything going on between you that you'd like to share with our readers?"

"You'll be the first to know, Barry," Nik said with a laugh.

"In your acceptance speech you mentioned you're a wife and mother—how many children do you have?" someone shouted.

"This press release is vague," another called. "Is there a reason for that?"

"What does your husband do?" another reporter yelled. "Where is he tonight?"

For every question, Nik had an answer. Some were truthful, some ambiguous, all gracious. It was clear he'd done this before, and Ursula was grateful she only had to smile and nod. Truth be told, she was frightened beyond belief, and she was concerned about her family. *What are they thinking? Where are they?*

Just as Arnie had predicted, the media were in a frenzy over the fact that Ursula Rhoades, aka Alexandra Arcano, wasn't a well-known singer.

"Do you really expect us to believe you're a housewife from Bel-Air?" Kathleen Carter from *Us* magazine shouted above all other voices—causing the room to grow quiet. "This question is for Ursula Rhoades to answer, provided she can talk as well as sing."

Lord, help me. "I suppose so, yes; why would we lie about that?"

"You've lied all along; why should we believe this?" shouted a man waving the press release in the air. She couldn't read his name tag.

"Let me handle him," Nik whispered.

"Hey, Bob! Nice to see you." Nik smiled. "Thanks for the question—but we've never lied to you. Alexandra Arcano does exist—she's right here in front of you—but most folks in the real world know her as Ursula Rhoades."

"So why the big pretense? No one uses an alias unless they have something to hide," Busybody Bob sneered. "So what is it, Ursula Rhoades? You know we'll find out anyway, Nik. Why not give it to us straight? What aren't you telling us? Who is this woman?"

Arnie quietly retreated to the back of the room to stand with Don, Victor, and Valerie. He quickly introduced himself to them, and they watched Nik deftly field one obtrusive question after another.

"It's only a matter of time," Kitty whispered to Arnie, pulling him away from the Rhoades family "before someone connects Don Rhoades, counselor to the stars, to Ursula Rhoades, Nik's mystery woman . . . especially with you standing here with them."

"What am I supposed do? Leave them to fend on their own? This is entirely your fault."

"My fault?" Kitty raised her eyebrows and her voice.

"Shhhh," Arnie hissed. "She was supposed to tell her husband in the limo on the ride over. This was your brilliant idea."

"No, it was actually Nik's brilliant idea, remember? I only helped with her speech to her family. It was a good speech—if she had told them, things would be decidedly different now, wouldn't they?" She crossed her arms defiantly and leaned back against the wall as Arnie shook his head, walked behind Don, and spoke over his shoulder into his ear.

"I'm sure this is a lot to digest all at one time," Arnie said quietly as Don continued to stare at his wife while holding Valerie's hand on his left and resting his right hand on his son's shoulder.

"How could she do this to us?" Valerie cried.

"Can we go up there?" Victor motioned, stepping forward as Don grabbed his sleeve.

"I don't think so, buddy."

"Ah, your father's right; it might not be a good idea right now." Arnie handed Don a copy of the press release. "We distributed this when they won. Ursula's real name has been revealed."

Don read the release with Victor and Valerie doing the same from either side as Arnie continued.

"But unless someone has already seen you, I doubt they've put two and two together that her Rhoades is the same as your Rhoades."

"So what if they do? Is that bad?" Valerie asked. "Is she ashamed of us? Why didn't she tell us?"

Arnie looked at Don and at the expectant faces of Ursula's children and felt a rush of embarrassment that he knew more about the situation than they did.

"I think that's something you need to ask your mother."

"She appears to be busy," Valerie snipped.

"Valerie, there is no cause to be rude," her father admonished.

"I'm sorry, Mr. Shapiro." Valerie looked sheepishly at Arnie, then hung her head. "This just doesn't make any sense." She began to cry. "Mom has always been honest with us. Why didn't she tell us, Daddy?"

Don put his arm around his daughter and squeezed. "Honey, she must have had her reasons. Let's give her the benefit of the doubt, okay?"

"She did have reasons, and very good ones. For one, she didn't want to bring undue attention on you during the trial. She was protecting you." Kitty spoke up behind them. "I'm sorry. I guess I should keep my nose out of it, but everyone's so upset about not knowing and no one appears to give a rip that she's just won a Grammy. This is her dream come true, for crying out loud!"

Arnie squinted his eyes and shook his head, saying "enough is enough" without saying a word.

Kitty shrugged. "I'm sorry, folks. I've got a big mouth. It was nice to meet all of you. I'm sure you'll get things all figured out when you have a chance to talk with her. She really does love you all. I'm going back to sit in the house. I don't want to be standing here when someone recognizes you." She pointed at Don. "You've got Nik handled—right, Arnie?"

"Yeah, I'll stay nearby. His next category isn't for quite a while. Come back then, okay?"

"You got it. Later!" And she was gone.

Don quickly turned his back on the press corps and pulled his children around with him, motioning for Arnie to come closer.

"Do you have a pen?" Don whispered. Arnie reached into his suit pocket and handed over his new Montegrappa. "Is there a driver who can take us home?" Don asked while scribbling a note on the back of the press release.

"Home? But—" Valerie quickly stopped as her father shook his head firmly.

"Yes, I can have Boris take you home." Arnie pulled a cell phone from the holder on his belt and punched in a number. "When do you wish to leave?"

"Now," Don said firmly, folding the note and handing it to Arnie along with his pen. "Nice pen."

"Thanks." Arnie smiled as he instructed Boris to bring the car around and then hung up.

"But, Dad," Victor said, "you can't be serious! It's party time after the Grammys, and our mom just won one!"

"I'm serious. You have to trust me on this, son."

Victor reluctantly nodded.

"Thank you for your help, Mr. Shapiro," Don said to Arnie, then walked toward the door with his children. "Please see that my wife gets that note. We'll meet her at home."

"Uh, Mr. Rhoades," Arnie said, "you don't have to go. You are welcome to stay. I have tickets for you to attend several events with her—I know she'd love to have you with her."

"Thanks, but I know what the press is like. I'm not ready to answer their questions right at the moment, if you know what I mean. I want to get out before someone recognizes me."

Arnie shook his head and extended his hand. "I understand. It was nice to meet you. I hope we'll have the opportunity to talk again when things calm down."

Don shook Arnie's hand and looked once more toward his wife. "Something tells me that could be a while." He ushered his children out of the room.

Arnie stared at the door for several moments before turning away. He had a letter to deliver, and he prayed it contained kind words, but he refused to sneak a peek.

"Is he here?" Ursula rushed over to Arnie as soon as they were released from the press gaggle—replaced by the next Grammy winner, who had just been escorted offstage. Nik stopped to talk with Lionel Richie, waving her on with a smile.

"Where are they? Are they still in the audience? Did you bring them backstage?" She craned her neck, searching for her family in the crowded room.

"They're fine. They're all proud of you. They just left."

"They left?" Ursula grabbed Arnie's hand. "What happened? Where's Kitty? What did she tell them? How did Don sound? Is he mad?"

"Calm down!" Arnie laughed. "Everything is fine. Kitty took a seat out front with some of her friends; she'll be back later. She didn't tell them much of anything—neither of us told them much of anything. Kind of like you, eh?"

"Oh, Arnie! I can't believe I couldn't tell him! But I tried. I really tried."

"I'm sure you did. Well, now he knows—everyone knows."

"I'm not sure any of the press corps has connected us. No one mentioned Don's name."

"Give them time."

"Okay, so what do I do now? Go back to my seat?"

"You can if you want to. Or you could remain in the green room for the rest of the show, watching on the big screen."

"Just like I was at home." She smiled, looking around her in awe.

"Just like home." Arnie grinned.

Ursula decided not to return to the auditorium, where she would surely face hundreds of curious stares, looking forward instead to witnessing the backstage excitement. A well-dressed young man appeared to escort her to the green room as Arnie wrapped her in a bear hug.

"Congratulations, you've earned this. Just sit back and enjoy it, kiddo. Bask in the limelight. Some singers wait their entire life for this. I know Nik has."

"He was great, wasn't he? Did you hear his speech? I can't believe it—we really won. Where did he go?" She looked over Arnie's shoulder but couldn't locate him. "Tell him where I went, okay?"

"Will do. Oh, Ursula? Here's something from your husband." He handed her the note Don had quickly scribbled on his way out. "I hope it's good news, sweetie. See you later."

She nervously opened the note as her escort walked her to the green room where she would spend the next several hours.

> Hon, I don't know how I'll ever top this for a surprise; but I'm already spinning my wheels trying to think of something— maybe the Pulitzer? Enjoy yourself. We're proud. Figured it best I lay low until the hounds get my scent—you're on your own until then. Stay safe tonight, okay? Call when you can. I'm sure we'll try to wait up for you, but don't sweat that. We'll see you in the morning. We love you—I love you—Me
> P.S. You could have told us. xo

It was going to be okay. *Thank you, God.*

Nik met up with Ursula in the green room. She didn't know how to approach his recent declaration of love and decided for the time being to pretend it never happened.

"So Arnie tells me the old man is okay with things?"

"My father?"

"Your husband."

"You can call him Don, or my husband, or the father of my children, but not old man." She wasn't angry—just high on love. His love note had buoyed her spirits. She gave Nik a piercing look. "He deserves to be called good names, not old man."

"Sorry."

"Apology accepted. And yes, he is okay. But I wish I could talk to him. My cell phone won't work."

"That's intentional," Arnie said as he joined them. "I'll get you a land line you can use, okay?"

"Thank you. I still can't believe it—this is amazing."

"Wanna hold it?" Nik asked, holding out the Grammy statuette.

She held the gold gramophone in her hand as tears slipped down her face yet again.

"I'm going to be a mess," she sniffed.

"What do you mean, *going to be*?" Nik laughed. She gently slugged him.

"I can't believe this. I'm stunned."

"Believe it!" Arnie cheered. "And if this is any indication, I think Nik will finally walk away with his own award for Best Male Pop Vocal Performance."

"Oh, I do hope so!" Ursula gushed. "Are you going back to your seat, Nik?"

"Nah, I think I'll stay right here. Where else can you get a bird's-eye view like this?"

She followed his eyes to a makeup mirror where Jessica Simpson was being primped to go onstage. Jessica caught Nik's gaze in the mirror and winked.

"Well, she's single now. You'd make a cute couple," Ursula whispered.

"Puh-leeze. That kind of drama I don't need. Anyway, I'm kind of spoiled on older chicks now. You gals have it together, you know?"

"Oh yeah, you've got that right. I have it all together. Ha!"

For now she would enjoy the wildest ride of her life. She felt like Cinderella at the ball.

53

It was that magical time in the early morning when everything was cast in the pale blue of sunlight awakening from a long night's sleep. Ursula leaned against the armrest inside the limousine, not the least bit sleepy, even though she had been up for almost twenty-four hours. Boris had long ago returned to the Prevelakis estate, taking Cristoff and Isabella home shortly after the Grammy program ended. She couldn't recall the name of the kind gentleman driving her now. The Prada heels Kitty had loaned her sat on the seat as she rubbed her tired feet. Nik's and her shared Grammy Award for Best Duo sat in her lap. Nik had taken home his own award for Best Pop Male Vocal. He said she could keep this one with her—that she'd earned it.

She was only a mile from her home but light-years away from her old life.

"Are you sure you're okay?" Arnie had asked as they left the final party of the night. "I'll gladly go with you, if you'd like."

"I'm fine, Arnie, really. I haven't had a thing to drink, I'm wide awake, and I really want to get home and talk to Don, see the kids."

"That's not what I meant. Do you want me to come with you and . . . explain anything?"

"You're sweet, but I think it's going to be okay. I managed to get a call in to Don, and he sounded fine—at least as far as I could tell in a three-minute conversation."

As the limousine turned onto Strada Corda Road, she could see cars and TV vans lining the street in front of her home.

They have made the connection! They know where I live!

She grabbed her cell phone and dialed Arnie's number, praying for him to answer.

"Arnie! They found out. There are TV crews in front of my house! What should I do?"

Her address had not been listed in the press release. There were hundreds of Rhoadeses in the phone book, but they were not listed among them. Clearly, someone had done his research. The driver, obviously used to this kind of thing, pulled over to the side of the road and awaited instructions.

"Calm down, Ursula; it's okay. We knew they'd find out—just not so quickly. Is your husband home?"

"I'm sure he is. Where else would he be? Why?"

"I imagine they've already knocked on the door. Has he talked with them?"

"It's four forty-five in the morning, Arnie. I didn't want to call and wake anyone up."

"Oh, I'll bet they're already up. Hang tight and I'll be right there. In the meantime, give him a call and tell him to get ready."

"To get ready for what?"

"To let you in."

She had no sooner hung up from Arnie when her cell phone began to play Led Zeppelin's "Stairway to Heaven," the distinctive ringtone for her husband.

"You're up?" she asked.

"Hard to sleep with the vultures circling the wagon. You need to know there are TV crews outside our—"

"I know! I'm sitting in a limo down the street. What should I do? Have they been there long? Did you talk to any of them?"

"A couple of them arrived an hour or so after we got home, but they've multiplied in the past hour."

"Arnie said it would only be a matter of time before they made the connection. He's on his way now."

"Who?"

"Arnie, Nik's manager. I called him."

"Ursula, what were you thinking?"

"He's used to handling things like this—"

"That's not what I meant. What were you thinking about this entire thing? Why didn't you tell me?"

"I want to explain, but can it wait until I get out of this car and into the house? And, just so you know, I was trying to protect you."

"Protect me?"

"Yes, Don! That was the reason behind the entire charade—I didn't want to upset your work on the Chesterfield case."

"That's thoughtful of you, Ursula, but what about upsetting my entire career? I'm waiting until a decent hour before I call Sam, although I'm sure he already knows—someone surely had to call him last night when they saw you on TV."

The next twenty-five minutes of waiting kept Ursula in tears. She had it figured out: Don had encouraged her with his fake love note at the Grammys because he was such a good man and didn't want to ruin her evening, but now that the evening was over and the truth was coming out—he was mad.

Arnie finally arrived, along with two security guards he'd hired, and rushed her from the limo into her home via the side door of the garage; he stayed on the lawn of her home to answer media questions. One guard took post at the front door, the other at the foot of the driveway.

Victor met her at the door. "Way to go, Momza!" He picked her up and swung her around the room. "Let me check it out!"

He gently put her down and took the Grammy statuette from her hands. "Awesome! Did you hear us cheering when you won this? You were amazing! None of us can believe we didn't recognize your voice. When we got home we played the CD over and over again—how did we miss it? What dorks!"

Don was sitting at the breakfast bar with a cup of coffee in his hands looking at her. Dressed in the same clothes he'd had on the night before—minus the tie, cummerbund, and jacket—he looked rugged, a bit of stubble on his chin and his hair slightly mussed.

"Did you guys sleep at all?" Ursula said as she sat next to her husband, placing her hand on his. "Where's Valerie?"

"She's asleep," Victor said. "We've been waiting up for you. Want some coffee?"

"Desperately."

She watched Victor prepare a cup of coffee for her as he'd done dozens of times before. There was tension in the room, and it was growing by the second.

"Son," Don said quietly. "I'd like to talk with your mother alone."

"Sure, Pops, no problemo." He set a coffee mug in front of his mother and kissed her on the cheek. "Congratulations, Mom. I'm proud of you. Prepare to tell me everything. I'm not going back to school until Wednesday." He walked out of the room smiling and wiggling his finger at his parents. "You two play nice, you hear? Don't run with scissors, and make good choices."

A delicate silence was quickly broken by the ringing of the phone.

"Don't answer it." Don raised his hand. "I feel like I'm on a TV show saying that—but it's a reporter, I'm sure. Who else would call at this hour?"

"Have they been calling often?"

"Practically nonstop."

"Why don't you shut off the ringer?" Ursula lifted up the phone and flipped the switch to Off. "And turn down the volume on the answering machine." She moved the lever to silent. "There. We can check messages later. Voilà!"

"It's not going to be that easy, Ursula. I wish you would have told me."

"I wanted to. You have no idea how many times I tried. I'm sorry . . ."

Don shook his head sadly, and Ursula couldn't decipher what he was feeling. "I know you did." He looked up at her. "I've been going over and over the past months—how many times you said that you had something to talk with me about. Was this it?"

She nodded.

"You should have made me listen to you." Before she could speak up he shook his head. "Not now. Why don't you go get showered. You must be exhausted. We can talk about this later, okay?"

"Thank you. I'll be right back. Arnie's outside talking to the press. Please let him in when he knocks, okay?"

After answering the questions flung at him with as much discretion as possible, Arnie turned toward the house and banged on the door. "It's me. Arnie," he called out.

Don appeared at the door, quickly closed it behind Arnie, and then held out a hand. "Nice to see you again. Didn't expect it to be so soon."

Arnie shook his hand. "We can thank the World Wide Web—the Internet has made everyone a successful spy. Your press coverage for the Chesterfield case is still fresh. You're one of the first Google references to come up when someone searches Rhoades."

Don just shook his head. "Go figure. Ursula's showering; she'll be down soon. Would you like coffee? Just made a fresh pot."

"I'd love some, thanks."

Don sat down at the breakfast bar after pouring the coffee. "Well, that was quite a surprise."

Arnie remained standing, feeling more awkward in the kitchen with one man than he had out in the yard swarming with media.

"Ursula tells me you've got a plan?"

"Well . . . yes . . . somewhat. We knew they'd eventually find out—just didn't think it would be this quickly. It seems one of the interns at the *L.A. Times* was on the Chesterfield case and recognized you last night. Got lucky with a Google search, like I said."

"I'm not sure how to take this entire scenario," Don said, staring into his cup.

"I can only imagine." Arnie shook his head. "But she was great! Don't you think so? Your wife was amazing, Mr. Rhoades—absolutely amazing. Her talent amazed Nik and me from the moment we saw her singing with Victor's group."

"Call me Don, considering . . ."

"Don, your wife has an incredible talent—they just won two Grammy Awards! This is a major accomplishment."

"So now what?" Don raised his eyebrows. "What happens now?"

"Nothing happens if your wife has her way."

"What do you mean?"

"She says this was a one-time shot—that she's done. Over. Fini!"

"And what do you say?"

"No offense, but I say she's crazy. Nik wants to record a follow-up album. I agree."

"Ah . . . Nik."

Don got up to refill his coffee cup. Arnie remained standing, not sure what to do.

"It's not like that, Don. There is nothing going on between your wife and Nik. In fact—"

"Stop! I don't think I need to have this conversation with you, with all due respect."

Arnie nodded his head. "Sorry. You're right. Okay, then, here's how I think we need to handle the varmints outside on your lawn. . . ." He pulled up a stool and was still explaining his strategy when Ursula joined them fresh from the shower. She wore a beautifully embroidered tunic over a pair of jeans with chartreuse sling-back sandals. Her hair was pulled back in a ponytail, giving her the appearance of a woman far younger than her years.

"Arnie thinks we need to have a press conference," Don said without looking at her.

"What do you think?" she asked her husband, joining him at the breakfast bar.

"Do you want something to eat? A bagel or something?" Don asked, shrugging his shoulders.

"Thanks, but I feel like I've been eating all night. I've never seen so much food! You should have seen the spread they had at the Sunset Tower."

"I would like to have seen it, but under the circumstances I felt it was best to get the kids home—I'm used to press hounds; they aren't."

"I think it's time for me to leave." Arnie stood.

"No, wait, please," Ursula said. "Don, I know this must look insane to you—and frankly there have been times these past months when I felt I was crazy! But all of this secrecy started because I really was trying to protect you. I'm not hiding anything because I'm ashamed or because I've done something wrong. I just didn't know how it would affect the case—and your career. I never wanted to jeopardize your chances with the firm. It didn't start out this way."

"How did it start out?"

She and Arnie were well into the story when yet another knock sounded on the back door.

"I'll get it," Don said.

When he opened the door, Arnie saw it was Nik standing there, rather well disguised, but his broad, dimpled smile gave him away.

"Come in," Don said with resignation in his voice.

"Get inside before they recognize you," Arnie said, feeling slightly panicked. "How did you get here?"

"Taxi dropped me off down the street. I walked through the neighbors' backyards—hope I didn't disturb anyone. I'm Nik Prevelakis. You must be Don," he said, holding out his hand. "Pleased to meet you."

"I know who you are, Mr. Prevelakis," Don said, taking his hand. Arnie hoped this wasn't the last straw. Don had been calm so far, but things could get ugly.

"Nik. Please call me Nik."

"Have a seat." Ursula motioned to the breakfast bar. "Arnie thinks we need to have a press conference and get it all out on the table," Ursula said as she poured coffee for Nik, dropping in one scoop of sugar with no cream. Arnie saw Don watching her closely and realized how Nik and Ursula's familiarity must appear to Don.

"At least as much as we're willing to disclose," Arnie said. "Before they start inventing things on their own."

"What do you think, sweetheart?" Ursula asked Don.

"Does it matter at this point, Ursula?" He sat next to Nik, and Arnie saw him sneaking glances at the young singer.

"Yes, Don, it matters. It matters very much."

"Perhaps you two should discuss this, and you can give me a call later, okay?" Arnie stood again. He hated to be in the middle of his own domestic spats—the last thing he wanted to do was join someone else's. "You must be beat. Get some rest and we can talk later. Let's go, Nik."

"I just got here. . . ." Nik complained as Arnie grabbed him gently by the elbow and pulled him up.

"Perfect timing too. You and I can talk on the way home."

"Yes, Don and I need some time together," Ursula agreed. "But, guys . . . congratulations!" Ursula's enthusiasm got the best of her, and she jumped up and down like a kid, hugging and laughing over their success. Then, remembering herself, she turned to her husband. "I'm sorry, honey; it's all just . . . such a . . . hoot!"

"That's a good word." Her husband put his face in his hands and rubbed his eyes.

"This is an exciting time for Don too, you know," Ursula gushed to Arnie and Nik. She turned to Don. "Please tell me you don't think Sam will pull the senior partnership away from you because of this. I couldn't bear it if that happened. I should think Sam would be happy at the added publicity. Please, honey, say something."

"It's a great album," Don admitted. "You deserved to win. Our daughter thinks you betrayed her, though. And she lost twenty bucks on a bet—she thought you were Celine Dion."

Arnie was relieved to see a reluctant grin on Don's face.

"Twenty bucks?" Nik scoffed. "With what you're going to make on this project, I'm sure she'll get over the loss. Your net worth just skyrocketed with that baby." Nik pointed to the Grammy statuette. "I can't believe you're serious about not recording another one, Ursula. Tell me you're not serious."

"Oh, but I am serious, dear friend. I told you from the start this would be it. We've worked too hard for Don's promotion. You have no idea what it's taken to get to this point—and what it's going to take once he gets his senior partnership." Ursula crossed to where Don was sitting, stood behind him, and put her hands on his shoulders. "All of the senior partners and their spouses will be dining here in less than two weeks, and we expect Don to be offered a full partnership. Right, dear?" She leaned down and kissed his cheek.

"That's correct."

"I'm so thrilled to have won a Grammy—I won't deny that. But I'm happy to go back to real life now."

"Why do you have to choose one over the other?" Nik pleaded. Arnie wished he could teach his client some tact. "Plenty of women do both. This is the twenty-first century, Ursula. Hello? You don't have to be just a housewife—you can do it all."

"You're wrong, Nik," Ursula said gently. "I can't do it all—not without someone or something suffering."

"Time to go now." Arnie once again put his hand on Nik's elbow. "You folks discuss the press conference thing, and we'll talk later, okay?" He informed them of the specifics regarding the security-guard detail he had coordinated as they nodded their heads. "You don't have to be prisoners in your home, but I'd suggest laying low for a couple days. You'll no doubt be the topic of discussion on TV shows and news programs today, so don't say I didn't warn you if you decide to watch. Take it all with a grain of salt—they're bound to say things that aren't true."

"Like what?" Don cocked his head.

"Who knows?" Nik answered with a laugh.

"I don't see the humor in this." Don ran his hand through his hair.

"Yeah, well, hang around awhile and you'll see that's the only way to look at it. Otherwise you'll go crazy."

After another round of good-bye hugs and handshakes, Ursula and Don were once again alone.

Suddenly they both spoke at the same time.

"Honey, I'm really sorry about not telling you."

"Baby, I have to admit I'm proud of you."

Ursula smiled. "I had the time of my life, Don—when I wasn't obsessing over you. I really did try to tell you—several times. You were always too busy to listen to me. Then, one thing led to another and it got harder and harder. I'm so sorry."

"I would have listened to you."

Ursula poured another cup of coffee and clapped sugar from her hands after sweeping the countertop with her palm.

"I could easily cite at least a half dozen times when you blew me off, Don—including the time I called your hotel when you were just about to go to Jean Georges with Celeste and the crew to celebrate. Remember?"

Don nodded. "Does Julliette know?"

"Of course not. I wouldn't tell her before you. Of our friends, only Dee knows, and she's been madder than a wet hen that I haven't told you. I was worried she was going to tell you herself."

"She did call me one day."

"She did?"

"I thought it was rather strange, but she didn't say much—just some lame excuse about your birthday."

"Don, I made a hundred thousand dollars recording the album, plus I negotiated a percentage of profits from sales. Arnie tells me it's topped a couple million in sales already. I think we're going to make a lot of money from this."

She heard a gust of wind whistle outside as the first bright rays of sunlight pierced through the stained-glass suncatcher hanging from the window above the kitchen sink. She held her breath, waiting for Don's verdict.

"You signed a contract?"

"Of course."

"Without me?"

She didn't answer him—neither apology nor accusation would make a difference anymore. She crossed to her desk nook in the kitchen, pulled out a file, and handed it to Don.

"Here it is, along with the cashier's check. I didn't know if you wanted it in the kids' education fund or if you wanted to pay off the house—or what."

He perused the contract as she quietly stared at him.

"The check is in both of our names," he said, waving it. "So is the contract."

"We're a team, aren't we?"

They talked at length about the project, the money, and about Don's career. She shared her suspicions about Celeste—and believed Don when he assured her nothing inappropriate had occurred in their relationship. She poured out her heart, sharing the anguish she'd felt lying to him all these months. She told him about Nik's feelings for her—feelings that were not reciprocated—and Cristoff's odd behavior. Exhausted, they finally rose from the kitchen stools two hours later and stretched the kinks from their backs.

The guards changed shifts, knocking to introduce themselves and to let Ursula know everything was "all quiet on the western front." Ursula could see several members of the press drinking coffee and talking by their cars at the curb—had they stayed up all night too?

She rolled her head from side to side as Don reached for her neck, and she leaned back into his hands, the tension easing from her shoulders. All around her, the world hummed with activity, yet her attention was focused completely on her husband, whose hands now soothed her, reassured her.

"What do you say we hang the Do Not Disturb sign, shut off the cell phones, and get some shut-eye?" Don asked, a gleam in his eye. "Can't say I've ever slept with a Grammy Award winner."

Ursula didn't say a word as she took his hand and led him up the stairs to their room.

54

The clock said four when she opened her eyes, trying to get her bearings. She rolled over to see Don fully dressed, sitting in a wing-back chair he had pulled over from the fireplace, his stocking feet propped up on the edge of the bed, her Grammy in his lap.

"Good afternoon," he said.

"When did you get up?" she mumbled, rubbing her eyes and stretching. "Is that clock right?"

"I've been up for a couple hours. Yes, it's four o'clock on Monday afternoon. You've had a good seven hours of sleep—time to get up and face the music, as it were." He reached over and placed the gramophone award on the pillow next to her.

It seemed but moments ago she had glanced at the bedside clock before falling asleep in her husband's arms—the digital display had said it was nine o'clock. Don had already fallen asleep, breathing quietly as she stared at his handsome face. She recalled the entire night and early morning and smiled, wanting nothing more than to escape back into the arms of her beloved once again.

"I'd rather have you next to me than this award." She pulled back the covers. "Hop in, and let's pretend we're on vacation," she teased.

Don got up and sat on the edge of the bed, taking his wife in his arms and kissing her deeply. She responded to his touch like a thirsty plant soaks up water.

"Sorry, babe." He pulled away, placing his hands firmly on her shoulders. "No can do."

She stuck out her bottom lip, pouting like a child. Then she heard voices downstairs.

"Is that the kids?" she asked. "Have you talked to them?"

Don moved his hands from her shoulders to her head, entwining his fingers in her hair and looking her directly in the face.

"Listen to me and listen to me closely," he said quietly. She gulped and nodded.

"Last night—rather this morning—was magical. It's how things should always be between us. There will be no more secrets, no more lies, no more games."

"I know. I'm sorry. I said I was . . ."

"Shhhh . . . I said listen. I didn't say talk."

She nodded again as he took her hands in his.

"I have loved you from the day I first laid eyes on you. We have been partners, working side by side in what I thought was every area of our life." She tried to speak up, but he silenced her again. "But last night you showed me that wasn't true. We were partners in my life and in the lives of our children, but we weren't partners in your life—in your dream—in your passion. And I'm the one who is sorry. I'm sorry you felt that you couldn't talk to me—that you couldn't share this secret with me. I'm sorry I couldn't celebrate your accomplishment with you last night."

"Oh, Don," she cried, tears cascading down her face as she leaned into his arms. "I love you so much. Will you ever be able to trust me again?" She sniffed as he handed her a tissue from her bedside table.

"I'm not going to lie and say everything is fine and dandy. I'm hurt, Ursula, but I can understand your crazy rationale. We'll get through this. But we have more pressing things to deal with right now."

She wiped her eyes just as someone knocked on their door. "Is Mom awake yet?" Victor whispered loudly.

"Hang on a sec, Vic. . . ." Don called out as he handed Ursula her dressing gown. He walked to the door as she got up, put on her housecoat, and sat back down on the edge of the bed, combing her hair with her fingers.

"Are you alone?" Don asked, opening the door slightly.

"Yeah, just me. The screaming hordes are outside," Victor said, smiling as his father let him in their room, closing the door behind him. "I thought I heard you guys talking." Vic looked at his mother, and with the exuberance of a child ran and jumped on the bed, knocking her over. "Way to go, Momza! This is so totally cool! I'm ticked you didn't tell me—tell us—but I am so proud of you! I can't stop thinking about it."

She hugged her son tightly, telling him how sorry she was for not being honest. They bantered like magpies for a few minutes, until a second knock interrupted their revelry.

"Uh-oh, that would be Val." Victor frowned and shook his head. "Just so you know, as happy as I am for you—she's at the other end of the spectrum."

"Thanks for the heads-up," Ursula said as Don opened the door for his daughter.

Valerie stood with arms crossed at the foot of the bed, looking at Victor and her mother like maggots on a dead carcass.

"Oh my," Ursula said, trying not to laugh. "That doesn't look good."

"There is nothing whatsoever funny about this, Mother. You lied to me—you lied to all of us. What do you have to say for yourself?"

"Yes, dear . . ." Don smiled, sitting back in the chair and putting his feet up on the bed. "What do you have to say for yourself? We are all present and accounted for—waiting to hear the whole truth and nothing but the truth."

No sooner had she started to explain when the clashing sound of falling pots and pans cut through her story.

"What's that?" She jumped up. "Is someone down there?"

"I think Winston is looking for a pan," Victor said.

"Winston is here?" Ursula raised her eyebrows.

Valerie sneered, "Is *someone* down there? Mother, the house is filled with someones. The yard is filled with someones. There are someones lurking in the bushes, for crying out loud! Surely you didn't think things would return to normal!"

"What's she talking about, Don?" Ursula walked to the window and peered out from the curtains. There were even more television vans parked on both sides of the street, satellite-dish extensions raised high into the air. People stood on her lawn, on the curb, and in front of camera crews, microphones in hand.

"Is that Arnie?" She peered.

"Yes, he's been here for a few hours—seems right at home out there, knows just what to say." Don leaned back in the chair.

"He'd have to, working for Nik." She smiled.

"He's pretty cool," Victor added. "Offered to introduce me to Willie Nelson. Seems they golf together at a place in Texas. What's it called, Dad?"

"Pedernales, I think. Something like that."

"Who else is down there?" Ursula asked excitedly. "Why didn't you get me up sooner? What have I missed? I need to get showered and . . ."

"Hel-lo?" Valerie shouted. "Can we stay focused, people? Let's be serious, okay?"

Ursula, Don, and Victor all looked at Valerie, who was trying hard to be serious. But she erupted into laughter as Victor pulled his sister onto the bed.

"Lighten up, chicky!" He tickled her. "Our very own momza is Alexandra Arcano. This is way beyond cool, and you know it! Stop raining on everyone's parade, got it?"

She gave in to his teasing as Don joined them, and they romped and rollicked like kids on a trampoline. Breathlessly, they lay back and looked at Ursula. She started in on her story—pouring out her heart and soul between laughter and tears.

"And that's how it happened," she said, sitting up on the edge of the bed. "And I pray you can all find it in your hearts to forgive me for not telling you sooner. I just didn't know how."

"Nik Prevel!" Valerie almost shrieked, sitting up. "All this time you've been working with Nik Prevel! Gee whiz, Mom . . ."

Ursula smiled, knowing how her daughter felt about him.

"Is he one of the *someones* downstairs?" Ursula asked.

"Not yet." Don looked at his wife. "He's holding court at his place. Apparently it's just as crowded over there. Arnie wants us to have a group press conference, the three of us—you, Nik, and me."

"What do you think about that? What does Sam say? Oh, Don, Sam isn't angry, is he?"

"He's downstairs." Don grinned. "He's ecstatic over the added publicity the firm is getting—right in his element strategizing with Arnie. He's offered to loan us the conference room at the office for a press conference—if we want it."

"Do we?" she asked quietly.

"Uh, maybe we should leave you guys alone?" Victor stood, grabbing his sister's hand.

"No. Wait," Don said, standing. "I know you are angry, Valerie, but I'm going to pray as the days go by that you and your mother can work things out."

Valerie nodded.

"And I'm glad to see you're being supportive, Victor. I can learn a lot from you—you've been encouraging your mother's gift of song when no one else was."

Victor kissed his mom and gave her a thumbs-up.

"Ursula, we are all proud of you. This is an amazing accomplishment. I think I can speak for all of us when I say we're sorry that you didn't think you could share your secret with us. That somehow we made you think that your dreams didn't matter."

Ursula looked at her family, her heart ready to explode with joy as tears streamed down her cheeks.

"I'm so sorry," she whispered.

"So are we, sweetheart, so are we," Don said as he enveloped all of them in a healing embrace.

———————

Arnie and Sam held a press conference the next morning, confirming Ursula's identity, recapping Don's position as lead counsel on the Chesterfield case, and stating unequivocally that neither of them would be making any official public appearances in the coming days. Nik, on the other hand, held a series of press conferences—including one with his father. Ursula smiled as she watched them together.

Don was surprisingly right at home as he strategized with Arnie and Sam about their options—including Ursula in all of the decisions and frequently asking her opinion. For the next few days, their home was filled with well-wishers coming and going at all hours, including partners from Don's firm and their wives, and committee members Ursula had worked with over the years—including Dee and her husband, Lyle. Nik had sent Winston to help with meals and to lend an air of calming control over the chaos. Deliverymen brought flowers, fruit baskets, candy, and telegrams. It was Grand Central Station, and Ursula was glad to see things quieting down as the week came to an end. She had not seen Nik since the morning after the Grammys—but they talked daily on the phone.

Victor went back to school midweek, excited to share his mother's victory with his friends and assuring her he'd be back on the weekend if he could hitch a ride with Blair. Valerie had managed to get over her anger and was now more intent on meeting Nik than she was on castigating her mother for not coming clean earlier and making her fear the worst. "I still can't believe you spent the entire summer with him. It's not fair."

"I didn't spend the entire summer with him. We worked on a project together. It was a job."

"Some job. Gee whiz, Mom—*I* have a *job*. Working at Fat Burger is a *job*. What you did was way beyond a job. So why hasn't he come over? Everyone else has been here."

"I promise you'll meet him someday—when you're fifty," Ursula joked, not really joking. She figured the reason he was making himself scarce had something to do with his impulsive declaration of love—that and the ever-present media hounds.

Nik called as she was sitting in the kitchen paging through cookbooks, trying to decide on a menu for the upcoming dinner party she was holding for Don's partners.

"It's an important night. We're pretty certain they are going to offer him the partnership," she told him.

"And that's what you want?"

"Of course it is; it's what we both want—what we've both prayed for."

"You actually prayed about his job?"

"We actually pray about pretty much everything in our life. You should know that by now."

"Tell you what, I just picked up a new cookbook. I'm heading down to the farmers' market. I'll drop it off. You'll find everything you need in it for your menu—I guarantee it. You won't believe this book. Clear the garage for me, okay? Be there in a jiff."

He hung up before she had a chance to respond. She looked out the window and didn't see any TV vans—probably because of the recent drama in the life of the blond pop singer whose name she never could remember. She and Nik were yesterday's news, at least for a little while. She moved her vehicle to the carport, leaving her garage stall open for Nik to hide his car.

———————

The kitchen smelled of garlic when he entered.

"*Mangiamo!* Are you sure you're not Italian?" Nik exclaimed as he came through the garage service door and walked behind the cooking island. He lightly kissed her on the cheek and then inspected what she was preparing. "Anyone else home?"

"Not yet. It's surprisingly quiet—first time in days."

"Welcome to the world of stardom."

He began to stir the concoction. "I smell rosemary and garlic and—what is this? Cilantro?"

"Good guess. I'm not sure what I'm making—just playing with some leftovers, trying to decide what to make for the big day. So what's this new cookbook?"

"But first I want to say something about what I said backstage at the Grammys. . . ."

That's really why he called. "Nik, you don't have to . . ."

"I do have to. I was wrong. It's just so hard trying to figure out what's acceptable and what isn't—the feelings I have for you. I'm not sure I'm cut out for the friends-only thing. I always want more."

"Who sings 'You Can't Always Get What You Want'?" She smiled.

"Mick Jagger."

"Wise man. Forget about it. I'm okay. I understand."

"I'm trying to get it all worked out." He sat down at the counter and sighed.

Could it be that Nik is actually growing up?

She thought back to a conversation she'd had with him when they first began to record *Blissful Love*. He was incredulous that she could be content with what he called her "middle-class lot in life," and was equally suspicious that she honestly believed her husband had been faithful throughout their entire marriage. She hadn't shared her suspicions about Celeste.

"It's just not in a man's nature to remain monogamous," he'd insisted. "I'm sorry, but I think you're living in fantasyland if you think it's possible."

"So what are you saying? That countless couples since the beginning of time are, what, deluding themselves? That there's no such thing as commitment?"

"That's not what I said. Commitment is possible; look at my parents. What I'm saying is that sexual exclusivity is more the exception than the rule. Trust me."

At the time she had still been getting to know him, and it was hard for her to speak frankly, but she believed she needed to give him another perspective. "Nik, I hate to be the one to burst your bubble, but I'm afraid the world you and your father live in is not the real world. Hopping in and out of bed with people you barely know is not the norm, despite what we see on TV and movies. It is not acceptable behavior for most of society." She had stopped there, determined not to get into a heated argument—she'd realized early on that Nik had a phenomenally distorted view of reality.

He'd shaken his head at what he called her "suburban naiveté," and their conversation ended there. But as the months went on and their friendship grew, she'd been certain—at least she prayed it was true—that he was beginning to understand how the rest of the world lived. That commitment, honesty, and monogamy were things to be cherished and fought for. That what he thought was liberating freedom was in reality a bitter and lonely way to live.

And she now prayed that his friendship with Pastor Doyle would continue—he needed a constant source of spiritual grounding. "So tell me more about the cookbook, Nik. Sounds like fun.

Is it the HBO Sopranos?" She knitted her brows as she paged through the book.

"One and the same. It's a totally amazing cookbook. Look at this."

They were laughing over the book when Valerie walked in.

"Hey, Mom, got off work early. What smells so—" She stopped dead in her tracks as she came face-to-face with her heartthrob.

Nik straightened up and bowed at the waist. *"Benvenuta, signorina."*

"Uh, hello," she squeaked as a brilliant flush began at her neck and proceeded quickly up to the top of her forehead.

"Nik, this is my daughter, Valerie."

Nik reached for her hand and kissed it lightly. "I'm pleased to meet you. I've heard a great deal about you and feel as though I know you already."

"Valerie, you need to breathe, dear, or you'll pass out, and that won't be at all attractive."

"Not in the least." Nik grinned.

Valerie mumbled another hello and quickly crossed to the refrigerator and opened the door, peering inside. The room was quiet as Ursula and Nik smiled at each other. Ursula had told Nik he had a big fan in Valerie, but she had also made it clear she was ultraprotective of her youngest child. Less than a year ago he probably would have made a pass at her. But now he didn't, and Ursula was pleased she could be witness to this one small change in his behavior.

"So, Valerie, your mother tells me you are enjoying our CD?"

"Yeah, it's pretty good." She grabbed a container of orange juice and closed the door.

"Pretty good?" Nik smiled. "Okay. I guess that's better than a stick in the eye."

Ursula laughed and handed the spatula to Nik to take over stirring. She walked to Valerie and put her arms around her. "Hello, honey. How was your day?"

"Don't ask. Some people are real jerks. Sorry, but it's true."

"I'll second that!" Nik said.

"Valerie is working part-time as a waitress," Ursula told him, sitting down with her daughter on the kitchen stools. "So who's a jerk?"

They spent the afternoon visiting and planning the dinner menu together—the three of them. And when Nik left several hours later, Ursula and her daughter went out to sip peppermint tea on the patio, enjoying the cool Southern California breeze, keeping an eye out for lurking paparazzi.

"Well, what did you think of your hero?" Ursula asked.

"He's not my hero."

Ursula raised her eyebrows.

"Okay, so I like him. At least I used to."

"Used to? Not anymore?"

"Well, you have to admit—it's not the same."

"No, I don't know. Tell me."

"He's kind of . . . well . . . normal, but not really, you know?"

"How so?"

"He's kind of lonely, isn't he? I mean, he seems kind of lost— like those guys we feed in the soup kitchen on Thanksgiving Day."

For years the Rhoadeses had volunteered at the mission in downtown Los Angeles, working with dozens of volunteers to feed the homeless. The line seemed to go on for eternity as one soul after another filed through. Valerie and Victor had grown up playing a part in this act of service, but Ursula hadn't realized how profoundly the experience had touched her daughter.

"He's all jokes and sex appeal—"

"Wait! What do you know about sex appeal?"

"Get a clue, Mother. I'm not a baby. He oozes sex appeal." She stopped to stare at Ursula. "You honestly don't think so?"

"Oozes? Oh my."

"Yeah, oh my. But once you meet him he's really not all that attractive. He's kind of needy—in a strange way. I never figured he'd be like that. Does he have a girlfriend? He really needs a girlfriend."

"When did you get to be so wise, my darling daughter?" Ursula leaned over and wrapped her daughter in a big hug.

55

Record sales continued to climb, and the album went from platinum to triple platinum, selling over three million copies.

It was hard to believe two weeks had passed since Ursula's Grammy Award win, yet the glowing golden statue on the mantel reminded her daily. She had decided to put the award upstairs in her closet for the night, not wanting to overshadow Don's momentous occasion.

Ursula had pulled out all the stops for this landmark event. She could host a dinner party for twelve practically in her sleep, but this was different. This was going to be an evening to long remember—the culmination of their shared dream—and she wanted everything, including the atmosphere, to be savored just as much as the sumptuous meal she had planned.

Don had left early that morning to play golf at the club, and just before he left, she'd surprised him with a gift of pampering after the game—complete with a massage, facial, manicure, pedicure, and a gourmet lunch. The Andrews for Men day spa in Burbank catered only to men, and she knew he would love the experience.

"I know it's been a difficult two weeks," she'd said quietly, "and I'm sorry . . ."

"Please, Ursula," Don had said while loading his clubs into the trunk, "you don't have to keep apologizing."

"Okay . . . but it has been difficult, and that's why I want you to have some time to yourself before dinner tonight—to relax and not think about anything except this promotion, and how much you deserve it." She handed him the spa certificate.

He'd been tense since the awards night—and understandably so. The press hovering around didn't help. But finally it seemed a weight had lifted from his shoulders. In fact, she'd overheard him whistling a medley of songs from *Blissful Love* as he got ready that morning.

"You should play your CD during dinner, Mom," Valerie had suggested when she heard her father whistling. "It's actually kind of perfect dinner music."

That might be, but she wasn't about to play *Blissful Love* for all the free Lancôme gift-with-purchase bags in Nordstrom. This was Don's evening, not hers. She'd had her day in the sun.

She wondered if her husband was enjoying his afternoon of pampering as she kissed her daughter good-bye on her way to work and then prepared to get ready herself for the important evening. She planned to wear an elegantly understated Vivienne Westwood cocktail dress of pale green satin with pearl-embellished Coco Chanel pumps. She would sweep her hair into a classic chignon, and Mikimoto pearls would grace her ears and throat.

Don was glowing like a hand-polished Rolls Royce on the showroom floor after his day of masculine pampering. And he had played one of the best golf games in his life, but he still appeared a bit on edge—or was it her lingering guilty conscience for the secret she had kept for so long? *Please, Lord. I know you've forgiven me, and Don claims to have forgiven me. Help me to forgive myself.*

They were able to spend some quiet time together before they both dressed, and she made a conscious effort not to apologize.

"I thank God for you," she declared sincerely as they toasted with ginger ale in crystal goblets. She had worked hard to make this evening special, including candles burning in their master bedroom suite, and music quietly playing from the multiple speakers situated throughout the house. She doubted that Don was ever consciously aware of the pains she took to develop the perfect atmosphere, but it was reflected in the comfort they both felt during these times of stress before a major business event.

"I'm the one who is thankful for you. Look at this place." He waved his hand. "You think of everything—don't think for a minute that I don't notice. Trust me, I do. And I've been noticing a great deal more these days."

He took her in his arms and began to gently sway her around the bedroom, dancing a slow and seductive waltz. She placed her head on his shoulder.

"Ursula?"

"Hmm, yes?" she whispered, still nuzzling his neck as they slowly danced.

"I need to ask you something."

She raised her head, looked into his eyes, and gulped.

"What is it?" They stopped dancing, but he continued to hold her.

"I know you never intended to intentionally lie to me; I know that. Sometimes I'm a buffoon. But I need to ask you something right now—point-blank—no holds barred."

"Yes?"

"And as God is my witness I want the truth. Not what you think I want to hear, but what you really feel"—he placed his hand on her heart—"here." He led her to the bed, and they sat side by side on the edge. "Ursula, do you want to continue singing? Not tutoring or taking private classes—but singing professionally. Do you want to continue?"

She felt so much love for him her heart ached as she took his hands in hers.

"All those months we were recording . . . that's all I wanted to do. But, Don, I came to see that Nik, and even Cristoff and Isabella, weren't half as happy as we have been all these years." She pulled him up from the bed. "Come on, we'd better get dressed before our guests arrive and find us in our underwear." They began to dress as she continued. "I've spent years with you and our children, and a few short months with Nik Prevelakis, and there is no comparison."

She turned so he could zip her dress.

"I loved singing with Nik. I loved the experience of recording *Blissful Love*." She helped him button the studs on his shirt. "And I love that people around the country—"

"Around the world."

"Okay, I love that people around the world are enjoying the songs on the CD. But, Don . . . ?"

"Yes?" he said, clasping her necklace.

"Those people don't see me in my underwear. They don't help me zip my clothes, or hook my jewelry, or—forgive my graphic description—wipe my brow when I'm throwing up in the bathroom from food poisoning. They don't know what makes me laugh or hold me when I cry. . . ."

She turned to help him with his bow tie.

"I've loved you since I laid eyes on you. God has ordained our union and we've worked for decades as one to get you where you are today. My little side trip to stardom is but a blip on the radar. . . . This is what matters. This is what counts." She completed tying his bow tie. "There . . . done. What do you think?" She stepped aside so he could see himself in the mirror.

"Thanks. I never can get that," Don said with obvious admiration. He sat on the edge of the bed to tie his shoes.

"Don, I had a great experience; it was mind-boggling! I won a Grammy! I can still hardly believe it—I fulfilled my dream. Now it's time for you to fulfill yours."

Don sat quietly—still looking at his shoes.

"Look at me, Don."

He looked up, a bundle of conflicting emotions in his eyes.

"I won't lie to you. I would love to continue singing professionally, but it's not as important as I thought it was. What's important is you—and us—and the fact that in a few hours I'm going to be the wife of a senior partner at Carpenter, Haggerty & Pillsbury!"

He smiled one of the megawatt smiles she loved.

"Now, if you can manage to finish getting dressed, I have to go check on dinner."

He dramatically threw himself back on the bed, hand draped over his forehead, and sighed heavily as she looked at him through the mirror of her dressing table.

She loved him so much—and she knew he loved her. For the first time since her secret had been revealed, she felt confident they would eventually heal. She felt a slight twinge that she would never again experience the adrenaline rush of recording, but what she had said was true: this mattered more. When she saw the peace in her husband's eyes as he prepared for this momentous occasion, she was deeply satisfied. It was true—love grows from sacrifice.

Thank you, God. For everything.

"Thank you, Don," she said quietly.

"For what?" He sat up on the bed, looking at her reflection in the mirror.

"For asking."

They stared at each other in the mirror for a few moments before he got up and kissed her.

It didn't take long for the press to realize that the Rhoadeses were hosting regular folks for dinner and not a bevy of Hollywood elite, and they departed from their curbside perch shortly after dinner began. But Ursula noticed Don had been unusually quiet throughout the first several courses. She figured it had to do with Julliette's continued comments about her Grammy performance. No matter how Ursula tried to deflect the conversation away from that night, Julliette was relentless.

"I still can't believe you had the nerve to walk on that stage!" Julliette resumed as appetizers were being served. "I mean, really! Millions of people were watching. What if you had fallen or missed a note or something like that? It's not like you are a seasoned professional or anything. I certainly give you credit, Ursula. You couldn't have paid me enough to do that."

Well, they sure paid me enough—one hundred thousand dollars and counting. Ursula smiled and changed the subject, and the conversation rotated from business to current events to politics.

It was becoming tiresome, the number of times she had to gently shuffle the conversation away from her work with Nik and back to other issues—she hadn't anticipated the level of interest the project had garnered from the guests.

"You simply must tell us what it was all like," Babette Lithgow encouraged. "How utterly decadent the entire mystery was!" She batted her eyelashes none too coyly.

"There was nothing decadent about it at all." Ursula smiled, all the while boiling inside at the insipid woman, whom she was still unable to like even after ten years, and no matter how much she prayed for grace to tolerate her. "It was a job, not much different from taking on a legal case."

"Isn't that rich?" Kelly Harper cooed while sipping her sparkling water. "As though winning a Grammy could be compared to winning a case."

"Speaking of winning a case, may I have everyone's attention, please?" boomed Sam as he stood.

This is it. Ursula caught Don's eye and winked.

"It's no secret why we're all here tonight." He lifted his goblet toward Don. "You have once again made the firm proud, Don. With the Chesterfield case, you exhibited a level of professionalism and talent that has consistently marked your career with Carpenter, Haggerty & Pillsbury. Bravo on a job well done."

Everyone applauded, and the gentle chime of crystal goblets being toasted filled the air. Those sitting nearby clapped Don on the back in admiration. Ursula was so proud of her husband it brought a knot to her throat as she watched him humbly accept the accolades.

This is your time, sweetheart. Enjoy the night. Yet she felt unsettled—sensing that Don was somehow uneasy, that something was wrong. He really had not been himself all night, and she couldn't put her finger on it.

"But that's not all I'd like to say," Sam continued, sharing how he'd first met Don and reciting a fifteen-minute speech that covered Don's entire career with the firm—a soliloquy worthy of repeating at, say, a fifty-year gold-watch celebration. He walked around the table, stood next to Don, and placed his hand on his shoulder. "Don, your wife may be the star of the air waves, but you are the star of our firm—and it would do us proud if you would accept our offer to be the next senior partner at Carpenter, Haggerty, Pillsbury & Rhoades!"

Whistles, shouts, and a bottle of champagne appeared from out of nowhere. The cork made a resounding *pop* as Sam shook hands with Don, clasping him boldly around the shoulders in the sort of masculine bear hug that doesn't linger too long.

When at last the melee had subsided and Don was able to speak, Ursula was left speechless at his response.

56

"This is indeed an honor," Don said, standing behind his chair, hands resting on the back. "I've waited a long time for this day— we've waited a long time, Ursula and I."

Ursula looked at her husband with love and pride, ecstatic for her partner in a way that only someone who had invested almost a lifetime in helping to make a dream come true could be.

"That is why this is a bittersweet moment." He cleared his throat. "Sam, it has been an honor to work with you all of these years, and I appreciate the trust you have placed in me with this offer of a full senior partnership—and a few weeks ago I would gladly have accepted it."

What is he saying?

"But I'm afraid I must decline." He smiled at her.

What?! Decline?

"As you all know, my wife surprised us with her recent 'summer job,' as we've come to call it around here. And her summer job has the potential to become a phenomenal career." He walked over to the stereo cabinet and hit Play. Ursula's chorus from "I Must Have Done Something Good" filled the room. "Listen to that. I have, over and over again these past weeks. You called me a star—but the real star is sitting right there." He pointed to his wife. "And if she'll have me, I've decided to leave the firm and go into private practice, taking on one exclusive client: Alexandra Arcano."

Knowing fully that Don was not a man who came to any decision lightly, Ursula's heart leapt to her throat with joy at this sacrifice he was making. *Can this really be true?*

"I don't expect many of you to understand this decision, and I really struggled with it at first, but the more I thought and prayed about it, the more right it seemed. My beautiful and talented wife has stood by me for years—making my dream her own—never complaining, always supportive. She's raised our two children to become fine, upstanding citizens—a better mother, wife, and friend I could never hope to find. Now it's my turn to sacrifice, and it's her turn to shine—and I intend to help her to do just that."

During his talk, he had walked to where she was sitting with tears streaming down her cheeks. As he reached her side he spoke directly to her, as though no one else was in the room.

"I'm sorry for being so monumentally selfish—"

"You weren't—"

"I have been selfish. What you've managed to do is nothing short of spectacular, and I want to see you do it again." He reached into the buffet cabinet and extracted her Grammy Award, placing it on the table in front of her. "I want to see this sitting proudly on a shelf in our home with more just like it, and never hidden in your closet."

He knelt down on one knee and took her hand. "I love you, Ursula Rhoades, and if you'll let me, I'd be honored to work for you—with you—to manage your singing career. What do you think?"

I think I love you more than I could ever believe possible.

"Can I have my people get back to your people?" She laughed, wiped away her tears, and wrapped her arms around his neck as the guests one by one began to clap and cheer—even Sam, who appeared befuddled at losing his ace attorney yet happy to see such inspiring love.

Ursula was still in a state of shock as the last guest walked out the door a short while later. When they were alone, she turned to her husband, and he took her in his arms. After a long kiss that left her breathless and a bit weak at the knees, she was speechless.

"Sit down, Ursula. You don't look well." Don laughed nervously. "Are you angry with me? Don't tell me you'd rather I stayed at the firm and sentenced you to suburban obscurity for life!"

"You could have told me—let me in on your secret. . . ."

They giggled at the deep meaning behind what she had just said.

"Are you certain this is what you want, Don? It will change our lives."

"Honey, our lives are already changed. You'll never be able to go back to teaching students in our living room. Oh sure, I have no doubt you'd try. And knowing your character, you'd be successful and relatively happy. But this Cinderella experience would always be in the back of your mind—you'd always remember that you'd grasped it once but then disappeared into oblivion. I don't want that for you—I don't want that for us. Honey, God gave you a voice that He's allowed you to share. I just don't think it's right that we tell Him, 'Thanks, but no thanks.' Do you?"

What could she say to that?

"Now, what do you say we go out for a nightcap?" Don asked.

"Now? But it's almost eleven."

"And your point is?"

"I have to clean this table . . ."

"The table can wait."

He pulled her up from the chair and swung her around the room. "We're all dressed up with somewhere to go. Let's celebrate! Let's go to the Pink Palace; it's been a while since we've been there—should be fun. I'll get your wrap." He left the room, leaving her standing with her mouth agape. The Pink Palace was what the locals called the famous Beverly Hills Hotel on Sunset Boulevard.

The valet took their car as they walked into the Polo Lounge. It was unusually crowded for a weeknight, yet they were seated in the dark lounge without a wait. Ursula could barely see five feet in front her now; candles flickered on each table and the brightest light in the room emanated from the empty stage on which a baby grand piano sat like a lone newborn infant in a hospital nursery.

"I wonder if there's entertainment tonight," she said.

"You could always sing for us."

"I don't think so." She laughed, playfully hitting his arm.

They ordered coffee and two Pellegrinos with lime.

"I'll have to call Nik and Arnie, to see if they even want me back," she said as they waited for their drinks.

"Like they wouldn't? They said they wanted to record another album. I heard them."

"Yes, but that was before I told them to find someone else. Oh my, Don—what if they have found someone else and don't want me?"

"That's my girl, always the optimist. Check it out." He nodded toward the stage. "Looks like we're in luck."

A lovely young woman in a canary-colored gown walked across the intimate stage and sat down at the piano. She adjusted the microphone and welcomed the audience while her fingers cascaded over the ivory keys like gentle raindrops on flower petals. She sang "I Love How You Love Me," an old Bobby Vinton tune that Ursula was especially fond of.

"She's good," Ursula whispered. "I wonder who she is."

The waitress returned with their drinks, and as she turned away, Don reached into his pocket and extracted a lovely white satin gift box and set it in front of Ursula.

"W-what is this?" she stammered.

She carefully untied the gold ribbon. Nestled in a tiny blanket of pink satin on a delicate chain was a small gold record, the size of a quarter. A sparkling diamond graced the center.

"I had it made especially for you. Do you like it?"

"Oh, Don, I love it! It's beautiful! Please put it on for me, would you?" She quickly removed her pearls, leaning her head down and holding the new necklace around her neck as Don stood to help. With Don blocking her view of the stage and focused so intently on the task at hand, she didn't notice the young man who seamlessly replaced the singer at the piano until he began to sing the chorus. She raised her head abruptly just as Don successfully clasped her necklace.

"Victor!"

Her son smiled and nodded her way as he continued to sing.

"Donald! You scoundrel! I can't believe I fell for your 'Let's go have a nightcap' ruse. You had this planned all along!"

"Busted." He smiled, then kissed her and returned to his seat. "Truth is, he actually has a gig here this weekend—got hired at the last minute. I figured no matter what happened tonight we'd stop by and say hello."

"What do you mean, 'No matter what happened'? You weren't sure if you wanted to give up your career? Oh, Don, maybe we should give this more thought. Call Sam and . . ."

"Whoa! Slow down. *I* was sure what *I* wanted to do. I just wasn't sure *they* were actually going to offer me the partnership— you know how Sam is. And I haven't given up my career, just a slew of clients who were driving me crazy, anyway. Not that you won't." He smiled and kissed her.

"Ladies and gentlemen, thanks for being with us this evening," Victor said from the stage, quieting the room. "We have a special treat for you tonight."

"Oh, Don, he's not going to call me up there, is he? I'm not ready for that."

"I don't know what he's going to do. Why don't we listen?"

"Please join me in welcoming to the stage . . . Nik Prevel!"

The room became instantly quiet, all eyes straining to see if the kid was serious. From behind the backdrop Nik walked onto the small stage, grinning from ear to ear and oblivious to the resounding applause as he smiled at Ursula and Don. Victor and Nik shook hands, and then Victor began to play "As Time Goes By" on the piano. The room grew silent again, and Nik began to sing.

Ursula could only smile and shake her head as she fought the tears from falling once again, knowing her husband had orchestrated the entire thing.

Halfway into the song Nik was joined by another voice, and the crowd went ballistic when the Great Cristoff walked onstage, microphone in hand, singing as though his life depended on it. There was no holding back tears now as Ursula watched father and son perform together in public for the first time in their lives.

"Ladies and gentlemen," Cristoff said as the applause ceased when their song had ended, "my son is here to make a special announcement, but I could not let him do it alone."

Ursula watched Nik beam as his father called him "son."

Nik smiled as the audience laughed, moving center stage into his father's spotlight.

"Leave it to a legend to upstage the upstart." Nik shook his father's hand.

Ursula laughed with the rest of the crowd as father and son went on to joke and even embrace as Cristoff left the stage to a standing ovation, giving Nik time to swallow his emotions as he addressed the audience once again.

"Ladies and gentlemen, the real reason we are here tonight is to make a special announcement about an exciting new project. By popular demand, *Blissful Love Part Deux* will be going into production later this month, and here to sing one of the songs from the original Grammy-award-winning album, *Blissful Love,* please welcome Grammy-award winner Alexandra Arcano!"

Don stood and held out his hand to his wife, nodding to her as the audience began to applaud once again. As she stood and began to look around, her eyes now adjusted to the darkened room, she began to make out familiar faces—Nik's band! And the boys from Victor's band. And . . . was that Valerie waving from a nearby table . . . with Dee and Kitty at her side?

As she walked onstage to join Nik, she could no longer contain her emotions—tears poured unashamedly from her eyes, even more so when she noticed Arnie, Isabella, and Cristoff applauding from the sidelines. It seemed the more she cried—the louder the applause became. Nik pulled her into a friendly hug and whispered in her ear. "We're singing 'Someone to Watch Over Me'—need the music?"

"Yeah, right," she said with a chuckle, remaining in his embrace, keeping her back to the audience as she held tight and tried to regain her composure while the applause continued. "How long did you know about this?" She had to practically shout to be heard.

"Not long. Don called me this afternoon from somewhere in Burbank . . . asked me to get on the phone ASAP. He just gave us a heads-up call a few minutes ago—said you were on your way. That husband of yours is some kinda guy. He's already wrangling quite a contract for your next project—I think I'm going to like working with him. Now, blow your nose, grab a microphone, and shut up and sing, would ya?"

Laughing while wiping her eyes with a tissue that Dee had thrust in her hand on her way to the stage, Ursula thought of something. She whispered to Nik. The applause died down when the audience saw Nik wanted to say something else.

"Ladies and gentlemen . . . I've made a mistake. . . . Please give it up for my partner and Grammy-award winner, *Ursula Rhoades!*"

They sang over the background applause. The entire time, Ursula stared into the eyes of her husband. She saw him mouth the words that made her heart sing—*I love you.* When she got the chance, she mouthed back, *I love you too,* oblivious to everyone in the room except him. As she sang and silently thanked God for the rich and wonderful blessing of this new journey in her life, one thought that sneaked into her head made her smile. *Not bad for someone who's just a housewife.*

With God, a loving family, and a forty-five-piece orchestra, anything is possible!

Acknowledgments

The longer I live and the longer I write, the more people I have to thank for making every book come to life. God has blessed me greatly with family, friends, co-workers, and an amazing publishing team whose encouragement, support, and love make all the difference in the world. You know who your are—thank you from the depths of my heart.

Yet without readers it's all for naught. Therefore, I wish to extend a heartfelt thank-you to my readers. I pray you've enjoyed Ursula's dream-come-true journey. I'd love to hear from you. Please drop me a line or send an e-mail to let me know if you've enjoyed this, my second novel. Have you read my first? It's called *A Stitch in Time*, and it's there that Ursula first shows up on the scene.

And, if you've never heard of our true short story compilation books called *God Allows U-Turns*, I encourage you to visit our Web site to find out more about them. In the meantime, thanks again for reading *One Little Secret*, and I hope to hear from you.

May God bless and keep you—and give you the desires and dreams of your heart.

Allison Bottke
P.O. Box 717
Faribault, MN 55021-0717

AB@AllisonBottke.com
www.AllisonBottke.com
www.GodAllowsUTurns.com

About the Author

Allison Bottke lives in southern Minnesota on a twenty-five-acre hobby farm with her entrepreneur-husband, Kevin. She is a relatively "new" Christian, coming to the fold in 1989 as a result of a dramatic life U-turn. The driving force behind the GOD ALLOWS U-TURNS books and ministry, she has a growing passion to share with others the healing and hope offered by the Lord Jesus Christ. Allison has a wonderful ability to inspire and encourage audiences with her down-to-earth speaking style as she relates her personal testimony of how God can change a life. You can find out more about Allison, lovingly dubbed "The U-Turns Poster Girl," by visiting her Web site at *www.AllisonBottke.com*